For Frances

PARIS TRIANGLE

An International Love Affair

James P. Harrison

iUniverse, Inc.
New York   Bloomington

PARIS TRIANGLE
An International Love Affair

iUniverse books may be ordered through booksellers or by contacting:

iUniverse
1663 Liberty Drive
Bloomington, IN 47403
www.iuniverse.com
1-800-Authors (1-800-288-4677)

Because of the dynamic nature of the Internet, any Web addresses or links contained in this book may have changed since publication and may no longer be valid. The views expressed in this work are solely those of the author and do not necessarily reflect the views of the publisher, and the publisher hereby disclaims any responsibility for them.

ISBN: 978-1-4401-4959-7 (sc)
ISBN: 978-1-4401-4958-0 (ebk)

Printed in the United States of America

iUniverse rev. date: 6/24/2009

Contents

CHAPTER ONE

PARIS AND THE LOVE OF MY LIFE

What a beautiful cool day in Paris! There were scudding clouds against a blue sky.

My arrival there had been in mid August, 2000, and I spent the first days enjoying myself with long walks, visiting museums and eating great food. My plan for this first sabbatical year was not only to teach two courses as arranged by my French hosts, but to research and start work on a planned book on French wines which I could finish after the year in Paris. So, as September approached, I decided to get to work on the wine project. My first stop would be the wine museum in the 16th Arrondissement.

Then I saw her! I was crossing the Jardins du Luxembourg from my nearby hotel en route to the Vavin metro stop when I noticed a beautiful blonde woman. She was looking at the bees in the apiculture center at the southern end of the garden, which was also a favorite place of mine. As I approached, I wondered which language to try? I decided to speak as best I could the language of where we were. Having had some practice with that from my schooling and trips with the parents to Montreal and Québec, I hazarded in my best French, *"C'est tres interessant, n'est-ce pas?"* To my delight, she asked, "Do you speak English?"

With enthusiasm I responded, "You bet! It's my first language. I like to speak my imperfect French in Paris, but it is with an accent."

"At least you can be understood. Though my mom is French, we didn't speak it much, and mine is mostly from several years at a girl's school in London. So it is not very good, although thanks to mother I have a good accent. I usually switch back to English when I can."

She looked at me with seeming curiosity, but a bit mischievously, I thought, as I noticed her sparkling eyes.

"The bees are so busy doing whatever they are doing and I am glad you have discovered them." Then I asked, "How about a drink?" I could delay my proposed trip to the wine museum since it didn't close until six, almost six hours away. "I know some good places nearby."

"Why not?" she answered.

"Marvelous! The places I know are over that way," I said, heading for the Rue Vavin exit. We passed more beautiful flowers, shrubs and trees and then the many boutiques lining the streets before we reached the Boulevard Montparnasse.

We took seats at the Café Rotonde, a favorite stopping place, opposite the more expensive and better known La Coupole and Le Dome Café restaurants. I said, "This is one of the things I love most about Paris. There are so many attractive places to have a drink and eat, don't you think?"

She replied, "You seem to know Paris quite well. How is that?"

"Well, I lived here several years when I was doing research for a book on the Vietnam wars. One of the reasons I chose that subject, which was hot then, was that I could research it in Paris. At the time, the subject was so painful I didn't want to work on the book in the U.S. with its continuous distorted reports on Vietnam. I frowned as I recalled the anguish of so many aspects of the Vietnam war.

"I certainly agree. Though I am not at all political, that was one subject that always drove me crazy. It was as if the people of Indohina were from another planet."

I thought I liked this lady more and more. We talked so easily, and she was so great to look at. We talked and talked.

She told me she was an aspiring artist, but to make ends meet was working in a London bookstore from which she was now on vacation. Fortunately, she would have not just a few days but a few weeks--- perfect for me, if things worked out as I was planning, with several weeks of preparation and research for my course in Paris before heading for Burgundy. I was heading there to study some leading vineyards for the hoped for book on wine. I wouldn't have to return for my teaching until mid October. How perfect for me as a history professor to meet an artist working in a book store. She told me she was staying in a hotel, the *Sevres Azur*, on the *Rue Abbè Gregoire*, not far away.

We finally got around to our names. She was Valerie Field and I told her my name, Chris Howard. She declined my invitation for dinner that day, but we agreed to meet the next day for drinks at a bar near *St. Germain des Près*. She bid me *au revoir* and headed off to shop at the *Galerie Lafayette*, just down the street.

I watched her go off, again admiring her wonderful appearance, and asked myself if I was jealous she might be seeing someone else tonight.

But no, I can't be like that, I told myself, even as I remembered that one of my major problems with the wife I had just divorced was my jealousy at her flirtatiousness. After eating a marvelous chestnut crepe with another glass of Sauvignon Blanc at La Rotonde, I headed to the Vavin stop and took the *Nation-Etoile* metro which arrived at the *Passy* stop close to the *Musèe du Vin.*. I still had two hours to go before the six o'clock closing of the museum. When I got there, I started with the exhibit they had on the *Clos de*

Vougeot vineyard. I thought that could be a good start for my wine researches.

But, soon I found so many fascinating facts to do with the history of the Chateau Clos du Vougeot, that I wondered if it would prevent my concentrating on the wines, or even on a fictional work I was considering trying to do as I told some of the history of French wines. As I was pondering that question, a rather handsome man asked in English how much I knew about the Clos de Vougeot. I answered, "almost nothing," and was delighted when he said he knew a lot as he was a taster, or *degusteur,* for a big English wine company. He said his name was Keith Weaver, and looking at me, had decided I probably spoke English. I asked him if I could talk with him a bit as I was hoping to do a book on French wines.

He agreed, and after a few more minutes walking around the museum, we went to the museum's own wine bar just next door. At Keith's recommendation, we drank two glasses each of a delicious *Meursault*, a white wine made just to the south of the *Clos de Vougeot*. Keith explained that the name came from the Roman soldiers two thousand years ago calling a narrow ravine running through that vineyard *"muris saltis,"* or jump of the rat.

It came to me that he looked very like one of my colleagues back in New York. Both were tall and slim with angular faces and full beards. Both had brown hair which was somewhat balding. After a half hour more of talking mostly about wine, I began to be bothered by Keith's leaning almost into my face to speak. Interesting as his stories were, I made up a white lie in order to take my leave. That was because I wanted to have dinner at a restaurant a friend had recommended on my way back to my hotel, and I wanted to be alone to reflect not only on the wine project, but on my recent meeting with Valerie.

Following another wonderful meal, I set out for my hotel and decided to have a drink at a wine bar I knew of almost next door to where I was staying. Its name set its style. It was the *Chai de l'Abbaye*, or wine shop of the church, *St. Germain des Près,* which was just up the street.

Who did I see on entering but Valerie with her friend. I went over to say hello, and Valerie introduced me. "*Bonsoir*, Chris. This is Mark Goden."

I did not like his looks and was further put off when he asked with a cold tone, "How long do you expect to be in Paris?" I responded as cooly as I could, "About a year," and briefly told him of my teaching and plans for research on wine.

He sat up high as he could and said stiffly, "Well, I'm in business. I do important stuff regarding English trade with France for a big export-import company."

"What do you deal in?" I asked.

"Mostly agricultural items. Our beef and woolens for their oils, wines and special foods."

I said, "That's good, maybe you can give me some information about the wine trade."

"I doubt it. Details on that might be secret, and besides I am allergic to teachers. My father was one," he replied with a frown.

Valerie blurted out, "now, Mark, don't be rude."

He rejoined, "I'm not being rude, just stating facts. Besides, no doubt Chris like most academics is a liberal."

Now, it was my turn to say as meanly as I could, "In fact, I am more of a radical than a liberal, and I don't much care for conservatives which most business types like you are."

At that point, Valerie grabbed Mark's sleeve, and winking at me, said, "Well, I see we should be on our way. Besides we have a party nearby to go to. See you tomorrow, Chris."

I needed to have a drink right away, as I watched them go off. They were obviously arguing with each other, which made me feel better. I ordered the special of the day, a *Chateauneuf du Pape*. I thought that was very appropriate as we were so close to the imposing Cathedral *St. Germain des Près*, and there is no better red wine.

The next day, a Thursday as I recall, I decided to get up earlier in order to do more reading in the small library of the wine museum before meeting Valerie as agreed that evening. Still, it was after eight when I awoke. I sleep later in the autumn, and it was already late summer. Moreover, my room on the courtyard was quiet and not very bright in the mornings, making it perfect for rising late, or having a `grasse matinèe' as the French say. Anyway, the sun comes up later in Paris than New York, given its position on the western edge of a time zone, and position on a latitude as far north as Montreal. After the usual ablutions and coffee, I was off by ten, quite early for me. Back home, I've always been able to schedule classes in the afternoon, and I sleep late most days. That day was as they say *variable* and I admired the scudding clouds. They were Stratus type at different altitudes, below the Cirrus clouds high above.

At the museum library, I found several books on the *Clos de Vougeot,* and dozens on its region, the *Cote d'Or*, to the south of Dijon. Along with Bordeaux in the southwest of France, it is the most famous wine region in the world. At least it was, prior to the emergence of the vineyards of Napa Valley and other now famous wine areas elsewhere in the Americas, Australia and around the world.

After a few hours of reading, I spotted Keith Weaver there again.

I invited him for another drink on me in return for his telling me more about French wines. We took our same places at the wine bar. This time I decided to ask him why he liked to lean so close to me to speak. He seemed surprised, and said he would try not to. He asked, "But why does that bother you?"

"Well," I said, "I guess I feel better when you keep your distance. You are such an attractive guy. Why cause problems, and please, don't hold that against me." He responded, "And I see you are quite particular, if also an attractive guy. I will have to see if I want to hold that against you."

After that, he leaned back with a smile and proceeded to tell me about how he had discovered that the English like their wines light. He explained their choice of the word claret, since the southern French called their lightest wines *clairet*. He went on to other fascinating information, including speculation that the name of the great bordeaux wine, Haut Brion may have come from an Irishman named O'Brien, who was involved in the wars that gave the British control of that region during the middle ages. He added that the first monk in Burgundy to start the improvements to the vineyard of *Clos de Vougeot* was from the Priory of *Saint Vivant*. That was in 1162, a generation before the founding nearby of the famous Cistercian monastery at *Citeaux*.

He went on to tell me about his tour of the region and its famous vineyards, monasteries and cathedrals a few years back. Since the *Clos de Vougeot* is about fifteen kilometers south-southwest of Dijon, he had decided to do a clockwise tour starting with *Citeaux*, the home of the Cistercians. He told me how fascinated he had been by the ruins of the monasteries and their history, including the development of wine making techniques.

Keith was puzzled when I spoke of my consternation that there was so much history involved with *Clos de Vougeot*. That was after I had added that I knew that St. Bernard ---not the dog !---had preached at *Citeaux*, most famously when he advocated the second crusade there in 1146. In my European history classes, I had also lectured about the saint's criticisms of Eleanor of Aquitaine when she was married to King Louis VII, prior to her marriage to the English King Henry II, Plantagenet.

I thought to tell Keith how I knew such things. I said, "This year I decided to pass my sabbatical in Paris. There were two good reasons which came together for that. First, it's my favorite big city, and second, in 2000, I was able to get a part-time teaching job here. That was part of an exchange teaching program established between the City University of New York, including my college, Baruch, and the Université de Paris. The *Institut d'Anglais* in Paris agreed for me to teach a course on American and Canadian history there, while one of their professors taught European history in my place at Baruch for this year, starting in September."

As for handling the complexities of history, according to Keith all I had to do was figure out a way to weave some of the details about Clos de Vougeot into my history of wine, or fiction about it. He complicated that further with still another story, this one about a man, Gaspard de Sterimberg, who used the wages he earned as a courtier to Queen Blanche of Castille, to buy a vineyard in the Rhone valley of Southeast France. There he planted a Syrah vine, that he had acquired from friends he had made doing a crusade in his youth. Those friends had installed themselves in Tournon, which was in the heart of what would become the Cote du Rhone wine region of southeastern France. They kept up contacts with the Middle East through a trading company, and Syrah became one of the more important grapes for Cote du Rhone and other red wines. Keith added that Blanche de Castille was the granddaughter of Eleanor of Aquitaine and mother of the famous French King, St. Louis.

By this time, thanks to Keith's fascinating stories and the mellowness of the wine, I was feeling no pain. I decided to ask Keith to join me and Valerie for the evening. I described a few things about Valerie, saying I was certain he would be compatible with her as both were English and with similar interests. He asked how I knew that if I had just met her. I replied that we had talked about wine some, and she seemed quite interested. She said she had sold many books about wine from her bookstore in London. So I told him of our rendez-vous at 7:30 at the Café Bonaparte. Keith thanked me and said he knew where that Café was and would try to make it. "Now, I have to go see some business people. So, I'll see you later."

I continued to work at the museum library and went back to my hotel about 5. After a little rest and a bath, I made my way to the Cafè Bonaparte for the 7:30 rendez-vous. Valerie was there and greeted me warmly. No sooner had we ordered our drinks than Keith showed up. I introduced them and noticed immediately how obviously Keith seemed taken with Valerie. I noticed also that as he kept looking at her, he seemed to avoid looking into my eyes. Another friend had told me "Never trust someone who doesn't look you in the eyes."

Then, it was Keith's turn to start asking questions of Valerie. "I hear you sell a lot of wine books from your store in London."

"Well, I see Chris has already started talking about me," Valerie said as she looked at me archly. "Yes, it's true. You know the English are crazy about wine, as well as beer," Keith remarked with a sour smile. "I am sure Chris also told you I work for a British wine company. That's why I'm here in Paris. And why are you?"

"Just a nice vacation, and I have to say, I am not bored."

I blurted out, "I should hope not! And I have a plan for the evening. After a drink or two here I propose we do a favorite restaurant just around the corner. It's called the Brasserie St. Benoit and is as cheap as it is good."

Keith said, "Maybe, but I prefer the Petit Zinc right next door."

"All right, then we'll let Valerie decide," I said with a nod.

Valerie came right back with, "Why don't we look at both and their menus and then decide."

Keith said with a big smile, "I can see how amiable, smart, and vivacious you are, Valerie. Tell me more about your work?"

I put in, "As I already told you, she works for a London book store."

"But, I asked her, not you, Chris. Why can't you let her respond?"

"All right, sorry. I guess I am already feeling protective," even as I was thinking that Keith asks too many questions, and was too obviously flirting with Valerie.

"And how do you think that makes me feel," Valerie said with a quizzical look at me. "You know, my job is not that interesting. Just being there to sell what you can, answer questions, and rearrange the position of books when possible. To tell the truth I am getting a bit bored with it."

"And what are you thinking of doing?" Keith asked. "If you want, I can recommend you for a position my firm is looking to fill. It is to talk more with London restaurants about what wines they serve and the like. The idea, of course, is to try to make them buy more of our wines."

Valerie said, "That sounds very interesting. Maybe we can trade cards."

Keith immediately began to dig in his pockets and found two cards in his wallet which he proffered to us.

Reaching across with a frown, I took mine and Valerie's as well, showing that I was not very happy with the latest conversation, although I thought it wise to give Valerie hers. Then, I said, "Don't you think it's time for the restaurant?"

As we got up, I noticed Keith's face. It had a large mole on the left cheek and a smaller one on the right, which were only partially hidden by his beard. He reached for his cane which he put on the side toward me as we started to walk. Valerie took her place by Keith's side as if to annoy me, but I hastened to walk around to be on her other side.

After that stiff beginning, Valerie loosened us up by talking about her day at the museum. She said, "I can't believe how huge the Louvre is. It makes the British Museum look almost tiny. I started at 11 in the morning with an exhibit on the

Etruscans. After lunch in that incredible basement complex under the museum and adjoining streets, I went back but could only see half of the Italian and Northern Renaissance collections. I love them so much, I will certainly go back."

By then we had arrived in front of the Petit Zinc, and studied its menu which was conveniently placed on the outside, as is the case with most Paris restaurants. We noted that the place was almost completely full. After that it was only a hundred paces to the St. Benoit, taking a left on the Rue St. Benoit from the Rue St. Apolinnaire, and the same exercise.

Since it was only three quarters full, I recommended we go in. Valerie agreed, but Keith drew himself up and said, "You all go ahead. I think I will go back to the Petit Zinc, and see if they have a place for me."

Valerie laughed, "So you are already tired of us? Well, enjoy your meal."

Keith bowed slightly and said, "No, I just think we may enjoy our meals more apart. I can see Chris does not like my talking to you very much, and I would certainly want to do that if I was with you."

In fact, I was delighted with the turn of events, and said, "Yes, you may be right. See you at the museum again. Or whenever. Bye."

Grabbing Valerie's arm, I steered her into the St. Benoit, as we turned partially to watch Keith disappear. Once seated, I ventured, "What luck for me that he's gone his way, and now I have you to myself. I thought he was going to try to take you away from me, and even that you seemed to be responding to his advances. I suppose because of the job offer."

Almost before I finished Valerie rejoined with, "No, you're crazy. I was just being polite, though to tell you the truth I may want to change jobs. But that's weeks off and I'm looking forward to that time, maybe with you." She gave me a ravishing smile, but again with a mischievous twist.

"Wouldn't that be wonderful," I said, as I stared at Valerie. She looked as beautiful as I remembered. She was wearing a pretty rose jacket, with beige blouse and skirt. They set off nicely her hazel eyes and lovely figure. I felt underdressed, even though I was wearing my best brown ascot, or *foulard* as the French call them. But, my beige jacket and dark trousers and shoes were all worn out and scruffy looking.

Never mind. Our conversation went beautifully. She asked about my life in New York and how I could stand the cold of the winters. I said it wasn't too bad, and that in fact I hated the heat of the summers more. I decided to tell her of the breakup of my marriage with Henrietta.

That got Valerie's attention, and she asked me to tell her how such a thing could be controlled. I told her divorce was indeed very difficult, but not too terrible if there were no children, as was the case with us. As for Henrietta, I told Valerie that I had never really known her. My original mistake was to marry in too much ignorance of what I was getting into. I did so because she was pretty and successful with her financial counselling. But as we started living with each other, it became more and more obvious how incompatible we were. What can you do in such a situation, except divorce, and all the more so, before there are children. It got so bad that I even wondered if I would agree with the quote, from Schopenhauer I think, 'To marry means to do everything possible to become an object of disgust to each other.' "Do you agree?"

She asked, "How can I know since I've never been married. Yet, I would guess that quote is an overstatement since there are some good marriages after all. Anyway, tell me more about what you were feeling when you decided to divorce, and as the divorce was proceeding."

"Well, you know, when you are living with someone, making love, going to parties and doing all the routines of daily life, some disturbances just pop up and make you lose your temper. At least, I have that problem. Is it that as you become aware of differences you realize how bad it is to be married to someone who thinks so differently from you."

"Can you give some examples of what happens in those situations?"

"Because it happened only about six months ago, the first example I think of was our last big fight. It came over a petty disagreement about how to set the table for a party we were giving. I wanted to sit next to a lady colleague that I like a lot. But, Henrietta put me at the other end of the table, and as we were preparing the table she proceeded to launch into criticisms of my friend. When I protested, saying, 'You're just jealous,' she fairly screamed at me, 'And you are a moron.'"

I stalked out of the house and ordered some drinks at a nearby bar. When I came back a half hour later, I could see that the guests did not believe my story that I had to go out for some more wine, but could not find what I wanted. The dinner was not very good and the conversation tense and boring. The next day my friend told me Henrietta had said I didn't want to sit next to her. A complete lie, revealing her jealousy I suppose.

"That's crazy," said Valerie. She added, "But, I see what you mean, as I've been through such scenes a couple of times too. Yet, with me, they were usually cases of drawing away and sulking, rather than leaving in a huff."

Just then our food arrived, and I said, "*Basta* to do with such difficulties. Let's enjoy our meal and afterwards, you can tell me about those experiences of yours. *Bon appetit.*"

The meal was excellent. She had a sole meuniere and me a rack of lamb. We chose, that is I proposed and she agreed, glasses of a muscadet wine to start and then a bottle of bordeaux.

She said, "I'm finding everything so great on this trip, I hope you won't spoil it," even as she gave me another one of her mischievous smiles.

I put my hand on her sleeve, and asked, "And what would spoil it for you?"

"I will tell you when you start to do so, and meanwhile just keep ordering such good food and wine. How did you learn to do that by the way?"

"Well, my father was very big on wine and good food. He was a school teacher in Asheville, North Carolina, where I grew up. He had wines every dinner and allowed me to start tasting when I was about sixteen or so. I loved to eat and soon got into choosing the wines myself. Naturally I love your challenge to keep ordering well. And tell me about your name. Valerie does not seem very English, though Field obviously is."

"You're right. My father is English, and as I think I told you, my mom is a *Francaise, de Limoges,* whom my father met on a trip. She didn't speak French that much with us, in part because she wanted to practice her English as well as avoid suspicion for being French, the traditional enemies of the English, at least until the first World War. That was too bad, and now my French is not much better than that of a schoolgirl."

"Oh, come on. I find your French excellent. We should speak it together more often."

She nodded and took another bite, but finishing it said in English, "As for the other problems I mentioned; once, I had a friend who was an architect. He invited me to use an empty room in his house, a lovely flat in Knightsbridge. I was to assist him with his work, which he did in the basement. It was full of computers, and he assigned me one. It was a new Compaq, and I was not familiar with it. That also frustrated me. But, mainly, I did not like the amorous approaches he started making. So after a difficult first month, I just told him, "Listen, this is not working out as I had hoped. I want to move out."

He talked me into a last dinner at a marvelous French restaurant nearby, *La Bouchèe.* The food was great, but his conversation further turned me off. So, I took my leave while he was still at the table, and left him to pay the bill. I had to go back to his house to get my things, and he came in before I had finished packing. We had more arguments and shouting matches. It was horrible, but he soon drank himself into a stupor and I was able to get a bit of sleep on the couch. The next day, before he got up, I took my things and moved in with a friend not far away."

"But, didn't you know you were risking his approaches if you moved in with him," I asked.

She said, "Well, he was very attractive. But, you are right, of course, and I will never make that mistake again."

"All right, so what other misadventures have you had?"

She continued, "Another time, I was with a fellow artist, but also making love at times with an academic, who taught a literature course I was taking at the University of London. I found out, I can't handle seeing two people amorously at the same time, even if I had worked it out so that one was in the middle of the week and the other on weekends."

"Which was which?"

"What difference would that make? Let me tell you something about my bookstore. But not until after we finish eating these lovely dishes and a dessert if you want one. And then I want you to tell me more about your wine history project and planned year in Paris."

So, we enjoyed the rest of our meal. We decided against dessert, and I asked her if before she talked to me about the book store, I could tell her about the bad experience I had also had trying to handle two lovers at once.

"Please do," she said.

"That was when I had just begun teaching in New York. I had begun dating and loving a nice woman who was a physical therapist. But, then at the library one day I became intrigued with the lady sitting opposite me. She was trying to read Japanese. As I had once studied that before giving it up as too difficult, I struck up a conversation. We went out for tea and one thing led to another.

But after about two months of imagining I was getting the best of both worlds, I began to feel badly. Moreover, I began to get bumps which made me wonder if they were some sexual disease. It turned out they were just pimples, but I decided to break with the second lady."

"How did you feel about it later, for example?"

"Not great. But, as time passed I thought *c'est la vie,* and a lesson to learn." In fact, I was thinking how enticing it was to think about making love with a beautiful woman like Valerie who also liked sex so much that she too had had two lovers at one time. But, I had to wait and see when that could be possible. So I said, "Now tell me about your bookstore."

"I see we do think alike, perhaps too much. Anyway, the store is called Lombard's. The owner is a great Italophile and he hopes to attract some business types who work nearby on Lombard Street, London's Wall Street. It was named for the medieval bankers who came there from from that region of Italy. The store is on Old Broad Street and at lunch time and after work, we get lots of customers and even more browsers--- oops---, I forgot that word now has more to do with computers. But, what else can you call them?"

"Indeed ! It's like `gay.' That used to be one of my favorite words. I still use it, but with a wink. I guess it's the same for `browser.'

"Exactly," Valerie continued. "Anyway, I love books and reading and so it's great work, even if quite hectic at times. I remember two weeks ago, this chap came in to ask me if I had a new book, to do with problems of world history, but he couldn't remember the name of the title or author. He said it was something like `*Germs, Guns and Civilization.*' Well, I happened to know that book because I had just bought it. I'm reading it on this trip and it is fascinating. He had mixed up the order of words. It's by Jared Diamond and called *Guns, Germs and Steel.*

"That kind of thing to do with my work is very satisfying. And maybe you should get that book too. It's a study of maybe the biggest problem in world history since the last ice age, namely how come we Europeans and you Americans got to take over the world, rather than some other countries like China or the Arabs taking us over. How does that strike you for cheek, to have the ambition to tackle something like that. A friend told me that another recent book, *The Wealth and Poverty of Nations*, by David Landes, tackles the same problem but from a more conservative point of view."

"That's fascinating, and maybe you don't want to quit a job that gives you insights like that. In fact, I definitely want to read those books and thank you for the references. I've tried to treat that very question in many of my survey courses at Baruch. Do you think I can find them here in Paris?"

"Probably, most likely at one of the English language stores here of which I hear there are several. And good luck. Now, tell me more about your wine history project."

"All right. Since I love wine, for several years I've been wondering how I could do a book on some aspect of wine history. It's really vast, you know, with all its history since the Greeks and Romans, and now with the growth in consumption all over the world. But, it seems that recently people are consuming less and less of it. Maybe that's another example of my luck in turning to a subject that will be harder and harder to sell. Vietnam, for example, was like that after I did my book on the wars there about ten years ago. For years after the American defeat there, it was a hot topic. But now only entrepreneurs and an occasional tourist give a damn about it."

"Oh, come on! I know a lot of people still fascinated by anything to do with the Vietnam war, and some are obsessed with anything at all about Vietnam. On my last trip to New

York, I had to laugh when I saw a car, parked not far from the play MISS SAIGON, with a sticker on the rear window, which said ʽUniversity of South Vietnam: Department of War and Killing.' And there must be still more people who are interested in anything to do with wine."

"Well, I've started serious reading about it, and think I may have found a way to tackle it. Since the subject is so big, why not choose an interesting and famous chateau in France and try to interweave its history with the story of improvements in wine making over the centuries."

"And have you come up with a chateau yet?"

"Yes. At least I think so. But, I'm stuck with the problem of too much history at the one I'm thinking of, Clos de Vougeot. I might also try to set a historical novel there, but whether that or a straight history, it is sort of overwhelming. Too many details, and there are an infinite number, which will probably get in the way of telling any story I can come up with."

"Before you go on, tell me more about where it is, and other relevant stuff."

"It's just south of Dijon in the Cote d'Or region. You know, the Romans were there, and then many Crusaders returning from their battles. Later some other soldiers composed the famous La Marseilleuse nearby on their way to fight in the Napoleonic wars. Anyway, I plan to go check out some of the chateaux south of Dijon in a few days, and in the meantime I'm spending my days in libraries and at the Musèe du Vin, researching the more interesting vineyards and related subjects. Tomorrow, as I've already done the latter, I think I will go to the national library, the Bibliotheque François Mitterand, or as everyone calls it the TGB for *Tres Grande Bibliotheque*. It is really enormous, and to the east of the Gare d'Austerlitz about a half hour southeast of here, by foot that is. Then, after my return from Burgundy, I'm scheduled to teach a course at a part of the Universitè de Paris, called L'Institut d'Anglais. That is attached to the Paris VII College, or Jussieu as it is called after the metro stop nearby. There's an exchange teaching program between the City University of New York and the University of Paris, and I was able to get the Baruch slot for that this year."

"How fascinating! Would you like a research assistant for the trip to Burgundy?" She said that with an arched eyebrow and another mischievous smile. I hesitated as I pondered my response. I was thinking I really liked my privacy, and yet she was so beautiful and nice, at least when she is flirting with me. "Are you serious?" I asked.

"Well, maybe. As said, I'm not sure how long I want to be working in the London book store. Along with the good moments, there are too many boring ones. I mean you can only spend so much time rearranging books, and trying to skim them until the next customer asks some boring question. Besides, I'd love to see more of France. As mother was already an orphan when she married dad, we only went to France one or two times; To Paris, Bordeaux and Limoges. So, I would love to see Burgundy." As she finished speaking, Valerie delighted me with an affectionate squeeze of my hand.

"Incredible! That would be so great. Yet, maybe I need to reflect a bit. Would it lead us to too much togetherness do you think?"

"I see you are afraid of commitment ! So, OK, forget I proposed anything."

"Look. Let's just spend a few days here in Paris, exploring things and getting to know each other better. And we can see. How about that?"

Unfortunately, I could see that the previous good mood had been broken, and wondered how to restore it. I had an idea.

"Tomorrow, I'd like to introduce you to some older friends of mine who now live here. I knew them in Asheville and New York, and I think you'll find them sympathetic."

"All right. But, it will have to be later in the day, as I want to see some more of the Louvre and other museums."

"Do you know all the other marvelous places to see?" I asked her. I couldn't resist citing to her chateau-museums that were lesser known, and their collections. "Some of them are off the beaten track," I continued, "I would like to take you to such marvelous places as Chantilly and Vaux Le Vicomte, which are both near Paris." My enthusiasm was contagious, and encouraged by her interest, I told her what incredible histories those places had, as well as how beautiful they are. "Chantilly's name comes from a Gallic Roman who first built a fort there. It was enlarged in medieval times, and the present splendid chateau was built mostly in stages from the fourteenth to nineteenth centuries. It became very famous as one of the best places in France to raise beautiful horses of all types, from walkers to racers."

She was still listening attentively, so I went on with my history lesson. "Nicolas Fouquet built Vaux Le Vicomte after 1656, but was arrested about five years later when he offended the new king, Louis XIV, by giving too regal a party at his chateau. The king thought only he could give such a pretentious soirèe and I guess he feared Fouquet's ambition. But, the chateau is a magnificent place." I finished by saying "I guess it or some member of that family gives the name of the restaurant on the Champs Elysèes, though I have never had that confirmed."

Meanwhile, the waiter kept circling us, evidently hoping we would leave to make way for new guests. In fact, by then it was almost eleven. We decided it was time, paid and left. That done, we walked back for a night cap at the Cafè Danton several blocks west on the Boulevard St. Germain des Près.

Over several glasses of their wine special of Pomerol, Valerie began to explore her feelings about me. She said she really liked me, but was also torn between letting her affection grow, and preserving her indepedence. She laughed as she said,

"I know I shouldn't have been so forward about proposing to accompany you on the trip to Burgundy. But, I thought it sounded like fun."

"It would be, I'm sure. But, I guess we have to wait a bit and see. I, for example, am wrestling with the old questions of any new relationship with a woman. Yet, how can I resist you? Anyway, we have a few days to decide. And now let's confirm the rendez-vous for demain. How about the Chai de l'Abbaye at 7:30; and I'll try to arrange for cocktails with the friends I mentionned. They are Clara and George Simpson, who live in the Place d'Italie area in the southwest of Paris. By the way, if you want to explore another area of the city, that's an easy ride from here, transferring to the Nation line at the Raspail stop. And tonight is still young. Before you go to your hotel, how about seeing my room at Hotel La Louisiane?"

"All right! In fact, I'd like to see a room in another sympa hotel. Who knows how long I want to stay in mine?"

Was that another hint, I wondered as I looked into her lovely hazel eyes with an intent stare. It did not hide my mixture of admiration, expectation and nervousness. I told myself to be careful, even as I looked forward to intimacy with one of the most beautiful girls I had seen, let alone met, in quite some time.

I took her arm. She pulled back, and said, "But, I thought we were going to be careful and take our time. Shouldn't we be platonic for awhile?

I'll look at your room for curiosity's sake, but then be on my way, all right?"

"Yes, maybe you're right. I promise to be a gentleman." Noting her acquiescence, I continued, "It's this way."

We crossed the Boulevard St. Germain and walked down the *Rue de l'Ancienne Comedie*, took a left on *Rue de Buci* and came into the *Rue de Seine*. The hotel is at number sixty on the west side of that street across from us. I had a corner room on the courtyard. The first thing Valerie said was "It's so small.

But, I see you are comfortable with a big bed and bath. And it's so well situated. You're just steps away from so many great places."

"Well, I certainly think so," I said as I helped her off with her coat.

Fortunately, there was an easy chair for her and I sat in the desk chair.

I ventured, "So, you want to put off a little love-making? We can, but on the other hand, I've never been in such a small place with such a beautiful woman."

Again her ravishing smile. And imagine my delight when she took my hand and led me to the bed. We kissed and I put my hand on her swelling breasts. She began to sigh. Our hands began to explore other intimate places, even as I began to unbutton her blouse. She stood up, saying "Let me do those buttons. They're so fragile."

That was all I needed to strip myself and we fell into the nice, wide bed for one of the best such times I ever had or could imagine. She let me run my hands all over, from her thighs to the sweet spot, to her neck and down again to fondle her glorious breasts. I had never experienced such a magnificent creature, and naturally I became harder and harder. But, I didn't want to rush such delights and took my time even as we resumed kissing. My only problem was to have both hands free for the caressing. I tried to imagine I was one of those Indian gods with four or more arms. One solution I found for my two, was to put one around her shoulder and on the right breast, while with the other I excited her down below. And she was excitable. I could resist no longer and we went at it with enthusiasm.

The next morning, when I awoke and sought her, she was equally responsive. This time she came on top of me, and before long that was in both senses of the word. I tried to restrain myself, remembering the night before and thinking about the book I had read about how Taoists and other Orientals limited their ejaculations so as to be able to perform more often.

I also did not want to cause a pregnancy, though Valerie had told me she was on the pill. The problem was picking the right moment to withdraw, and then there was a slight let-down. A small problem to say the least, and what bliss. I wondered about Aids, but thought that I could wait to ask her about that later, hoping we had not already blundered into it.

An hour or so later, toward nine, I proposed we do breakfast, which I then ordered. A few minutes later, the chamber maid brought in one *café au lait complet,* which included a croissant and some jam. But only for one, which I considered fortunate, as I did not want them to start charging me for a more expensive room for two. But now they probably would.

The serving lady, who was a bourgeois looking, middle aged brunette, winked at me but with a somewhat suspicious air. I supposed she would tell the direction downstairs. I remember thinking I had better concoct some story for the front desk, and decided to ask Valerie to leave first. She said she would start with another visit to the Louvre and I planned to go to the TGB library further up the Seine at Tolbiac.

"All right, *cherie.*" I said with deliberate understatement, "That was not a bad step forward in our friendship. But, could you leave first, so I can try to keep my single room rate, and I will see you as agreed at 7:30 this evening?" She nodded and said, "*D'accord.* Have a great day and see you then."

As I watched her leave, I thought I could not believe my luck. But, also I was wondering if we had gone too far too fast. No doubt I should have waited until our trip before bedding her. But how did I know she wouldn't disappear before that, and then I would have missed a great opportunity.

Time would tell, and I quickly dressed and went down to try to cover myself and save the thirty euro less my room cost for one person, as compared with the double room rate of one hundred twenty euro. At the desk I said in my best French, "*Bonjour. Il fait beau n'est-ce pas? C'était une petite amie de passage, et je serais absent presque toute la journèe.*"

It was a bit disconcerting to think how much I had gotten in the habit of telling white lies such as that one about only having a sometime friend in my room. And that had been one of my problems with Henrietta, who had a woman's instinct about such falsehoods. But, in Paris white lies usually gave me no trouble. To be sure, I would have to see if that would be the case with Valerie.

The lady at the desk said, "*No problem. Bien sur, Monsieur Howard, on comprende bien ces choses la. Pas de probleme, et bonne journèe.*"

My best way to the Tolbiac library was bus no. 89, which passed across the street on the other side of the Boulevard St. Germain just before the Odeon metro stop. It came rapidly and I arrived at the library before eleven.

It was really too huge. You could see the four enormous towers housing all the books and reading spaces from a considerable distance. The

Towers were at least 100 meters apart, forming a rectangle around a large garden. I imagined if it was in America, local youth would rapidly make a mess of the perfect lawn with their careless discarding of junk. But, I wondered if maybe Americans are getting neater. At least I hoped so.

Perhaps, if the planners had made the whole space smaller, the place would have seemed far more agreeable. But, the government said it was building a library big enough for the new century and all the students, researchers and library lovers who would be using it. Maybe, I thought, but what a grandiose project! I feared that rather than being "a library for the 21st. Century" as the signs proclaimed, it would discourage even more people from going to the library. Was this an example of the bad side of

France? Was too much ambition for edifice complexes ruining their usual good taste? It is said that each new leader has to create his own colossal monument. This was one of Mitterand's, as had been I.N. Pei's pyramid in the courtyard of the Louvre and the awful stone statues marring the esplanade of the Grand Palais. They are so-called "Grandes Travaux," and good luck to them. At least, there was only one skyscraper, the Tour Montparnasse, which is very out of place among the beautiful other buildings in the center of the city. But, how about keeping the graceful lines of the metropolis? There are other problems in the suburbs, but central Paris is still one of the most beautiful cities.

It took me over an hour to find which tower housed the books on wine history. First you had to pass the security controls with the annoying emptying of your pockets. I wondered if such security checks were one of the biggest damages to bourgeois society inflicted by terrorists. Then there had been the stop at the information desk and the trip down a long hall to register for using the library. So much paper work!

Once in the history tower, it took more time to figure out the very different system for ordering the books I wanted. The computers were the latest and required considerable time to understand the proper commands. Typing was a whole other problem for foreigners, as the French keyboard and orthography seem strange to say the least. To begin with, they have the letter "a" where the "q" should be? And the "w," "m" and other letters are all in places different from those used by anglophones. I supposed the best solution was simply to go back to typing one finger at a time.

Finally, some books arrived and I began to feel less frustrated. There was a new one for me on the *Clos de Vougeot,* and I was struck again with how much history it had. Maybe it would be better to try to do a fictional account where I could make up my own stories instead of having to research so much. How nice it would be not to have to do footnotes and all the academic paraphernalia that had encumbered my previous few books.

By then it was almost three in the afternoon, and I thought I could read for another hour or so. But, I continued to reflect on the quandary about whether to do the non-fiction I knew I could do, or to try figure out something new writing fiction. I liked the latter idea and thought maybe I could be helped with that by a new love. Still, I kept seeing fascinating new stories to do with the *Clos de Vougeot*. For example, the pages I had just read related the medieval story of a good way to curry favor. The Cistercian Abbot, *Jean de Bussières*, whose neighboring monastery controlled the vineyard, in 1359 sent thirty kegs or over 9000 bottles of *Clos de Vougeot* burgundy to Pope Gregory XI. Four years later, Jean became a cardinal of the church. Talk about the politics of gift giving!

That made me think of Valerie, as if I needed inducement. I returned my books to the front receptacle for that, and set out by foot for the hotel. It was over a half hour walk, again by lovely places. I followed the Seine which shortly led to the *Jardin des Plantes*, which was just after the *Austerlitz* train station. It had been the Royal Medicinal Herb Garden in the *Ile de la Citè* near Notre Dame until Louis XIII moved it across the river to its present location. He opened it to the public in 1640, eight years before his death. Great botanists headed by *Buffon*, who died in 1788, made it one of the world's preeminent sites for the observation and study of natural history, plants, and trees. I enjoyed walking through the garden with its beautiful flowers and all the rest.

Then I went back along the river towards my hotel, enabling me to look to the left at the University of Paris VII where I would be teaching. It and the nearby metro are called *Jussieu* because of three botanists of that name who worked in the *Jardin des Plantes* before and after the time of their great colleague, *Buffon*. As mentioned I had audited several courses there on the history of Vietnam at Jussieu ten or so years ago.

And this year they have asked me to do courses in American and Canadian history at the *Institut d'Anglais*, which is across the river, but administered by Jussieu.

Next, I passed the eastern terminus of the *Boulevard St. Germain* and stopped at the entrance to the famous restaurant, *La Tour d'Argent*. I looked at its menu and my mouth watered, thinking of the *Quenelles de Brochet* to start and then one of the duck dishes for which the restaurant has been famous for centuries. I probably could not afford it, however, and took consolation by looking down the Seine at the splendid rear portions of the Notre Dame Cathedral with its great flying buttresses and noble lines.

From there it was an easy ten minute walk back to my hotel, again by many interesting spots. I detoured via the hotel my mother used to stay at, the *Colbert*. Then I decided on a drink at another favorite bar, *Au Trois Mailletz*, just across the river from Notre Dame. Buildings, however, blocked the view from that bar of the beautiful church.

By six I was back at the hotel, and soon ready for my evening rendez-vous at 7:30. I arrived at the *Chai de l'Abbaye* at the appointed time. My friends, Clara and George Simpson, were already there and we exchanged the usual pleasantries. About five minutes later Valerie arrived.

I could see George's favorable appraisal, but noted before long a certain coolness on the part of Clara. At first, they had greeted each other with cordiality, but as we talked a certain mutual disapproval seemed to develop.

I guessed several factors were at play. Clara was not a bad looking brunette, but was the jealous type. She may have been turned off by Valerie's blonde beauty as well as by her praises of Paris. It seemed the Simpsons had had a disastrous arrival two days before from the trip they had taken back to New York to see Clara's parents. Because they came back on an early flight, they arrived at the airport at seven in the morning and at the *Hotel d'Angleterre* by ten. There, they were told they would have to wait until at least noon for their room. They were staying at the hotel for three nights until they could check on the work they had ordered done for their apartment on the *Avenue Soeur Rosalie* near the *Place d'Italie*. They were jet-lagged, and Clara became angry at losing what she said was her favorite scarf. She claimed she had given it to the hat check girl at the bar they went to in order to pass the time until their room was ready. She thought the girl had stolen it, and got into a fight with George when he said she had probably left her scarf on the plane.

I wondered if that argument had to do with the shaky state of their marriage, which I had already noticed when I knew them in the States. I had met George back in Asheville and as a fellow student at the University of North Carolina. Then I got to know him better when I was doing my doctorate at Columbia. He became an insurance salesman in New York and had made good money by the time he met Clara. She was a psychiatrist who could be either charming or difficult according to her mood. George told me those moods changed frequently and were beginning to bother him. But, he hoped they could stay together for the sake of their two children.

In any case, as Valerie was saying how much she was enjoying seeing Paris and its museums and restaurants, Clara barked at her, "How can you say that? Everything has gone badly for us here since we got back. A hat check girl stole my scarf as we were waiting to get into our hotel room, and last night I had one of the worst meals of my life. It was supposed to have been good as it was at a Michelin one star restaurant near us on *Rue Grands Augustins*, close to the Seine, called *Relay Louis 13* or something like that."

She had a thick accent and *Relais* came out Relay, but in this case, it was no problem as they mean the same and sound alike. She continued, "The lamb chops I ordered were so rare, I thought they were raw. The string beans were undercooked and the dessert too sweet."

Valerie interjected, "Excuse me, but I think that's all wrong. Lamb chops are supposed to be rare and the haricots verts green and tender. Anyway, the scarf you are wearing is very pretty."

"Well, thank you. It's my only other scarf, but I preferred the one that was stolen. And, I disagree about the lamb chops. I thought I told the waiter I wanted them medium or well done. I also like my beans better cooked."

That cleared the air a bit, and I said '*a chacun son gout.*' George did more by saying he would buy another scarf for Clara. I added that, "I was glad they were meeting Valerie, who though a very new friend was quite close." I restrained myself from winking at George as I said that, but think he got the idea. "Let's have a glass or two here and then go to a nice restaurant I know of not far from here."

"And what might that be?" George asked. "Do you think we should reserve.?"

"No, I don't think so. Parisians don't go to restaurants until about 9, and there are several other possibilities nearby. So, we risk nothing."

It was at the *Bistrot Mazarin* on the street of that name, a few blocks down and towards the Seine. Arriving, I saw Keith had just come in, and asked if he would like to join us. He said yes, and we found a table for five. The food was wonderful. Even Clara complimented it. But she continued to be rather frigid I thought, especially towards Valerie. Keith thought he was making up for that by continuously smiling at Valerie and asking new questions.

I thought, oh no, there he goes again and tried to steer the conversation to something else. I asked them what they thought of all the talk about terrorism and Islam. Keith said he thought it was all overblown, but George said he was not so sure, as athorities kept making new arrests. I said I agreed with Keith, and always wondered why they made so much about the few terrorist deaths when so many people were killed by other things, including cars.

Keith said he thought that was crazy as people driving know they are taking risks. "But," I said, "If you are killed you are killed, whether by bomb or car. And do you know that in United States well over 100 people are killed every day on the highways?"

"Well, that proves it. I will never drive with you," Keith asserted.

"Who said I would ever ask you to?"

Valerie asked, "Why are you two fighting again? I thought this was to be a fun evening."

Clara interjected, "Well, you can see they like a good argument."

To which George said, "I don't see any dispute, just a disagreement. And back to the terrorism, I think I would rather be killed that way, than by a car. It would probably be quicker."

"Not necessarily," I said. "Depends on the speed and where you are sitting and so many things."

At this point Valerie said, "Whichever way you die, it's all a matter of fate, and we just have to see what will happen next. In any case I am tired of all the talk about terrorism."

As that was before the September 11, 2001, attacks on New York and Washington, I had to wonder if Valerie was psychic. In any case, Clara tried changing the subject by saying that in her work she only talked of personal subjects which are so much more interesting. I wondered about that, but did not want George to talk of his work in insurance. I couldn't wait to be alone with Valerie again. I changed the subject to tourism in Paris and then seeing their boredom with that, was glad when George proposed we call it the end of "a pleasant evening."

It was indeed a beautiful evening and we passed a happy crowd at the bar/restaurant, the Palette, almost next door to the Bistrot Mazarin. Then I said, "We turn left here," as we reached the corner of the Rues Callot and Seine. I hoped very much that Keith would not follow us to my hotel which was just up the street. Fortunately, he continued on with the Simpsons, saying he would look for a taxi. Before he went off with them, he turned around to tell us another of his usually interesting anecdotes. This time it was that the Café Flore, opposite which was the taxi stand he would go to, was named after the Café Florian in the Piazza San Marco in Venice. But, I wondered if it showed Keith preferred the company of the Simpsons since an equally good place to find a taxi was closer by on the Boulevard St. Germain just beyond our hotel on the Rue de Seine. Possibly he had forgotten that, and in any case, I happily watched them go on their way down Rue Jacob.

CHAPTER TWO

BURGUNDY and WINE

After a new night of fabulous love making, Valerie and I spent the next few days going our separate ways, she to museums, me to libraries and the evenings discussing the pros and cons of taking off together for Burgundy. As promised, the next day I did lunch with the Simpsons. It seemed Clara continued being unhappy in Paris and was also frequently fighting with George, as several times during our lunch. When in the men's room, I asked him how he could stand to stay with Clara. He replied that he was not sure if he could, but that he wanted to stay with her for the sake of their two kids. He said, "If she does not become more reasonable, I will have to divorce her."

That evening, I finally convinced Valerie and myself of the desirability of making the trip to Burgundy. We planned it for three days later, which would be Thursday, the seventh of September. That day, we went to the Gare de l'Est and took the 14:54 train for Dijon, which arrived at 16:35.

The first problems were easily solved. We found a nice inexpensive hotel and proceeded the next day to rent a car for the trip to Clos de Vougeot. As we drove south, Valerie could barely contain her enthusiasm and it matched my own. There were fields of wheat, often with stands of beautiful flowers on the edges of neighboring pastures. We looked at frequent fields of red, yellow, brown and green blooms, with groves of trees all around. They made beautiful kaleidoscopes of colors, both brilliant and subtle.

We soon came to the village of Vougeot, only 17 kilometers, or just over ten and a half miles, to the south-southwest of Dijon. Following the Michelin red guide, we found a room in a lovely hotel two kilometers to its east, the Chateau de Gilly. It had been a Cistercian Abbey, and possessed a superb restaurant and cellar of wines. We enjoyed both days we were there.

On Saturday, Valerie took our rented Renault to explore the environs and the Chateau de Vougeot. I stayed behind to research what the hotel reading room had on the local wines and to interview the owner and staff about what they knew. I found a few books on the Cistercians and their work in the nearby vineyards. The latter was among the things helping to make their order so famous. Among other things, I discovered that by the time of the completion of the Clos de Vougeot chateau in the fifteenth century, they had built a wall around the 125 acres of the vineyard, presumably to protect it from the numerous marauders in the area.

But then came worry! Valerie had said she would be back by later in the afternoon, and when she still had not returned for the eight o'clock dinner, I became increasingly alarmed. I parried the questions as to where she was with the white lie, "She has a headache."

After a hurried dinner, I called the police to see if I could find any relevant news. To my horror, an inspector told me there had been a report of what sounded like a kidnapping. Worse, it might well have been Valerie, as the witness who gave the information described a woman shouting, `Help, Help! Au Secours! Let me go,' as two men forced her into a truck, described as a grey pick up. I said, "I fear that sounds like the lady I am traveling with, who said she was going to see the Chateau from our hotel which is nearby."

"And where is that?" the inspector asked.

"It's the Chateau de Gilly."

"Interesting, as the woman was assaulted about eleven, not far from the Clos de Vougeot, between it and your hotel. Can you come to the Poste de Police Centrale? It's on the main street."

"Yes, certainly. I'll be there in about five minutes."

Oh happy day! When I arrived by taxi Valerie was there, but looking quite battered. She had bandages around her head and right leg. I rushed up to her, asking "What happened! I am so glad you are there, but how much does it hurt?"

The policeman standing beside her stepped between us, and asked, "Who are you?"

I replied, and then he said, "She can't talk to you now. But, she will be all right. We need to ask her some more questions and then you can go on your way."

"Of course. I'm just so glad to see her." I gave my best smile, and took a seat as indicated. Valerie tried to return the smile, but her face was badly twisted from a bruise on the right cheek, I feared from a blow to the head.

The policeman asked if she could identify her attackers. She started to speak, though with difficulty. "I couldn't believe it when these hooligans pulled in front and forced my car off the road. They were in their twenties or going on thirty and quite average looking. They were both dark haired and one had a full beard and moustache. I couldn't understand what they said, but it didn't sound much like French.

"Luckily, as they were driving away, another car ran into them at the next intersection. They promptly jumped out, as did I. Then, I greeted the people who came running up, and the police were not far behind. I directed them in the direction the bandits had gone. So, here I am, even if a bit battered. One of them couldn't resist taking a swing at me, leaving me with this swollen jaw and black eye. Maybe, because he didn't like my accent for the few French words I used! Thank God, they ran off without taking my purse."

The policeman smiled with the statement, "*C'est très bien que c'est passè si bien que ca.* You were very lucky. And now you can go on your way, after you give us a telephone number. If we can catch them, we will contact you to be a witness at their trial. Tell us before you leave town."

With a "*Certainment, et merci beaucoup,*" we wrote down our cell number, and were on our way.

We went to look at the car, about three blocks away. It had a dented front end, and obviously needed some repairs. We walked over to a nearby gas station. There they told us the number to call for repairs. Since it was past nine in the evening there was no answer. We called the next morning and they told us to go to the car and wait for their tow truck. We walked over, and when the tow truck arrived the driver said it would take several days before we could get the car back.

That gave us the chance to spend the time enjoying the charming village of Vougeot and our hotel. "How bad can it be?" I said, hoping Valerie would agree. She did, and said "What luck. Now, we can really profit from this delightful place." I hugged her, and we walked back to the hotel which took about twenty minutes.

We spent a lovely weekend, walking around and doing this and that. On, Monday, September 11, we walked over to the Chateau de Clos de Vougeot, which Valerie had not seen before her kidnapping. Now, all she had as evidence of that fearsome event was a huge black eye, swollen jaw, and sore leg. There was a huge bruise mid way down her left thigh. She could walk, if slowly, and still had some trouble smiling and talking. She said she was aching a bit, but not too much now that she was on the mend. I told her how brave I thought she was.

Examining the chateau, we found that it had been built mostly in the

14th and 15th centuries, and after damages in the Revolution restored to its present splendor in the 19th. I was especially interested in the plaque describing the Confrerie des Chevaliers du Tastevin, which had bought the Chateau of the Clos in 1944, ten years after the Confrerie had been founded to promote the fortunes of local wines. The hotel owner had told me the day before that their annual meetings were renowned for the splendor of their feasts, as well as for the high jinks of many of the high livers among them.

Valerie and I went out into the garden of the Chateau which was surrounded by Plantain trees. Just looking at my lady, despite her bruises, made me want to caress her. I contented myself with taking her hand and asking how she felt.

She replied, "much better, thank you." And, as if she read my mind, asked, "Shall we go back to the hotel now, maybe with a meal on the way?"

"Great idea," I said. "It's almost lunch time and a glass of wine will be wonderful, even if it's not of the order of the 1970 Clos de Vougeot, which we just saw featured on a plaque of the Chevaliers du Tastevin."

In fact, we did a much cheaper, but still very good 1997 *Cote du Rhone,* called *Beaume de Venise.* The waiter said the name came from the original makers who had been on a crusade or two in the twelfth and thirteenth centuries. That was at a small bistrot we had seen on the walk from the hotel. We got into a friendly dispute over who had ordered the better dish, her mountain trout or my Lac Lèman perche. Both were excellent and followed by marvelous cheeses and salad. That set us up for the walk back to the hotel, another round of caressing, a nap and dinner.

We had only one more day before getting the car back and deciding what to do with it, whether to go back to Paris or stay awhile longer in Burgundy. We decided to do the latter, and the day of waiting passed happily, with reading, walking, eating and sleeping. The next day, the car seemed perfectly repaired and I proposed to use it to explore the itinerary that the English wine taster, Keith Weaver, had outlined to me. Valerie happily agreed and we prepared to set out. First, we had to go by the Police Station and give them the number of our cell phone, in case they caught the two hoodlums who had attacked Valerie.

Then, before going south as Keith had done, I wanted to go north to see three other famous wine locations, the village of *Chambolle-Musigny*, and the towns of *Gevrey-Chambertin and Vosne-Romanèe*. The first owed its name to a corruption of the Roman words, *Campus Ebulliens*, describing the spring flooding of the stream which runs through *Chambolle Musigny*. About two miles to the north is *Gevrey-Chambertin*, which is bigger and better known. Its great wine, *Chambertin*, was the choice of Napoleon who drank more of it than any other after he discovered it. The French national song was first sung nearby after soldiers from Marseilles composed it in 1795, and it has been known ever after as the *Marseilleise.*

Next, we went the five kilometers southwest to *Vosne Romanèe*, a small town at the edge of *Romanèe-Conti* and other famous vineyards. Its name went back to 312 when a Roman wrote to Emperor Constantine about a "famous canton distinguished for its culture of the vine." The vineyards there developed further in the middle ages and *Romanèe-Conti* became so famous by 1760 that it fostered a dispute between Madame de Pompadour and a Bourbon prince. The latter used his prestige and connections to acquire the vineyard against the wishes of Madame de Pompadour, a favorite of Louis XV. She had looked forward to having it as another summer retreat.

After a quick look at each of these places, we decided to turn around and try to find the original site of the Cistercians. We were told they were called that after the Latin name, *Cistercium*. To get there we had to drive south to *Nuits St.*

Georges, which is another famous wine town. It was bigger than the previous ones, though still small with about 6000 people. As the leading town of the Cote d'Or vineyards just south of Dijon, *Nuits St. Georges* became a center for wine dealers and shippers, along with Beaune, fifteen miles to its southwest.

The famous medieval Abbaye de Notre-Dame-de-Citeaux, the home of the Cistercian order, is about ten miles to the east of Nuits St. Georges. A certain Robert de Molesme, a Benedictine abbot, founded the Cistercians in 1098. It stressed absolute poverty and manual labor in opposition to the extravagant life styles of the monks of Cluny and the Scholastics of Paris. The Cistercians criticized the opulence of Cluny monks and the Scholastics, and sought to emulate the life of Christ and his early followers. After the appointment of St. Bernard as abbot of the Abbey in 1142, the order rose to such fame that by the middle of the 12th. Century, it rivaled Cluny as a center of Christianity. After 1162, the Cistercians turned much of their energy to wine making and were instrumental in establishing the fame and quality of vineyards like the Clos de Vougeot. By the eighteenth century their successors became known as Trappist monks.

After several hours looking over Citeaux and the ruins of the old monastery, we went to the major wine center at Beaune some twenty kilometers further southwest. We easily found another small hotel, the Cloche. It was not far from the Hotel-Dieu, founded as a charity hospital in 1443 by one of the last Chancellors of Burgundy. The Hotel-Dieu is said to be one of the best examples of Burgundian-Flemish architecture, housing some of that school's finest paintings. The fact that it was first built as a refuge for the poor led King Louis XI, who incorporated Burgundy and many other areas into an expanding French monarchy during his reign from 1461-1483, to make a witty comment. He said that the Chancellor, Nicolas Rolin, an advisor to the Duke of Burgundy, must have "built the Hotel-Dieu for the poor, since he has made so many of them." Later, upkeep was paid for in part by annual wine auctions.

The next morning, we spent exploring these and other wonders of Beaune, a town of some 22,000. We started with the Musèe du Vin de Bourgogne. It contained more information on the history of the region, from the Gauls to the establishment there of the Roman town of Belma, which became the flourishing Medieval wine city of Beaune. From that museum, it was just a step or two to the Hotel Dieu, which we wanted to examine at leisure. With its ornate façade, polychrome tile roof and gabled courtyard, it resembled a fairy tale castle. Its most famous work of art was the Last Judgement by Roger Van der Weyden, whose striking scenes of hell are said to be worthy of those of his more famous contemporaries, Hieronymous Bosch and Breughels. There were other lovely paintings and many yards of intricately carved small statues of saints and other figures along the walls.

Our lunch at the nearby one star restaurant, Le Jardin des Remparts,

was hard to believe, with oysters, foie gras, duck, steak tartar and other delights. Despite some drowsiness from a half carafe each of delicious white one from Meursault, and a red Cote de Rhone, known by its location on the map at latitude 45, we continued on. That was to Pommard, just to the south. The most famous wine of the area along with Meursault, Pommard is also plentiful and the most widely consumed of all red Burgundies. The estate was dominated by an impressive eighteenth century chateau. After wandering around that, we went to get our bags which we had left downstairs, and headed for Meursault to the southwest of Beaune. We were guided to it by the spire of its fourteenth century church. I recalled to Valerie what Keith Weaver had told me earlier, about the name of Meursault coming from the latin for mouse's jump, or *muris saltus*, to describe the crossing of a stream flowing through the town.

Meursault produced the most wine of the region after Pommard, a fitting coincidence for those like us wanting to enjoy both those splendid libations. After a glass of one of each at a nearby café, we decided to drive by two other famous white wine vineyards just to the southwest of Meursault. They were Chassagne Montrachet and Puligny Montrachet. Their white wines are considered superior even to those of Meursault.

We stuck to our pleasant habit of sampling these well known wines at a bar or café as close as possible to where they are bottled. That worked out perfectly, as we discovered the Montrachet Hotel, which even had a splendid restaurant. The timing was also good as it was late evening, and, fortunately, they had a room. We took a bath, rested a bit, and went down to as good a meal as you can imagine. We each did one of their specialties to start, namely me the escargots de Bourgogne and Valerie, the *Oeufs en meurette*, with both of us following with the main course specialty of *Blanc de Volaille de Bresse au foie gras*. The escargots were delicious and Valerie said her eggs with red wine sauce were about the best she had ever had. The chicken also was something to write home about. Understandably, we accompanied the meal with a half bottle each of Chassagne Montrachet and Puligny Montrachet. We agreed we would have to economize to make up for the bill, but I thought 'what the heck, you only live once.' I asked Valerie, "How can we not live like this? With so much good travel and food, not to speak of the company." I took her hand with a squeeze. She returned it, with the comment, "I certainly agree, but we have to figure out how to afford it. Never mind, we will figure that out later." I smiled, and we went upstairs for another night of incredible lovemaking, talk and sleep.

The following day we set out to continue our clockwise circular tour back to Dijon by driving south about twenty miles to Chalon-sur-Saone. The most famous things about that town, aside from its proximity to other great vineyards, were its Roman origins, and that it was the home of one of the principal founders of photography, with the curious name of Nicèphore Niepce. He produced a primitive camera as early as 1816. But, the town, at the junction of the Canal du Centre coming from the northwest and the Saone River coming from the northeast, was too industrial for our tastes, and we continued on to the south. We soon passed a commune called Chardonay, evidently the origin of that famous white wine. It is just to the south of Tournus, about 55 miles south of Dijon and 18 miles north of Macon.

The latter was to the southwest. On our way there, we passed through miles of beautiful pastoral landscapes before reaching Macon, a city of

about 30,000. After buying some cheese and a half bottle of Meursault for our lunch, we went southwest a short distance to the towns of Pouilly and Fuissè. They are the site of the famous Pouilly-Fuissè wine, also made of Chardonay grapes. After enjoying our cheese and wine, we kept on to the south, soon reaching the famous wine region of Beaujolais. Its rolling hills of vineyards were all the more welcome, as to reach it we had to get off the autoroutes we had been taking some of the time.

The first town we stopped in had the charming name of St. Amour, or "holy love." It produces some 800,000 bottles of the wine of that name every year. The bigger wine town of Julienas is one mile to the south of that and it produces several times as much again. We stopped at the recommended restaurant, the Coq au Vin, in the marketplace in the center of Julienas. Its lavender blue shutters set off perfectly the pleasant interior, not to speak of its marvelous specialty, the Coq au Vin dishes that we both had.

Just to the south of St. Amour, was Chenas and the neighboring Moulin a Vent, with their equally well known wines. We decided to spend the night in the next village to the south. That was Romaneche-Thorins, where we found another pleasing hotel, Les Maritonnes. After a welcome siesta, we were told to go to a little restaurant on the Saone river. There we ate an incredibly good dish of crayfish from waters in the marsh adjoining that river.

The next morning, we drove a few miles further southwest through Fleury and other towns to Mont Brouilly, the site of the most reputed Beaujolais. Their estates produce over four millon bottles a year!

So much wine! But just as well since the Beaujolais was the first red wine I had discovered back in North Carolina. My father bought it more than any other as it was the cheapest of the good wines, or so he said. He allowed me to start sipping it when I was about fifteen. Now, Valerie and I stopped for a few glasses at the restaurant of the Hotel Mont Brouilly in the village of Quincie-en-Beaujolais, just to the northwest. After another delicious meal, we decided to keep on in that direction in order to get to the famous medieval monastery of Cluny. That meant continuing northwest, rather than south to Lyon and the Cote du Rhone wine region to its south. Too bad since the latter has become my favorite red wine.

After about ten miles we came to the village of Milly-Lamartine, where the well-known romantic poet, Lamartine, lived most of his life from 1790 to 1869. He became foreign minister briefly after the February, 1848, Revolution, and was a prominent member of the French Academy and Parliament.

Another ten miles to the north and we arrived in Cluny, which was about sixteen miles west of Macon. As the mother abbey of the powerful church order of Benedictines, it was larger than any church in Rome from its founding in 910 to the building of St. Peter's in the fifteenth century. After that, the Cluny church remained the second largest in Europe until the late 18th. Century when it was almost completely destroyed during the French Revolution. In 1823, orders finally came to preserve what was left of it.

Given the historical importance of Cluny, we spent a night in the aptly named Abbaye Hotel. The following morning we walked around the ruins of the monastery trying to imagine what it must have been like to be a monk or nun there a thousand years ago. Valerie said, "I've always wondered that also. I think I would have liked the peaceful times, at least until the plague struck. But, how would one have passed the day. I can't imagine praying all day."

"It is difficult to imagine. But, of course there were several hours of gardening, or other chores. And I suppose one enjoyed the repasts such as they were, though I read once it was mostly cabbage, cauliflower and beans, with chicken or meat only very rarely."

"I once tried being a vegetarian, but didn't like it very much. Maybe, attending angels helped distract the monks from their lack of hedonistic pursuits. Anyway, speaking of food, or the lack thereof, how about lunch?"

We walked over to a nice lawn under some trees and took out the cheese, apples and pears we had brought.

After eating and resting a bit, in about an hour, we continued northwest another hundred miles to Vèzelay, a lovely hill town with a complex of churches. Pope Jean VIII consecrated one of them in 878, a generation before Cluny. But it came under the control of the latter shortly after the founding of Cluny in 910. A century after that, a wondrous new church was begun in Vèzelay, which became the Basilica of Ste. Madeleine. A major fire in 1120 destroyed its nave and buried up to a thousand pilgrims in its ashes. By 1215 the Basilica was completely rebuilt to become one of the greatest of all cathedrals, beautifully situated on the 1000 foot hill overlooking the village. We spent the night at a hotel we reached three kilometers before the village. Another wonderful meal, with a cheese souflet and Turbot, preceeded some of our best love-making yet.

We spent some hours the next morning examining the wonders of the Basilica. They included some of the best representations ever made of Christ and the Saints. Then, we set out to the west for Sancerre, a village of 2000 people who produce that famous white wine. Next it was northeast about thirty five kilometers to the site of still another famous white wine, Chablis. It lies directly south of the Champagne capitals of Reims and Troyes, and just west of the headwaters of the Seine River. In Chablis, we found a restaurant with a beautiful garden. The escargots and sandre fish we had set off the wines which accompanied the meal. Not surprisingly, the enormous amount of garlic that came with the meal, served as a marvelous aphrodisiac. I soon prooved that to be the case, in the room we booked above the restaurant.

The next day we drove along the Serein River southeast to Dijon to turn in our car. That completed our more or less circular tour which had been in the shape of a boomerang or bow tie in that lovely part of eastern France. An easy walk from there took us to the train station, and the train back to Paris arrived on schedule at the Gare de l'Est. It was Saturday afternoon, September 23 and our metro left from the lower level of the station. We reached the Odeon station and La Louisiane Hotel with ease.

No sooner were we in our room than Valerie asked me if she could ask a personal question I might not like. She wanted to know if I had the money to pay her as an assistant for my teaching and writing.

"The problem is," I hazarded, "I don't have much money, and think perhaps we should wait until after I start my teaching in a few weeks."

"Well, I am increasingly anxious to make a change in my life, and I was wondering if you might be the man to help me do that. But, I see you are still hesitating. Shall I go my way and do something else in Paris until I see whether you have changed your mind? Anyway, if I get a job, that could help with the money side."

"That's a great idea! Do it, and I will keep this room while we both look for studios. I need one for my teaching job and other work, and you should probably get one while we figure out if we have a future together."

"Wonderful!" said Valerie. She then added with a smile, "Why don't we celebrate this solution with a little caress?"

That made me think again how "cute and sly" Valerie was. I thought of that formulation from the description of a French word, *dèlurè*, I had just sought in a dictionary. Naturally, I took her in my arms and we started to kiss. That led to other things and removing our clothes, we settled on the bed and went at it with enthusiasm. I explored her curves, narrow waist and plump derriere. She responded with her supple hands all over me and our mutual pleasure seemed very natural and mutually reinforcing. As I was wondering how we could ever stop, we both were overcome with the completion that resulted from such love-making.

Such heavenly passion is all too short lived. As I lay back with luxurious satisfaction, I began to think how dumb I had been to put off Valerie. I appreciated more than ever how wonderful she was. I mumbled softly, "Forgive me for my stupidity. You are so great. I can't let you go even for a few weeks. Let's look for a flat together, starting tomorrow. OK?"

"Well, how do you know I don't want to explore Paris on my own," she teased, fortunately again with a smile. I considered that, but then said, "OK, we'll both explore Paris a little more and see each other as we can, and then our love making will stay fantastic. I entwined with her again and it was another hour before we put on our clothes.

The next day after breakfast, we went our separate ways, having decided to look for apartments in different areas of the city. But, we decided to keep our room in the hotel for awhile longer until we could find other digs. I thought I wanted something nearby in the fifth or sixth arrondissements, and Valerie said she wanted to look near the Square Monceau in the Seventeenth Arrondissement just north of the Arc de Triomphe, and the Eighth all around it, on the other side of Paris. She said a London friend who knew Paris well had recommended that area and she liked what she had seen on a trip or two just after her arrival. We already had cut out a few apartment ads from Le Figaro, and thought if we had problems we would have to go through an agency.

The next evening Valerie came into the room in great excitement.

"You will never believe what I have found. A beautiful apartment on the Rue de Vèzelay. Can you believe it? Vezelay was the most impressive of the many sites we saw on our trip, and here I can live on a street of that name. It's just to the east of Park Monceau, or Square Monceau as it is called officially."

"Is it big enough for me," I interjected. "I saw nothing I liked, and how can I do without you?"

Valerie replied, "So, you are changing your mind again. I don't know what I am going to do with you." But she added, "I think it's big enough for the two of us, if you promise to behave."

She came over to embrace me. I was all too eager. But, Valerie quickly pulled back and started talking again.

"You can't believe how elegant and well located it is. It's on the third floor, or deuxième as they call it here, of a walk up. As you enter the apartment there is a hallway going back to the kitchen, with the living room off to one side and the bedroom on the other. The bedroom looks out on a small courtyard and is thus very quiet. The location is incredible. You get to the Monceau Metro stop just across the east end of the Park. Within steps you get to streets with the names of many of the great cities of Europe, Athens, Constantinople, Bucarest,

Lisbon, Madrid, Florence, Milan, Rome and I don't know what. And it's walking distance from Montmartre."

"That sounds perfect. How did you find it."

"Again, you can't believe my luck. I was walking along that street, thinking how much we had loved Vèzelay, when all of a sudden I saw a piece of paper stuck on a gate entrance to the house. It said 'chambres a louer.' So, I went in and asked the lady who came to the door if I could look at her rooms. It was great practice for my French and she seemed to understand me. I found her easy to talk to. She is a good looking lady, in her fifties I would guess. And so nice. She showed me the apartment and I had to restrain my enthusiasm. I could hardly believe how little rent she asked, 5000 francs a month. That is only about 500 pounds."

"But, that is about half what I will be getting at the Institut d'Anglais. How will we manage?"

"Well, I will try to get a job, and I have to anyway since I signed a lease with her."

"To start when?"

"In about a week, the first of October. But, that is a Sunday and maybe we should tell her Monday, the second. What do you think?"

"Let's do the second. We only got back from our trip to Burgundy two days ago on September 23, and I start to teach on Tuesday, October 17. We had better tell the hotel, and we will save the cost of that at least. Maybe you will have a job soon and we will be all set."

For our last week on the Left Bank, we decided to explore the Jardin des Plantes and a bunch of other galeries, museums and restaurants we wanted to see. One of the best was the Musèe de Cluny, officially the Musèe National du Moyen Age, just up the Boulevard St. Michel from the Place St. Michel. It was the Paris residence of the abbots of Cluny next to the ruins of the Roman baths. It includes many masterpieces, most famously the six tapestries of *La Dame a la Licorne*, or The

Lady with the Unicorn. Five tapestries depict earthly senses and the sixth shows the lady putting her necklace in a casket to symbolize the renunciation of sensual pleasures.

A week later, on Friday, the 29th, I planned to stay in and do some organizing of my teaching notes. Valerie said she would do a few bookstores and if she had time go back to the Louvre to see some things she had missed. We agreed to meet later in the afternoon at another favorite bar of mine at the northwest corner of Place St. Michel. It is called La Perigourdine and has a splendid view of the front of the Notre Dame Cathedral.

I got there first and ordered a Tuborg. It was one of the only places that had that wonderful beer. As I was looking at the façade of Notre Dame, marvelous from that distance, my pleasure increased as I saw Valerie walking across the end of Pont St. Michel coming toward me.

After greeting me, she said she wanted a white wine, and the waitress suggested and brought her a Sauvignon. We clinked glasses, and I asked her what she had found.

She said, "My luck continues. You must not love me very much."

"On the contrary, I couldn't wait for you to arrive."

"Well, you can't believe it, but I already found a job. It's at that well-known book store, Shakespeare & Co., which I am sure you know. As I was looking at it, I asked someone if they needed any help. They say I can start two weeks from next Wednesday, which will be perfect for us, as just after our move. They will try to get me a carte de sejour so I can be legal here. Do you think you can get one?"

"That's a long story. It's a perfect Catch 22. I went to the French consulate in New York with my letter from the University inviting me to teach at the Institut d'Anglais. But, they told me it did not have the official stamp and therefore could not be used to procure a longer visa. So I thought I would do it here. And guess what? Here they told me I had to get it `*sur place,*` meaning back in New York. Can you believe that?" In fact, I plan to go to another country every three months in order to stay legal with my tourist visa. How about a trip to Belgium or Italy?"

"All right. Why not over Christmas, when you should have some time off from your teaching. Anyway, I hate Christmas now, especially in a big city, with all the commercialization at that time of year. And since we have no family here, why not do Bruges and Ghent then, and maybe we can do Italy in the spring."

"I was thinking of doing Italy first, but you are undoubtably right. It will be winter in both countries in December, but spring starts earlier in Italy. Besides, I've never been to Belgium, except the Brussels airport. But, for final plans, let's wait till we've moved and I've started teaching."

The time passed agreeably, and on Sunday the first of October, we packed our few things and enjoyed our last day at La Louisiane and seeing its lovely neighborhood. In the afternoon we visited again the Jardins de Luxembourg, our favorite park and gardens. At the end of September it was at its most beautiful, with still green grass, beautiful flowers and trees, which were beginning their autumn colors. We walked to the lovely seventeenth century Fontaine de Medici constructed for Marie de Medici, and admired the fish, shrubbery, trees and the beautiful statue at its end of the Cyclops, called Polyphemus. He is waiting to crush the lovers Acis and Galatea in the act of embracing below him. I told Valerie I would certainly want to come back to see such things as often as possible, even as we explored Parc Monceau and other places in our new location. She said she certainly agreed,

and asked me if I knew Handel's music titled, Acis and Galatea. I said I didn't and she said it was one of his best, if lesser known works.

CHAPTER THREE

NEW AREAS OF THE CITY OF LIGHT

The next day, Monday, October 2, was our day to move to the new apartment on Rue de Vezèlay. We got up relatively early and were packed and ready to go by eleven. Taxis are not easy to find in Paris. But, there is a taxi stand on the Boulevard St. Germain, a long block to the west of hotel La Louisiane. So, after saying goodbyes to some of the hotel people, we toted our bags over there, and found one. It took a twenty minute drive via Place de la Concord, to arrive at 15 Rue de Vezèlay, the address of the apartment.

The first thing we had to do was to decide who could put what where. I already had a big pile of teaching notes, and said I would need the bigger desk in the living room. Valerie agreed, but said she would need one too, if smaller. That would be another project, and Valerie asked where we should go for that. I said I knew a good place to try when we had finished unpacking.

About two hours later, arriving at that great department store, La Samaritaine, the choice seemed impossibly complicated. While deliberating, I proposed we go to Notre Dame, only about three blocks up the Seine, for a few prayers of thanks and to help us make our choices. Fortunately, the lines to get into the church were not too long, and we spent a good half hour there. The stained glass windows are so incredibly beautiful. They are another of those wonders of the past which seem impossible to find today

without visiting the originals. Their secret seemed to have died with the Middle Ages, and one wonders why such works cannot be reproduced.

Back at La Samaritaine, the desk we finally chose was a relatively inexpensive mahogany one, with drawers on the left side. They said they could deliver it by the end of the week. For the trip back to our apartment, we took the metro from Chatelet to Etoile, and then to Courcelles in the direction of St. Denis-Basilique. From there it was another marvelous walk, through the Park de Monceau, passing its Metro stop to the Rue de Vezelay, just beyond the eastern end of the park.

By then we were hungry and decided to do a snack at home. We had bought some cheese, fruit, salad and wine, and enjoyed our first meal in the apartment. Then, we arranged the placement of a few more things, from our four suitcases of stuff. Since I had come for an academic year I had also sent a trunk from New York, filled with books and more teaching notes. It was in storage at Debaux Transit, where I sent it asking them to hold it until I called. And now I had a place to deliver it. When I did call, they said a driver could bring it Thursday a week later, or October 12.

Now, early evening, we decided to explore our new neighborhood. Valerie was right. The apartment was really well situated. With the Parc de Monceau to the west and the Champs Elysèes to the south, we discovered a host of interesting streets all around, all with the names of world cities. Going east, we walked down streets with names like Lisbonne and Madrid, and crossing Rue de Rome arrived at the Place de l'Europe. From there it was left on the Rue St. Petersbourg, which we followed to the Place de Clichy. Then we took Rue Bruxelles to Place Blanche, and a left on Rue Lepic to the Rue des Abbesses, which we followed to the church of St. Jean de Montmartre.

Paris is a really wonderful place to walk, and since it was close to dinner time, we decided to hell with our resolution to try to economize. We would dine and wine in Montmartre which was just above the church of St. Jean de Montmartre. To get there we took a small street to the funicular which climbed to just below the more famous church, Sacre Coeur, built just after the defeat by Germany in the war of 1870. Once there we had one of the best views in all of Paris from the front of that church. Much of the city was laid out to the west and was easily seen if there were not too many tourists blocking the view. From there it is an easy walk to the Place du Tertre, the place where many famous paintings were done by famous artists. These included many of the Impressionists, and most of all Toulouse Lautrec, who lived many years in Montmartre.

I knew from my first trip there, before I met Valerie, of a restaurant with a marvelous name, Au Clair de la Lune, just to the west of Place du Tertre, on Rue Poulbot. After dinner there we went back to the Place du Tertre for some more wine. There were the usual mobs of tourists and the pedlars trying to sell whatever they could. Many tourists were having their portraits done by aspiring artists, and I asked Valerie if she wanted one done. To my surprise, she said yes, and took her seat. The artist circled her several times and then started to paint looking at her face. He was Asian, probably Chinese, and very skillful. The likeness was done in about fifteen minutes, and captured very nicely Valerie's beauty, as well as her coquettish side.

Following that, we went for a nightcap to a bar on the other side of the Place du Tertre. After a calvados each, we passed Sacre Coeur again and made a circle around its back on Rue Lamarck to Rue Caulaincourt and the Metro stop called by those two names. From there it was only two stops to Pigalle and our train in the direction of Porte Dauphine for the Monceau stop. We were very happy to get to our new home and settled in for a needed good night's sleep.

The next day I went again to the Musèe du Vin which was an easy metro ride with a change at the Etoile for the Passy stop. I wanted to look up more about some of the ideas I had on my trip about the wine book. One idea was to try to find enough information about what new techniques the Cistercians had brought to the improvements in wine making at Clos Vougeot and other vineyards.

Just as I was getting into that in a book on the monks and twelfth century wine making, Keith Weaver came up and started to talk. He proposed a drink at the next door wine bar. I accepted, but said it would have to be in an hour which would be about lunch time. That gave me time to finish what I was reading, and find a few other items in several books. Then, we went to the wine bar, and ate well with dishes again accompanied by glasses of that marvelous white wine, Meursault.

When he asked me if he could treat Valerie and me to dinner two days later, I accepted. He said we should meet at La Mediterranee just opposite the Theatre de l'Europe up the street from the Carrefour d'Odeon. I wondered if I had been wise, but Valerie thought it a good idea and at the appointed time about nine, we arrived, and found Keith had reserved a nice round table looking toward the Theatre. Keith jumped up to give Valerie a warm hug, saying how glad he was to see her again. No sooner were we seated than he said he wanted to repeat his offer to see about getting her a job with his company in London. As before, I became nervous hearing that, and all the more so, when Valerie said she might want something in a few months. She added she had just found a job at Shakespeare & Co., and was enjoying Paris too much to leave any time soon. I squeezed her arm, saying I hoped so.

As we were finishing our sole and turbot, Keith asked us about our trip to Burgundy. I said, "In fact, we followed more or less the itinerary you outlined to me back in August. But at the beginning we also went north to see those double name towns, Chambolle-Musigny, Gevrey-Chambertin and Vosne-Romanèe, and their famous wines." Savoring my glass from the marvelous bottle of Pouilly Fouissè that Keith had ordered, I added, "I guess it's a good thing we all like wine."

Keith enjoined, "You can say that again. After all it's why we know each other, n'est-ce pas?"

I couldn't help saying, "I thought it was because you are trying to seduce Valerie."

Valerie said, "Excusez-moi Chris, but don't you like that. Having other men chase after me? Especially, if they are as attractive as Keith."

"Well, thank you Valerie. It's your first compliment for me. I hope it won't be the last."

"And what am I supposed to make of that?" I asked.

Keith replied with what I thought was a nasty look, "Whatever you wish."

Valerie again had to intervene, and say, "Now, guys, let's not ruin a nice evening. And, now that we have finished here, how about a night cap or two?"

"OK. Anyway, you can see why I am so crazy about Valerie. How about Cointreau or Marie Brizzard, and we can have them here." Keith added, "But, I prefer Whiskey, if you don't mind"

"Why should we mind," I replied. "What I mind is your constant flirting with Valerie. Can you at least reduce that?"

Again, Valerie stepped in to moderate. "I don't see why you two keep fighting over what every woman likes, attention, attention, attention. So, do as you like, for all I care. She squeezed both our hands."

But, I was still annoyed, and thought that later I would have to ask Valerie to keep it cooler with Keith.

As we got our Cointreau, Marie Brizzard and Whiskey, Keith said he was going to Bordeaux in several days to try to buy some of the *grand vins* for his company to distribute in England. "By the way, my company is called The International Wine Shop, Ltd., and they are paying for my trip. I can call you two my assistants and treat us all to a trip to Bordeaux. How would that be?"

"Since Valerie has just gotten a job and I have to start teaching in two weeks," I said, "We had better do a rain check. How about next summer."

But, Valerie put in, "Shakespeare & Co. told me I didn't have to start until Wednesday, October 11. So that could work, even this weekend? I would love to see Bordeaux, and Chris will just have to trust me if he doesn't want to go."

I looked at the moles which I remembered were on either side of Keith's face as I debated my response. Maybe I should let Valerie go on her own and see whether I could settle the question of not being so jealous that I might risk losing her. I decided to do so, and said, "All right. Valerie will go,

and tell me all about it when she comes back. I have to see if I can trust you out of sight with a man you find attractive. But, don't betray me."

Valerie responded by leaning over to kiss me on the cheek, saying,

"Don't you know me well enough yet to know I want to both enjoy myself and find the man who can save me. If you can trust me enough, why shouldn't that be you?"

Again she gave sly looks bordering on winks at both of us. And I again noticed Keith looking fondly at Valerie but seeming to avoid my eyes when he looked my way. Then, looking again at Valerie, Keith asked her if she could meet him in two days, Saturday, October 5, about noon at the Gare d'Austerlitz for the high speed train that left at 12:30 for Bordeaux.

Valerie replied, "Oh goody, I get to go on one of those superfast trains and see a great new city. But, as said I will have to start work early next week. So, can we return by the following Tuesday at the latest?"

"Of course," Keith said. "I've got meetings with various wine guys Saturday evening. So that should be perfect. Maybe, I can even take you to some of the great vineyards on Sunday and we can come back Monday afternoon."

"Sounds like a wonderful trip," I said, even as I wondered what else might transpire between Keith and Valerie. "I wish I could join you but had better prepare my course. I look forward to hearing all about it. And I mean ALL, if you get my drift."

Keith gave me a look that he tried to make neutral but that I suspected hid his envy of me and plans to get even by trying to seduce Valerie this weekend. He stood up, saying, "Let's be on our way then. And see you, my dear, Saturday noon at the Austerlitz station. I will get the tickets and let's meet just in front of the ticket windows."

Leaving the restaurant, we walked down the Rue de l'Odeon to the metro just below, which we took while Keith walked back to his hotel on Rue Bonaparte.

Back at the apartment about midnight, I said, "Now, it's my turn to ask you something personal, Valerie. What are you expecting from Keith on this trip?"

"Do you want me to have an affair?"

"What do you think? The fact you can even say that makes me all the more worried. I hope at least you will take separate rooms."

"I should think so. He probably likes to charge his company extra, and that way he can say he got an extra room for his assistant. As for me, if I sometimes mention the possibility of having an affair, don't you see I am just trying to tease you. This time there will probably be nothing more than a kiss on the check."

She walked over to give me a rather passionate kiss, and I embraced her, suggesting we do a tumble. Her reply was to lead me to the bed and another wonderful prelude to a good nights' sleep.

The next morning, I felt more relaxed and told Valerie I very much hoped she would enjoy the trip. "But, watch out for Keith. I am not sure I trust him at all."

"Well, you don't mind picking his brain for information about wine. He doesn't seem dangerous to me."

"All right, but be warned. I fear that I am the jealous type."

She again came over to give me a *bisou* as the French call a peck on the cheek. "Don't you know how women like their men to be jealous?"

Saturday morning, I escorted Valerie to La Gare d'Austerlitz. We walked to Etoile at the head of the Champs Elysèe for the line to Nation. Before the metro reached the Grenelle stop, we took the correspondance for the metro line to Austerlitz station. The metro came onto an above ground track just in time to cross the river and see a stunning view of the Eiffel Tower on the other side of the river. Then, with the change at La Motte-Piquet-Grenelle, we reached Austerlitz about fifteen minutes later. It was 11:30 and I hoped Keith would not arrive for another twenty minutes.

Yet, there he was already, sporting a bowler hat and tweed suit. In fact, he looked quite dapper. I greeted him coolly enough with a "*Bonjour, ca va?*"

To my consternation, with barely a glance and bonjour for me, he walked over to hug Valerie. I was thinking 'watch it old boy,' but decided to say nothing. Valerie disengaged after a moment and asked, "Have you got the tickets and which track do we go to?"

As he replied, I saw the same information on the bulletin board announcing departures, '*Bordeaux: 12:30. Voie 14. A l'Heure.*' Keith took Valerie's arm and began walking toward track 14, which was at the far end of the station. Thinking, he's wasting no time, I said "How about letting me continue to talk to Valerie, at least until you get on the train?"

Keith apparently recognizing that he should be gracious to show his appreciation for taking my girl friend off for a weekend, said "Of course. So sorry old boy. I agree you can talk all you want with Valerie for the next few

minutes. Then, it will be my turn."

Valerie squeezed both our arms, saying "What a pleasure to be fought over by two such smashing men. I don't know how I can be happy without such attention. So, keep it up."

I grimaced when I heard Keith say, "Soon, it will be my turn."

But, I hugged Valerie and said as cheerily as I could, "Bon voyage and have a wonderful trip." I added "Hurry back," with a fond look at Valerie as she boarded the train. Keith followed her and we exchanged final glances, mine with barely concealed disapproval of Keith.

Back in the apartment, I lost no time getting out my teaching notes and trying to lose myself in the mysteries of history. Yet, as this was to be the first time I taught American history I let my mind wander back to my earlier teaching in New York about Asia and Europe, which I thought were far more interesting. Many of my courses had been on Chinese history, my first specialty. Now, my best thoughts were about trying to do a history of wine and all the great history to do with that in France. But, fortunately I then saw something interesting in the pages I had brought with me for one of my courses on American history. They were about France's loss of Canada to the English, culminating in the Seven Years War of 1756 to 1763. It was good to spot those pages just then because it came to me that that would be a logical place to start my course. Here in Paris, the students would be more interested if they saw a French connection at the beginning. Then I could flash back to the Indians and arrival of the first Europeans, and come forward to the rising English dominance of the world, including most of North America.

The next days passed well enough for me. I made a start on writing the notes I would need to start that class, which was to begin the week after next, only ten days off. Meetings with the faculty would start before then, and I would have Valerie to come home to. So, I passed the days working at home and the first two nights walking to nearby restaurants. On Saturday, I decided to go to Montmartre. Enjoying another good restaurant, food and wine at the Place du Tertre enhanced my reminiscences about the evening I had spent there with Valerie just five days before. In addition, the restaurant was most interesting. It was *Chez la Mere Catherine*, proudly announcing it had been *fondé en* 1793. That meant it had started at the height of the Revolution, but continued to become a marvelously successful bourgeois enterprise still flourishing over two hundred years later. There were over a hundred fellow diners there, mostly at tables on the Place du Tertre facing the rooms of the restaurant itself across the street. How marvelous it all was, including my meal of quiche lorraine, moules and creme caramel. Even better I thought, in two days Valerie would come back. Then, I could hear about her time in Bordeaux, and I hoped about how she had kept her distance from Keith.

The next day, getting up late, I again took to my notes hoping the time would pass quickly. Since I did not know which train they would take, I would have to await Valerie's arrival on Monday evening. That day by six in the evening I started to worry, and decided I would take a walk hoping to find her chez nous on my return. The Parc Monceau was the obvious choice although I regretted not having come earlier before the closing of the Camondo and Cernusci museums. On further reflection, I thought that was just as well since it would be better to see them with Valerie. As it was I walked round and round the garden and sat to read in a chair under a street light which had just come on. As I got up, I noticed I was on the Allée Garnerin, and walking towards home, noticed a placard explaining that name. It seemed that André-Jacques Garnerin at the age of 28 had made the first parachute jump in history, from a balloon, on October 22, 1797. It landed in the Parc Monceau presumably somewhere near the sign. As a student of the history of aviation I took notes on that, and tried to imagine flying without a parachute. I wondered how long it took to make parachutes practical after that first jump in 1797.

Returning home at eight, I was troubled that Valerie was still not there. All I could do was read, and if she was still not there at ten go out for something to eat. That happened and I thought to have a drink or two after the dinner to give a bit more time and be that much more relaxed.

When I came back close to midnight I was very pleased to see Valerie as soon as I opened the door. She was unpacking and said she had just got in. She said they had not left until the six o'clock train and it had been an hour late, "But, you know I rushed home as fast as I could though the metro seemed slower than usual."

"Well," I said, "It was one of those times I wish we both had cell phones."

"I guess so, but in fact, I hate cell phones. They are so erratic and expensive. Though you are right, when you really want to get in touch with someone they work very well."

"Agreed. I will go get us some wine, and then you can tell me all about your trip."

As I was getting and pouring the Sauvignon Blanc, Valeried began to talk.

"Do you want to know everything, or just the good parts?"

"Everything of course. Especially if you tell me how horrible you found Keith."

Valerie smiled and said "If I tell you he was horrible, how do you know if you can believe me?"

"Test me and try."

"All right. Here goes. Most of the trip down on the train was good. I admired the speed of the TGV as they call that High Speed Train for its initials for *Train Grand Vitesse.* It went up to 270 kilometers an hour! That is 168 mph, if you can believe that. And the scenery was lovely, passing woods and fields and lots of cattle, horses and sheep. Keith was civilized at first but kept moving closer and closer to my nice window seat. When he leaned over and put his hand on my arm, I told him to stop and asked him to please keep it correct between us. He said all right but then you wouldn't believe it, he asked me if I could stay in his room. I told him certainly not, as strongly as I could say it, which made the last part of the trip more tense. So much so that at one point I toyed with the idea of trying to soothe him by saying `maybe later' or something like that. And would you have liked me to have an affair, just to know how superior you are?"

"I do wish you would stop having such thoughts, and if you do, please don't express them. Anyway, where did you stay? And how far was your room from his?"

"We stayed at the Claret Hotel, and wouldn't you know that it was just off the Garonne River on the aptly named property, called the Citè Mondiale du Vin. Given Keith's wine business, that presumably is why he chose it. And I don't see why you object to my teasing you about sex. Don't you see how much I like it?"

With that I got up and put out my hand. "In that case let's go to bed." We did, and after making love slept until late the next morning. After breakfast, I asked Valerie if we could talk more about Bordeaux, in part because I had been there for a weekend several years ago. I remembered fondly the Musèe d'Aquitaine, the museum called the Maison du Vin and the Hotel des Vins, where they sold that nectar of the gods. I saw also the vineyards of Chateau Haut-Brion, on the western edge of the city,

St. Emilion to the east, and so many others. How much did you see of such things?"

"I'm glad to hear you went to Bordeaux too. It's such a great place. After dinner in the hotel the first night, we went to some of the vineyards you mentionned and some others. Leaving the hotel Sunday morning, we went to Chateau Haut-Brion. The guide, a lovely lady, told us some amazing stuff. It is a sixteenth century Chateau and came to be owned by Talleyrand, that foreign minister of Napoleon, who was so skillful that he was used by kings before and after Napoleon. It is said that he prevented the defeats from costing France very much at the 1815 Congress of Vienna in part because Napoleon's chef, equipped with wines from Haut-Brion, so wowed the leaders of the coalition against France, Alexander I of Russia, Castlereagh of England and Metternich of Austria, that they made many concessions disguised as compromises. It appears that is another example of the power of wine. The guide also repeated the information that the name Haut Brion might in fact be of Irish origin, from a soldier, named O'Brien. He fought in the wars that gave England control of so much of western France until the time of Joan of Arc. The guide also mentionned that the diarist Pepys described having a French wine, called `Ho Bryan' at the Royal Oak Tavern on Lombard Street in London on April 10, 1663. I took some notes as I found those details so fascinating."

"Then, the next morning, it was St. Emilion, about 25 miles to the east. Its name also has a curious appelation. Supposedly it comes from an eighth century hermit, Emillion, who arrived from Brittany to spend his adulthood in the village that came to bear his name. The village is quite charming, and as you can imagine we drank some very delicious wines."

"Fascinating," I said. "Indeed. I still remember my wine tastings on the trip I did in 1993. In addition to those at the vineyards, at the Hotel des Vins, salesmen offered tastings of dozens of great wines. In fact, that was where I discovered that

Pomerols were my favorite wines. But, tell me more about you and Keith."

"You never give up, do you? Asking about whatever man I might have talked with. Well, that is all I did with Keith, talk."

"And do you find him agreeable to talk with?"

"As you know, he is witty. But, I became irritated with all his chatter about business successes and female conquests in London. I know one of the ladies he mentioned, and will certainly ask her about Keith when I get back to London."

"All right, brava! I guess you have passed my exam, to know whether I can trust you. Now, you make me think I can, and I greatly appreciate all the info about the wines. Forgive my stupid jealousies."

"Thank you, cheri. And let me add a few more details relevant to that and my trip. The first day, as I told you, I had to tell Keith I would not share his room or do anything intimate with him. He mostly accepted that, but liked to buss me on the cheeks whenever he could. The afternoons he was working, I went to the Cathèdrale St. Andrè, and the two museums just to its west, the Beaux Arts and the Aquitaine. So, it was one of the best trips I ever had. Again, thank you for allowing me to go, even if it was with that other man."

The next day, Wednesday, October 11, Valerie started her work at Shakespeare & Co. Since I was to start teaching a week later on the 17th, I went over parts of my notes again. In the afternoon I did some shopping for dinner and other items, and wondered about working out with Valerie a schedule for our dinners. That would be needed since by next week, we both would be working.

When Valerie got back that night about eight, she told me they had assigned her to work from the opening of the store at ten to seven in the evening with an hour off for lunch. Even better it would be only week days, though she might be asked to work weekends at times to replace other people on vacation.

"You wouldn't believe it," she said, "Guess who came in my first day?"

"Surely not Keith," I blurted out.

"I'm afraid so, but he said he would be off to London tomorrow."

"So, you told him where you'd be working? He'd better not be there too often or I will have to hang around there myself. Anyway, tell me about the other things your first day."

"You know, it was the usual being there just to answer questions when people come in. And the boss asked me to smile and go out on the sidewalk to wave people in as I could. Since it is in the middle of that small street between the Rues St. Julien and Petit Pont just above and across from Notre Dame, there are always people going by. Many of them do look in and too many of those step in to start browsing. So, it is quite busy, but I like the boss, the views outside are lovely, and Keith didn't bother me too much. I think I will enjoy working there, more than at my London store, in any case."

"Marvelous. And now, how about helping me prepare the dinner? Since you are a working girl, I thought to buy some things. And we have to work out a schedule to do with such, and also to figure out how often we want to go out to eat. D'accord?"

"All right. I hope you have some haricots verts, which are my favorite vegetable, and I can do them while you do the meat. What will that be, by the way?"

"As you can guess it's my usual, lamb chops. I will do them with some herbs, maybe garlic and rosemary, OK? And I do have some string beans, but let's have another glass of Sauvignon Blanc before starting."

"Wonderful, but as we will have red with the dinner, shouldn't we start with that also?"

"I love starting with a white, which seems more like a cocktail to me. So, don't argue and try it."

After I poured the wine, she said "You're right. It's delicious."

"So, why did you tell Keith where you would be working?"

"There you go again. Why can't I have other friends? Anyway, it just came up in one of our conversations in Bordeaux. And as said, he is off to London tomorrow."

"Did he say when he would be returning?"

"Maybe in a couple of weeks. By the way, he again offered to recommend me for that job. I told him to wait a few months and I would see if I wanted to come back to London. That, of course, depends on whether I tire of you, or not."

Again, she looked at me with that mischievous smile. I smiled back, if with some strain. We seemed to be getting in the habit of teasing each other, in part by the nature of our smiles and looks at the other. I have heard that that is one of the best ways of communicating. And I have been noticing how much French, and I guess Europeans in general communicate that way. And with less conversation than Americans normally do.

After dinner, we decided to do a night cap at one of the cafés close to Parc Monceau. The Cointreau she had and my Marie Brizard anisette were marvelous. Once more the evening passed with great walking, food, wine and love making. I was very happy and Valerie seemed to be also.

The day after that I went to my first orientation meeting at the Institut d'Anglais. The name was appropriate as it was for the school attended by students studying English and the history of the anglophone countries, But it was located in a very Parisian looking neighborhood. It was on the Rue Charles V in the fourth arrondissement in a rectangular courtyard that several centuries before had been a residential compound for well to do, if not rich, bourgeois types. It was between the Rues du Petit Musc and St. Paul, at what would have been the middle of a triangle formed by the Bastille, the Metro St. Paul and the Seine River.

In the amphitheatre designated for the meeting, I observed the people who would be my colleagues for the year. The speaker giving the introductory remarks was a middle aged man of average stature, but with a strong face and aquiline nose. He was director of the school, a man called Richard Dhuiq. He spoke about twenty minutes, explaining that the school had been set up after the war for the increasing numbers of young people who wanted to learn English. He said that somewhat to the regret of "We French, English has replaced our language as the lingua franca of the world." He dated that to the first world war and America joining with England to be the dominant powers on earth. The English to be sure already had been that after the Seven Years War and even more after the defeat of Napolean. But, he said he thought that until the 1920s, the English and Americans still acted, in Europe at least, with some deference. English power in various overseas territories remained supreme as in the statement, "the sun never sets on the English Empire." But in France, especially, he said, the anglophones often felt culturally inferior, in part at least since they rarely knew the language. He concluded, however, that that had changed after the second World War and the Americans above all had started to act like the lords of all that they surveyed.

I thought his remarks were interesting even if understandably somewhat French-centric. The next speaker was a lady, named Nadine Bruyere. She was the assistant director in charge of the language programs. She briefly outlined the requirements we teachers were to fulfill. Those included giving grades at the end of the courses, which could be based, as desired, on a combination of papers and exams. As she was speaking, I noticed a very handsome gal with light brown hair, who presumably also was one of the teachers. I decided I would try to make her acquaintance as soon as I could.

That opportunity came quickly as the meeting was soon adjourned and we were invited to partake of the spread of wines, cheeses and other odd delicacies. I went up to her and asked what she taught. She replied advanced English courses, and asked me my name. I happily replied "Chris, *et vous?*"

She said "Claudia Chevalier. *Et vous enseignez quoi.*"

I replied in my best French, "They asked me, as an American, to do the history of North America. But I have taught mostly Asian and European history at my school in New York, Baruch College of the City University of New York."

She said, "How interesting. And have you taught about Vietnam?"

I answered, "Yes, it is my favorite course. In fact, that is why I know France so well, because I chose to do a book on Vietnam, knowing I could research it in France. That was back in the early 80s."

"Incredible. I was in Saigon back then, teaching French, and sometimes English, at a Lycèe. It was on the old Rue Catinat, now called Tu Do or Liberation Street. Have you ever been in Saigon, or Ho Chi Minh Ville, if you prefer the new official name.?"

"Yes. I went there for a short trip at the end of the American war." "How long did you stay in Saigon, and tell me more about it?"

"I was in Saigon for five years and loved it. It still has some of the airs of an old French city. The students were smart and usually well behaved."

"Unlike so many of ours! At least in New York. You know when I was in Saigon it was really surreal, in part just because that was at the end of the war. You cannot believe how Orwellian it seemed. For example, there were posters of peasant soldiers shooting at jets with Communist insignia, as if everyone didn't know that it was American jets bombing everywhere. And then, on the armed forces radio, I heard an antiwar guy, say, 'Before the news I want to give a public announcement. For thousands of years man has used fire. But fire can be dangerous. Watch what you do with your cigarettes. Do not throw them away and cause destructive fires. And now the news. This morning American bombers unloaded over fifty tons of bombs and napalm on the Mekong Delta provinces around My Tho.' Can you believe that?"

"I guess one has to believe almost anything regarding what the Americans did in that war."

"You can say that again. The more I learned the more horrible it seemed. And now there is all the talk about the 58,000 American casualties with almost no mentions of the over two million Vietnamese killed in the American war, not to speak of the million or so they lost in the French war. At least in the American press. But enough of such horrors! Tell me more about what you expect in the coming semester?"

She did, but quickly said, "Now, I have to go talk with Madame Bruyere, *justement* about my courses."

As she took her leave I again admired her appearance, and wondered if I would get into trouble with Valerie if I kept flirting with her.

I decided to follow Claudia, but then speak also with Madame Bruyere about the course I was supposed to teach. Since I was doing a sabbatical year, I was glad I would only have one course to teach each semester, as against my usual three. Getting some more wine and a piece of cheese I walked slowly, and exchanged a few pleasantries with several others before arriving near the corner of the salle for my hoped for conversation.

Claudia recognized me coming and introduced me to Madame Bruyere. She then said she would be on her way and looked forward to seeing us both in the coming weeks. I had to put my too enthusiastic thoughts about Claudia aside and concentrate on the questions I had for teaching my course. The conversation went well and Madame Bruyere asked me to call her Nadine and *tutoyer*, or use the intimate form of conversation if I wished. I thanked her for saying that since most of my French conversations, such as they were, had done that. She complemented my French, but noted that "As you know, all our courses are in English, to give the students the practice." She went on to suggest I assign the students weekly small papers and give as many exams as I wished. Since no one likes grading papers I thought to limit myself to a mid term and final exam, and make the papers as short as three to five pages. But I kept that to myself and took my leave of Madame Bruyere, Monsieur Dhuicq and the rest.

Imagine my delight when on Friday I went back to the Institute and found that they had assigned me the best possible hours, namely Tuesday and Thursday afternoons from three to five. All the better, I saw on the schedule of classes that Claudia had the same hours. I wondered if that could be a plot. If she had had different ones, I was sure I still would have looked her up. But, this way we would almost be forced to see a lot of each other. Of course, I knew that that would be my choice if I really pushed it. One side of me thought, I had better take it slow, but another played with the idea of how nice it would be to have not only an English love, but a French lover, or at least friend, as well. Oh, well I can enjoy Valerie this weekend, and hope that I am shrewd enough not to screw up my friendship with her.

The same evening Valerie and I walked back to the Claire de Lune Restaurant near the Place du Tertre in Montmartre. That was an easy half hour trip if you take the funicular up from Place St. Pierre to the Basilica Sacre Coeur. Over dinner, I told Valerie about my schedule and asked if she would like to come to audit a course or two. She said it sounded like a good idea and would see.

"How about when you are talking about the Americans taking up arms against the English. I would love to hear about the humiliation of my still arrogant country."

"All right, you are on. I will tell you when that comes up, probably about a month from now."

Then, she asked me about who I had met at the Institut d'Anglais. I told her about the director and vice director in charge of the courses, but decided not to mention Claudia. After all, I had barely met her. So, I asked myself, why should I keep thinking of her? I asked Valerie to tell me more about her first days at Shakespeare & Co. She shrugged and said she was already getting bored, except that she could look at the incredible side of Notre Dame with its flying buttresses by just going to the front of the store or out on the sidewalk. "But the rainy days will be the worst, as you can imagine," she said. After dinner, we did the usual nightcap, or *digestif* as they are called, at the Place du Tertre. Walking back home was easy as it was all downhill.

The weekend was in fact rainy and we stayed in most of the time, reading, talking and, of course, making love. Monday, I prepared for my first course as well as I could, and arrived an hour before the start of the class the next day on Tuesday, October 17. It was easy to get there, taking the metro to the Etoile and then the direction Chateau de Vincennes for the St. Paul or Bastille stop. It was an aproximately five block walk from either one to Rue Charles V in the middle between them.

I found my cubicle, which I could use for storage, a desk, and rest as needed. The course was in a room across the courtyard and I walked there so as to arrive just before the class time of 15 hours as they say much of the time in Europe for 3 o'clock.

The room was about two thirds full, or with something like thirty students. That was almost the perfect size, and some would no doubt drop out, thereby reaching the nice number of twenty or so attending. First came the passing out of a layout page of the room, which I had marked with slots for the students to put in their names to indicate who and where they were. Then, I did the roll call from the official list of students, which I said I would continue doing until I became more familiar with the students in the class. The names ranged from simple, like Celeste, to bizarre such as Tesfaye Bizuayehu. The latter was one of the students from French West Africa. After the names, the class went well enough. As planned, I began with references to the natives in North America, and then about the coming of the French after the Spanish, Dutch and English. I spoke of the first French to go to there, from Veranzano, an Italian who sailed for France in 1524, to Jacques Cartier, the foremost discoverer of French Canada a decade later. After that came the rising tension in America between the English and French. I was still discussing that and the beginnings in the mid eighteenth century of the Seven Years war when the class ended.

Who should I see going into my cubicle but Claudia Chevalier. I said, "What a coincidence we have the same hours and cubicles almost next to each other. Do you think they are trying to be matchmakers?"

"If so, maybe we should not disappoint them," said Claudia.

"How about a drink in an hour or so?"

"Pas ce soir. J'ai un rendez-vous. But maybe next week, all right?"

"I hope so and *bonne soirèe,*" was all I could think of to say as I entered my cubicle and heard her shut the door to hers. I could not help recalling how way back in late August, Valerie had put me off when I asked for a first date because of her rendez-vous with Mark Goden.

After arranging my things and taking what I needed to prepare for the Thursday class, I made my way to the closest appealing bar I could find. It was on the tiny street, Rue de l'Hotel St, Paul where it ran into the Rue St. Antoine. The bar is called the Fontaine Sully. There, I struck up a conversation with the bartender. He was sympathetic and about my age or possibly a little older and in his forties. I realized with a shudder, I would be 40 next July 10. What can you do, and after all, that is still young, relatively speaking.

The barman and I got into a discussion about the neighborhood and its history. Since I was teaching nearby on Rue Charles V, I asked him what he knew about King Charles V. He explained that it was under Charles V, in the late 1300s that the Marais, as the area is called, was incorporated into the city of Paris. The king became known as the wise king, *Charles le sage*. The bartender went on to say that there had been huge satisfaction with various reforms launched by Charles V, after the putting down of demonstrations and protests by Etienne Marcel nearby in 1356. He continuted, "Etienne Marcel became the name of a Marais metro stop. The king's reforms had been facilitated after 1360 by a lull in the Hundred Years War between England and France, which had begun in 1338. When the war resumed in 1368, the king went on to win some of his battles against the English, using an early version of guerilla tactics. He thereby became one of the more beloved and important kings of France."

"Very interesting," I said as I asked the bartender his name. He said it was Charles, but in fact named after an uncle, not the king. "Still, who knows, my uncle may have been named for one of the other kings, named Charles. I think there were at least eight of them in the history of France. And let me tell you a few things about the later history of the quarter. Many of the impressive buildings around here were put up from the fourteenth century on, and our first Bourbon king, Henri IV, gave orders for the building up of what became known as the Place des Vosges just on the other side of the Rue St. Antoine. The whole area became a center of Parisian life until the Revolution, after which much activity shifted to the Left

Bank. You might want to try a restaurant in what claims to be one of the oldest buildings of Paris not far from here. It may be just west of the Marais, as it's on the Rue Montmorency off of Rue St. Martin. But, it's well worth going to, and called the *Auberge Nicolas Flamel.* It seems he was a thirteenth century guru and alchemist, who I hear was the inspiration for one of the characters in those incredibly popular Harry Potter, children books by A. K. Rowling."

"Thank you so much for all that fascinating info. But, now I have to be on my way. *Et à la prochaine.*"

I decided to walk back via the St. Gervais Church, two blocks to the west, just off the right bank of the Seine River. It was named after a Roman officer martyred by Nero and was started just after the baptism of the king of the Goths, Clovis, who established his capital in Paris in the early sixth century. St. Gervais was rebuilt in the seventeenth century and I especially liked to enter the church from its rear off of the Rue des Barres. The interior is in stunning Gothic and houses the oldest organ of Paris. On Good Friday, March 19, 1918, a German bomb hit the church killing and wounding 160 members of the congregation. Reading about that, I decided I needed another drink and descended to another favorite bar-restaurant close to the Pont Louis Philippe, logically called the *Café Louis Philippe.* From there I walked back to the Pont Marie and took the metro to the Opera, from where it was an easy half hour walk back to the apartment.

Arriving about seven, I looked in the fridge and saw we had almost nothing to eat. I wondered if I should wait for Valerie, and decide whether we would go out to eat or buy something to eat in. While waiting I had a wine and sat down to read. I tackled the Oxford History of the American People, which I had brought along for reference for my teaching. I resumed my reading after page 154 where the author, Samuel Eliot Morrison, proceeds to talk about the wars of England and the colonists against Spain in the south of what became the United States, and the French in the north. Valerie came in just as I was getting into his description of the French in Canada.

"Hi," I said, "Do you want to go out to eat or shall we buy something to eat here?"

"Now that we are both working," Valerie said, "Why not go out? I'm guessing we will eat out most nights. In fact, back in London, I got in the habit of eating in only on Sunday and Mondays."

"You're kidding. I did the same in New York. We really are too much alike. That is, if opposites attract. What do you think?"

"Maybe that is a perfect combination. Some things just alike, others very different. For instance, I'm not sure I like your politics."

"Oh, come on. You just mean my interpretation of the Vietnam war, *n'est-ce pas?*"

"No. It's more to do with your comments about politicians, here and in England and America. You may not know it, but I am quite conservative. Like my father, I guess."

"Why was your father conservative?"

"Well, you know he was in heavy combat in World War II, as a Colonel in the British army in North Africa. After that, he decided he could only back smart conservatives, like Churchill. I guess I was much influenced by his conversations, and now only go for such politicians."

"That would sound very reasonable, except for me such politicians are generally unsympathetic types. Maybe especially in England and America. And my biggest problem with them, is that they seem to favor the rich. I am more for the poor. Although, you have to watch their actions more than what they say, don't you think? And war hero Churchill was defeated by Labor's Clement Atlee in the July, 1945 election."

"Yes. But, let't just leave it that we can always agree to disagree, all right?"

"You are so persuasive, *ma belle. On verra.* Now, how about dinner?

I propose Montmartre again. But, I discovered a nice Italian one on the way there when you were in Bordeaux."

"Marvelous. Let's go, or *andiamo* as the Italians say."

"You're right. I like that word so much, and the Italians invented so many great words, *basta, ciao, farnienti, magari, schifoso,* etc. How much Italian do you know?"

"A few words only from my trips there. I've been there about four times. And you? And what do *magari* and *schifoso* mean?"

"Magari's a favorite word. Something like `would that it were so.' Schifoso means disgusting. I've done Italy only once. About ten years ago, and I'm looking forward to the next time, I hope with you."

We got a nice corner table at the Tratoria Alceste on Rue Ravignan between the Metro Abbesses and Place du Tertre. The pasta dishes were wonderfully tasty, and once into them, I asked Valerie what she had liked most in Italy. She said, "Everywhere I went. It would be hard to rate one place better than the other. But, I didn't much like Milano. It's too much of

an industrial city, despite the great art you can see there. I went from there to Florence and stayed in a pensione on the left bank of the Arno.

Fortunately, it wasn't raining and it was in July. A walk across the Ponte Vecchio was most appealing. Then, the great museums of the Pitti Palace and Galeria degli Uffizi were sensational. I especially remember the dinner I had in the Piazza della Signoria, looking at copies of statues by Michelangelo, while an actor was reciting from Dante. Of course, I couldn't understand the Dante, but was told it was from the Comedia, or Divine Comedy as we call it, his masterwork. From there I went to Ravenna and after that to Venice. I haven't done

Rome, and maybe we could do that in the spring. What do you think?"

"Magari. You see, one can use that word all the time, and it sounds so nice even as it gives an idea so succinctly."

We finished the dinner and walked up to the Place du Tertre for our usual night caps. Then it was the nice walk home and more of the usual.

Two days later was my second class. I decided to start it by asking one of those great might have been questions.

"Let me start by asking, how do you think history would have changed if the French had won the Seven Years War?"

It was a good question because about ten students raised their hands.

Naturally, I chose the prettiest girl to do so. She was Isabelle Avrillon, who said predictably, and in decent English, "It would have changed everything.

And what do you think would have happened, if France, not England had come to dominate the world?"

"Indeed, Isabelle, as you say everything would have been different. What would we anglophones be like if French was the lingua franca? But, a great thing about history is that you have to accept the consequences of whatever happened, however unlikely it might have seemed at the time. As you all know, France was the dominant European country, and hence of the world precisely until England's victory in the Seven Years War. So, we have to go back to that, and outline the growth of English power not only in the Americas, but in the rest of the world."

The class ended discussing the decisive battle of Quebec in 1759 giving the English control of Canada, despite the death of the leaders of both armies, the Marquis de Montcalm and James Wolfe.

After arranging my notes and getting my coat, I knocked on the door of Claudia Chevalier, and was delighted when she opened. Even more delightfully, she accepted my invitation for a glass of wine at the

Rue de l'Hotel St. Paul bar. Once there, I asked her to tell me more of her life, starting with the question, *"Est-ce que vous etes Parisienne?"*

She replied, "Not at all. I was born and raised in Orleans. That is

132 kilometers to the south, and a wonderful city. Do you know it?"

"No. But, I would love to go some time. Maybe, you could show it to me.?"

"Not this semester, anyway. But, tell me your background?"

"Well, I came to New York from the town of Asheville in North Carolina. It's in the west of the state, with mountains, but many miles from anywhere very interesting. Still, it was a good city to grow up in."

"So, you must be a great hunter, no? I ask that because my father loved to *chasser le gibier autour d' Orleans*. We especially had a lot of pheasants, and even *becasse*. I believe you call that woodcock. It is very delicious."

"I'm not a bad hunter, but less good than my father was. He loved especially to hunt ducks and quail which abound *chez nous* in the fall and winter. In the warm months. we did a lot of hiking and fishing, which I preferred to hunting, and, of course, swimming." "How great! Maybe you could take me there sometime?"

"Sure! But not this term, to return your comment. If we can't do any trips together for awhile, what else might be possible for us as new friends?"

"I do enjoy seeing you, Chris. But, I should tell you, you are not the only guy pursuing me."

"Well, that's another thing we have in common, since I have a girl friend. And how serious are you with your friend?"

"In fact, not very. I may be breaking up with him before long. And you?"

"My friend is English, and we met in the Jardins de Luxembourg at the end of the summer. She was doing a vacation, but decided to stay in Paris, and see what happens with me and her new job. That's at Shakespeare & Co, which I am sure you know."

"And how serious about her are you?"

"I love her, but sometimes find her too mysterious. For example, she just told me she was maybe too conservative for me, which seemed the opposite of what I would have thought."

"That is also a rather dangerous formula. Two people in love with each other, but having different politics. How leftist are you?"

"Sometimes, very. At other times I am also quite conservative. But, I get troubled by other things with Valerie. That's her name by the way. For example she likes to flirt, and claims she is doing it to tease me. Do you think I should believe her?"

"That obviously would depend on the circumstances. Does she seem sincere or tricky? She sounds interesting. When can I meet her?"

"Well, she may be coming to one of my classes. Perhaps after that. And now, I had better be on my way. She will want to know what kept me so long."

"All right then. See you next week."

We embraced with kisses on both cheeks, or bisous as they are called here, and I accompanied her to the St. Paul metro stop. We went off in different directions on the number one line, me towards the Etoile, her towards the Bastille. She had said she lived on Rue des Tournelles, towards the Chemin Vert metro stop.

As I neared our apartment, I wondered if Valerie would in fact be there after her work. And again I debated if I should mention my new friend, Claudia. I guessed not, but supposed I would have to wait and see how our conversation went.

Valerie was there, and said she got off work early. She came over to welcome me and suggested we sit in the foyer. I was no sooner seated when she asked me how my class went. I related that, bragging about my might have been question for the students, about what would have happened if France had remained dominant after the Seven Years War, and the lively discussion that followed that. I also mentionned that I would have to go to a department meeting on the next Wednesday, and wondered what I would find. I thought that the director, Richard Dhuiq, and vice director, Nadine Bruyere, seemed such opposite types that I imagined they would have diffculties functionning smoothly together.

Valerie said, "And guess who came in to my shop today?"

"Surely not Keith."

"No, but that other Brit you like even less, Mark Goden."

"Oh, my God. Is it possible he knows Keith?"

"In fact, I asked him that. He said everyone in his business knows Keith. That is people who deal with wine."

"What else did he say about him?"

"That he enjoyed talking with Keith, but thought he was a crook. He wondered if he was using some of his wine contacts in France to deal drugs on the side."

"Oh come on! Keith seems to me like the epitome of honesty, even if too pretentious and smug. And did you and Mark make another date?"

"In fact, yes. It's next Wednesday, the day of your department meeting, which you might enjoy if you want to do something else that night."

"Well, remember my jealousy and keep your distance. Now, how about a dinner, and why don't we try a restaurant we haven't done together which I am sure you will like. It's even in the clothes and fashion part of Paris, in the Tenth

Arrondissement. There are two great possibilities, the Brasserie Flo, in the *Cour des Petits Ecuries* and the other on the easier to find *Rue de Faubourg St. Denis*."

"Great. And what does *Ecurie* mean."

"Stable, for horses that is. Which restaurant do you think you would like?"

"I must say, *La cour des Ecuries* intrigues me. Let's do that one."

"Wonderful. It's a favorite! If it is too crowded, or not to your taste, it is an easy walk to the other one."

Our metro route was to take the no. 3 line to Strasbourg-St.Denis and then one stop to *Chateau d'Eau.* From there it was a very short walk, but to an almost impossible place to find, as the entrances to the 'Court of the Stables' were tiny doorways, disguised by surrounding buildings.

By now it was 9:30 p.m. and not surprisingly, the Brasserie Flo was *complet.* They said there would not be a place for two until 11, and I proposed, and Valerie agreed, that we go to the other choice, Julien. It was at 16 *Rue de Faubourg St. Denis*, and the exit from the *Cour des Petits Ecuries* led directly into that street. It was a five minute walk to the west and fortunately they had a nice table for us.

We were in a corner looking down the long hall of the dining room. There seemed to be lots of models and assorted types, as well as a group of what seemed to be American tourists at a long table near us. As we were drinking our initial glasses of wine, a couple came in that I thought I recognized from my previous time in Paris. But, I couldn't remember who. "That's so annoying, not being able to remember people you have met. And that happens more and more often. Am I coming down with Alzheimers?"

"Oh, come on," said Valerie. "Everyone does that all the time."

Suddenly, I remembered. It was one of the teachers of the seminar on Vietnam at Univesitè de Paris VII. His name is Pierre Hemery, and Julie that of the wife. After dinner, I proposed that we go over and say hello.

The restaurant had the tasty seafood, Coquille St. Jacques, and we shared a dish of it to start. Then we both had marvelous lapin or rabbit dishes in a cream sauce. Our waiter was an amusing middle age man, who danced around as he waited on the incredible number of people in his section. That included us, as well as the group of American tourists who came in just after us and took an enormous, oblong, adjoining table just off to our side. The waiter imitated some of the terrible pronunciation of the dishes the tourists ordered, and other waiters passing by had to restrain their laughter. We spoke enough French that we could understand and make our own jokes in that language about such embarrassments without the neighboring table understanding us.

Finishing our meal, we walked over to the Hemery table at the other end of the restaurant. I remembered the last time I had seen Pierre. That was in 1982 at Jussieu, in the tower where the classes I took on Vietnamese history were held. He was walking briskly to the elevator as I was coming in to talk with his colleague, Georges Brocheux. We stopped to talk a bit, and I told him I had started writing what became my Vietnam book. He wished me luck and made a suggestion. It was to start at the end, with the drama of the Communist victory in 1975. I liked the idea so much, I decided to restart my writing to do that.

Now, after I had introduced Valerie, Pierre asked me what had become of my book? I answered "Not much to do with the sales. But, I was happy with the reviews I got. Part of that is no doubt due to you and Georges and Daniel, and thank you for all your information and perceptions. I really enjoyed those classes." Those two had taught the seminar with Pierre, and Pierre thanked me in return for having been an attentive student, even if I was afraid to speak up, given the state of my French.

Julie asked if we could bring up chairs and join them for a drink or two. We agreed and got the waiters to help with that. Julie went on to ask Valerie what she did. When Valerie replied that she worked at Shakespeare & Co., Julie gave her equivalent of 'it's a small world.' It seems she had worked there also ten years ago. Valerie asked, "And why did you stop?"

"I got a better job," said Julie.

"What was that?"

"In Galeries Lafayette, the one at Montparnasse. Selling men's clothing."

I asked,"Did you meet any men who could match Pierre?"

"Certainly not. You know how attractive my husband is."

I thought that's a good one, as if marriages between attractive people didn't break up. But, rather than say anything to do with that, I said, "Well, it's good you two are still so happy. Now I am too, with Valerie." They gave me a knowing look, and Valerie smiled nicely.

As we were exchanging a few more sentences over our glasses of muscat, we were surprised by another sort of embarrassment, this one by another French waiter. He began shouting at the Maitre D', who shouted back. "*Ca suffit! Vous etes fini ici! Allez vous-en.*" Fortunately, the waiter left calmly, with dirty looks at his boss. Another waiter came over, apologizing and explaining that the fired waiter had been fighting for days with the boss. He said he was not sorry to see him go, but regretted the disruption. We said "Oh, it's nothing," more or less with one voice. After finishing the muscat, we said our good byes and went our separate ways.

The next days passed calmly and Wednesday arrived. It was the day of my department meeting and free night, given Valerie's date with Mark Goden. I wondered if that meant I could see Claudia Chevalier for a longer time than had been the case with my first meetings.

The meeting was uneventful, and afterwards I went back to my cubicle hoping I would see Claudia on the way. She was already in her office and opened when I knocked.

"*Bonjour. Ca va?*"

I wondered why French invariably said that when they saw someone. But, soon understood that it was like our "How are you?" After her "tres bien," I replied "Not bad. At least the class went all right. Can we do another drink, and maybe dinner?"

Claudia said, "A drink anyway. I don't know about later until I call a friend who mentioned something."

"And, when do you think you will know? In any case, I have the evening free for a change. So, I hope you can join me."

"*Bien*. I will knock soon as I know, and no later than 6:30 or so. *D'accord?*"

"*D'accord. Et bonne chance pour moi,*" I said as I closed the door of my cubicle. There, I unloaded my teaching notes on the desk to arrange them for the next class. After that, I re-examined the second reference book I brought over for my class, a two volume text book by six authors, titled *A People and a Nation*. As my specialties were Asian and European history, I had asked colleagues for the best such reference books for American history. For the Canadian history, I had only one book and wondered if I would need to get more, but doubted it given the brevity of the course and limited expectations of the students. There would be even less of a problem for my few mentions of Central American and Mexican history, and that only when the U.S. became involved with them.

At 6:30 there had still been no knock on the door. I thought I would wait another fifteen minutes and then redo my request, opening my door on to the hall in anticipation. I had only read two more pages when I saw Claudia emerging from her place next door. She smiled brightly and said, "*Ca va, on y va?*"

"Wonderful, and I hope for dinner also. I have a lot I want to tell you."

As we exited the courtyard on to the street, I debated whether I could take her hand. After a few paces, I did so and she willingly squeezed mine in return.

As we walked along Rue Charles V, I saw a nice looking bar/café at the corner, and proposed we stop there for a drink, before deciding where to eat. She agreed and over glasses of chablis I asked her what restaurants she liked in the neigborhood. She said she knew of some in the Bastille area. Just then, I remembered the St. Paul bar guy's recommendation of the *Auberge Nicolas Flamel* and asked if she knew of it. She said yes, and had heard it was very good. I asked if she also had heard it was said to be in one of the oldest buildings of Paris, and if she would like to go. As the response was positive on both counts, we paid up and set out for the Rue Montmorency. Claudia knew that the quickest way there was via the Rue des Franc Bourgeois and Rambuteau, until a right on the Rue Beaubourg to the Rue Montmorency.

As we walked, I expressed admiration for her knowing all those little turns, and we arrived in about fifteen minutes. Fortunately there was a table and we happily installed ourselves.

After ordering, and over a nice bottle of Merlot, I asked Claudia how she was finding her class this term. She replied, "It's quite interesting, as I have some students who seem *très intelligent.* One of them, I think a *Provencal* girl, asked me an amusing question today."

"What was it? I love it when I get good questions."

"She wanted to know why the English ate so badly. It seems she had gone to London last summer to study English and was horrified at the food."

"And what was your answer?"

I said. "Maybe, It's because they are so isolated as an island country. Or maybe their taste buds are not developed." I said that with a smile, and then suggested more seriously to the class that we explore that question in our studies of English literature. "In other words what did English literature show about cooking, food and its quality, and could there be any connection between the awfulness of English food and the greatness of their literature?"

She asked, "Is that true of America as well?" I answered that she would have to see for herself when she came to the U.S.

As our plates arrived, I wondered again what troubles I was building for myself by becoming so familiar with an attractive other lady. Would it go too far? How would Valerie react if she learned of it. Since she liked to flirt herself, would she ignore it, or even treat it as an enticement? In any case, I thought I can enjoy this meal and see Claudia this semester at least, and then see what happened.

We enjoyed the patè we both ordered to start, followed by a filet of sole for Claudia and a rouget, or red snapper, for me. The wine flowed freely and I asked, "What exactly are you teaching now."

Claudia answered, "A comparison of the Arthurian cycle in British lit with the Chanson de Roland and works of Chrètien de Troyes in medieval France."

"Sounds fascinating! And will you get into the historical works of Shakespeare? I wonder if I can mention some of those to do with my current discussion of the wars with France, and the later rise to dominance of England."

"Yes, certainly there will be references to the King Henry plays and a bit more to do with Richard 111. But, I doubt if there will be anything to do with American history."

"Well, I don't suppose I will have any problem filling the time for my course. There is so much to talk about. I have started with the French explorers and their settling of Canada. Then, I cover England's victories, and after that the colonists' increasing opposition to 'taxation without representation' and the war against England, and after that the march to the Civil War. In the spring semester it will be the twentieth century. But, as said I really prefer Asian and European history. That will be a consolation for my return to New York. And bicycling is another."

"So, you do the velo also?"

"Very much so when I'm in New York. I don't know how people get around without bicycles. In Paris, however, I have only done it about twice. Some time I would love to do a tour in France by bike."

"This summer, I plan to do one. To Aquitaine and beyond."

"How great! And when do you leave and for how long?"

"It's really to be a history and scenery tour. Depending on what happen's with my boy friend, we might leave in June and do much of the summer. The plan is to go southeast to the Vallèe de la Loire, via Chartres, Orleans and Tours to Angers. From there southeast again to Poitiers, and Saintes, and then southwest to Perigueux and Sarlat. We will take trains for some of the longer stretches. You know you can take bikes on most French trains, though sometimes there is a small extra charge. How is your knowledge of such places?"

"Very limited. I've done the Loire valley towns but only read of the wonders of some of the other places you mention. And if you break with your boy friend?"

"We'll see. Would you like to replace him?"

"Maybe. *On verra.*"

"Anyway, a girlfriend also wants to go. So, why not be the second man, if not the first?"

"You really tempt me. But, I don't think my English friend will agree. But, then why don't I ask her if she wants to do such a trip. Would that be OK, to have another couple along?"

"Why not? The more the merrier. But, it gets tricky on some roads, especially when there are a lot of cars. Then, we have to go single file, and keep up with each other. And/

or know where the next stop is going to be. And then if it's just you with me and my girl friend, your Valerie might get jealous."

By then we had finished eating, and I debated how to respond to that and simultaneously disengage from Claudia.

"Well, I hope you don't break with your boyfriend, or at least until after the trip. How about if we pay up here and go to Centre Pompidou for a nightcap. Or do you have other ideas?"

Claudia agreed and after settling the bill we proceeded down Rue St. Martin the several blocks to Beaubourg as that enormous futuristic building and its square is usually called. Beaubourg was the name of a village in the then north-eastern edge of Paris at the time of Philippe Auguste, towards 1200 when it became the name of a street. President Pompidou chose that street and its neighborhood as the site of the cultural center that would bear his name when completed eight years later in 1977. We chose a bar restaurant on the hill overlooking the square and building complex from the west.

What should we see walking across the top of the square on Rue St. Martin but the projection of a film against the western wall of the huge building. We learned from a waiter that it was *Rashomon* by Kurosawa, one of the greatest movie directors. There were no loudspeakers for the Japanese dialogue, only French subtitles below. In any case, the images somewhat distracted us from any serious conversation.

Still, Claudia told me some more things about places she wanted to visit on her bike tour. That was over several glasses each of a nice and relatively inexpensive port. She said one of their first stops would be Poitiers, near the site where Charles Martel defeated the Saracens in 732. About a hundred kilometers to the southwest she said they would arrive at Saintes, on the Charente River southeast of La Rochelle. It had been one of the largest towns in Gaul in the Roman era and the capital of the region. It had monuments from Roman times

as well as an Abbaye and Cathedral from the middle ages. Claudia went on to mention a few details about the medieval towns of Perigueux and Sarlat.

"How marvelous," I said. "I hope I can work out something with Valerie and join you on that trip. Shall we leave it at that, and talk more about those possibilities in a few days?"

She waved for the bill and said, "I hope you can, and I would love to meet Valerie, whether or not you can join us."

We shared the bill and went our separate ways, she to the east and me to the west.

I decided to walk back across the Pont des Arts over the Seine River to St. Germain des Près and another drink at the Cafè Bonaparte to reflect on these latest developments. It was a nice clear night and I got there fortunately before the illumination of the St. Germain church disappeared. Normally they turn off those lights at midnight. It always comforts me to see the soothing lines of the façade and the ancient tower. Even with that I felt confused to say the least. I couldn't ruin my best love yet, with Valerie. Still, I also liked Claudia very much and wondered about the wonders of exploring parts of my favorite country by bike. So, I was faced with two, or three, if I counted the bike trip, of life's greatest pleasures, as well as possible love complications. I risked ruining some of them by trying to do all of them. *Que faire?* The Marie Brizard finished, I could only go back to my obvious compromise of deciding to try to have the best of all worlds for at least the rest of the semester, hoping things would arrange themselves as well as possible.

CHAPTER FOUR

CLAUDIA AND JEALOUSY

When I got home via several metro transfers, I was delighted that Valerie was already there. I asked her when she had gotten in. She said, "About an hour ago. And what were you up to?'

"I had a nice dinner with a lady I met at the Institut d'Anglais.

"And who was that?"

"A fellow teacher, who happens also to be an attractive woman."

"And did you score with her?"

"No. Certainly not. You don't think I want to ruin my chances with you, do you?"

"With men, you never know. And I've noticed you have an eye for other ladies."

"I can't deny that. But, now I'm being more careful, since I love you so much. Still, meeting this lovely colleague at our meeting and with a free evening, understandably, I asked her to dinner."

"All right! I hope your meal was more agreeable than mine with Mark Goden. I think he's all right as a person, but he has no education. Because of that it's frequently hard to have a conversation. And he's always talking about this or that movie star. But, you'd better watch out! His politics are more like mine."

Again, she looked at me with her mischievous smile.

I asked, "And, how did you find out you had similar politics?"

"He asked me what I thought of England's joining the European Union. I told him, I thought it was a very bad idea and hoped we would continue to resist switching to the Euro. We agreed on the idiocy of being controlled by bureaucrats in Brussels."

"But, don't you see that is what the U.S. did by uniting our colonies, when we started becoming the greatest country on earth. Of course, we didn't have the baggage of all the history older countries have, and we managed to get rid of most of the Indians while defeating the French, Spanish and English. And, of course, we were helped in all of that by our poor black slaves."

"If you think like that, I can see why you are so radical."

"Maybe so, and I have been turned off by our foreign policy after World War II, especially with Vietnam."

"But look at all the good you did, the Marshall plan, NATO, and all the rest."

"Of course, you are right, as always, or almost. How about hitting the sack?"

We did that and enjoyed another great night of love making. The next day, which was that of my fourth class, I decided to play it cool with Claudia. All the more so, since I had only mentioned her to Valerie, but not given her name or any other information. So I was relieved when I did not run into Claudia. After class, discovering by phone that Valerie was not home, I decided to do a Bastille evening before going home. I had a white wine at a Cafè on the way, and dinner at Boffingers Restaurant off to the western side side of the Bastille.

The weekend passed nicely. Valerie and I did more walking in our new neighborhood with several outings to various bars and restaurants. On Saturday night, October 28, we were joined by Keith, who had called to invite us to dinner in Montmartre. That was at a place he knew of about halfway betweem the Basilica Sacre Coeur and the Lamarck-Caulaincourt metro stop on the Rue Lamarck. It was the Beauvilliers Restaurant, with a one star rating in the red Michelin, meaning it was very good. It had been founded way back in 1784, and had handsome mid 19th century décor. It was so expensive I was delighted when Keith said it could go on his business account.

He said, "That is the least I can do after you let me go to Bordeaux with Valerie. And the International Wine Shop is happy to pay for such, I might add."

"Well, thank you very much," I said, as I noticed Valerie smiling her accord.

Keith ordered a bottle of Chablis to start, and it came promptly. The glasses poured, he turned to us and asked, "Now tell me about your latest, starting with your new digs, and jobs?"

Valerie took over and briefly described our apartment. She gave some details about Parc Monceau and the museums there and then told about her job. I was glad she did not say she was bored with it.

I added, "As you can see, we love coming to Montmartre for all the restaurants and bars there are."

"Well, I'm glad I got in on that and could introduce you to one of the best of the restaurants around here. Now, tell me more about your teaching, Chris."

"So far I've done four classes and they have gone well enough.

I started with the possibility that France might have taken over America, which poses an interesting might have been question."

"What a fascinating idea," Keith said.

Valerie said, "But, Chris did it by talking down us Anglos as we pushed to dominance with the Seven Years War and all that. It's true that it started with what Americans call the French and Indian wars, but in fact it was more about the attempts of the European powers to dismember the old Austrian and new Prussian empires."

Smiling broadly at Valerie, I said, "I didn't know you were such a historian, my love."

Keith said, "You never cease to astonish. But, why do you think we Brits came to take over most of the world back then?"

"Because we are the best, naturally," Valerie said with a wink.

That gave me the chance to say, "And what about the way you treated Ireland? And how come you were the ones who forced the opium wars on China and shipped more slaves than anyone else?"

"I told you he was too radical for me, didn't I, Keith?"

"Unfortunately, he's right," Keith said. "Moreover, we went on to massacre the Boers in the Transvaal."

I put in, "At the same time we Americans were massacring the Indians and Philipinos."

"Basta, basta, you two," Valerie almost shouted. "Let's order and find something more amusing to talk about."

We decided to do their specialties, Valerie and me the duck with figs and Keith his favorite, the sweetbreads..

"How delicious, and I have another question for you, Keith.

Why didn't you and Valerie go to Pomerol on your trip to Bordeaux?"

"Because we didn't have the time, rushed as we were. Let's see, we did St. Emilion on Sunday morning, didn't we, Valerie?"

"Yes, and I loved that village. I wish we could have stayed longer."

Staring at Keith, I said, "Since Pomerol is almost next to St. Emilion, I still don't see why you couldn't go there as well."

"Because we had to take the autoroute to the train station for the six o'clock train."

"Well, it's too bad, as the village is beautiful and the wine is my favorite Bordeaux. Of course, I can't afford the Chateau Petrus, or anything half as fine as that. Did you know the name, Pomerol, comes from the Latin word for the goddess of fruit trees, Pomona?"

"All right, I'll have to add that to my repertoire of factoids about wine."

I asked, "When do you go back to London?"

Keith said, "In about a week. Is there any chance you two, or at least Valerie since she's from there, will get to London soon?"

"Certainly not. I'm teaching, Valerie is working and I'm not letting her out of my sight. But, I want to propose another trip to her, and by bicycle, yet."

"Wouldn't that be fun," Valerie said in a louder than usual voice. "I love to bike. But where to, and I thought our next trip was going to be to Belgium."

"It will be. That's over Christmas and then Italy for Easter.

But, it's an idea my new friend at the Institute proposed for next summer. So, it's some time off, but as I just heard about it, I'm thinking of it."

Keith put in, "So, I see Chris is making new friends, and maybe that gives me a chance with Valerie. And again, Chris, why do you keep answering for Valerie when I put questions to her?"

Looking crossly at him, I said, "And why do you keep flirting with Valerie? Are you trying to increase my normal jealousy?"

Valerie again saved us by changing the subject. "And where would the bike trip go?"

"My friend, an attractive lady colleague named Claudia, who maybe Keith should look up, proposes a trip with other friends to the Aquitaine and some cities there as well as a few other places I've long wanted to see."

Keith immediately asked me to give the name and co-ordinates of Claudia. As I looked in the address book at the back of my agenda, Valerie said, "I would love to see that part of France. Does it include the Bordeaux area?"

"No, I think it will be to the north and east of that, and we'll do part of the trip by train. The French have a good system for taking bikes on such trips."

"And how do you know your friend will accept to have another person, meaning me, along?"

"I thought of that and already asked Claudia, who said she would love to have you come along. Keith, here's her telephone number, but I don't know where she lives."

Keith said, "I'll call her some time before I return to London for sure."

"Please do, so I don't have to keep worrying about you and Valerie," I wondered at my tendency to tell white lies, this time, about not knowing Claudia's address.

"Before you two start fighting again, tell me more about what sort of job you think you might help me get, Keith."

"You're so diplomatic, aren't you," he said, as he almost fell into Valerie's lap leaning over in her direction.

"There you go again," I said, "leaning into people as you talk to them. You told me you were going to stop doing that. How about it?"

"Sorry, I guess I'm sometimes clumsy. Anyway, the perfect job for you, as I said, would be to charm more restaurants and bars into buying our wines."

"Well, you give me something to think about," Valerie said. But, I definitely want to wait awhile and see how my job here goes and if I can stand Chris much longer."

She poked me in the ribs, and smiling at me, added, "And, now I also want to see what happens with that bike trip next summer."

"For that jab, since I've already finished mine I'm going to take a last bite of your canard aux figues, my love." Then, turning to Keith, I asked, "And how was your ris de veau?"

"One of the best sweetbreads I've ever had," he said, wiping his mouth. "When and where do you expect to go in Belgium and Italy?"

Valerie said, "We don't know exactly, but certainly Bruges and Ghent in Belgium and at least Rome in Italy. We leave for Belgium about December 20 or whenever Chris can stop teaching."

"How long a trip do you think you can take?"

I replied, "Again, that depends on my teaching schedule. I think classes start in the second week of January, which for me would be Tuesday, January 9. So, we might come back the weekend before that. Or we might do a shorter trip, just over Christmas."

Keith put in, "Can I propose some other places you should go to in Italy, other than Rome, if you haven't already been to them?"

"For me, that includes Florence and Venice, and we'd love to see other places," I said. "I think Valerie also has been to only a few places. So, go ahead and give us your advice."

"Well, to the south you have to see the beautiful Amalfi coast, and then towards Florence, the cities of Siena and San Gimignano. As well as Ravenna south of Venice."

Valerie came in at that point to say, "But, I like to see one place thoroughly before flitting about to other sites. That will be especially true if it's 'the Eternal City.'"

"I agree, and as it will only be for at most two weeks, we should probably stay in Rome. But, I have heard how gorgeous the Costa Amalfitana is and hope to do that some day. Now, shall we do dessert or a nightcap? I suggest the latter at the Place du Tertre."

"A great idea," Keith said. Turning towards a waiter, he called out, *"S'il vous plaît, l'addition."* Then to us, he continued, "That is

something I love about France. You can always get the waiter's attention by saying *'s'il vous plaît.'* As soon as they hear that, they come running, whereas in England saying 'please' does no good at all."

"I agree, and certainly it's also like that in the States. But, I've wondered if it's just because they are so much better trained for restaurant service here than they are in the anglophone countries."

"In any case," Valerie said, "Let's be on our way as soon as the waiter takes care of the bill."

That happened more or less immediately, and we made our way up the Rue Lamarck and around the front of Basilica Sacre Coeur and then to the nearby Place du Tertre. There, we went to one of the first bars and installed ourselves around a nice round table. Valerie and I ordered a green Chartreuse and Keith a Chivas Regal whiskey on the rocks.

Since Keith had paid the far more expensive restaurant bill, I offered to pay this one, and did so right away. Looking up, I noticed the literally dozens of artists surrounding us, and remembered having asked one to paint Valerie's portrait not long ago, but resisted mentioning that. Sure enough, Keith asked her if she wouldn't want one. Fortunately, she said, "No way, I had one done a few weeks ago."

"Was it any good?" Keith asked.

"Not bad," Valerie replied.

I said, "I like it a lot. It shows a beautiful woman, but with something extra, vivavious and a bit coquettish."

"When can I see it?" asked Keith, and I immediately regretted my comments. All the more so, when Keith went on to say, "You should see the picture my ex-wife did of me in London. I left it with her and hope she has thrown it out. It features the moles on my cheeks and makes me look even fatter than I am, with a round face."

"You don't seem that bad," said Valerie.

I added "There you go again being polite, and maybe too polite."

Keith said, "You can see why I prefer Valerie, can't you? And I've noticed some spots on your trousers, old boy."

"How about drinking some and stop acting like school boys," Valerie said, as she raised her glass for a toast, "Santè, and good times. No more bickering, OK?"

As I was struggling to think how to change the subject, Keith said, "D'accord, and let me tell you something about the wines I've been buying on this trip."

"Please do," Valerie said with an expectant look.

"One of the biggest batches I bought, ten cases worth in fact, are Gigondas, a marvelous Cote du Rhone. Of course, the quality varies by the year. The most expensive wines I bought are two cases of Haut Brion, 1995, and in between those are another ten cases of St. Emilion, 1996. In addition, I ordered thirty cases of cheaper Languedocs, of varying *etiquettes*. Do you know that word?"

I looked at Valerie who was shaking her head, and said, "I have heard of it but am not really familiar with it. Do vintners use it all the time to refer to their wines?"

"It means label, and we use either that or more commonly, we call the bottle by its brand of whatever year. Still more often we just refer to whatever region, or locality, the stuff comes from."

"And how many places besides France do you get your wines from," Valerie asked.

Keith pulled himself up as if he were the CEO of the company, and said, "From all over: Australia, Africa, Latin America, the U.S., even various parts of the ex Soviet Union. However, over half our wines are from Italy and France, more or less equally divided between them."

Then, I asked, "How big is your warehouse for all those imports, and where is it located? How many bottles do you have from the various years, and at what point is the storage area called a '*cave*'?"

"The last is an interesting question," Keith observed. "I am not sure what the etymology of the word is, though I think it's from the Latin word for hole in the ground. And in the middle ages, people discovered that wines aged best underground. But, nowadays, that can only be the case with the rich who have enough space for a separate cellar or room for their wine. At last count, we had about eight hundred cases of wine, with some going back to the sixties. As for where our warehouse is, as you might guess it is outside London, near Chester. Do you know that town, Valerie?"

"No. Is it worth going to?"

"Very much so, it has some of the best of Roman and medieval remnants in England. It still has pieces of Roman walls and ramparts."

"Very interesting, Keith, but it's time we are on our way. It's already after the witching hour and I need to do some more work preparing my lectures for next week," I said.

We all stood and took our leave, Keith with the usual too ardent embrace of Valerie. I had to restrain myself from threatening him but only said, "You don't have to look as if you are going to rape her when you give her a parting hug." He ignored the remark, and fortunately, took the metro at Abbesses instead of the one we were going to. We walked on to take the metro from the Blanche stop, which was on another line. We took that for three more stops, including one called Rome. We got off at the Monceau stop for the short walk to the Rue de Vèzelay.

The next morning, after working on my notes, I asked Valerie if she felt like going to the Louvre again and doing a walk in the Tuilleries afterwards.

She said, "That's a great idea. I'm very ready for an outing. All morning I've been reading in the Diamond book, *Guns, Germs and Steel*. In that, by the way, some of the last pages were really extraordinary. Did you know that the language on Madagascar off of northeast Africa, called Malgache, is Austronesian?"

"You must be kidding? I know almost nothing of such places, but across such a vast ocean, how could that be?"

"Well, according to Diamond, archaelogists have proved from iron tools, livestock and crops, that there was an Austronesian colony there by 800 A.D. His book is convincing about so many incredible things. And, by the way Shakespeare & Co. has that book. So how about that, for a Christmas present?"

"That will be wonderful. Now give me a hug, and let's have some cheese and wine and then be on our way."

As Valerie prepared the cheese, salad and wine, I got out my Guide Michelin Vert for Paris and discovered that it had over 38 pages on the Louvre, the biggest section of the guide by far. I asked if I should tell about what I read. Valerie said, "Please do."

"Well, it seems the museum now is on the site of the Roman victory over the Parisii in 52 B.C. The Normans also camped there for their siege of the city in 885. A Fortress existed from early times and imposing buildings started appearing by the fourteenth century. Great early kings, including Philippe Auguste (1180-1223), Saint Louis 1X (1226-1270) and Philip the Fair (1285-1314) established themselves nearby, but protected by water, on the Ile de la Citè, on the site of what is now the Palais de Justice. They also resided in palaces in the Marais, or outside of Paris in one of their chateaux. About 1190, Philippe Auguste began construction of a fort that became the Louvre. The museum's enormous collections began with François the First in the early 1500s, but that king lived mostly in the valley of the Loire River. He induced the great genius, Leonardo Da Vinci, to come to a chateau at Clos-Lucè near Amboise on the Loire, for several years before his death in 1519. Moreover, Leonardo's men carried the incomparable painting, Mona Lisa, and other works with him on the backs of mules to France on their arduous trip over the Alps. Fortunately, no great storms damaged them and they are now mostly in the Louvre."

Valerie interrupted at that point, "How incredible that the world's most famous painting was carried over the Alps on foot!"

As Valerie brought our two plates and a bottle of Muscadet to the table, I asked her if she wanted me to go on. She suggested I stop during lunch and then summarize other highlights while she did the dishes.

"Perfect, as usual," I said. "Now, tell me what you most want to see that you haven't. That is after we eat as much as we wish."

She started and after a bite or two, said, "I think, the Roman period, since I've already done the Etruscans. And the great Italian and other Renaissance painters again as one never gets enough of them. *D'accord*?"

"Very much so. And the rest of the history can be quickly finished after we do these bites." When, Valerie started on the dishes I went on to describe how, after Louis XIII died in 1643, Louis XIV became the '*Sun King*'. He added many more works of art, but preoccupied with Versailles, stopped new construction for the Louvre. A century later came the Revolution, and after that Napoleon completed the Cour Carrè at the eastern end of the Louvre, as well as the Arc du

Carrousel to the west. The latter inspired the building of the Arc de Triumph at the other end of the Champs Elysèes. It was begun under Napoleon but not finished until the 1830s.

As Valerie was finishing the dishes, I said, "You know, aside from the Etruscan stuff, the Louvre has very little of Roman art, but enormous amounts of Egyptian and then Greek materials. Then as you said, we should see the Renaissance art, which has the highest rating of all."

She agreed and I said, "All right, after all that info, let's go to the great museum."

As we walked to the Champs Elysées and the George V metro stop for our trip there, I continued to talk about stuff in the guidebook. "Do you know that there is an original Sphinx in the Egyptian collection of the Louvre. Why don't we start with that."

"Very good," Valerie said, locking arms with me. Before long we were entering the metro. We got out at the Palais Royale to go into the underground complex there. That is an interesting walk with views of opulent shops in a mall surrounded by copies of art works. It led directly to an entrance into the crypt of the Sphinx in the basement of the Louvre. I said, "How appropriate that we start with the Sphinx, the symbol of so much mystery in the ancient world. It is appropriate that France acquired it about the same time Champollion was figuring out the mysteries of the hieroglyphics from Egypt."

Valerie agreed, and we proceeded upstairs to the Greek antiquities and the noble statue of the Winged Victory of Samothrace. "That is so incredible," I said, "As if it is flying with its one remaining wing. You know, I use pictures of that in my teaching about aviation. Did I tell you I do that?"

"I don't recall that you did. And why do you teach about flying?"

"In fact," I said, "Way back there, I was a pilot myself and loved it. So, after I became a history teacher, I thought why not teach about the history of aviation."

"Will you take me flying some time?" Valerie asked.

"Maybe, but now let's do the Renaissance paintings before it's too late."

Still on the ground floor, we came to sculptures by Michelangelo among others, and then going up to the second, saw innumerable masterpieces, mostly from the Italian Renaissance, including Leonardo's Mona Lisa.

Valerie asked, "Why do you suppose it's called *la Joconde?*"

"Beats me. I think it is to do with an Italian word of the time for an ambiguous smile or something like that. Anyway, let's move along and not be too late to see all we can before the closing. I read that they have all the greats, from Cimabue, and Giotto to Botticelli, Fra Angelico, Leonardo, Raphael, Caravaggio and all the rest. Then, there's the Norhern Renaissance School and who knows how much later stuff."

We went along and by the time I looked at my watch, it was already going on towards the seven o:clock closing time. "How about a glass or two at La Perigourdine, *ma belle?*"

"A great idea. All the more so as it is just over there across the river. I go there quite often from Shakespeare & Co., and love looking at Notre Dame from a seat in front. It's been quite awhile since I was there."

We exited from the east end of the museum through the Cour Carrè onto the Rue du Louvre facing the neo-Renaissance church, St. Germain de l'Auxerrois. From there it was along the right bank of the Seine to the Pont Neuf which we crossed half way to turn left through the Place Dauphine on the Ile de la Cité. Then it was just a few steps passing the Palais de Justice to the bridge leading to the Place St. Michel. Entering it, we noticed a large crowd of people. We saw that an entertainer was amusing onlookers gathered in the only free area in the place. Valerie wanted to see what it was and guided me over to it, even as I was tugging her in the direction of the bar. She won, but we only looked at the entertainers and crowd about two minutes. It was several guys and a good looking woman doing various somersaults, handstands and the like.

At the bar, we found a table with a view of Notre Dame and did our usual white wines. No sooner were they brought than Mark Goden, that gauche English guy, ignoring me fairly shouted 'Bonjour Valerie'. He finally said, "Oh hello, and remind me your name. Can I join you?"I thought, what nerve this creep has. Barging in on us and demanding to sit down when he doesn't even know me. He is worse than Keith, for God's sake. I looked at Valerie trying to indicate my displeasure. I was very relieved when she said, "There's really no space, Mark. How about another time?"

But, he said, "Well, I can find another chair, and I have something to ask you. All right?"

"Well, go ahead and ask it, but we want to be by ourselves as I'm sure Chris agrees."

Mark hesitated and I guessed he had improvised to say that he had a question. After a considerable pause, he said, "I was just wondering how long you were thinking of staying in this too leftist country?"

Valerie replied, "At least another six months. I have a good job, and Chris and I are planning some great trips. If things keep going this well, I may even overlook French leftism."

I said, "How can you say it is leftist with Chirac in the Presidency, even if he had to choose a socialist prime minister?"

"There you go again like most academics," Mark said. "All you hear are what you take to be leftist comments, no matter who says them, as even Chirac does from time to time."

"I didn't know you knew French, Mark. So, how do you know what they are saying. Or were you just listening to us?"

"I know enough to tell that. But, I see I'm not welcome company for you. So, I'll take my leave and call Valerie later."

To my great relief he went on his way, turning right towards the Boulevard St. Germain.

Valerie said, "What a relief he didn't stay, and I am sure you agree even more."

"You can say that again. I was thinking what a creep he was as soon as he started talking. I hope you never see him again."

"Me too! But, I can't help it if people I don't like come up to talk. All I can do is try to show them how to back off, as just now."

"Yes. You're right and congratulations on your success. Where would you like to eat when we finish our drinks?"

"There are some good restos behind where I work, and why don't we try one of those?"

Naturally, I agreed and shortly we were walking across to the other side of the Boulevard St. Michel. We took the Rue St. Severin to the church of that name where Valerie led me to the right, saying "I really want to try a restaurant they say is wonderful on a little side street over this way."

We reached Rue de la Parchminerie and turned right to find the recommended restaurant of that same name. She had the Turbot, and I a somptuous Soufflè de Fromage. The restaurant was unpretentious but had its charm with a lot of affiches or posters. As we were both somewhat tired after all the walking, we decided to head straight home by metro. We took a different route from the metro stop at St. Michel on the number four line towards Porte de Clignancourt, with a change at Barbes Rochechouart for the train headed to our stop at Monceau.

The next day was quiet and on Tuesday I made my way to my class ahead of time for my first 'office hours.' Sure enough there were two students waiting for me. They were Erica Celeste and Isabelle Avrillon, my two favorites in the course. The questions concerned recommendations for books on some topics they were considering for the papers due at the end of the term. Erica was thinking about a paper on the early history of Quebec city, and Isabelle about something on the

French and Indian wars. I told them I would have to look up the books to recommend, but went into some more discussion of the subjects and said we would look up those subjects on the internet. Since they were good topics, we easily used up the time we had. To have a few minutes to compose my thoughts, I sent them on their way about ten minutes before class time.

The class was mostly devoted at first to the history of the explorations. When I reached the seventeenth history, I started with Virginia history after the landing by John Smith and his crew at Jamestown in 1607. I could do that easily enough, having grown up near by in North Carolina. The latter part of the class got into discussion about the pilgrims landing in Massachusetts and some of the early history of what became the United States. The next class would begin with a narrative of the French and Indian wars and the significant role played in them by Virginians, including George Washington. Isabelle, and others, asked good questions and it was a lively class.

All the better, since as I was coming out of the room, I almost bumped into Claudia. We did the usual preliminaries while we walked to our cubicles. A little later, at my request, we decided to go to the bar on Rue de l'Hotel St. Paul again. There, I asked her how she was enjoying her class.

"Oh, you know. It's the usual mixture of sweet and sour. Both for me and the students. Some are good, most boring, and it varies a lot each time. But, I love it that we teachers get to talk about what we want."

"Today, for example, you taught about what?"

"I have just gotten to some Shakespeare. Before that, in this semester's first couple of classes we did the usual introduction and then Chaucer and a few of his contemporaries and successors. I especially like doing Wycliff because of all the subversive influence he had. He was an inspiration for the English peasant uprising of 1381, led by John Ball and Wat Tyler. Have you ever read a book called the Pursuit of The Millenium?"

"Can't say I have. Why do you mention it?"

"Because that's where I got the information about the last mentionned characters. Beyond that, he has really fascinating pages about the egalitarian rebels of the middle ages, from the Anabaptists and Cathars to the Levelers and Ranters."

"And you can link all that to John Wycliff? I thought he was an Oxford teacher."

"He was. But, his preachings and writings went far beyond that, influencing the Lollards at the time of the 1381 peasant uprising and later others, like Jan Hus and Luther."

"And what Shakespeare are you doing? As I told you, my friend is working at Shakespeare & Co, and I am wondering if I can make references to some of the great bard's works."

"I do Hamlet, King Henry V and Romeo and Juliet. That should give them a good sense of the master. But, of course, we only touch on those great works. Still, they get a sense of his genius, from drama to history to romance. As I told you, I don't think you can make any connections with American history."

"I can see you are a good teacher, just from the words you use. I can at least mention Shakespeare at some point. And the semester is not very long anyway." I said that even as I was thinking how fortunate that was, given my travel plans with Valerie. "What do you teach next semester?"

"Later writers, obviously," Claudia said with a smile. "A lot will be on the novelists and poets, from Dickens and Keats to Shelley and all the others."

"You know. *demain est Toussainte*, or Halloween as you call it. Tonight I am doing our celebration with my sister, and tomorrow mass with the parents at Notre Dame des Champs. They live near Montparnasse, and so I have to leave."

"And what will you do *ce soir*?"

"With my sister, we do a combination of Halloween and commemoration of the dead, as intended by the *Fete de Toussainte*. That is we will start with another drink or two and something light to eat, near the Bastille. And then a midnight mass or part of one. Would you like to come?"

"I don't think so. Valerie and I are planning dinner for a change near the Champs Elysèes. But, it's not even six. We have plenty of time for a drink or two before the evening activities."

"Yes, you're right. I'm not meeting Annette until nine, and anyway I have another restaurant to show you, where we can have a drink. It's toward La Bastille, d'accord?"

"Wonderful, I always love to see new bars and restaurants. What's it called?"

"It's the Brasserie Bofinger, which you get to on Rue Bastille just before the square. It's one of the oldest restaurants of Paris, with a nice, if small bar."

"Wonderful. I discovered that restaurant a couple of weeks ago, and will be very happy to go back."

We walked down the Rue St. Antoine, and reached the restaurant just before reaching the Place de la Bastille. We did a drink at the bar, and I asked Claudia more about her travels. "Tell me about your five years in Saigon"

"I loved Saigon, and especially the school where I taught and the students there. In addition I went to a few other places in Vietnam. They included some nice summer visits to Dalat, in the mountains north of Saigon, and also Nha Trang and Quang Ngai on the coast and the Imperial City of Hue. They were all quite beautiful, as was Hong Kong where I did a week."

"You must be kidding. I spent a few months in Hong Kong doing research on China. Where did you stay?"

"A small hotel in Kowloon. And you?"

"I rented a flat on the other side. It was so marvelous, looking at the mountains of China and all the boats in the harbor. I think it's one of the most beautiful cities. You know, Chinese for landscape is 'mountain and sea,' and Hong Kong has that in spades."

"I agree. But, there are many other cities in that category also. Rio, Palermo, Athens, Paris and Rome. Even though the latter two don't have mountains and sea, but hills and rivers."

"Indeed, and have you ever been to Venice?"

"No. Should I?"

"For sure, it is up there with the most beautiful cities. And more or less unique, in that it's almost the same as it was five hundred years and more ago. You know, it was built in and over the water, stone by stone, to get away from the barbarians way back there. And after the fall of Rome and Ravenna, it was the first metropolis of Europe until the take off of Paris and later London. Now, the only sounds you hear are the boats and occasional construction. Venice is still a great city, even though smaller than it was a few centuries ago, and with tourism its only big industry."

"I see you know it well. How is that?"

"Along with studying Vietnam in Paris, I researched my course on Marco Polo in Venice. That was mostly in the 1980s, and I guess I was there several months in all."

"What were your favorite places there? I should make notes for when I can go."

"The usual ones are all in the guide books. I swear by the Michelin green guide. As you know it gives the most interesting places three stars, which they define as 'not to be missed.' The first things that strike you in the *Serenissima*, as it was called for centuries, are The Grand Canal and the basilica St. Marco. You get to the latter on a Vaporetto or marine bus, which is one of the best sytems of transportation on earth, and probably the most scenic. In the Piazza St. Marco there are three, three star places, the square itself, the Basilica and the Palazzo Ducale. In addition, there is the Campanile or tower at an angle facing the Basilica St. Marco. Moreover there is an excellent museum in the Piazza. It has a unique fifteenth century statue of Marco Polo, of which I showed pictures in my class, The World of Marco Polo. Then across the canal is another great church, Santa Maria delle Salutè. That's one of my rare disagreements with the Michelin. They give it only one star. It was built to commemorate the ending of a plague in the mid 1600s and has a magnificent dome. When I was there I lived on the top floor of a three story, sixteenth century building just behind that church. From my window I could see the laundry hanging in several courtyards in the direction of its dome."

"Well, you certainly make me want to visit *Venise* as we call it. The Italian name is *Venezia, n'est-ce pas?*"

"You are right. And I really would love to go there with you some time. Yet, now I see it is already past eight, and suppose we should be on our way."

"D'accord. Have a great weekend and see you Tuesday."

I decided I wanted to do another drink while I contemplated my temptation with Claudia. I took the metro at the Bastille for the two stops to the Hotel de Ville and the short walk to my favorite terrace bar, the Cafè Louis Philppe, looking out at the rear of Notre Dame from across the bridge of its name. My problem was a real *casse tete* problem to use the expression for 'head breaker.' I had only seen Claudia about four times and already felt in love with her. Not only for another beautiful lady, but for her spirit and experiences in Vietnam. There were so many things to like. But Valerie was equally wonderful and I had known her somewhat longer. I was thinking what to do? Again, unsurprisingly, I decided to go along with both ladies for the foreseeable future. I paid up and took the metro home.

Valerie came in just after me, and we embraced. She asked, "What is that smell. You've been out with some woman haven't you?"

"You're right. I had a drink with my favorite colleague, Claudia Chevalier. But, I don't see how you can smell anything, unless it's from my kissing her on the cheek."

"Maybe. I have a sensitive nose and you'd better be careful. What do you like about her?"

"Well, she does English lit and I like to hear more about that. Also, she taught French in Saigon for five years and we have a lot to talk about to do with that."

"Oh yes, now I remember, you are a Vietnam nut."

"How can you not be. It's about the only foreign policy problem one heard about growing up and in school. Because of that, I decided to make up a course on it. I forget if I told you, but it's called 'The Vietnamese Revolution and Wars.' I have taught it two times at Baruch and it gets a lot of student interest. So, naturally I want to talk to someone sympa who has lived there, even if well after the end of the war."

"All right. But, I'm not sure I believe you did nothing but kiss her on the cheeks. I'll have to see if I notice any changes in your behaviour towards me."

"That's a challenge! And I love it. You know I was always a frustrated actor as I suppose most teachers are. Great actors are certainly great teachers. I wish I had a film of Laurence Olivier narrating some stories in U.S. history. I remember being so affected by his playing Henry Vth in that film twenty years ago, that I almost switched from studying Chinese history to English history."

"In that case we wouldn't have met, since you wouldn't have gotten the job you have here. By the way, I've heard that the French only talk of England and its history from their own perspective, and with their own teachers."

As Valerie spoke, I found myself wondering if I was becoming more and more bothered by her frequent put downs of France while promoting England. I never liked promotions of favorite subjects, whether of yourself or your friends, city or country. No doubt, I do the same about France as my favorite country, and I have to ask myself if I am letting the memories of my times with Claudia prejudice me against Valerie.

Just then, as if she was reading my mind, Valerie asked, "Who is teaching English history at the Institute.?"

"I don't know. I will find out, maybe from Claudia."

"Why do I have to keep hearing that name? Do you want me to speak only of Keith and Mark? Or better, of the man I met today talking about American literature. He is so knowledgeable about it, even if not an American."

"Valerie, please don't be jealous. That is one of the things I like best about you. Until now, you have never objected to my speaking of past girl friends or about my marriage to Henrietta. Is it because Claudia is a new friend? But, you need not be jealous. I promise there is nothing between us, and will not be. And tell me more about this non-American who knows its literature so well."

"So, you want to hear about an acquaintance of mine to even the tables? All right. In fact, he is a good looking Français, who studied American literature at Harvard a decade ago. His English is so good that some Americans in the store asked him how he could speak such good French when he spoke with a colleague at Shakespeare & Co. They thought he was an American."

"Do you plan to keep up with this prodigy?"

"I never thought about it. Should I? To keep up with you?"

"You already are keeping up with me, with Keith, Mark and who knows who else. By the way, I am trying to work on my problem of being too jealous. So, go ahead. What's his name?"

"It's Gregoire. Do you like that, as a name?"

"Not bad. I have a cousin named Gregory, but as always in Amercia everyone shortens things and calls him Greg. What does Gregoire do besides try to seduce attractive ladies?"

"He's a teacher, of course. I'm not sure where. But, he says he will come in often to check up on what his students can buy and so on."

"And what's the latest with Keith and Mark?"

"Mark called me at work to say he was on his way back to England, but that he would be back before long."

"And Keith too, I suppose."

"No. At least, he told me he might not be back until mid December."

"All right. But, in any case, let's not screw up our Christmas trip with all these flirts. Now, it's after midnight and to bed. D'accord?"

We did, with the usual love making.

But, then I had a remarkable and unsettling nightmare. It was after I had gotten up to pee, and rather late in the night when I dreamed I had come home without the small bag, or *sac*, I almost always carry around my neck. I realized I had led left it in the department store I had just been in, and got up to rush back to that store. I retraced all the places I had gone and finally found it with two sales ladies in the third place I'd been to, at Printemps, the store's name. It was on the ground floor where I had bought a pair of shoes. However, one of the sales girls told me she had taken it to lost and found, saying she had to report such things. She never came back from the lost and found, and I asked the other girl where she had gone and she said to the administration behind a door she pointed to. I went there and went in but was unable to find the girl or my bag. At which point, I woke up from this dream and realized it was a nightmare. But, I also wondered if the dream wasn't trying to tell me something. Namely that I was losing my way, and had better watch out, or would lose Valerie.

In part because of that, I decided to keep my distance from Claudia, and the next days passed with no new adventures. Best made plans and all that, and of course, I slipped again ten days later. That was on November 9. After my eighth class, Claudia knocked on the door of my cubicle and asked if we could talk.

"I have a problem I want to ask you about. One of my students related that on a trip to the U.S. last summer, she had met a guy who said he had been accused of raping a minor in the state of Virginia. He was to go to trial about now, but said he thought the case would be thrown out as he believed the girl was already sixteen. My question is, what is the age considered adult in America?" "It depends on the state. For sex, it's usually sixteen, but drinking doesn't start until twenty one. My acquaintance with that was having to lie about my age, precisely in Virginia, at Virginia Beach where we went for summer vacations. We had to falsify driving licences and so on. Did your student know if charges were pressed against the alleged rapist?"

"She says he says no, but would have to see what happened at the trial. He says he thinks it was the parents who wanted their daughter to take action. In a way, she says, she hopes that next summer if she goes back as planned, she can see him again, and if he wants, meet her parents. She is obviously still taken with that Virginia boy."

"That reminds me of a scene I saw the other night here in Paris. There was a really beautiful young girl who I would only have noticed in passing, except that she was with one of the ugliest and most uncouth guys I have ever seen. He was Asian, maybe Filipino, and I couldn't imagine why the girl was with him. Until I heard what she said."

"They came into the bar and the guy asked the bartender in English to give him a box of cigars off to the side of the liquor bottles. The bartender said it was not for sale. But, the guy kept demanding it in a loud voice. The bartender shook his head and said something in French which neither of those two idiots spoke. The guy reached over and grabbed the bartender by his collar, and the girl started shouting, 'You'd better do what he says. Do you know who he is? He's one of the richest men in the world and he always gets what he wants.' At which point a bunch of French rushed up to rescue the bartender.

But the Asian, fat as he was, knew some karate, and let fly a couple of kicks. The French pulled back in surprise and the two idiots ran out. The girl also seemed about sixteen and, of course, was with the boorish guy for his money."

"That's quite a story," Claudia said, "though I don't see what it has to do with the rape problem."

"Nothing. Just that it was a beautiful girl getting into a scrape. Anyhow, how about a drink or two? I'd like to go back to that Bastille restaurant, Boffinger or some place near there. What do you think?"

"All right, but there's another place I want to see first. As it's only 5:15, we should wait and read for an hour or so. Besides, I need to prepare some stuff for my next class. How about seven?"

I agreed, and when Claudia came for me, she said the café she wanted to go to was on the way to the Beaubourg complex in the opposite direction from the Bastille. On the way, I asked her if there was anything new about her bike trip next summer. She replied, "Certainly not. That's still over six months off. And what about your trip to Belgium with *ton petite amie*? Are you still friendly with her?"

"Very much so, though I must add, she has started to get jealous of you. Moreover, I'm beginning to get irritated with her over praising Britain and criticizing France. But, yes, we are leaving for Bruxelles, most likely on December 20. Then we will do Ghent and Bruges for several days and return here for the *nouvelle an*."

"How could she be jealous of me? As you know, we haven't even touched."

"You know women. Last week when I came in, she smelled your perfume, or said she did. Asked who I was seeing, I told her that I had seen you, but only done some bisous as you call those pecks on the cheek."

"Oh bother. That's all I need. A jealous lady. If that keeps up, I may have to withdraw my invitation for the bike trip.

Meanwhile, here's the bar I wanted to show you. As you can see, it's on the Rue du Roi de Sicile at the corner of the Rue Bourg-Tibourg. I came here often when I worked down the street on the Rue Pavèe at the Bibliotheque Historique de la Ville de Paris. Which by the way is very much worth seeing. It's in one of the handsomest buildings anywhere."

"Claudia, you really do tempt me too much; not only with your brains and beauty, but your experiences and memories of beautiful places. Not only did you spend five years in Saigon, but you have so many places in Paris to talk about. What am I going to do with you?"

"We'll have to see about that. Meanwhile, I think I'll do a kir. And you?"

We ordered two, and over the drinks observed the stylish crowd. I asked Claudia how much she biked in Paris, as against her trips elsewhere by bike.

"I bike everywhere. I live nearby on the Rue du Temple, so I can walk to the Institute. But, I often bike there in order to have it for trips later across the river or wherever. Today, I didn't because I thought we might be walking. But, I don't know how people get around the city without a bike."

She said that with a radiant smile, again making me both thank my luck and wonder what I was getting into. Our drinks finished, we set off for the Bastille. Claudia said she wanted to show me another restaurant, which turned out to please me a lot. We found it after a walk along the infamous Rue de la Roquette on the other side of the Bastille, until it turned right on the Rue des Taillandiers.

The restaurant, le Piton des Iles, was a beauty. It had an apartment-like layout, with four rooms arranged along a hall way. The room where we got a table was the biggest, with two French windows looking out on to the street. I began the conversation. "I want to hear more about biking in Paris. As said, I do it all the time in New York, but wonder how you navigate the narrow streets here."

Claudia replied, "I'm sure you'd get used to it. You just have to stop on the most narrow streets and wait for threatening cars to come by. You have to be careful, and on two lane streets I always stay on the driver's side, so they can judge where you are more easily. But, the other day this British car almost got me, not far from here. It was on the Rue St. Bernard, where I was going to another restaurant to meet some friends. This bastard, who was on the other side of the car, British style, turned on to that street, sharply off the Rue Charonne and almost hit me. Rue St. Bernard is very small and he misjudged the much smaller street."

"Yes. You're right. You have to not only be very careful, but have good luck as you did then. And let me tell you about the time I got hit. I was biking across East 52nd. Street in Manhattan, and had barely turned onto Lexington Avenue when this idiot hit me. But, he had braked enough so that he barely glanced me at about five miles an hour. He stopped and asked if I was all right, saying he had to brush against me in order to avoid the car passing him on his right. Anyway, I am a fatalist about such things. If it's my time, then I have to accept it. As for the summer trip, I really hope we can do that. I love biking, I love you and what could be better than taking a trip like that with the two women I love."

"How do you know I won't be jealous of Valerie? Of course, she being English, I can curse her in French without her knowing it."

"Don't be so sure. Her mother is French, and she might understand, though she grew up in London speaking mostly English. But, that would ruin the whole trip. Anyway, we have to see if the trip is going to happen, *n'est-ce pas?*"

Claudia nodded, and I proposed we be on our way. I embraced her, and she said she would walk home. I decided to take the metro from the Bastille to the Etoile and then to the Monceau stop and our apartment.

Unsurprisingly, Valerie greeted me by saying, "I see you've been with Claudia again. That is, I can smell her perfume. How was it this time?"

"Not bad," I replied, but wondered why she had to notice every time I saw another woman. Even though I do the same if she looks at another man, I couldn't help thinking again how much simpler it is when you are on your own. Should I break with Valerie, I asked myself. I questionned her, "Why do you keep asking me about other friends I might be seeing? That is beginning to annoy me. And I told you I would be home late tonight."

"Well, your flirting with so many women has begun to annoy me," she said as she went into the other room, slamming the door behind her. As it was about ten o'clock, I decided to go out again and have a drink or two. I went to a bar I discovered on the Rue de la Bienfaisance, wondering if its ambiance could help me. It was a typical late night bar scene. I took the only remaining free stool, and looked around. There were a bunch of men to my left and two rather handsome couples to the right. There were about five tables of four eating in the bar room, and I could hear the sounds of pool balls striking, as well as loud comments of the players and some spectators in the back room.

After ordering my drink, I got up to go look at the pool room. Just as I approached, one of the dozen spectators pulled a gun from his pocket, and demanded the stack of euros on the table. They were about four inches high, with a twenty on top. The five players immediately grouped together and one of them shouted "You must be joking. There's almost nothing there! Do you want to go to jail for a hundred euro?" Signaling for everyone to join him, he approached the would-be robber. But the latter was too quick and snatched the notes, even as he kept the gun pointed at the others. But, as he turned and ran, the others ran after him with shouts of 'stop him.' One of the men at the end of the bar jumped up and was immediately shot, as the thief cleared the door and started running down the Rue de la Bienfaisance, turning right on the Boulevard Malesherbes. Two men from the bar chased him but came back several minutes later to say he was too fast for them and had escaped into the Metro St. Augustin. Others in the bar tended to the wounded man and called an ambulance. It arrived maybe three minutes later and took him away. The wound was in the chest, and I learned later the poor man had died in the hospital Lariboisiere, just to the northeast in the Tenth Arrondissement.

After this excitement, I went back to the bar and my Marie Brizzard anisette. Its taste was very good, and I mused on the idea that a man getting shot put my stupid quandry into perspective. What is a confusion of thought about two loves compared to such suffering. Still, I was troubled by the last scene with Valerie. Since I was very attracted to Claudia I had to think maybe Valerie was right to be jealous of her. And what were my thoughts about Valerie's handsome new French friend? I could more or less ignore her friendship with Keith and Mark, since they did not seem that seductive. But, if she took up with a slick Français, what would I do? I was not sure at all, and took some more sips of my drink.

Just then the police arrived to investigate the scene of the shooting. Immediately after them another guy came into the bar saying he had witnessed the chase on the Boulevard Malesherbes, and thought he recognized the person being chased. The policeman closest to him asked who he thought it was. The newcomer said, "It's Mario Grimal. He used to be in my school, and I heard he had turned bad."

"Do you know where he lives?" asked the policeman.

The guy replied, "I don't know, but can ask some friends." At which point the policeman took out a pad and took down the coordinates of the newcomer, writing in big letters at the top, 'MARIO GRIMAL.' He and his two colleagues rushed out the door into their car double parked at the curb with its blinking lights.

The newcomer, a rather handsome man whose looks I liked, took the seat to my left, vacated by the guys who had done the chase. I asked the new guy his name. He said it was Francois, and we proceeded to talk several minutes about the shooting incident. Then, I asked him if he had a girl friend. When he said he did, and that he had married her, I asked him if he had problems of jealousy with her.

"With her or me?" he asked.

"Either one," I said. "Because at the moment I am having both problems. My love just slammed the door on me when I told her I liked a colleague I had just met. So I have come out to cool off. Only to see this shooting!"

"Just now, we have no problems. But, I have had them. So tell me yours."

"First of all, I am the jealous type. When I first met the mentioned colleague lady friend, I was a bit jealous of Valerie to do with various guys she was seeing. I had mostly gotten over that, when I met another girl I also really like. That is where I work, teaching history at the Institut d'Anglais. I resisted speaking of her to my older *amour*, Valerie, as she's called. But, then, one evening about a week ago, Valerie said she smelled perfume and asked me who else I was seeing. I confessed that I had a new friend at work, called Claudia, but had only kissed her on the cheek, which was true. She more or less accepted that, but is now continually asking me about Claudia, so much so that I am getting quite annoyed. Moreover, she has made me jealous again by talking about a new friend of hers. Worse, he is supposedly a handsome Frenchman, named Gregoire, who speaks perfect English and frequently comes into where Valerie works. That is at Shakespeare & Co. She says he does that because he is teaching English at Nanterre. So, I feel in a quandary to do about all that, though now I am beginning to feel better thanks to this drink."

Francois said, "My problems were something like that also. That is, my wife and I both had other friends. But, after the usual arguments of first one, then the other not believing the latest story about what one was doing with those friends, we decided we loved each other too much to risk that by such stupidities."

"I was thinking the same way until this recent jealousy on Valerie's part. She says she has an especially sensitive nose, so that now I wonder if I can even give *bisous* to old friends, if they happen to be women wearing perfume. But, *basta*! Let me change the subject and ask what you do?"

"I'm a pilot, with Air France."

He paused to see the effect the statement of such an impressive job might have on me. Sure enough, I smiled broadly, saying "How wonderful! All the more so, as I am a pilot myself, though with nothing like your credentials. Tell me about flying with Air France. Which routes do you fly and so on."

"I'm on the European routes. My last flight was to Moscow and back. That was yesterday."

"Wow. How exciting! Tell me the times and the rest so I can try to imagine it."

"It was very routine. We left at eleven and came back at 19:00 h. The flying time is three hours for the almost twenty five hundred kilometers to get there, and about three and half hours for the return against the wind. So, that gave us four and half hours in Moscow. Some rest as well as refueling and the like. What is your flying experience?"

"Oh, me, I started 'low and slow' back in the late 1970s. But, I liked it so much I kept it up, and started teaching about aviation history in the 90's. Maybe I will ask you to come and talk to my class, now that I am teaching in Paris, though about the Americas rather than about flying."

"I don't think my English is good enough for that. But, I do like to talk about flying. For example, on this last flight, the take-off from Moscow was fantastic. The Air Bus 340-300 climbed as usual, to 35,000 feet in under twenty minutes, and the clouds were so beautiful. That was because they were 'broken,' that is with enough of them so that you are constantly going through them. But at the same time it was not a solid overcast and you could also see the beautiful colors of sunset and the cirrus clouds above."

"I can see you love your job! And you have a lot of time off and can go anywhere in the world for almost nothing. What's not to like?"

"It does have its advantages, especially as I like to travel. And there are girl friends in many different places." He said the last phrase with a wink, which I appreciated.

"What does it take to get into such a job? For my next life that is. And how many hours do you have now?"

"I just passed 4000, which is about average for my five years with Air France. And you."

"Almost a thousand, and none in jets since I didn't have the money to upgrade to them."

"Well, that's not bad. You can still claim to be a pilot, for your class at least. And tell me how you speak such good French?"

"You know, the usual school classes. But, I much improved it when I was here for several years in the early eighties researching a book on Vietnam. Could you give me your co-ordinates, and can I call you some time?"

He gave me his telephone and e-mail address, and I saw that his family name was Dutroux. Then he said he had to be on his way. We shook hands and he went off, saying "Let's do keep in touch." I looked at my watch and saw that it was past eleven. So, I settled my bill and went back to the apartment. Fortunately, I thought, Valerie was asleep and I tried not to awaken her, as I sat and read a few pages before stretching out beside her for the night's sleep.

The next day, she went off to work as usual and with no sign of irritation at the misunderstanding of the previous night. At first I worked on my American history course, and in the afternoon, resumed thinking about the idea of a book on the Clos de Vougeot and wine. It had been over a month since I had given that any thought, and after several hours agonizing over my notes from the trip back in September, I decided to go back to the Musèe du Vin. There I looked up some more on Burgundy wines, but was just getting into it when the museum announced its closing. It was already six o'clock. On the way back, I tried to plan what might be possible, such as relating a love story that also told some history of wine. But, more immediately I thought of Claudia and Valerie and my confusion about the two loves of the moment.

When I got home, I was delighted to find Valerie there, and decided I would try to put Claudia out of my mind, and concentrate on preparing for our Christmas trip to Belgium.

"How was your day, my love?"

"Not bad, and yours?"

"Uneventful, though I did some more thinking and research for my wine project. But, yesterday evening a lot happened after our quarrel. I didn't wake you or bother you with it this morning when you went off. Shall I tell you about it now?"

"Please do."

"I discovered this bar new to me, called La Bienfaisance. Do you know it?

"No."

Well it's on the street of that name just to the east towards the Gare St. Lazare. While I was waiting for my drink I went back to the pool room and withnessed a guy trying to steal the money on the table, followed by another guy getting shot when he tried to stop the robber. He was taken away in an ambulance, and after that I met another and really interesting man. His name is Francois and he flies for Air France. So, we had an interesting discussion about flying and other things. I want you to meet him at some point. But, also I have been thinking more about us. I want to get back on best terms with you, and plan our trip to Belgium. D'accord?"

"Sounds like a good idea. But, first tell me more about the shooting."

"It was like out of a grade B movie. While waiting for my drink, I had gone back to look at the pool room. There a kibitzer pulled out a gun and demanded the money on the table. The pool players shouted at him, but he grabbed the notes, said to be about a hundred euro, and ran out to the bar. There a guy rushed to stop him and got shot. An ambulance was called and took him to a nearby hospital. Later I learned he died there of his wounds.

I decided to change the subject, and said, "As for the trip, shall we do it all by train, or just to Brussels and rent a car for Bruges and Ghent?"

"Why not both. I like to watch new scenery from the windows of both trains and autos. Can you reserve a car for December 22? That would give us two nights in Bruxelles, and over a week to see Bruges and Ghent."

"But, maybe we want more time in Brussels. In fact, maybe Christmas there, and then we can do the other places. So I will reserve the car for December 26, and to the 30th or so. That is, if we want to be back in Paris for the new year. In any case I start teaching Monday, January 6."

I went over to put my arms around Valerie, and asked her, "Where shall we do dinner tonight?"

"How about the Chinese just down the street?"

We did that with some rice wine, which is sweeter than saki, and almost like sherry. As we ate, we discussed what we knew about Belgium, which was not much. But, Valerie knew that Jan Van Eyck, an important early fifteenth century Flemish artist was from Bruges, as well as certain other things about the famous tapestries made nearby. After a good and different sort of meal, we returned home by midnight.

There was still more than a month to go before Christmas, and I spent much of the next days pondering how to avoid messing things up with Valerie. I decided my best way was to tell Claudia honestly that I didn't want to screw up with Valerie, and therefore would only say hello when I saw her while teaching, but not go anymore to bars and restaurants with her. At least until after our Christmas trip.

The next Tuesday, November 14, I ran into Claudia after class. I asked her if we could talk in one of our offices. She said that would have to be after some consultations with her students. About an hour later, she knocked on my door, and I asked her to come in.

"You know, I am geting more and more anxious about our friendship. That is, I want to remain friends, but think that as my trip to Belgium with Valerie approaches, we should keep our distance more. What do you think?"

"Interesting that you should say that just now. Because I have just met a man I really like. His name is Guy, and he is an artist and philosophy teacher, who lives on the Rue des Artistes, in the fourteenth out near the Porte d'Orleans. Can you believe an artist lives on a street of that name? But, in fact he is more of a teacher and only an occasional artist, with water colors, I think."

"In that case, we have no problem. How, might that change our proposed bike trip next summer?"

"I've no idea. *On verra*. Who knows how long this romance will last."

"All right, as you said, we will see. And so now, I'll be on my way, and see you around, with or without social meetings." We embraced and she went back into her cubicle, while I went down the stairs into the courtyard. Skipping the usual after class drink, I walked to the Centre Beaubourg library. It is the largest in central Paris now, with the transfer of the

Bibliotheque Nationale de France from its beautiful site on Rue Richelieu to the new monstrous BNF on the other side of the river.

Fortunately there was no line, as there often is, to get into the library. Passing the usual security I was able to find numerous books on wine. After several hours reading there, I returned to our apartment and found Valerie eager to tell me some more about our trip.

"Can you guess what I want to see most in Belgium?"

"Let's see. The porcelain, or some paintings?"

"No! Where they did those incredible tapestries, such as for the Dame à la Licorne that we saw in the Museum of the Middle Ages. I understand that was done mostly in Brussels, or nearby. I have read that there were 1500 tapestry weavers in Brussels by 1500."

"Very good. I made our reservation for the car there for December 26.

It's supposed to be a Renault V, the cheapest good car I could rent. It will only cost us about 200 euros for the five days to the 30th. I am really looking forward to that, and it is only a little over a month off."

"Me too! But, I sometimes wonder if you are going to be as nice as you were on the Burgundy trip."

"Why wouldn't I be?"

"It's just that our arguments, about new friendships, and to a lesser extent about politics, have made me more cautious about you."

"Oh, don't be silly. I have decided to put those disputes, or whatever they are, behind me and concentrate on being as nice as I can. And loving you even more."

So saying, I went to put my arms around Valerie who was standing on the other side of the room. She accepted my embrace and we ended up making love and going out to dinner.

CHAPTER FIVE

HOLIDAYS AND OUR FIRST TRIP

The next day, I called Francois to ask when we could meet again. Fortunately, he remembered me and proposed that I come to the Fifteenth Arrondissement where he lived, the following Friday evening, November 24. He said he was flying to Stockholm on Thursday, and to Prague early the following week. The date came rapidly and I took my favorite route to his home at 23 Rue Dantzig. After reaching the Etoile stop, I did the line to Nation which goes above ground with its incredible view of the Eiffel Tower until the Dupleix stop where I got out for the walk to his apartment. Francois greeted me and after a bit said he was hungry and wanted to go to a restaurant. He proposed the Clos Morillons on the street of that name, which was nearby. We dined in style and relatively inexpensively. After the usual small talk, I asked him to tell me about his latest trips.

"The Stockholm trip was quite interesting in fact. I just got back several hours ago, as there were complications due to a big storm. We were told to divert to Oslo which the storm had already passed. But, at Oslo there was still about a foot of snow on the runway, and we requested clearance to Amsterdam. We spent the night there and this morning went on to Stockholm without problem. I met a really classy gal there in addition.

I was not sure I was going to make it back for my rendez-vous with you, but I got home about an hour ago."

"Tell me about it, and also about what you expect on the next trip, which I think you told me would be to Prague."

"Well for Prague on Tuesday there should be no problems, although given the weather this time of year, you never know. It takes only a little over an hour to get there, and after the usual lay over for refueling and whatever, we should get back by evening. As for the gal in Stockholm, she seems perfect. She's called Erica and is the right size, with a beautiful face and smile and nice curves. We only had tea, since one can't drink on layovers. But, we exchanged addresses and I look forward to the next time."

"And when do you expect to do that, and will you have new problems with your wife?"

"In about two weeks, and I hope I can avoid new jealousies. Next week, I fly to Rome and Venice."

"I must say, you seem to have quite a life. But, now let me tell you the latest about me getting over my jealousy problem and planning for a Christmas trip."

"By all means do, as now I may be getting into the same situation of having two *amours*?"

"It's not easy, as you are discovering. But I have decided for now to concentrate on keeping my older love, Valerie, who I met last August. All the more so, as we are planning this first trip to Belgium and a spring trip to Rome. Too bad we don't have free air fare like you. But, in fact I prefer land travel for short trips like those where you can see the landscape up close. Unless you're driving, and run off the road because of that."

"You're right. But, we pilots do a certain amount of that too, driving that is, hopefully without running off the road. I, for example, frequently drive to see my parents in Normandy. They live in St. Malo, which is about 400 kilometers away. Since I share a small plane with my wife, we fly to Savoy as well, to see her parents, who live there."

"Where else do you fly with your wife?"

"When we can which depends on our vacations, we usually fly south to the Midi or beyond, a nice way to avoid the traffic jams. Last September, we went first to Lyon. Then Milano and Venice, before flying back to France. As you know, it is beautiful to fly over the Alps as well as see all the other stuff from above. Then, you can drive by later and get both perspectives."

"I certainly agree and have done that several times. For me, that means observing from an airliner window. I always sit in the rear, where I can see as much as possible of the plane and the ground below, or the clouds as the case may be. I've flown across the Alps about four times now, several of them in clear weather, where I could see the beautiful mountains. Then, two years ago I did a great trip by car, from Rome to Paris, via a bunch of interesting towns. Shall I tell you about that trip, which was one of my best ever?"

"Please do. I not only love to travel, but to hear travel stories as well."

"Well, driving north from Rome, I first came to Orvieto where I spent the night and had a few glasses of their famous white wine. The next day, I turned east to see a colleague and friend, named Michael, in the mountain town of Montecastello. To get there I had lunch in another lovely small town half way to it, called Todi. Michael is an artist who spends part of each summer at the teach-in for artists held at the castle in Montecastello, bought by an American foundation, with ties to his college, Haverford. The day after that, Michael and I went to the famous art center, Spoleto, about an hour to the southeast for lunch.

Two days later, I continued north, via the well known medieval towns of Perugia and Gubbio to Urbino, all of them terrific places. Not only that, but off to the side of the road to Perrugia I saw what must be the place name for the melon, Cantaloupe. It was a village named Cantalupo. After a few days in Urbino, I went west to Sienna, via Arezzo. From there I should have gone to the home town of the great painter, Pierro della Francesca, in San Sepulcro, considered another tourist must see. Arezzo is the only place to access San Sepulcro and I now greatly regret I did not go there. But the day was getting late, and I felt too exhausted. So, I continued on to Sienna and found a hotel there. But, the next day, I could not find my car which I had left on some narrow street. I walked for hours looking for it, and got very dizzy following so many narrow and winding streets. Finally, I had to get the help of a *carabinieri* who spoke some English, to help me find it. Then I went north to Florence, and spent almost a week there, seeing its great museums and art works. After that it was east to Venice. On the way, I went via Ravenna to its south. I spent a night there in order to see some extraordinary churches and other sights.

In Venice, I spent another week, seeing some friends and the fabulous architecture of that city. Then I headed west again to Verona, where I saw an opera, and more great sites. Following a couple of nights there, it was north and west, via Bellagio to Montreux, Switzerland, my favorite lake and mountain resort. I had studied French there for several months during my first sabbatical year a decade ago. From Montreux I went to Strasbourg, where I have a cousin who married an Englishman who works for the Council of Europe. Like the American friends in Venice, they now love living in Europe, which I can easily understand. From Strasbourg, I drove to Paris via some smaller but also remarkable places. They were Toul, Troyes and lastly the marvelous chateau at Vaux le Vicomte, just outside of Paris. It was quite a trip, and I can't recommend those places too highly."

"Francois said, "It's a good thing we both like to travel. And tell me where you plan to go in Belgium, and later in Italy."

"I think just doing trips with Valerie, whom I love so much, will help a lot with my jealousy problems. We plan to take the train to Brussels and spend Christmas there. Then we will rent a car, and go to Bruges and Ghent. But, tell me more about your wife, and what you think is going to happen now that you are attracted to a *Suedoise*?"

"I just have to see. Maybe, the next time I see the Swedish lady she will tell me she already loves someone else, or I will have second thoughts about her. As you can imagine, that has happened quite a few times already. Now I have to go home and get some sleep before my next trip which is to Warsaw."

"Enjoy it, and I really liked seeing you again. *A la prochaine.*"

It was about eleven, and I made my way home. Valerie greeted me like old times, and I was very glad to see that. The next month passed uneventfully. The classes went normally, with the usual rush to finish the semester's material. I only exchanged pleasantries with Claudia, and was eager to leave for Belgium with Valerie.

The day for that arrived and we took the early afternoon express train, arriving in Brussels at five on Friday, December 22. We found a nice, cheap hotel just off the Grand Place, on Rue du Marchè aux Fromages. After unpacking, we explored the square and saw an affiche for the Sunday *marchè aux oiseaux*, or bird market. I wondered if that meant only to buy them, or also to eat some. We thought we would go to it in any case, as we had long admired the feathered species and wanted to see how many different ones they had.

The imposing Gothic Hotel de Ville, begun in the thirteenth century, was already closed when we got there. So we admired its imposing 300 foot high tower and other later pre-baroque and Hispano-Flamand buildings built after the Spanish took control of Belgium in the sixteenth century. There was also the statue of Charles of Lorraine, recalling the earlier Burgundian and Hapsbourg presences in Belgium. From there, we walked to the handsome, medieval Cathedrale St. Michel. It was still open, and we admired its interior and exterior created from the thirteenth to the seventeenth centuries. After that, we went in the direction of the hotel and found a nice bar-restaurant on Rue St. Jean. Drinks and dinner were marvelous and we made it back to the hotel before midnight for another great night of love-making and sleep.

The next day, we went to the best rated Musèe d'Art Ancienne with its splendid collection of works from Van der Weyden to Bruegel and Rubens. Then we saw a fourteenth century church, Notre Dame du Sablon, built after a statue of the Virgin was discovered there. The Square du Petit-Sablon, with many remarkable statues, was just across the street from the Church of the same name. Following lunch, we did the Parc de Bruxelles and the Palais de la Nation, where the Belgian parliament and Senate meet.

We decided on a quiet last evening in Brussels. After drinks and dinner, we returned to the hotel early to plan the coming days. We took out the map we had bought for the trip, and saw that the best way to Ghent and Bruges was via Route E 5 to Ostende on the coast. It is only fifty kilometers to Ghent and another forty or so to Bruges. Christmas was on a Monday that year, or only two days off, and we decided to spend it in Ghent, rather than Brussels as we had previously thought.

The next day, Sunday, the 24th, we had to get the car first. That meant going back to the same train station at which we had arrived, the Gare du Midi, where we arrived about eleven. The Renault 5 was ready for us and we set out, arriving in Ghent in time for a late lunch. Leaving our bags at the Hotel check-in, we found a nice restaurant in the Centre Ville, where we could eat our favorite Belgian specialties, including that wonderful bouillabaise, called Waterzooi de Poulet. We decided we would only stay the one night and Christmas morning in Ghent, to leave time for Bruges and other places. Even though the most famous Hapsburg emperor, Charles Quint (V) was born in Ghent, our guide book showed relatively little of interest there. After lunch we toured the Citadel Park and the Musèe des Beaux-Arts off the side of the park. In the museum, we admired especially the works of Hieronymus Bosch, one of my favorite painters. That night we did a walk through the old city where lovely illuminations highlighted the many beautiful buildings, and especially the Hotel de Ville and Cathedral.

After dinner, we returned to the hotel and got into a lively discussion with an English couple about the pleasures of tourism in Europe. The couple had taken their car by ferry to Sweden, from whence they drove to Norway, Denmark, and Holland, before arriving in Ghent. We told them about what we had liked best in Brussels, their next stop. After several cognacs, we took our leave thinking we would leave for Bruges just after the Christmas noon mass in the Cathedral.

We arrived in Bruges towards three, and stopped in the Hotel Notre Dame close to the Grand Place, called *Markt* in Flemish. That name reminded me of the strangeness of Flemish, whose sounds seemed so un-euphonious after the French we had been hearing. We checked in and after undoing our things, set out for drinks and dinner. They were not hard to find, given the many bars and restaurants near the hotel. Towards seven, we started on cocktails and found a splendid restaurant not far from our last bar. I enjoyed my rabbit, done with haricot verts and carots, and Valerie said her filet of sole was the best she had ever had. After dinner, we went to look at the thirteenth century beffroi, an imposing bell tower with a carillon of 47 chimes, which gave a short ten o'clock concert we loved. We decided to save the two top rated museums for the next day, and spent the rest of the late evening walking through handsome little streets back to our hotel. We decided to turn in by midnight and as usual thoroughly enjoyed our double bed.

The next day, our first stop was at the Groeninge Museum, featuring the great Jan Van Eyck, who in the early 1400s was the first painter to use oils in his paintings. That technique transformed the history of art after it was learned by the great Italian Renaissance masters by the end of the century. After several hours there, we lunched and went to the Memling Museum, separated from the Groeninge by the thirteenth century church of Notre Dame. We were most intrigued by the Memling work of the mid 1400s, called Sainte Ursula's Hunt. It shows scenes from the extraordinary journey before the martrydom of that saint. According to tradition she went all the way from Cologne to Rome and back, accompanied at times by up to 11,000 virgins. After that remarkable trip, in the third century, on her return to Bruges, she was murdered by the Huns. The museum had other beautiful works, mostly from the fourteenth and fifteenth centuries. From there, we walked the short distance to the *Begijnhof*, or *bequinage de la vigne*, which had been founded in 1245 by the Countess of Flanders, Marguerite of Constantinople.

After a nice evening of the usual cocktails and wine at a bar and restaurant, we decided to go to Antwerp for another day and then drive back to Brussels to turn in our car and head back to Paris.

Checking out of the Hotel before noon, we had to return the same way we had come. That meant going to Ghent, and then taking Route E 3 to Antwerp. We crossed the river Schelde into the Old City of Antwerp and easily found a hotel which we checked into by mid afternoon. After unpacking, our first stop was at the Cathedral, the biggest of Belgium, built over two centuries after 1352. It has numerous works by native son, the great artist Pierre Paul Rubens (1577-1640). Its central tower is a marvel of rich and ethereal decorations, with a splendid steeple or clocher, housing 47 bells. We were told there would be carillon concerts Fridays and Mondays, which we would miss given our stay only until Wednesday.

Of the three museums we wanted to see, we decided to do the 16th century Plantin-Moretus that afternoon. As it closed at five, we had to hurry to it for a one hour visit. It had beautiful furniture and tapestries and lovely paintings, mostly portraits by Rubens. After our usual drinks and dinner, we turned in early. The next morning, we visited the Rubenshuis, with its collections of that master's work, and then the Mayer van den Bergh museum. The latter featured paintings by Jan Brueghel, another favorite painter of ours, who had been a pupil of Rubens.

Then, we checked out of the hotel and drove back to Brussels.

Arriving at the station, we turned in the car, and took the five p.m. express train back to Paris. It was Wednesday, the 27th.of December and we arrived at the Gare du Nord close to 6:15. From there we took the metro, with a change at Barbes-Rochouart. We arrived at the Monceau stop and made the short walk back to our apartment.

The next days, we took it easy, with walks in the Parc Monceau and a visit to the Musèe Cernuschi there, with its marvelous Asian collections. It was founded by an Italian banker, who started his collections on a trip to Asia from 1871 to 1873, before settling in Paris to avoid the Austrians whom he had fought as a young man. There were especially beautiful Chinese works from the second millenium before Christ to the thirteenth century, and an enormous Japanese Buddha from the eighteenth century dominating the entrance to the museum. We also went to the nearby Nissim de Camondo Museum, a house, which had been made into a museum in 1936 by the father, Count Camondo, to honor a son killed in World War 1. It had a splendid art collection of eighteenth century furnishings.

On Friday, Saturday and Sunday evenings, we did Montmartre.

Sunday was New Year's Eve, and about ten, we decided to go to the Palais Royal for the *Reveillon* as the French call the turn of the year party. It is one of the biggest celebrations of the year in Paris and we got to it by taking the metro from Montmartre to the Madeleine stop. It was a short walk from there, but we went slightly out of our way to pass by the beautiful Opera Garnier building. There were already big crowds in the Palais Royal when we arrived there about eleven, waiting for the magic moment. I decided to go into their midst from the back where it was less crowded. That meant taking a route I had discovered when working in the library near there on my Vietnam book. It was like navigating a maze. We went up the Rue Richelieu to the Bibliotheque National and then round its back to the Rue Vivienne. From there, we walked back west to cross the Rue de Petits Champs, and into a little back street off of the Rue de Beaujolais. That led through a small gate into the garden of the Palais Royal.

Many of the people were in costumes and masks as if they were there for Mardi Gras, not New Year's Eve. We made our way through the crowds to the central fountain. There we got into a conversation with another couple. I asked where they lived. She answer we live in the third, near Centre Pompidou."

"What a nice location," I said. She answered that it was indeed "*tres bien situè*. And my name, by the way is Chantal, *et mon ami s'appelle* Robert. Et vous?"

"I'm Chris and my friend is Valerie. *Enchantè* to meet you. Why are you not in costume as so many others, and what do you plan at midnight? We didn't even know people would be in costume and, in any case, we don't have any with us. I'm American and Valerie is English."

"We are saving our costumes for Mardi Gras," Robert said. "The people wearing them tonight are probably going to be away then on a winter vacation or whatever, and wanting to do that now when they are in Paris. We have no special plans for the bewitching hour. And you?"

Valerie answered with a sly look at me, "Why don't we do exchange kisses like in those children's games, but just on the cheek. Our partners first and then we switch."

"I love it," Chantal blurted out. It was now about only about two minutes to, and I wondered again at Valerie's naughtiness. Robert was a handsome guy, and here she was making me jealous again. I said, "You betta watch out, Valerie. How do you know I won't get carried away kissing Chantal?"

She was in fact a striking woman, though too brunette for my tastes. But, she had sensuous lips and nice breasts. Chantal said, "Oh don't worry, Valerie, I am too happy with Robert to cause you any trouble. But, I like to kiss others just to enjoy kissing Robert more."

"A likely story," I said.

Robert came in at that point, saying, "You'd better believe it. Chantal and I are champion kissers. Not to speak of what happens afterwards."

De toute facon, I can't see that part, but I am going to observe you kiss Chantal, before I kiss Valerie. Only then will I decide if I want to go on with this game."

Just then, the chimes of Notre Dame and other churches began to ring and their sound reached us in the Palais Royale. Robert swung Chantal around and began kissing her. I decided what I had said earlier was stupid, and did the same with Valerie. We went on, and on, and on. Several minutes later, as some of the chimes ceased, we disengaged.

"Oh la, la!" I said, as I eyed Chantal and Valerie. Chantal was already making a lunge for me. I said, "Wait a minute at least. You don't want to interfere with the great vibes I am feeling for Valerie, do you?"

She gave me a dirty look, and went back to kissing Robert. At that point, I grabbed Valerie's arm and pulled her away. We slipped into the crowd and were soon well away.

"What did you make of that, *cherie?*"

Valerie said, "I loved kissing you and was glad when you told her to wait. I regretted I proposed that. I don't know what got into me, except that I liked Robert's looks. But I like yours too, and it is good we are on our own again."

"You can say that again. I didn't much like them, good looking as they are."

"I agree. And now what do we do to celebrate the new year?"

"Why don't we walk down to Notre Dame, and see if it is open, which I doubt."

I proposed a nice way there. It was about six blocks out of the way, but well worth it for the views up the Seine to Notre Dame and beyond. Valerie agreed to follow me, and we walked down to the Rue de Rivoli. We followed it to the opening of the Louvre, which we crossed to walk through the Cour Carré to the Seine. There we had to go about a hundred yards west to cross the Pont des Arts, one of my favorite walks anywhere. On the other side of the river, it was East along the Quai de Conti, where some book dealers were still open. It was nice that so much was still open, despite the hour, which of course was because of the New Year. But, I wondered if the metro would go later than the usual closing about one, and thought we had better not risk it. Notre Dame was still open, also exceptionally. After a prayer or two, we exited and made our way to the metro stop at the Hotel de Ville, admiring that beautiful structure on the way. Fortunately, we got what must have been the last train. We got off at the FDR stop, for the walk back to our apartment.

Another nice night, but the next morning I wondered what would happen when I saw Claudia again. That would not be until Tuesday, January 9, but that was only a week and a day away. If she was still seeing her new love, there would be no problem. I would have to see, and decided to call my pilot friend, Francois, and see when we could meet again. He was

137

there, and proposed that Friday. I asked if he could do lunch, and he said he could and proposed we meet at the restaurant, the Clos Morillons at one thirty.

The time passed quickly, and I was glad to see Francois in the back of the restaurant. He waved me over, and I took a seat beside him at a square table for four, the best sort for conversing with someone, since you are just off to the side of the person you want to talk to.

I started by asking him about his latest trips.

"Interesting you should ask, because there were some adventures involved on my last flight, Tuesday. We were en route to Venice over the Alps at 8000 meters when Air Traffic control called us to ask if we were aware of the weather at our destination. We said that all we knew was that when we left Paris, it was said to be overcast in the Veneto, and forecast to remain that way, possibly with snow showers. The controllers said that the weather was deteriorating rapidly with snow squalls and increasing wind. Visibility was down to a hundred meters and the ceiling was zero. They advised us to divert to another airport. We asked what alternatives were still above minimums, and were told that most of north Italy was in a blizzard. They recommended we proceed either northeast to Vienna, or south southwest to Rome, or return to Paris. We opted for Rome and landed at Fiumicino without problem, except that about a dozen of the passengers complained bitterly to us after we had shut down the engines, and were on our way out of the cockpit. 'So, what did you want to do,' I asked. 'Crash and spend your time in Venice in a hospital?' One guy, a fat man of about sixty, said he was a pilot, and he would have taken the flight in. I said, well maybe it's a good thing you weren't flying. At which point, he started cursing at me in Italian."

"Well, there are all types, and I am sure you will enjoy your stay in Rome, no?"

"In fact we got in about four in the afternoon, and Air France asked us if we could take the next flight to Paris. I protested, and we were allowed to stay overnight on condition that I pilot the noon flight the next day. So, I went to the Internazionale Hotel, which we use there. It's on Via Sistina and I had a great dinner nearby at the Ranieri Ristorante, just down the Piazza de Spagna steps."

"I'm envious. And meanwhile what's happening with your new love?"

"Not much yet. But, I've called her several times and she is coming to Paris next week. So, I will have more to tell you the next time we meet."

"How do you plan to avoid problems with your wife?"

"You know, one has to figure out such things as the situation develops. Since Erica is staying in a hotel in the Eighth it should be easy to arrange a few meetings, that is, if I don't run into wife Sophie on a shopping trip there."

"Well, I will be most interested to hear what happens. As for me, I had a great trip to Belgium with Valerie and now am very happy with her. But wondering what will happen when I run into my colleague, Claudia, again. I cooled that off after she told me she had a new friend, named Guy. I hope she is still seeing him."

"Not Guy Fillon surely? He is one of my best friends, from our days at the Universiity of Orleans. He is a good artist and a teacher also. I am not sure where he is teaching now."

"I've no idea, but I doubt it as Guy is a common name, no? But, I will ask Claudia the next time I see her. Do you want a dessert?"

We had finished our omelets and Francois declined a dessert as did I. We took our leave, and I accompanied him to his street, on the way to the Convention Metro stop. My route was to Montparnasse and from there to La Madeleine, a ten minute walk away from our apartment.

Back home, I decided to look at my wine notes again. They were now in two manila folders which I had arranged more or less alphabetically according to the names of places and wines. The Cote du Rhone called Chateauneuf-du-Pape struck me as maybe a better source of elaborating the history of wine than the Clos de Vougeot I had been thinking of earlier. Its creation by Pope John XXII, the successor of the French pope Clement V who had moved the papacy from Rome to Avignon in the early 1300s would surely provide many stories, not only of the wine, but of the history of the times. For example, I had always wondered exactly why that shift of the Papacy from Rome to France had happened, although there were good stories about the crises in Rome which could have precipitated the move. Doing the Chateauneuf-du-Pape might also provide information about a neighboring wine, I had just fallen in love with, called Baume de Venise. I sampled that marvelous Cote du Rhone many times at the Chai de l'Abbaye bar near St. Germain des Près on previous trips. There was no information about the wine on the label, but since it was produced only a few kilometers to the north of Chateauneuf-du-Pape, I thought it was reasonable to hope I would find some references.

My notes also provided the information that the origins of the *appellation controllèe* system had started in the Cote du Rhone region in the 1920s. The system, to guarantee a wine's origin and quality was adopted by all French wine regions by the mid 1930s. Then, the retreating Germans blew up Chateauneuf du Pape in 1944, fleeing the advancing allies. After the war it was restored and the wine makers continued their centuries old traditions of planting, harvesting and aging their wonderful wines.

As I was speculating about these possibilities, Valerie came in. She greeted me and the night passed quietly with dinner, talking and the usual lovemaking afterwards.

The next evening, a Saturday, she proposed we go to the Champs Elysèes to see if the Christmas lighting was still on. I agreed, and we walked down the Rue de Vezelay to the Rue de Miromesnil and on it to the Rue du Faubourg St. Honorè. Crossing that, we took the Avenue de Marigny to the Champs Elysèes at the Place Clemenceau. From there the view was splendid, looking up to the Arc de Triomphe, or down to the Place de la Concorde. Sure enough, the Arc de Triomphe was brilliantly illuminated and seemed to rise above all the Christmas decorations still lining both sides of the wide boulevard.

We walked up towards the Arc de Triumphe, at first on the right side of the Boulevard. Before long we came to one of my favorite stores, a Prix Unique, which has some of the lowest prices in Paris. We entered the store and Valerie proceeded to look at the ladies' stuff, and me at the male sections. She bought a lipstick and maquillage or makeup kit, and me some socks. While telling ourselves to avoid the usual losing of our shopping bags, we proceeded on our way. Continuing on past the beautifully named streets, Colisèe and La Boetie. On the Champs Elysée we came to the Gaumont, the Galerie du Claridge and Arcade du Lido. The latter houses the famous night club, and all three have attractive galeries and shopping spaces. Then, we crossed over to the left side of the Champs and went up past Japan Airlines and various well- known watering holes. Those included the restaurants Ladurie, the Deauville and Fouquet's. Passing la Rue George V, we reached the Office du Tourisme de Paris and Air France. and arrived at the Drugstore Publicis. It took the name Le Drug Store to mock the American developments of pharmacies with their enormous choices of everything from aspirin to washing bowls. It had a wonderful site looking west to the Arc de Triumphe and a restaurant with the best Steak Tartares in Paris, which we decided to have for our dinner.

After that, I proposed we reverse course and do a dance or two at one of the best discos of Paris, Le Club 79. It is at 79 Champs Elysées. The entrèe used to cost 120 francs each, which after the switchover in 2000 had become 20 euros apiece. The music was good and got better when they went into Italian and Spanish dance music. We swayed and swayed, and as is the style in France if not most of Europe, danced on our own much of the time. The floor became very crowded. Since we could easily walk home, we didn't have to watch our time and soon it was one in the morning. Though the dancing was at its peak, we decided to leave. We got home before two, and promptly hit the hay for another night of loving and sound sleep.

The next day we slept late. It was already January 7, and my class would restart in two days on Tuesday. I would have to spend most of the time until then preparing my next subjects. But as it was Sunday, I also

talked a lot with Valerie through midday. Then, we decided to do our walk through the Gardens of the Tuilleries after seeing some areas around the Place de la Concorde. To save our energy we took the metro to Place de Clichy for a corresponance to Concorde. We decided to first look at the

Jeu de Paume Museum. It no longer houses the great works of the Impressionist painters, which have been moved to the Musée d'Orsay, but does mostly special exhibits. The current one was on the great actor Charlie Chaplin, and especially his wonderful comic creations, which the museum dubbed *Charlots*. We enjoyed that and then exited into the northeastern corner of the Jardin des Tuilleries. We descended the stairs to walk around the octagonal pond of water just in front of us, observing the crowds of people sitting around it and watching the carp and gold fish and occasional ducks that landed there. Then we walked back down to the next pond which was almost as far east as the Louvre. Turning around, we retraced our steps, looking at the other great museum building to the left on the northwest corner. That was the Musée de l'Orangerie. It was closed and had no exhibits, but looking farther west we could see two other well known Paris museums, the Petit Palais and beyond it the vast, Grand Palais. We decided not to go that far, but walked onto the Place de la Concorde. There we observed the splendid Obelisk given to France in 1829, and installed in the center of the square several years after that. It was by now well after six, and we took the metro home from the same Concorde stop where we had started.

The next day, Monday, Valerie went off to work while I spent the day preparing for my next courses. That night she came back to tell me Gregoire had come in again, and that he had proposed we do a dinner with him next Friday, the 19th.

"Great! I'd like to meet him. Do you know where he teaches?"

"Yes. I thought I told you that already. He teaches at Nanterre."

"All the better. I would like to know someone from there, as it is an important campus in the University of Paris system. Where does he propose for us to meet?"

"He said he will tell me the next time he comes in. I must say, I do enjoy seeing him a lot."

"Are you trying to make me jealous again?"

"Not unless you want to be. As I recall, you make love even better when you think you are jealous."

Hearing that, I went over to embrace her and we ended up in bed. Dinner and a good night's sleep followed.

CHAPTER SIX

IN THE AIR with FRANCOIS

After working on my teaching notes most of the next day, On Tuesday, January 9, 2001, I was off at about noon for my class at three. At lunch in the cafeteria, who should I see but Claudia.

"*Ciao Claudia. Comment ca va?*"

"Not bad, and you?"

"Never better! I've been wondering what's new with you. How was your Christmas, and are you still seeing Guy?

"Are you jealous?"

"That depends on your answer. Which is?"

"In fact, he has asked me to marry him. But, I'm not sure. I like most things about him, but am not sure I love him enough to tie the knot. I'd like to stay free for a few more years, I think."

"You are right to want to keep your freedom. But, I hope you stay with him awhile longer, so I won't be tempted to ruin the good vibes I've worked out with Valerie. What class do you have coming up?"

"I'll start with a resumé of some of last term's work, and then move on to the writers after Shakespeare."

"Such as?"

"I'll start with Spenser's the Faerie Queene, followed by William Blake, Alexander Pope, Daniel Defoe and then the nineteenth century greats.

There are so many of those it'll be hard to get to the twentieth century and the end of the course."

"Well, I'm sure you will do a great job of it. And now I should get ready for mine. I'm up to the pre Civil War period. So, see you later."

Having grown up in North Carolina, the class was relatively easy for me. Since I had never understood how my ancestors could have owned and exploited slaves, I naturally thought the North was on the right side of that war. Still, as a Southern boy, in school I heard mostly the Civil War side which taught that it was a matter of States' Rights which the North was violating. And that, the war came when the Yankees invaded the South without good reason, since all the South wanted was independence.

When I got to discuss the Dred Scott case, decided by the Supreme Court in March 1857 in favor of slavery, things got more complicated. It was followed by the John Brown rebellion against slavery in October 1859 and my favorite student, Isabelle Avrillon asked, "How could your people have been so stupid?" I told her that would be a good question, if asked by today's standards. But, she had to realize that back there, the Southerners were equally convinced of their arguments, which was why they formed the Confederate States on 8 February, 1861. I told the class to bear that in mind as we discussed other general background to the war.

I described how the U.S. had grown from several million only at the time of the war against Britain after 1775 to over twenty million by the time of the Civil War. Over eighty per cent of the population was still in the countryside, as the cities had just begun to grow. Almost twenty per cent of that population was non-white, and twelve per cent were still foreign born. Blacks had increased to about four million from the 345,000 slaves who survived the arduous and deadly trips from Africa to the United States. Greater numbers reached the Carribean Islands and still more the countries of South America. In the U.S. South, a minority of the 4.4 million inhabitants were slave owners. Some 484,000, they made up one third of the adult males of the South. In fact, up to half of the American Caucasian population had been indentured servants when they arrived from Europe, as they signed up for four or five years service to pay their way over. But, then in the South many of them became slave owners.

The slaves, of course, were used for all kinds of labor, but increasingly it was to grow and harvest cotton, especially after Eli Whitney's invention of the cotton gin in 1793. There were over 200 slave rebellions before the Civil War, most famously in 1800, 1822 and 1831. But, despite the rising abolitionist movement to ban slavery, the march to war was inexorable, and complicated further by the westward expansion across the continent. The immigrants to the west continued the struggle between pro and anti slavery, and there were previews of the war to come in "bleeding Kansas," and elsewhere in the 1850s.

The bigger fighting began in South Carolina, which had been the first state to secede from the Union on December 20, 1860. There, on April 12, 1861, Confederate soldiers opened fire to take Fort Sumpter, just north of Charleston, beginning the biggest war in American history. There were more than a million casualties, with over 600, 000 killed. It seemed a preview of World War 1, with the first wide scale use of machine guns and trenches.

After some more questions and discussion, I dismissed the class and went back to my cubicle. Leaving the door open, I saw Claudia pass by on the way to hers.

"Bonjour," I said. "Anything new?"

"No. Not yet anyway. I'll see Guy shortly and we will see. I'm sure nothing much will change for awhile."

"Glad to hear it. If you have a moment, I would like to report a few new things in my life."

"I have a while. So, tell me."

"Well, back in November I witnessed a scuffle at a bar where a guy shot a man. But, in part because of that I met an interesting man, who is a pilot for Air France, named Francois. We have become friends and get to talk about aviation. That is great, given my love of the little flying I have done. Moreover, he says he has a friend named Guy Fillon, and I wonder if that could be your Guy. So, that and my good trip to Belgium with Valerie over Christmas are what's new for me."

"Interesting. I will ask Guy whose name is indeed Fillon if he knows an Air France pilot, named Francois. I have been to Brussels a couple of times, and want to hear more about your Belgium trip. But first, tell me more about the shooting."

I narrated both briefly, and then took my leave of Claudia. I went straight home after a glass at the nearby bar on Rue de Hotel Saint Paul.

Valerie greeted me, and asked how the class had gone. I told her that I had started on the Civil War, one of my most interesting subjects. She agreed, and said she would like to know more about it. "Maybe you can give me some reading about it. Meanwhile, today Gregoire came in, and proposes the Bistrot Mazarin for our dinner on the 19th. Will that be good?"

"Wonderful. As you know it's a favorite restaurant."

The time passed quietly until that dinner, which was only a week from the Friday coming up. We got to the Bistrot Mazarin at the suggested time of nine and Valerie saw Gregoire at a table in the back. We went over to it and Valerie introduced me.

I said, "Bonsoir. I understand you are a teacher also, and at Nanterre. I'd like to hear more about both what you teach and about Nanterre, which I've never been to."

"Well, my teaching is mostly English and American literature. My dissertation at Harvard was on one of Hemingway's books, *A Moveable Feast*. Have you read it?"

"Yes. I loved it and want to re-read it. And you, Valerie?"

"Very much so. I always want to read descriptions of Paris and France. They have become my favorite places, in part thanks to Chris here."

With that she poked me in the ribs, and I poked back.

"You'd better watch out old boy," Valerie said looking at me. Then, turning towards Gregoire, she asked, "Tell us more about Nanterre? We've heard you have some great classes and students there."

"It's a typical Paris suburb, in the Hauts de Seine thirteen kilometers to the west. But, Nanterre is a good sized town and the University buildings are partly in the town. That is good, because the students have better places to socialize. But, sometimes it leads to problems, especially in the spring when trouble makers get too inebriated at some of the local drinking spots"

"What are your favorite courses?" I asked.

"Twentieth century American literature, as you might guess, because then I get to talk about Hemingway and other specialties. I also enjoy doing the earlier English literature where I can show links with the Chanson de Roland, Chrètien de Troyes and the whole Arthurian cycle. Valerie told me, you are also a teacher."

"Yes. My specialties are Asian history, especially China and Vietnam. But, back in the States, most of my students are in European studies, where I do survey courses. And here, the Institut d'Anglais asked me, as an American, to do U.S. and Canadian history. It's the first time I've done that, so I am learning a lot, showing how little I knew before."

"As we know, the best way to learn a subject is to teach about it," Gregoire said.

I noted that as Valerie had said, Gregoire was a good looking man who spoke perfect English. He had thick, reddish blond hair, was about my height, and had an infectious smile. That was all the more attractive as he did it so seldom. As I observed him, I wondered again if I should be jealous. The waiter arrived and asked what we wanted. We ordered their specials, which included artichokes, gigot d'agneau and sole. We all started with the artichokes. Then, Valerie did the sole and me the lamb. Gregoire asked for the cervelles, or brains, which was also on the menu. We also asked for a bottle of Cote du Rhone. Again it was our favorite, Parallel 45, named after the location of that wine in Southeast France..

Gregoire recognized a couple coming in and being seated in the front of the restaurant. He excused himself and went over to exchange a few sentences. When he returned, Valerie asked him, "Who are they? I think I have seen them come into my store."

"A couple I knew in my days before going off to Harvard, when I was at the Sorbonne. He has become a meteorologist of all things, and she works in a store."

"Which one?"

"The Printemps on Boulevard Haussman, I think. If you need advice or help with shopping there, ask for Nadine Savage. Her husband's name is Paul."

"And where on earth does a meteorologist work," I asked.

"At Meteo France in the Seventh, near Latour Maubourg."

"Maybe, I will go look him up some time. I have long been fascinated with meteorology, all the more so as I am now getting back into my interest in aviation."

"By all means do, and you can say I told you to look him up. What is your interest in aviation?"

At that point our food arrived. After it had been placed before us, I answered, "I became a pilot back in North Carolina where I grew up. Then, recently I have become friends with a pilot of Air France."

"Can you go flying with him, or elsewhere?"

"Air France allows me into the cockpit with my pilot's card, but of course I can't touch the controls there. But, my friend Francois has his own plane and told me I could come and fly it with him. I think I will do that shortly, although, of course, now the winter weather is at its worst of the year."

Gregoire said, "That would be wonderful. I have always wanted to learn to fly and have many pilot friends. But, with my academic training and work, that has never been possible. Tell me how you learned to fly?"

"Growing up in Asheville, North Carolina, it was easy enough once you got the inclination to do it. When, I was still in high school, I decided to learn. I had just gotten my driver's license and the parents let me use their car. So, one day I went to the local airport and signed up with a guy there who taught piloting. It took me eight hours to learn to solo, and from there it was a matter of building up enough hours to get a license. The first one is given after forty hours, and I went on until I got a commercial license after 250 hours."

"Well when you get to fly in Paris, tell me about it. I might like belatedly to get into that, and that would give us something else to talk about."

Valerie interrupted at that point to say, "How do you know I will let you fly anymore? It can be so dangerous, especially now when as you say it's the worst weather of the year."

"I didn't know you could be so bossy, my love. In fact, I already know where Francois keeps his plane. It's at Toussus le Noble in the Essone just to the south. The airplane is called a Robin for some reason. It must be American or British made as that bird is *Rouge Gorge* in French. I hope to go with Francois there and maybe fly next week. At least he invited me to do so, next Friday, January 26."

"If you insist on going, can I come to? If only just to watch," Valerie asked.

"I suppose so, but you will get bored I am sure. I think there are only two seats in the plane, in which case you will have to stay behind."

"Oh, that's all right. I'll take some reading, and see a different part of Paris. But, I'll have to ask at Shakespeare & Co. What time will you go?"

"In the early afternoon, probably about two. It gets dark so quickly this time of year."

By this time, we had finished our dishes, and I asked if anyone wanted another round of drinks.

Gregoire responded, "I would love a cognac. And you?"

Valerie said she would do a port, and I decided on another glass of wine, a bordeaux this time. Our conversation drifted back to books and teaching. Gregoire said he was looking forward to his upcoming class on Chretien de Troyes. He would start with Lancelot, the hero of *le Chevalier à la Charrette*. He said the students would know the name Lancelot, but probably not where it came from. Or that the word *Chevalier*, or Cavalier, first came into prominence with the writings of Chretien de Troyes. Before that the latin word *milices*, from which comes our word, militia, was used.

"How interesting," I said.

Valerie added that she had read Chretien de Troyes and the *Chanson de Roland* in English translation, but not really understood them. She asked if she could come to his class. "When and where do I come," she asked.

Gregoire said, "It's next Wednesday, the 24th, at 16 hours."

"Well, again I'll have to make an excuse at the store. And where do I come?"

"It's on the second floor of the main classroom building, in room 226. See you then, and now I should be on my way."

So saying, he stood up, said *au revoir* and started walking to the exit.

As Valerie and I followed him, who should we see coming in, but Keith. He said, "*Bonsoir*. So, I have missed you for dinner. But, why not do a nightcap with me before you go off?"

I looked at Valerie with some trepidation, but she said, "All right, but it will have to be short as we have already been here several hours. On the other hand, tomorrow is Saturday. So why not."

It now being about eleven in the evening, many people were in the process of leaving the restaurant. Valerie saw a table for three in the front of the restaurant, and led us to it. Keith said, "Let me ask if we can use that table for four over there which will be more comfortable, especially with our coats for the extra chair."

He did, and with the waiter's agreement we went to it. Keith started the conversation, asking us about our Christmas trip, which it seemed Valerie had mentionned. That described, Keith renewed his offer to get Valerie a job with his wine firm. He said he had just increased the interest of that by getting his bosses to agree to open an office in Paris.

"Maybe, you could be our manager for the Paris office. That way you can stay in Paris, and I would get to see more of you."

He looked at her meaningfully, and winked at me.

"What do you mean by winking, you old lecher," I said.

"And your jealousy spoils your sense of humor and proportion," Keith rejoined.

Valerie again came to the rescue, saying, "You two are so tiresome!… Can't we get our drinks and talk about something else?"

A waiter appeared just then and took our orders. Valerie did another port and Keith said he would do a good bottle and give me a glass or two.

He chose a Chateau Margaux 1982, and it was fantastic. Even I knew that that was a good year, and everyone knows that Chateau Margaux is one of the best wines anywhere. Valerie did her part to change the subject by saying how glad she was that I had met and liked her friend Gregoire. She added for Keith's benefit, that he had left just before he came in.

"So, you have a new boy friend, Valerie?" Keith asked.

"He's not yet a boyfriend, but who knows. He's so good looking and charming, I might be tempted."

"There you go again, Valerie," I said. "What am I going to do with you."

"I don't know Chris. Maybe you had better stop being so jealous. Especially, as now I think I do want to work for Keith. If I can stay in Paris, that is."

"Well, if you behave yourself, we can stay friends. But, please don't taunt me with so many compliments about Gregoire, or Keith either for that matter."

"That is going to be very interesting to observe," Keith said. "I am in the process of seeking office space on this trip. So far, I have found one nice place on the Rue de la Chaise. Do you know it?"

Valerie said, "I like the name but don't know it. Is the location as good as its name?"

"In fact, yes. It's just into the seventh, off of Rue Grenelle near the Sevres Babylone Metro stop."

"That is a great location," I said. "Just steps from the Bon Marchè, my favorite store. Maybe, that will lessen my jealousy if you work for Keith in such a great location." I gave Valerie a smile, and she returned it. Then I asked Keith, "When do you think this might get going?"

Keith said, "I will go by to sign a lease tomorrow, and find out when it will be ready. When I get back to London, I will tell them I found a terrific lady to manage the office."

Hearing that, I finished my glass of the Chateau Margaux, and suggested to Valerie that we be on our way. She agreed and we both thanked Keith for the drinks, me adding that it was one of the best wines I had ever had.

He said, "I don't doubt it. It is a rare treat and I am glad you have left me almost the whole bottle. I will call you, Valerie, when I have news about when you should start. And Chris, please relax and stop picking fights with me everytime I talk to Valerie. All right?"

"All right, providing you don't provoke me or try to be too intimate."

Keith said, "That will be up to Valerie, won't it?" He said that with another snide smile, which I ignored.

With that, we stood up and left. On our way out, Valerie smiled at Keith, but I gave him an imaginary fist in the elbow gesture. We went home and straight to bed. We had the usual results, even though I was a bit put out with Valerie for having been so open to Keith, as well as giving me cause to fear her friendship with Gregoire.

The next days passed without incident, until Valerie described her visit to Gregoire's class on Wednesday. She said he related many fascinating things about Chretien de Troyes. For example, that he had been inspired by the Breton legends of the king of Wales and his knights of the Round Table. That's where the tales of Lancelot and the quest for the holy grail originated. But then she made me wonder about her again, when she said Gregoire had taken her for drinks and dinner. All the more so, as she seemed very vague about which restaurant they had gone to.

"Well was it in Nanterre or back in Paris?" I asked.

"In Nanterre, at a little nondescript place not far from the school. It was delicious, and afterwards Gregoire asked me back to his place, not far from there. I went, but told him not to try anything---at least for awhile."

"Am I supposed to suggest you should try him in awhile?"

"Would you like me to?"

"You really do like to flirt, don't you? And to taunt me with your stories about doing so."

"Don't you think this is an old story?" said Valerie. "I see you really do like it when I do that, even though you say it bothers you. But, you wouldn't keep bringing it up unless you took pleasure in doing so, *n'est-ce pas?*"

"Maybe you are right. To prove it, how about showing me your affection for such a tolerant guy."

With that I went over to embrace her and we went off to bed.

The next day I did my class as usual. As I had proposed to go flying the day after that, on Friday, January 26, I called Francois as soon as I got home. We worked out that I would come to his apartment at noon, and we could go to the airport for the afternoon flight. I worked out with Valerie that I would go alone this first time. I was on time and Francois took me to his car parked in a nearby garage. He told me he was not sure about the weather as a front was due to pass Paris later in the afternoon. He said we would have to check out the latest weather reports at the airfield.

At lunch on the way, I asked him about the visit of Erica and if he had had any run ins with his wife. He said Erica had only been three days in Paris, and he was only able to see her once, fortunately, unbeknownst to his wife.

"Did you make love to Erica, if I may ask?"

"We did and it was fantastic. I am not sure what happens next. If I have some flights to Stockholm, it may get serious."

"Well, watch out. You know that can cause problems in your situation."

"Of course, you are right. But, I will have to see, and don't really want to talk about it. Now let's finish up here and get to the airfield and see what's happening with the weather."

"Great, I am really anxious to see if I can still fly without problems."

It took us another half hour to drive to the air field at Toussus le Noble. Francois went straight to the operations desk and asked for the latest weather. They said the front was due to pass the city towards five with rain preceding the front, and some snow following it. I asked if that gave us enough time.

Francois said, "No problem, as I think we will only go up for an hour or so. That will give us enough time for you to see something of the city from the air and the immediate surroundings."

"Wonderful. I will follow you to the plane."

Francois exited the terminal with me in the rear. We walked to the group of planes parked to the left. His Robin was there in the front row. I thought it resembled somewhat a Piper Cub. At any rate, it was a small high wing plane. But it seated four with side by side seating, unlike the Piper with its tandem seating for two one behind the other. Francois said he would take the right, or co-pilot seat, but do the flying until he told me to take over. He did the pre-flight and we got in. He started the engine and as the wind was from the south, we taxied to runway 20. The takeoff was smooth and we were airborne in less than a minute. I noticed that the speed of takeoff was about 80 kilometers an hour, and then we climbed at 100 kh. (112,5 mph). When we reached 300 meters (960 feet), Francois turned toward the north, and told me to take in the view.

It was superb. I could see the Seine and before long the back of Notre Dame, with the Eiffel Tower in the distance. Soon we were at 2000 meters (6400 feet) and Francois said we would level off there. Just beyond Notre Dame, he turned west, and he told me to take the stick and fly a little. I asked him if I could make some turns, and change the altitude. He said all right for the turns, but to hold our altitude and keep an eye out for any other plane I might see. Just as he said that, I saw another approaching from the north at more or less our altitude. I asked him if we should go up or down. He said up, and I did a climbing turn to 2200 meters (7040 feet) which went smoothly enough, as he told the tower our new altitude. To the west, I could see the Montparnasse tower and decided to make a turn around it. That went well enough, I thought, and Francois said, "Tres bien, though you wobbled a bit at first. Now let's head back before the front overtakes us."

The clouds were thickening and beginning to lower. After several minutes, Francois said he would take over and do the approach, but let me do the landing if I wanted. I eagerly agreed and sat back to enjoy the view. He spoke to the tower and we descended to 500 meters (1600 feet) up. After he had confirmed with the tower that the winds were still from the south, he took us to the south of the airfield and turned east, descending to 300 meters (960 feet). After a minute or so, he turned left at 90 degrees towards the north putting us on the downwind leg and told me to take over. That meant going another kilometer or so as I began to descend some more. Then I turned another 90 degrees to the west onto the base leg for a few hundred meters before turning left again to the south for the final approach. That lined us up with the runway to land into the wind from the south. Francois lowered the flaps to 30 degrees, which increased the rate of descent and before long the runway was right there. I began the flare out to round out our descent, and we landed not too roughly. Francois said, "I see you haven't forgotten too much. But, now let me take over, so we don't screw up the taxi back to the ramp."

On the way, I told Francois that I was glad that it had mostly come back to me, and that I could still fly. At least, I remembered the rectangular landing pattern, which facilitated my moves for the *atterrissage* or landing, which seemed to have gone all right.

In several minutes, we reached the end of the taxiway, found our space, and shut down the engine. We got out and went into the terminal to file our flight report. Francois entered the extra hour in his flight log, bringing his total time in the Robin to 1550 hours. That done, we drove back to Paris. He dropped me off at the Concorde metro stop, on his way to his home in the 15th. The rain associated with the front was changing to snow as I arrived home about six. Valerie said that she was sorry she had not been able to come, but asked me how the flight went. I told her how pleased I had been with it, and that the next time she would have to come, as the plane, in fact, had four seats, not the two, I had thought.

The next weeks passed quietly, except for the weather which featured several winter storms. My teaching went well enough and Valerie continued to work at Shakespeare & Co. She told me that both Gregoire and Keith came in regularly, but that she had not responded unduly to their flirting. I asked her about the job Keith had talked about. She said that it was still on, but would not begin until May after they had finished preparing the new office on the Rue de la Chaise.

"How perfect," I said. "That means we can do our trip to Italy in mid April without disruption."

"Exactly right, Chris. And until the end of that trip, let's not even mention Keith, let alone Gregoire or Mark, OK?"

"Agreed." On a late evening about mid February, I proposed to Valerie another evening in Montmartre. This time, we found a new restaurant on a little street off of the Place du Tertre, the Bistrot Tartempion. I couldn't believe it, but as soon as we were seated I saw Mark Goden over in a corner. I wondered if we should get out of there, but as we were in a different part of the restaurant, I thought to stay and hope he ignored us. For most of the meal he did, but when he got up to leave, he saw us and came over.

"Well, look who eats in one of my favorite Paris restaurants. How are you both?"

I thought to say, 'wonderful, until you saw us!' But, I let Valerie respond. She said, "Things are not too bad. When did you get back from London?"

Marc said, "Just two days ago. It's another trip, this time mostly to buy some cheese for our stores in London . I see you are still eating, so I will go on my way. I will probably stop in Shakespeare & Co. when I get over that way. In fact, one of the places I will go for the cheese, is the Marché at Maubert Mutualité close to there.

So long for now."

As soon as he was out of hearing, I said, "Thank God, he's gone. He really gets on my nerves. I am so sorry he discovered where you work. Please, watch out, and don't let him get too close."

Valerie asked, "Are you afraid of him talking politics with me?"

"That would be the least of my worries."

We finished our dinner and walked back to the apartment.

The next days went rapidly and it was already March. I called Francois to ask about another ride in the Robin. He suggested the following Wednesday, March 14, and asked if I could come to his place by noon. He is always so polite. He could have told me to forget it or to meet him at the airfield. I told him how happy I was to hear that and that I would see him on the 14th. I asked if I could bring Valerie along, and he said, 'by all means.'

Arriving at his place on that date I found he was slow to open the door, and when he did I could see why. He had a cast on the bottom of his left leg, and walked with crutches. He explained that the day before, arriving from a new flight to Warsaw and back, he had slipped on the ice and badly strained his ankle.

"It was so stupid. They made us park the plane out on the tarmac, and sent a bus for the passengers. Air France sent a limousine for the crew.

As I was going down the steps to get into it, one of my favorite hostesses called to me. Turning around to answer, I lost my balance and missed the next step, tumbling onto the ground with a twisted ankle. So, I guess we have to do a rain check for our flight. I hope you can come too, Valerie. How about a month from now?"

"I would love to, but let's wait two months, as we are going to Italy in mid April. Anyway, I'm so sorry about your mishap. The weather has been so awful, one has to be really careful of the ice after that last snow on Monday. And what is happening with your love life?"

"I was in Stockholm a week ago and spent a night with Erica, which was wonderful. But, I still don't know how far that is going to go. A lot depends on wife Sophie. I have been getting impatient with some of her behaviour. She shops too much, and can hardly carry on a conversation without talking about what she has just bought or plans to."

"Well, keep us posted, and we will leave you now to your convalescence. How long will it lay you up?"

"They told me about three weeks. That's too bad as I had another trip to Stockholm coming up."

"Can you call Erica to tell her your news?"

"Not easily. If I do it from home, Sophie might see the number on a phone bill. But, as she is at work now, maybe I will after you leave. Or I can go to Le Drug Store and call with my credit card. If I don't overdo it, I can always explain to Sophie that my trips are to see some of the Swedish pilots I know."

"What does your wife do?"

"Wouldn't you guess. She is a hostess with Air France, but fortunately flies internationally. So, we don't have to work together."

"Oh, I see. But that can be difficult anyway, to be married to someone in the same profession. 'Don't mix business and pleasure as they say.'" Meanwhile we will go to Italy in a few weeks. I'll call you when we get back. Good luck with your recovery."

Leaving his apartment, we went to the nearby Clos Morillons for lunch. After a nice pasta with wine and an expresso to finish we decided to walk back. In ten minutes we reached the Ecole Militaire and then the Champ de Mars. From there it was via the Tour Eiffel and over the bridge to the Palais de Chaillot. Then we walked on Avenue Kleber to the Etoile, where we took Avenue Hoche straight to the Parc de Monceau and home. The walk took close to an hour.

Valerie and I talked more about the accident of Francois and the postponement of my next flight with him. Then, we talked of our proposed trip to Rome. That was almost exactly a month off, as that year Easter was April 15. I said I would do reservations on Air France for Saturday, the 14th, and asked how long she could stay in Italy. Valerie said she thought she could do two weeks off, and would ask for that. In my case, there was only one week off. But we could come back on Monday, April 23rd. as my class would begin the next day on Tuesday. That would give us more than a week in Italy.

CHAPTER SEVEN

ROME and RENEWED LOVE

The time passed quickly, and I felt that I had barely gotten the Air France tickets at the Champs Elysées office before it was time to go. In fact, I had gotten the tickets before the end of March, but it seemed only days ago. On April 14, we took the metro to Les Halles, and from there the train to Roissy and the Charles de Gaule airport. That took about an hour and cost very little. As we had left home at eleven, we still had plenty of time before the three o'clock flight. That was great because we were able to have lunch at Maxim's, the new branch at the Charles de Gaule airport of the famous restaurant near the Place de la Concorde. Feeling flush, we started with smoked salmon and then had the rack of lamb. We did a glass of Chablis with the salmon, and then a half bottle of cote du Rhone with the lamb. We felt wonderful by the time we went through security and found our gate about 2:15.

We had the usual difficulty getting by people on our way to the rear of the plane. There are always types who carry their bags, and then have to wrestle them into the bin above, or put them under a seat. Finally, we reached our row with an aisle and window seat, 38 rows back. Valerie asked if I would like the window, and I proposed that I take it for the takeoff, and then give it to her for most of the flight. That was because I am obsessed about the takeoff of those giant airplanes. Ours was an Airbus 320, and soon the stewardess began the usual information about the plane and flight. The engines started and we taxied for about five minutes around the vast airport. When we stopped, and the pilot came on to say we were third in line for departure. We were on the right side, and could see the three planes taking off before us to the northwest. I always like to watch them gather speed and then lift off and climb ever more steeply, finally at an angle of close to twenty degrees.

I asked Valerie if she understood how the big jets could climb so fast, and if not if she would like to know what I had learned. She said please, and I told her that I had researched that for my teaching. I found my best example of the miracle of aviation in the astonishing statistics to do with the takeoff of a Boeing 747, the biggest passenger jet until the projected Airbus 380. The 747 weighs over 437 tons, or 875,000 pounds, and yet can cliimb higher than Mount Everest in less than half an hour. Then it cruises normally at a speed of about 640 miles per hour.

"You know, it really is a matter of the speed of the air passing over the curved surfaces of the planes' airfoils. It's like the force of hurricane winds which tear off roofs when they are over 100 mph. The 747 takes off when it reaches 154 knots, or about 177 mph."

"Thank you for some fascinating information. Now let's watch our takeoff."

I gave her arm a squeeze since that was exactly what I had been thinking. The captain asked the staff to take their seats, and applied full power. The plane began to inch forward and rapidly picked up speed, I was told later, the takeoff was at close to 150 knots. The lift off of the Airbus 320 came in about forty seconds as the plane began to climb into the air. That day, the wind was from the north and I had chosen to sit on the left side to be able to see what we could of the Alps, and with luck, Mount Blanc. That would depend on the exact course the pilot chose, and when I had seen it before, it was on the left instead of the right which side we were now on. Soon I could see the wheat fields below as the pilot commenced a turn to the right. He kept turning until Paris came into view off to the southwest. I told Valerie to lean over me to look as she liked. From where we were, we could barely see Sacre Coeur and the Eiffel tower. I could also see the rear of the wing and the two engines, which was why I liked to sit in a window seat at the rear. Of course, I could not see the force of the air blowing out of the jets, but felt I could given the fact I felt pressed back into my seat and could see the expanding distance between us and the ground as well as the increasing speed of the jet as the objects on the ground whizzed by.

Then came the best part of any flight, as the stewardesses started passing out the drinks and dinners. That was a disadvantage of sitting in the back as along with causing you to be among the last off of planes that had no rear door, you were among the last to be served a drink and meals. But, as a sometime pilot, I overlooked those small problems for the pleasures of being able to see more of the flight with a big part of one wing and some of the engines from the rear.

When the stewardess asked us what we wanted, I nodded for Valerie to speak first. She ordered a champagne and the fish course, a sole meuniere. I ordered a Chablis and two more Bordeaux for myself, another one for Valerie, and then my main course of steak and frites. Among the advantages of flying Air France are free drinks and wines and that most of the time you get good food.

Waiting for those things to arrive, I began to see the hills becoming the pre-Alps, and asked Valerie if she wouldn't like the window for the rest of the trip. She agreed, and stood up in the aisle while I slipped out and came in after she took the window seat.

We had just started to eat our appetizers, when Valerie said, "Oh look! There are some big mountains."

She had exaggerated, but the peaks were getting higher. Just then, the Captain came on to say that we were passing over Lyon and next would pass Torino en route to Rome. We were seeing some beautiful mountains rising above scattered clouds, and I hoped we would be able to see Mont Blanc. In the plane, also I observed some interesting looking people. There was one guy in a khaki suit, possibly decked out for some kind of adventure in Rome. He was looking at a bunch of beauties spread out in the middle pages of Paris Match. He spoke French, and putting down his magazine, started trying to flirt with the pretty hostess just passing him. He asked her if he could have another wine, and when she brought it, got

her interest with some kind of chatter. I saw him pull out his address book, and add her name and no doubt telephone number. She left him with a big smile, and I supposed they had made a rendez-vous for after the flight, somewhere in Rome.

After we had passed the highest mountains and the scenery became less interesting, I decided to leaf through the Air France magazine. It featured various Asian cities, but also had pages of maps of cities around the world. I tore out the one of Rome, wondering if it had any features not in our guide books. I had a Michelin guide for Italy and Valerie had a Lonely Planet for Rome.

As I opened my second Bordeaux, the pilot came on to say he was beginning the descent into Rome, and to please be seated and attach seat belts. I asked Valerie if she could see anything interesting, and she said not really as there was too much haze. But, then she saw a sizeable lake and asked if I knew what that might be. I said no, but turned to the map in the Michelin, and saw that it was probably Lago di Bracciano. If so, that reminded me of a great story I was told by a wine bibbing friend. He said that in the late middle ages, a German mercenary of the French army invading Italy liked a wine he was having on the shores of that lake so much that he named it 'Est,Est,Est,' meaning this is the place, for the best of all white wines. That became the name of the wine.

"Maybe, we could go up and try it," Valerie said.

I replied, "Not likely, unless we can combine it with some other sightseeing. I think we are more likely to go east to Tivoli and the Villa Adriano."

"So, I see you have already been studying your guidebooks and maps."

I leaned over to whisper in her ear that I had for a long time, and had been looking forward to this trip for a long time. Kissing her on the cheek, I lightly caressed her bosom and then sat back to get ready for the landing. That came, and we kept our seats as most of the passengers stood up listening to the usual announcements to not forget one's things, and watch out for this and that. After the walk through the plane and into the aerodrome, we looked for the train our guide books told us would take us to the main station, called Termini. From there we took a taxi to our hotel, the Teatro di Pompeo. It is a good hotel on a fascinating spot, said to be where Julius Caesar had frequented a theatre before being murdered by Brutus and others in 44 b.c. It is also perfectly situated just off of the Campo dei Fiori, and within an easy walk to the Piazza Navona and so many other incredible places also recommended by our guide books.

After we had undone our bags and put away most of the things, I proposed we go out for the evening as it was already close to seven. We started with a Cinzano at the Campo dei Fiori. Then we walked to the Piazza Navona, and ate at the marvelous restaurant on the nearest corner, called the Ciampini. We went back to the hotel and spent another great night of love making and sleep.

The next day we planned a walk to the ancient Roman sites to see what was left of that center of the Roman Empire. That lies between the Colosseum on the southeast, the Foro

Romano to the north of it, the Capitoline Hill to the northwest, and the Palatine Hill to the southwest. Leaving about eleven, first we came to the Palatine Hill.

As we neared it, we heard a guide telling some English tourists that our word for 'palace' originated there, and that they would start with the most interesting palace, namely that of Livia. She was the consort of the great emperor, Augustus. Understandably, we decided to follow the English tourists and soon came to the House of Livia. I wondered why they called it a house if it had been the residence of Augustus, and the word palace came from the Palatine Hill. It was, in fact not very big, and the guide explained that Augustus lived a simple life. But there were impressive medallions, remains of paintings and other objects. From there the guide led us to the southwestern edge of the hill overlooking the Circus Maximus and the Baths of Caracalla beyond. There was a platform overlooking the Circus, with stumps of columns, which the guide told us was all that remained of the Temple of Apollo. Beyond that was the huge oblong of dusty spaces where Roman performances and races took place, watched by up to 200,000 people according to our guide books.

From there we broke off from the group and made our way to the Roman Forum, to the northeast. There among the ruins still stood some impressive monuments. First we passed the beautiful Temple of Saturn, whose remaining eight columns give on to the Via Sacra which led to the equally beautiful Temple of Vesta, where the Vestal Virgins guarded the sacred flame. To its right, stood the Temple of Castor and Pollux. That in turn was just steps from the Temple of Antonino and Faustina, which was just behind the Arch of Settimio Severo. As we were following mostly the Michelin green guide, we debated whether we agreed with their listings of three stars for the first three, and two stars for the latter two. According to their definitions, three stars means 'not to be missed,' and two stars 'worth the trip.' Valerie said she would reverse their ratings for the Arch of Settimo Severo and the Temple of Anonino and Faustina, since she preferred the former over the latter. I said I thought the Temple of Vespasiano which was in the middle on the left side of the Via Sacra was worth more than the two stars the guide gave it. Deciding to move on, we walked back toward the Colosseum and came to another two star, the Arch of Titus, which was at the other end of the Via Sacra. In any case, we had now seen three three-stars and three two-stars in ten minutes of walking, which certainly was not bad for anyone's sightseeing.

Yet, we had just begun. We decided to see and walk around in the Colosseo next and then if not too exhausted walk back to the Capitolene Hill, or Campidoglio, all crammed with three star sites. The Colosseum was just beyond the Arch of Titus. It was now after two, and we found a food stand in the Piazza Collosseo. After eating a few bites, walking towards the Colliseo, we were amazed to see the remaining splendour of the Colosseum, now partially restored. That chef d'oeuvre of ancient architecture included the three classic levels, including columns in the Doric, Ionic and Corinthian modes. As we climbed the stairs, we imagined watching the gladiators facing the lions, and their fights to the death in those incredible bread and circus spectacles.

We exited toward the Caelian Hill and the Church of San Gregorio. As it was Easter day, we entered for prayers and a bit of rest. Then we circled back on the Via of its name past the front of the Colliseo and the three starred Arco Constantine. The arch had been built in 315 to commemorate that Emperor's victory over Maxentius three years before. A few steps to the north and we jogged right to reach the Via dei Fori Imperiali, which we took toward the Campidoglio. Along the way, we admired the forums of Trajan, Caesar, and Augustus. The first was designated three stars because of the magnificent scenes of his war conquering Dacia, north of the Danube, early in the second century. The latter two had two stars each to do with their handsome columns from two thousand years ago.

Just above Caesar's Forum which we came to last we saw to its left in order, the beautiful church of S. Maria in Aracoeli, and beyond that the inimitable Capitoline Hill. The steps up to S. Maria in Aracoeli were lovely and led into the interieur of that thirteenth century church, with its fifteenth century frescoes. We heard a guide saying in English that before the church had been built the site had housed the Roman Senate and been a favorite place of the nobility. As we exited toward the Basilica later turned into a museum, we saw just beyond it the second century statue of Marcus Aurellius mounted on his horse. Beyond that were three ancient buildings, partly rebuilt and arranged by Michelangelo. They included the Capitolene Museum, the Senatorial Palace and the Palace of the Conservatori. Tired as we were, but imagining our imminent return to the hotel, we walked more rapidly now. We relished especially the famous statues of the she-wolf and various warriors, emperors and a Venus. The Senatorial Palace was closed to visitors.

It was now already five in the afternoon and we headed back to our hotel. It was a fifteen minute walk, starting via the Piazza di Campitelli. We had a light snack at a trattoria on the way to restore our strength. When we got to the hotel, all we could do was collapse onto the bed and rest enough to get the strength to get into the tub. I told Valerie to go first and she happily complied. After my bath I went to bed for another rest and saw Valerie was asleep. Looking at her, I again thought how beautiful she was and how lucky I was. Thank goodness, I didn't mess this wonderful trip up with either my jealousy of her, or by seeing too much of Claudia. I snuggled up to Valerie and put my arm around her. When she awakened about fifteen minutes later, I asked her what she wanted to do for the evening. She asked, "I'm sure we can find a good restaurant to go to in a different part of the city, don't you think?"

"Marvelous. I've already researched a few. One is the Passetto just the other side of Piazza Navonna, on the Via Zanardelli. It's in the Red Michelin hotel and restaurant guide. And there are some others near the Pantheon. Or if you want to go farther, there is one towards the Via Veneto."

"Oh, let's do the latter. I want to see the Via Veneto, and tomorrow, we can start with the Pantheon, and then do the Piazza Navonna and lots of other things."

"Great. In addition, that other restaurant has a good name, the Capricio. It's on the Via Liguria which leads to the Via Veneto. As we have walked so much today, let's see if we can get a bus. Or failing that, a taxi. With all the ancient buildings, I don't think there is any metro nearby."

We walked to the Corso Vittorio Emanuelli, and found a bus stop. But the map of bus routes showed too many complexities, and we decided to get into a taxi at the stand nearby. The driver took us to the Via Liguria, barely avoiding several crashes, which seemed to be a problem with most taxis in Rome. We found the Ristorante at number 38, and happily debarked, paying only six euro, with one as a tip.

We started by sharing a *prosciuto e melone* and then did two *alla Romana* dishes, Valerie the *Tortellini* and me the *Gnocchi.* They were wonderful and mine all the better because I had them change the tomato for a cream sauce. We talked about the wonders we had seen and speculated about the next day. After the dishes had been removed, I spread my map of Rome out on the table to study that further. Then, using the green Michelin, I could see that we could do three, three star sites easily close to the hotel. We could start with the Farnesi Palace, then the church of Jesu, and last the Pantheon. Then, after lunch in the Piazza Navonna, it would maybe be a good time for us to walk via the Trevi Fountain to the Borghesi Gardens, and see the marvelous museum there. With those thoughts we left the restaurant. Strenthened by our meal, we thought we could do a tour of the Via Veneto area, then have a drink, and go back to our hotel via the Spanish steps.

We began by taking the Via Emilia up to the Porta Pinciana. We passed street after street of handsome stone buildings and came up to the Porta Pinciana. It was too dark to see into the Borghesi Gardens, but I wondered if we would go into it the next day from there or from the Piazza del Popolo off to the left. We turned right on to the Via Veneto, and walked down that broad and handsome boulevard, admiring more villas and appealing shops. Before long, we arrived at the imposing Hotel Excelsior, and decided to stop at the café just beyond it. I had a favorite drink, Punt e Mes, and Valerie the similar drink, called Cynar. With more good conversation and people watching, we paid up and set off following the curve of the Via Veneto until we got to the Piazza Barberini. From there we took little streets to the Via del Corso, and from there a left on the Via del Plebiscito. As we had done it the day before, it was an easy walk back to the hotel.

It was already Monday, April 16, and we had one more week in Rome. As planned, we started by walking to the Palazzo Farnese via the Campo dei Fiori. Now the embassy of France, it boasts two three star attractions for the sixteenth century building itself, as well as for the frescoes in the Grand Galerie. The Palazzo was built after 1515 by the Cardinal who became Pope Paul 111 from 1534 to 1549, with work by Michelangelo among others. After walking around the handsome courtyard and garden, which were all that were open that day, we walked back via the Campo dei Fiori to the Corso Vittorio Emanuele. There we turned right for several blocks to the magnificent Chiesa del Gesu. It had been built after 1568 at the height of the Counter Reformation, and became the principal church of the Jesuits in Rome, with a splendid altar dedicated to their founder, Saint Ignatius Loyola. After admiration of that and the interior, we prayed a bit and then made the short walk back to the Pantheon. I told Valerie, who agreed with me, how I was again greatly struck by how many wonders there were in such a small area of this incredible city.

The Pantheon also demonstrated the other half of that thought, namely how many ages there were. It had been built first by Agrippa in 27 B.C., and then reconstructed by Hadrian after 127 A.D.. You enter by a porch with sixteen columns, and see its interior, another masterpiece of the ancients. In the seventh century it was transformed into a church, and there are beautiful chapels, as well as the tomb of Raphael and other greats.

Following our guide books we found the church of St. Louis-des-Francais about fifty steps to the left and then right. Its highlight was a chapel with beautiful Caravaggio paintings. As we were close to the Piazza Navonna, for lunch we walked via it the few blocks north to the Ristorante Passetto. There we had some lovely pasta, wine and coffee. Then from there, it was back toward the east to the Trevi Fountain, one of the most popular tourist sites in Rome. Built in the eighteenth century, it became known as the place to throw two coins into the basin of the fountain below its statues. The first would be to guarantee a return to Rome, and the second for a wish.

To enter the Borghesi Gardens, we had to decide whether to go northwest to the Piazza del Populo or northeast to the Porta Pinciana. As we had done the latter the day before, we headed northwest via the Piazza di Spagna and soon reached the people's square. Also laid out several centuries ago, it contained the Renaissance church, Santa Maria del Populo. There we saw some more marvelous paintings by Caravaggio and others. By now it was mid afternoon, and we hastened into the Jiardini Borghesi just to the east. We took the paths lined with plane trees, the pines of Rome and other plants. Passing the pond more or less in the middle of the park, we had to ask our way to our next target, the Galleria Borghesi, one of the greatest museums on earth.

Arriving there via paths to the Viale del Museo, we studied our guide books and the map of the lay out of the museum. First we saw the Canova statue of Pauline Bonaparte. Considered a masterpiece, it had been done as a wedding gift from Prince Borghese, who later came to detest that sister of Napoleon. Moving on, we were stunned by the paintings of Titian and other great artists, and still more so by the exquisite statues of Bernini. The most impressive of all, and surely of all creation, is Apollo and Daphne. Its beauty and grace are dazzling, and to imagine that it could be made out of marble.

Soon, it was closing time, and we walked back to the Porta Pinciana and turned onto the Via Veneto for a drink at a café bar. This time we took the west side of the street. No sooner had we ordered our drinks than I heard my name being called. It was Harold Lewis, an old colleague from New York, who taught European history at City College.

"What brings you here, Hal?"

"The usual Easter vacation in Rome. What else?"

"Please join us," I said pointing to a chair just off to the side. "This is Valerie. We are doing a vacation here from our jobs in Paris. Did you know that I got an exchange teaching job for this sabbatical year?"

"No, I didn't. Before more about that and everything else, let me say how glad I am to meet you, Valerie." Hal, who had always been gallant, kissed her hand, and sat down.

Valerie replied with a smile, "So glad to meet you too. How do you know Chris?""

I came in, saying, "That's an old story. But, briefly, we met at a party in New York, and hit it off as fellow teachers in the City University. In addition, I liked to pick his brain for information about European history for my teaching those survey courses."

Valerie said, "In that case, maybe Hal can clarify some arguments Chris and I have had about European history. He says that feudalism was more exploitive than creative, whereas I argue that it led the way to the great developments of European history. What do you think?"

"You are both right. It was exploitive but also creative. Maybe the bigger question is, was the creativity enabled by the exploitation?"

"I see that like Chris and all historians, you can't give a decisive answer," Valerie said. "I guess you see too many contradictions, nuances and subtleties. But, for me, the development of the forts and chateaux led to the cathedrals which led to all our greatest art."

"Hold on Valerie," I said. "The cathedrals already started in the twelfth century and most of the great chateaux came long after that."

"All right they developed more or less simultaneously." Valerie said. "A more concrete question is, shall we eat here or try to find a restaurant?"

Hal said he knew a good restaurant not far away. He led us back several streets to a restaurant at the corner of the Via Emilia and Via Lombardia. I had noticed that restaurant on our walk to the Porta Pinciana. We had some more good pasta, salad and wine. I told Hal what we had seen so far, and asked him how well he knew Rome.

He said, "This is my third trip, and I hope not my last. And when do you see the Catacombs?"

Valerie said, "How about tomorrow? But, we also have to see the Vatican and Castel Sant' Angelo and so many other things. What do you think Chris?"

"Not only all that, but we should also do Trastevere across the river, the Quirinale and Santa Maria Maggiore. At least that is what I have been told."

"I see you have gotten good advice. Is it from people or guide books?"

"Both. Our hotel concierge is also very helpful, and my Michelin and Valerie's Lonely Planet tell us the high spots. How have you gotten around here?"

"Much the same way. And if you can find it, read the best book of all about Rome, *A Traveller in Rome*, by H. V. Morton. If you can't find it, I can get you a copy back in New York. Now I am going to leave you two and go home to prepare an early rise. I go to see an old friend of mine here, who got cancer and is now in a hospital. The visiting hours start at ten, but I have to leave before they start some treatments at eleven or so."

I asked, "Before you go, tell us more about your friend and her cancer. How serious is it?"

Already standing, Hal told us, "It is very serious. She first got a tumor in the lower parts, I'm not sure where, and it spread. She has already done two operations and may have to do a third. She is Italian, named Giuletta, and so I don't really know the details, but it is serious, obviously. So, goodbye. I'll call you when I can. Where are you staying?"

We told him and the phone number, and watched him go off. Valerie asked me about seeing the Catacombs, and if I thought we should do them first, or after the other places I wanted to see. I suggested we do them first the morrow, and that we go back to the hotel to prepare for that. I said we could do Trastevere for dinner after the catacombs, or the following day after we did the Quirinale and Santa Maria Maggiore. We still had almost another week, so we could do the Vatican and Castel Sant' Angelo later in the week.

When we got back to the hotel, we asked the concierge about getting to the Catacombs the next day. He told us to take a taxi, or if we were trying to save money, to walk to the Termini train station and take the metro a few stops. Eventually, he said we would get to the Via Appia Antica, and should also see the Basilica of San Paulo Fuori le Mura nearby. If we had the energy, he said, we could do the Baths of Caracalla and San Giovanni in Laterano, all in that part of southeast Rome. We thanked him and went to the hotel library, where miracle of miracles I found the book Hal had recommended, A Traveller in Rome.

Back in our room, I started reading it and found it really fascinating. Looking up the places we wanted to see, I found an example of that fascination in Morton's description of St. John Lateran. Named for St. John the Baptist, it seems that the building is on a site that had been owned by a notorius playboy, who had been a lover of Messalina, the wife of Claudius. She helped to murder Nero, back in the first century. Later the property came into the hands of Constantine the Great who gave it to the Pope who built St. John Lateran, that 'mother church of Christendom' in the fourth century. A guide book said it was reconstructed in the seventeenth and eighteenth centuries. As I told some of these details to Valerie, she said, "Stop reading, and come give me a caress." As we were already side by side in the bed, that commenced without delay. Before long we were satisfied and drifted off to blissful sleep.

The next day, we got up late. After having the cafè complet breakfast, we went out, still unsure whether to go by metro or cab. But we decided to walk to the Termini metro stop, and there we took a train to San Giovanni. From there it was a short walk to San Giovanni in Laterano. As we approached St. John, we were struck by the huge statues of Christ, St. Jean the Baptist and others on the roof. Inside we read inscriptions which described Constantine's building of it as the first great church of Rome. Its altar houses the heads of St. Peter and St. Paul! Statues of the apostles, ancient columns and a later restored ceiling dominated the interior. It was the home of the papacy for close to a thousand years before the building of the Vatican in the fifteenth and sixteenth centuries. A plaque says some twenty eight popes are buried there. Historically, it is linked to the three other 'great' churches of Rome, Basilica Santa Maria Maggiore, San Paolo fuori le Mura, and

St. Peter's.

After lunch nearby, we walked south to the Catacombs, one of which we were told, begins under the Basilica of San Sebastiano on the Via Appia Antica. That church in honour of St. Peter and St. Paul also dates from the fourth century. A short way off lie the earlier Catacombs of St. Callixtus, named after a deacon of the pope from 217 to 222. Another sixteen popes are said to be buried there. Not far away lie the Catacombs of San Domitilla, which are the oldest of all. As we walked in those lugubrious caverns, the feeling of death seemed omnipresent to us. But, later, I would read in the Morton book that all those martyrs remained incredibly hopeful and optimistic, with the words 'rest' and 'sleep' everywhere, and no references to 'farewell' or death. How great their faith must have been! Morton also cited historians saying it was estimated some six million Christians had been buried mostly from the second to the fourth century in close to fifty catacombs. If placed end to end they would stretch over hundreds of miles.

After close to an hour or two of wandering in these caverns, and listening where we could to guides speaking in English or French, we looked for an exit. Finding one, we asked the way to the Baths of Caracalla, which were off to the northwest. As we arrived there we tried to imagine bathing with the sixteen hundred people one of our guide books said could do that at one time, after its opening early in the third century. It must have been quite a bath! We saw the signs advertising Aida and other operas to be held there in the open air in the summer, and thought we would have to come back for that some day. Next, it was farther west via the Porta San Paolo to the great Basilica of San Paolo Fuori le Mura, built by Constantine after the completion of St. John Lateran. It was the first church to have its apse in the rear facing east, and houses the tomb of St. Paul, minus the head which was sent to the Lateran. The church burned down in 1823, but was fully restored by 1854. After admiring its magnificent interior elaborated over the centuries, we sat down to pray and have a bit of rest. It was now after five, and we left and fortunately were able to find a taxi which got us back to the hotel by six.

After some more rest and bathing, we decided to go to Trastevere for dinner. As it seemed to be at most a half hour away from our hotel, we wondered if we would have the energy to go by foot even after our extensive walking earlier in the day. We thought we could and set out before nine. Again passing the Campo dei Fiori, we came to the Ponte Sisto across the Tiber, or Tevere, River. Taking picturesque streets filled with shops and cafès, we arrived shortly in the Piazza San Calisto. A fountain there gives way to the fourth century Basilica Santa Maria in Trastevere, thought to be the first church ever dedicated to the blessed virgin. We wanted to see the mosaics in that twelfth century church. It was closed, but some mosaics were visible on the outside. Not to worry we thought, given all the incredible things we had already seen.

We went to the bar/restaurant in the middle of those that lined the eastern edge of the square. The drinks, wine and food were marvelous and so relaxing. I asked Valerie if she thought we should move to Rome, and she said that might be a very good idea. "But, only after I finish my teaching in June and the other things we want to do," I said, and she agreed. Some people next to us spoke English and we got into a cursory conversation. They asked us if we had seen the church of Santa Cecilia in Trastevere. They said it contained a wonderful medieval painting of the Last Judgement and had been the dwelling of the third century patron saint of music of that name. It is said Santa Cecilia invented the organ to express the heavenly sounds she heard when meditating and praying. We said we would go to it another day and took our leave to walk back to the hotel. There we turned in by midnight, with positive thoughts of seeing the Vatican and still more sights on the morrow.

That would be Wednesday, April, 18th, and we still had four more days after this one. I wondered if we should relax more those days, and only do remaining 'must sees' in our guide books, including the Vatican and the church of Santa Cecilia. After our morning coffee, bread and jam, we set out for Castel Sant'Angelo and the Vatican. We thought to start with the Castel, as it was on our way, and reached it in another half hour of walking, via the Piazza Navonna and the Sant' Angelo bridge. The Castel was a huge fortress, built in 135 by the Emperor Hadrian. As we entered, we learned that Pope Gregory the Great had built a chapel there in the late sixth century to commemorate an angel credited with ending a plague. Later popes added to it and frequently resided there. A lift to the top floor was constructed in 1513, operated by pulleys and winches powered by teams of men. Popes often had to seek refuge there, as did Clement VII at the time of the sack of Rome by troops of the Holy Roman Empire in 1527. That occurred when 34,000 Imperial troops mutinied because of lack of pay after their defeat of a French Army allied with the Papacy and some Italian cities in a war against the Holy Roman Empire. They forced their commander to lead them to Rome and pillaged the city for three days. The papal apartments on the top floor of Castel Samt'Angelo are beautiful. They somewhat make up for the gloom of the dungeons and tombs on lower floors.

After about an hour of wandering through the vast Castle, we took the Via del Conciliazione to the Vatican. We arrived first in the Piazza

San Pietro with its superb colonnades and ancient obelisk in the center. After admiring those across the vast space of the Vatican, we went on into the Basilica of San Pietro. After 322, Constantine commissioned its building near the spot where St. Peter had been crucified in 64. From the fifteenth to seventeenth centuries Bramante, Michelangeo, Raphael, Bernini, and other great artists replaced the collapsing remains of the original building with the present magnificent structure. Michelangelo, above all, contributed most impressive work, including finishing the dome, conceived by Bramante, the exquisite statue of the Pieta, and the astonishing Sistine Chapel. He painted the frescoes on the ceiling of the latter from 1508 to 1512, and thirty years later the wondrous Last Judgement on the altar wall. Some of Raphael's greatest paintings and Bernini's greatest sculptures also are found there and in the

Vatican Museum. The latter in addition houses an important collection of Etruscan art and the works of many other masters.

We had some pasta and wine before going to the Museum of the Vatican, and spent most of the afternoon there. When we got back to the hotel, there was a phone message from Hal Lewis. He proposed we meet for dinner and call him to arrange the details. I did that and we fixed on meeting in the Campo dei Fiori at eight, at a bar called Da Pancrazio. He was with a stunning blonde, called Bianca Donatella. Her English was good and she said she had lived some in London and knew Hal from one of his previous visits to Rome. We did our cocktails and conversation, and Hal proposed we do the restaurant, Vecchia Roma, nearby on the Piazza Campitelli. We agreed with his choice, and especially liked its name for 'Old Rome.'

It was a ten minute walk from where we were, and I asked Hal how he had discovered it. He said it was in all the guides of places to eat, and that he had often eaten there. He recommended their risotto and lamb dishes, which was just what I thought I wanted. We ordered those and others and continued talking. Bianca said she was a journalist with *La Republica* and that was how she had met Hal. It seems that he knew another journalist in Rome who had invited him to a party where Bianca was. Hal asked us to describe our latest sightseeing which we did. Then, Bianca asked Valerie how she had met me. She did and said how wonderful our world was, where you could meet attractive people of the other sex so easily. I agreed but pointed out how much luck figured in that.

"For example, I never would have met you unless I had decided to walk that day to the metro via the Jardins du Luxembourg, where if the day had been raining I would have taken a closer one. And you had to have had the idea of looking at the bee hives there."

"Naturally, dear, and fortunately you noticed me and wanted to flirt."

Hal said at that point, "It's a good thing we like to flirt, or we wouldn't meet such beautiful girls."

Bianca said, "And what will you do with us when we stop being beautiful? The fear of that is why we like to get extra men to have on the side." Hal asked, "And who are your extra men, Bianca? Do I know any of them."

"No, I don't think so. You are only here several weeks a year, though you may have met some of them, for example, at the party where we met. But, I wouldn't say their names in any case."

"That is wise of you," I said. "And Hal, tell us more about your earlier trips to Rome."

"All right. As you know I teach European history, and my specialty is Italian history. My PhD was on the restoration of the Papacy from Avignon back to Rome in the fourteenth century. So, naturally I came here for a year or so to do research for that. And fell in love with Rome, as well as Bianca, and I vacation here as often as I can."

I said, "You can see why I like Hal so much. Our tastes are very similar, which is very useful for a colleague. How long are you going to be here this trip?"

"Unfortunately, I have to go back on Sunday, as our Easter break will be over by next week. Would you like to dine again Saturday night, perhaps near where I'm staying in Parioli on the other side of the Piazza Verdi. It's in the Hotel delle Muse."

"That would be a great idea, and give us a chance to see another part of Rome. But, as we leave on Monday, I might be too jealous of my time with Valerie to do it. What do you think, Valerie?"

"Why don't we? As you say it's where we haven't been, and I like your friend," she said with a smile.

"All right, you're the boss. Do you already know where to propose for dinner, Hal."

"A favorite restaurant nearby is Al Ceppo. It also has great lamb and pasta dishes. Let's say at eight if that's all right with you."

"Wonderful. See you then and now we'll be on our way, as the witching hour is approaching."

In fact, it was only about eleven, but I wanted to savor my time alone with Valerie. We walked back to our hotel, buying a small scotch on the way. In the room, I embraced her, but then disengaged, saying, "Let's do our nightcap, shall we?"

Valerie agreed, liking scotch as much as I did. We talked about all the wonders of Rome we had seen, and speculated about what more we should do tomorrow, which was the Friday of our last weekend in Rome. I proposed we do Santa Maria Maggiore and San Clemente, and after lunch Santa Cecilia in Trastervere. Valerie said that sounded wonderful. She added that she had read we should also do the Aventine hill and a church there called Santa Sabina, and that maybe we could do that Saturday. I agreed and the scotch finished, we headed to bed, more embraces, and sleep.

The next day, I found that Santa Maria Maggiore was not far from the Termini metro stop. We walked up to the Spanish Steps for the line going there and rapidly got a train. Exiting from it, we went on the Via Cavour to the church. It had been begun before the mid fifth century with later additions. It had three different, three star ratings in the Michelin guide, for the church itself, its interior and the mosaics. The latter had fifth century scenes from the bible, and was among the most ancient Christian ones in Rome. They were among the most beautiful we had ever seen, or were likely to, anywhere.

Exiting the church, we were forced to take the Via Merulana until we could take the first right, and then a left to find the Imperial palace, Domus Aurea. From its other end, it was only a few yards to our next destination, the Chiesa San Clemente.

Its entrance is off of the Via di San Giovanni in Laterano on the other side of a courtyard with a central fountain. As you go in you become aware it is on several levels because of later constructions. Originally, there was a temple to the pagan cult of Mithras, the god of the sun. In the fourth century, the newly legitimized Christians built a lovely church on its ruins. The Normans destroyed that in 1084, fighting forces of the Holy Roman Emperor, Henry IV. It was rebuilt in the twelfth century preserving its frescoes and with beautiful mosaics covering its dome. Built in honor of St. Clement, thought to be the third successor of St. Peter, the church was given to the Dominican Order in the seventeenth century, and soon taken over by Irish Dominicans. We read of all that in a brochure we found at the entrance to the church.

After an hour of looking at the interior and prayers, we left and sought a nice place for lunch. That involved walking back past the Colosseum, where we found a tratoria on Via Marco Aurelio. When we finished it was almost three, and we walked again the Via dei Fori Imperiali past the Forum. From there, we crossed the Tiber further to the south than we had before, across the Isola Tiberina. On it, our guide books told us, was the Church of St. Barthomew, founded in 1100 as well as a famous hospital, founded in 1538 by a Portugese soldier who had recovered from a battle wound. The site was dedicated to the Greek god of healing, Aesulapius. The story was that after a plague in 291 B.C., a delegation had gone to his temple at Epidaurus on the Aegean Sea, and brought back a snake from there which took refuge on the island. The snake was credited with miraculous healing and the church and hospital were constructed there later. The 'do good brothers' (fate-bene-fratelli) also established a famous pharmacy for the poor on the island and became well known throughout Italy for their good works and healing.

Continuing on our way, we took the Via Antica to the Via dei Genovesi, and then a left and a right to our next destination, the Church of Santa Cecilia in Trastevere. Built on the site of the palace of the patron saint of music, martyred about 232. It had numerous later restorations and fine art, headed by Pietro Cavallini's Last Judgement of the late thirteenth century, as well as a famous statue of the saint lying on her side. We admired the handsome interior and altar, said some prayers and left for the walk to Santa Maria in Trastevere and another drink in the square facing it. It was now late afternoon and the perfect time for that. This time we were able to see the marvelous Mosaics in Santa Maria that we had been unable to see when we were there Wednesday night. Then we did glasses of wine in the same café as before. We walked next towards the Ponte Garribaldi, north of the Isola Tiberina, and found a trattoria in the Piazza just before it. After another nice dinner, we made our way back to the Piazza Navonna for a Sambuca Romana each, my favorite nightcap. We got to the hotel before midnight and turned in for the usual. I wondered how I could be so lucky, to be with such a beautiful woman in such an exciting city.

The next day was our last Saturday of this incredible trip, and I struggled to get up earlier than I usually did. Over breakfast we decided to go to the Aventine Hill as Valerie had suggested in order to see the churches there. We took the usual path to Campo dei Fiori and then a succession of streets to the edge of the Tiber which we followed until we got to the Aventino Hill and the Lungotevere road by the Tiber. The first church was Santa Maria in Cosmedin, begun in the third century with many layers added to it. Especially picturesque is its twelfth century bell-tower or campanile, just behind its right side. In the early centuries, bread was distributed to the poor from there. A big circular stone on its porch, contains the 'mouth of truth,' a popular attraction, with the story that an adulterous woman put her hand into its hole avowing innocence, only to lose a finger.

Next was Santa Sabina, built 422-423 at the summit of the Aventine Hill on the site of an Etruscan temple to honor a Roman lady converted to Christianity by her slave. Both were martyred under the Emperor Hadrian about 125. Its original wooden doors are still intact and carved with scenes from the bible. As we were looking at them, a bearded man with a beret asked us in Italian if we wanted a guide. We asked if he spoke English or French, but he looked at us as if we were crazy. Ignoring our 'non grazie,' he proceeded to almost push us to the crucifixion scene at the top of the left door. As best we could understand him, he said it is thought to be the earliest surviving representation of the crucified Christ. We looked that up later and saw that the guide books said the same thing. In the otherwise simple interior of the church, two dozen Corinthian columns along the sides and splendid ninth century windows, make it one of the best examples of the early Roman churches. There is a story that St. Dominic and St. Francis, who were near contemporaries in the early thirteenth century, may have met once in Santa Sabina, or its adjoining monastery. St. Dominic resided there before his death in 1221, as later did St Thomas Aquinas who died elsewhere in 1274. The Vatican gave Santa Sabina to St. Dominic three years before his death, and it became a center of that order of preachers.

It was now close to noon, and after studying some more the beautiful carvings on the doors, its interior, and doing some prayers, Valerie and I left to wander a bit more around the hill. We took the picturesque path leading to the Piazza San Alessio in front of the church of that name. Arriving there we found a trattoria for lunch. After another good pasta, we continued on to the north to take a last look at the many marvelous sites of the Palatine Hill, Circus Maximus and Foro Romano. Arriving back at the hotel in mid afternoon we decided to take it easy before our last Saturday night in Rome.

Towards six thirty, we went to Campo dei Fiori for drinks. This time, Valerie started with a Martini Bianco, and I did a Punt e Mes. We debated whether we should join Hal Lewis at the Al Ceppo or find a typical restaurant we had not been to, and a place to dance afterwards. One thought was that we might as well go back to the Vecchia Roma. It had so many nice dishes, its great name, and moreover was very close by. But, then we thought Hal's choice might be the best idea, and besides we had told him we would do that. Valerie agreed and repeated that she had liked him a lot. We took out our map, on which we had already marked where the restaurant he recommended was. It was quite far, at the edge of the Villa Ada park and gardens. As there was no metro in that direction, we would have to take a bus.

We went back to the Corso Vittorio Emanuelli and bought two round trip bus tickets each at the Tabacchi on the corner of Via Argentina. Studying the bus map at the stop across the street, we found one that would get us there, passing the Capitol, Quirinale and Borghesi Gardens to the Via Salaria. One came and we tried to ask the driver to tell us where to get off, but he didn't understand us. So, we took seats in the back and took out our map, hoping we could figure it out. The first part was easy because of all the famous buildings, some of which we recognized. The tricky part was after that, on the long Via Salaria. We went to the front of the bus, and got off as soon as we saw the tree lined park of the Villa Ada. Fortunately, the restaurant at 2 Via Panama was right there close to the bus stop. We were only about ten minutes late and glad to see Hal and Bianca seated at a nice table for four.

Joining them, Hal stood up and asked if we remembered Bianca. I said, "Of course. How could we forget such a pretty lady."

Hal said, "I suppose not, since I remember how much you like pretty ladies, Chris. And don't we all?"

Bianca smiled, but Valerie added with a frown, "See how they have already forgotten our previous conversation."

Bianca added, "I remember it all too well. I even have nightmares about it. What happens to us when we get old and ugly? As we said before, that is why we try to collect extra men. Though I am a bit out of practice just now."

She looked around the room, and pointing to a table full of men, said, "Look Valerie, there might be some new beaux for us."

At which point, Hal said, "Don't point, my beauty. And, I don't know what I am going to do with you, given all your flirting."

Thinking how familiar that sounded to me, I said, "Instead of all this flattery, flirting and disputes, why don't we get a little wine and order?" I got the waiter's attention, saying in a loud voice, " Cameriere, prego." They were two of the only words of Italian I knew, and very useful in a restaurant. I told our foursome how I agreed from its ambiance with the red Michelin description of Al Ceppo as *'caratteristico.'* I thought so all the more when I looked at the dishes, Ossobuco, Agnello Paesano, Vitello Francese and Spaghetti Carbonara. When the waiter came over, we each ordered one of those, with salad and vegetables. We did several bottles of Chianti to go with our wonderful meal.

While the girls talked about shopping and this and that, Hal and I got into a political discussion. He asked me what I thought of the first months of the Bush Presidency. I restrained myself to say that I neither liked the President, nor cared much one way or the other. "I became apolitical way back there, and disgusted with the conservatism and frequent stupidity of American politics, and I suppose all politics."

Hal objected to my use of the word 'conservative,' saying "Everyone wants to conserve the good. So, it's a misnomer, as are the other terms, left, liberal, right, etc. Words should be more exact as to what they mean, especially for politics. So much of our confusion comes from the vagueness and misuse of words."

Valerie said, "I couldn't help overhearing some of that, and I agree that it's all confusing. Worse, it's so boring! Can't you guys find something better to talk about."

"You have a point, my dear, as so often,. How about something on aviation?" Shall I tell Hal and Bianca the story I told you about the latest flight with my Air France pilot friend?"

Hal said, "By all means. Please do. Did he let you fly some?"

"Yes, he did. He even complemented my turns, the approach and landing."

Bianca said, "Hal never told me you were a pilot, Chris. Where did you learn that? Or did he do it all for you?"

"Back in North Carolina where I grew up, as I thought I had mentioned, or maybe that was only to Hal. Anyway, I only have about a thousand hours, not in jets, but in 'low and slow' jalopy planes. I wanted to go into jets but I didn't have the money to do it privately. Anyway, at the time, I would have been too tall for jets, or so another friend who had been in the Air Force told me. But, he says now they have redesigned their cockpits to enable pilots even taller than me. He said he had met some F 16 pilots, flying with a national guard unit in Richmond, Virginia, his home town, one of whom boasted of being over six foot, six. At this point, obviously, I am too old to become the pilot I wanted to be. But, it's great that I have this new friend who flies for Air France, and can tell me about it. Even better, he even lets me fly his plane out of Tousssus le Noble Air Field here."

Hal said, "In fact, I remember you telling me you taught a course on aviation history, and now I can see why you do. When we get back to New York, you have to tell me more, and maybe teach me to fly. How would that be?"

"Nothing would give me more pleasure, if I ever go back to New York, that is. I have loved this year so much, I may try to stay in Europe."

Both ladies raised their eyebrows at this, and Valerie said, "That raises all sorts of possibilities, doesn't it?"

Bianca said, "Maybe Chris will move to Rome. Then you all would be here much more, and that can't be bad."

I said, "Wouldn't that be nice. But Paris is more likely since my French is far better than my Italian. In fact, my Italian is more or less non-existent."

Hal said, "And I think you are just bluffing after all the wine you've drunk. In any case, I have to be off, as I go back to New York tomorrow. Come on Bianca, let's go."

It was only close to ten, but I breathed a sigh of relief, wanting as much time alone with Valerie as possible. I asked her what she was thinking now.

She said, as if reading my mind, "It was a lovely dinner and now how about finding a place to dance?"

"Wouldn't that be fun. Let me ask that sympa looking waiter over there if he knows of a place."

I waved at him to come over, and he did. We stood up to pretend we were dancing, and tried to make it known we wanted to do that. He said OK, and took out a pen and tore off a piece of the paper table cloth to write down an address. Taking the slip of paper, I had to ask him about some of his writing, which in typical European style was full of curly Qs. It designated a disco, called the Pala Cavicchi, nearby off of the Piazza Verbana. He told us how to go there by pointing to the left of Via Panama, and then indicating to take another left a little later. I got out a Euro and thanked him, as Valerie gave him a kiss on the cheek. He smiled brilliantly, saying 'Ciao, Ciao,' and some other words we didn't understand.

We found the disco without too much effort about ten minutes later. They charged us twenty Euro apiece for us to enter, which included a drink each. The disk jockey was playing some marvelous Latin music and I led Valerie straight to the dance floor. She said it was a rhumba and she loved to do that. She did it beautifully and I did my best to match her. There is something about dancing to good music that makes you feel so vibrant, and somewhat electrified with all the vibes. We glided, stepped and weaved as we circled the floor, spaced with about five other couples. The music changed to a more conventional disco piece, and a lot of new couples, as well as several single men who got up to dance. After a few minutes of that we went to the bar for our drink. I had a Sambuca, and she a Cynar. Asking for a taste of hers, I found it another good example of the marvelous Italian liqueurs. I asked her what she wanted to do our last day in Rome.

Valerie said, "I think we should go back to the Vatican museum and maybe the one in the Borghese Gardens as well."

"A good idea. I also want to see again so many of the places near our hotel, from the Campo dei Fiori to the Gesu church and the Farnese Palace. But, maybe that will overload us our last day.

"Well, we can see how we feel tomorrow and what the weather is, and so on. Now, how about another dance?"

So saying, she got up and took my left hand. With my right I finished my last sip of the Sambuca, and happily followed her onto the dance floor. The DJ was now playing some romantic fox trots, which we did with the usual moves, sways and twirls. As we weaved around the floor, I couldn't help admiring Valerie all the more. I thought she was by far the prettiest lady there, and I mentally thought again how lucky I was. Stopping, I hugged her and suggested we go. She agreed and we headed for the door and then back the way we had come to look for the bus stop going the other way. After a twenty minute wait it came and we settled in comfortably for the ride back. In a half hour we were back in our room for another night of love and sleep.

The next day was cloudy but rain free. We managed to do all we had thought of, starting with the Vatican Museum and lunch. After that it was the Borghese Gardens and museum. We saved the Campo dei Fiori for drinks and dinner and finished with a walk by the Farnese Palace and the Jesuit church of Jesu. Then it was back to the hotel. Since our flight back to Paris did not leave until four in the afternoon of the next day, we hit the hay, thinking to pack in the morning.

When that came, it took us only an hour or so to pack and we had time for lunch in the neighborhood before heading to the airport for our four thirty flight. We decided on the Vecchia Roma again. Valerie had a risotto del mare and I did my favorite dish, the spaghetti carbonara, accompanied by frascati, the standard Roman white wine. We gloried in all the pleasures we had had on our short trip, from the food and wine, to the monuments and museums, and of course being with one's love in the Eternal City. Looking at my watch, I said we had better get our bags, check out and head for Fiumicino.

We got the taxi a little after two and arrived at the airport over an hour ahead of our flight. Checked in and past security, we were able to have another glass of frascati at the bar before going to the gate. Entering the Airbus 320 we found our usual seats in the rear. This time, I had gotten us on the right side to look east and north, and Valerie took the window seat as agreed. We hoped with luck to see Mont Blanc. At least it was clear in Rome, but as we climbed out, I could already see a few clouds. After the plane leveled off, the pilot came on to say we were at 10.000 meters or about 32,000 feet. Fortunately, it remained more or less partly cloudy with good visibility, and only ten minutes later Valerie said she was starting to see the mountains. They were scattered all over and as I leaned over closer to the window, I wondered how much longer it would take to come close to Mont Blanc. Five minutes later, the pilot solved the problem, saying those on the right side would be able to see Mont Blanc about two miles off and below us in the coming seconds. Its altitude of 4807 meters meant the mountain seemed to rise almost half way up to us, and we could clearly see the principal glacier and the Aiguille du Midi, the jagged peak off to the side of the massif of Mont Blanc. Next came the flight over Geneva and we could see the lake off to its right. Valerie congratulated me for getting us on the correct side for seeing the best sites on this flight.

From there on the mountains became smaller and soon disappeared. Our next views were of the French countryside. We passed Annecy lake and its surroundings, reminding me of the pleasant times I had spent there. But, that was with my first wife. I asked Valerie if I had told her about that.

"No, I don't think so. Please tell me now."

"Well, way back in 1987 when I had just finished Columbia, Henrietta somehow got me to marry her. We had some good times at first, and some great trips. One was to a hotel I discovered by accident in the red Michelin guide. It was a best quality hotel at a good price in a part of France I had heard was very beautiful. It is called the Hotel Beau Site at Talloires, a lake side village midway down the lake we just went over. So in the summer of 1989 we made our way there, via a flight to Paris and train to Annecy. That's one of the great things about teaching, that you get summers off. And I was already doing some courses, at first, at Columbia and then at Baruch. We arrived in Talloires in mid July for a week, which was followed by another week in Paris. I became addicted to life in France with that trip, and when Henrietta and I divorced that autumn, I decided to come back to Paris for my research on Vietnam.

Anyway, the hotel down below at Talloires is sensational. It has about three buildings and a garden which leads down to the water. So, you can lounge about, or play croquet or tennis, and then go swimming in Lac d'Annecy right in front. The food was also great and you had a choice of signing up for the daily menus, or ordering a la carte as you liked. I want to take you there some day, all right?"

"Sounds lovely. Maybe in June or July."

"If we don't do that bike trip instead. Or, maybe we can do it later

in the summer. But, I also want to look into trying to get a job here, or decide if I have to go back to New York and the job at Baruch. As much as I love France, not to speak of you, that will be a difficult choice."

As the plane flew on, we came over some clouds. I said, "What good luck, now that there is no longer anything much to see, we run into clouds, or rather, over them. We should arrive in a half hour or so."

Valerie smiled and said, "Yes, it was so beautiful. The Alps and just looking at the lake from above, I can imagine how lovely it must be. But, if you were there with another woman, maybe we have to do another hotel."

"Very possibly. I need to think that through and check my guide books, and now I feel like reading some."

Giving her a quick caress, I took out my copy of the Guns, Germs and Steel book, and made myself as comfortable as possible. About ten minutes later, the pilot came on to say, "We are beginning our descent. We will land at Paris in about fifteen minutes."

The stewardesses immediately busied themselves with picking up trays, bottles and all the rest. I put up my book, saying, "With all the sightseeing and love-making and trips, I've made very little progress with reading this book. But, never mind, there will always be time for that later, if I don't get too bogged down with my teaching."

The plane descended but remained in the clouds. As comfortable as I was flying, I always started to worry when before landing you stayed in the clouds until you wondered if you were about to hit a hill or the ground. Just then, Valerie said "Now I can see the ground. How high up do you think we are?"

"Looks like maybe two or three thousand feet. I am happy we can land now that the pilot can see the runway."

Less than five minutes later, the pilot told the crew to prepare for landing, and we turned right onto what I gathered was the final approach into a north wind, as we seemed less than a thousand feet up. In minutes we were over the runway and touched down smoothly. The designated hostess said 'bienvenue a Paris,' enjoy your stay. That was in French, and then she, or others, did the same in English and Italian.

There was the usual wait for all the people in front of us to leave us room to go forward to exit the plane. That done, with the usual thank you's to the staff, we made it to the baggage pickup without difficulty. From there, it was the long walk to the train to Paris. We reached the ticket window in about five minutes, got our tickets and took the express whose first stop was the Gare du Nord. We got off at Chatelet/Les Halles and took the metro to the Etoile for the local in the direction of St. Denis. That enabled us to get off at the Monceau stop and we were home by shortly after eight. Not bad, to go from door to door from Rome to Paris, in under five hours. That reminded me of a friend's story about taking the Concorde from New York to Paris and walking in the door of where he was staying there in six hours. He explained that the three hour flight matched the ground travel in both cities. It being Monday, and with me having a class on Tuesday, I got unpacked as quickly as possible and told Valerie I would see her in bed. It worked like that, and despite more love making, I could not go to sleep until after midnight.

CHAPTER EIGHT

TEACHING AND FLYING

The next morning, I reviewed what I would be teaching about, and thought how glad I would be when I got to the twentieth century when the U.S. became so much more involved with the rest of the world. In fact, after several sessions, I would get to the Great War and America's belated entry into that. But, today I had to talk about Reconstruction, the forcible induction of the South into the Republic, the impeachment of President Andrew Johnson in February, 1868, and other late nineteenth century subjects. The course went as planned. As a Southerner, I thought I should not have much trouble with those subjects, and as I was teaching in France, would not have to fear some Yankee back biting about what I said. The course started as planned, with my favorite student, Isabelle Avrillon, asking me why the southern slave owners expected to be treated humanely after what they had done to the slaves. I told her it was a good question, but that she had to realize that many slave owners thought they had treated their slaves very well.

"That's the way it is with history, you know," I said. "It depends on who is telling the story and why. In this case, as usual, both sides were sure they were right. As a boy in the south, I could see the old confederate point of view. But, now,

I agree more with the intent of your question. Since I did my dissertation on questions of historiography I pay special attention to such problems. As they say, the victors always write the history of the wars they fight, and to a great extent that was also the case with the civil war. Are there any more questions about reconstruction or the Civil War?"

This time it was Erica Celeste, who asked, "Why did the South win most of their first battles, but the North most of them after 1863?"

"Again a good question, and I suppose it was mostly to do with economics. That is, when the war started, the South had a prosperous economy, in part based on slavery, and had been preparing for war for several years. They also had good leadership and expected help from Britain. But, on the contrary England sided with the North. After the war started, the North with British help was able to blockade the South. The North steadily increased production and expanded its armies and equipment. Therefore they won the war and it was over by mid April, 1865."

The class over, I figured it would take me about two more classes to reach the twentieth century. I would need to sketch the outlines of the enormous economic development, the expansion of the trans-continental railroad, the final defeat of the Indians and development of the west. Then another class could deal with the Spanish American war of 1898 and the buildup to World War I. As I walked back to my cubicle, who should I see but Claudia Chevalier going into hers. We exchanged greetings and I asked her how she had spent her vacation. She said she had remained in Paris, seeing her new boyfriend, Guy Fillon.

"How are things going with him?"

"He still wants to marry, but is giving me a few months to decide. He says I have until September. Then, if I say no, he will start looking for some other likely girl when the fall semester begins. He is a teacher too as well as an artist. Did I tell you that?"

"What does he teach and where?"

"He does philosophy at Paris Quatre, the Sorbonne."

"Well, I guess that's a good combination, art and philosophy. On the other hand, I'm not sure one wants to be the lover of someone in the same profession. What do you think?"

"I wonder about that also. But, most of the time we get on famously. Where did your pilot friend know him?"

"He told me, I think at his university. I forget where that was, and I will have to ask him again. But, now I remember, he said his friend taught at the Sorbonne. So, for sure, it is the same guy. Are you still planning on the bike trip in the summer?"

"Very much so. Guy also bikes all over and likes the idea. But, my girl friend who was going to go says she can't now since she got a summer job. Will Valerie want to go?"

"She says so. Do you know when you want to start?"

"I think, probably in August, when everyone goes on vacation. But, just because of that, maybe we should do July. What do you think?"

"I would favor July. That might give me the time to figure out afterwards what to do when the next school year begins. I have a job in New York, but would love to get something here. Do you have any ideas for me?"

"Have you asked here already?"

"Yes, but predictably they say I have to go through all those channels, and they tell me normally they only hire French for teaching positions."

"That's true, unless you become famous enough, that they can override those restrictions. They do that when they want some well known person to be a full professor."

"That pretty well excludes me, for a while at least. Maybe I can get a job teaching English or some business thing. I was even a journalist once, and I should ask at the Herald Tribune, or somewhere. Do you want a drink? It would be nice to recover from our classes and catch up a bit. I can tell you about our trip to Rome."

Claudia said, "D'accord. Let's do the nearby bar on Rue de l'Hotel St. Paul. I don't have much time, but we can do that for an hour or so. I have some things to do in my cubicle, so I will come get you in about half an hour."

We walked around the corner and got to the bar by six. We got a good table and ordered a half 'pitcher,' as they call a carafe here, of sauvignon blanc. I had always wondered why in Paris they used the word 'carafe,' for the water you want, and 'pitcher,' for the wine. It is the opposite of the case in America, as in so many things. As soon as we were seated Claudia asked me to tell her about Rome.

"It's such a fantastic city, you know. With so much history, sites and monuments all combined with very agreeable walking, great food and even some nightlife. I think, however, Paris is probably ahead for night life and for the food. But, *chacun a son gout,* or everyone to do with his taste, to do with things like that."

"And where did you stay?"

"A hotel to match the city, except for the price, which was several times what I usually pay. It's the Hotel Teatro di Pompeo, ideally located just off of the Campo dei Fiori and close to the Forum and all the other incredible sites in *Centro Storico* as they call historic Rome. Our room was in the annex next door to the hotel, which was a little cheaper. It had air conditioning and you walked up to our room through a courtyard, with fragrant rosemary bushes and charming birds singing all the time."

"You make it sound so wonderful that I want to go right now. But, I guess I have to wait for another time."

So saying, she moved close to me and put her hand on my arm, saying, "If we break up with our current friends, maybe you can show me Rome. Will that be possible, do you think?"

"*On verra*. But, as of now I would have to say not likely, since I am getting on so well with Valerie."

"Well, good trips can do that. I remember that was the case with about half of my previous affairs. I had a German lover once, for instance, who took me to Baden Baden and various other lovely spas. There's nothing like making love, after you've seen new things and luxuriated in new beautiful surroundings."

At this point, Claudia said she had to be going and stood up. I rose and kissed her on the cheeks, saying, "See you after class on Thursday, or whenever. Don't do anything foolish unless you want to."

"We'll see, and *a jeudi*," she responded as she walked briskly out of the bar. I poured what was left in the pitcher into my glass and took it to the bar. The barman was there, and I asked him, "*Quoi de nouveau*, Charles?"

"Nothing much. *Plus ca change, plus c'est la meme chose*, as they say."

"Yes, you're right, especially at my age. But, I'm just back from a wonderful trip to Rome. That should set me up for a nice finish for my semester of teaching."

"Well, enjoy it," he said and promptly started to pour a drink for another customer. I finished my glass and set out for home. When I got there, it was about seven, and Valerie, who said she had just got in, asked if I wanted to go out for dinner. I agreed and we did another nice meal and drinks in Montmartre. The next day, I called Francois and asked him when we could meet. He suggested a drink at seven at the Deauville on the Champs Elysées, the next week on Wednesday, May 2nd, and I readily agreed.

That came quickly. When I arrived, he greeted me, and asked about my trip to Rome. I told him a few of the details, and then asked him when we could go flying again. He suggested the next week on Thursday, but I told him that was a teaching day, and we settled on the Wednesday after that, which was May 16. Then, I asked him how his love life was going, and if he had seen Erica recently. He replied that indeed he had seen her on a recent layover in Stockholm, but only for tea as he had only a couple of hours and couldn't drink before his flight.

"Still, it was great to see her, brief as it was. I really like looking at her and started to get an erection. I had to get up and go to the bathroom to hide that, and fortunately she didn't seem to notice. But, on the other hand if she had, it might have been good, to do with the next time I can make love to her."

"And when might that be?"

"She said she would try to get a week off and come to Paris in June. I will really look forward to that, and hope I can work out a few visits without ruining my marriage."

"What's the rest of her name, by the way. Erica what?"

"It's Erica Jacobson. Why, do you want to look her up?"

"No. It's just that I met a really attractive lady from Stockholm a few years ago. But, it was on a street here, and we only did a drink or two before she went back to Stockholm. I tried to call the number she had given me a few days later. But, I was told, 'You have the wrong number.' She must have given me a fake number or something."

"If you give me her name, I can ask Erica to look her up."

"If only I could remember it. I had wondered if it was also Erica something. But maybe it was Ingrid. Anyway, now that I am getting on so well with Valerie, I shouldn't be into such games."

Francois said that was probably wise, and we turned our attention to watching all the people passing by on the Champs Elysées in front of us. I asked Francois what would be his next flight. He said it would be to Amsterdam on Friday at four with return to Paris at nine. I asked him how such frequent trips worked with his marriage. That is, making it so difficult to schedule dinners together and the like. He said it was not easy, and that since he and Sophie were increasingly distant anyway, it only exacerbated the problems. I looked at my watch and saw it was approaching eight, when I had asked Valerie to join us.

Just at that point, Valerie came walking up, looking beautiful as ever. I introduced her to Fancois, and I could see his appreciation of her. We had been drinking Ricards, but when Valerie requested a sauvignon blanc, I decided to switch to that. Francois had a Perrier. Valerie asked Francois if he had children. He replied no, and I supposed that was just as well, given all his absences from home for flying, and the apparent state of his marriage. She then asked about his flying, and if she could accompany us the next time.

"Sure, why not?" he said. "Obviously, I'm used to passengers, and I don't suppose Chris will mind."

"Indeed not. But, I hope the weather will not be bad, and that I will not disgrace myself. The last time was all right, and I seemed to remember a few things, *n'est-ce pas*, Francois?"

"In fact, I was surprised at how well you did. I assumed that like many small plane pilots, you probably would mess up the landing. But, you did it quite well. As it is getting on, may I suggest we eat at Ladurée, a belle époque restaurant just next door?"

"Wonderful," I said, "and as you Parisians mostly eat after nine, we should have no trouble getting a table."

Francois asked for the check which we shared, and that paid, stood up to go. Francois said, "*Apres vous, Mademoiselle,*" and we followed Valerie out. It was just to the right towards the FDR Metro stop and away from the Place de la Concorde. Sure enough, we found a lovely table for four in the corner looking toward the Arc de Triumphe.

No sooner seated, the waiter asked what we would like to drink, and we replied, "*du vin*." We ordered a bottle of Burgundian Pinot Noir which was surprisingly cheap, at eight euros the bottle. Then, we ordered; I had duck, Francois lamb and Valerie, fish. The dishes were all delicious.

Over the wine, of which we ordered a second bottle, I began to talk about my idea for a book on wine. I described briefly the trip Valerie and I had taken to Burgundy just after we had met, noting that the Pinot Noir bottle came from one of the places we had visited, near Beaune.

"Will you be making more trips to do with that," asked Francois. "And when do you plan to start writing?"

"I'm not sure on either count," I replied. "Nothing much will be done this spring, as I am too busy with the teaching. Maybe, I will break off from the proposed bike trip to the southwest, and see the Bordeaux wine country. If I can afford to stay in Paris, then I will start writing next autumn."

"Can I stick with you when you do that," asked Valerie?

"It would be marvelous if you stay with me, and you could tell me some more of the things Keith told you about wine in Bordeaux last October. By the way Francois, Keith is an English buyer of wines who is a friend of ours. What is his news, Valerie?"

"I haven't seen him since we got back from Rome, but he left me a message on a call from London, saying that he hopes to get to Paris in May. What should I tell him the next time we communicate?"

"You might invite him to a dinner at a good time. Do you have any interest in such social life, Francois?"

"Sure! Let me know, and I would like to learn more about wine. I have always liked it, and an uncle in Normandy tried to grow and make it, but without much success. That was on a farm he owned near Rouen, where I grew up."

With that, as we had finished eating, we asked for the check. It was rather expensive, but since Valerie was working, we could split it three ways as we had done for the cocktails, which made it easily possible.

Outside, I asked Francois if we should come to his place on May 9 or meet him at the Toussus le Noble airfield, and at what time. He suggested we come *chez lui* at eleven or so for an afternoon flight. That decided, we went our separate ways.

The next days passed without incident, though Valerie informed me she had made a date with Keith for us to have dinner on Wednesday, May 23. That was perfect, a week after the flight with Francois, who we could invite to join us. On May 16, we left a little after ten to make our way to Rue Dantzig, and Francois greeted us with enthusiasm. "It's a great day for our little venture. Perfect weather for flying with a few clouds and light winds. Let's go, and my garage is only a few steps away."

But, wouldn't you know, we got into a traffic jam just outside of Paris. That delayed our arrival until after one. Then, as we were hungry we had a sandwich at the airfield cafe and got to his plane shortly after. Valerie climbed into the back as instructed and I took the left seat, and Francois the right or co-pilot seat. Francois told me to try to do whatever I wanted with the flight, saying he would be watching closely and take over if any problem arose. Francois started the engine, and I taxied over to the takeoff spot at the southern end of runway 310, headed to the northwest. The takeoff was smooth and as we reached cruising speed, Valerie said, "How wonderful, I can see why you like flying so much. And there's the Eiffel Tower just over there. Can we go by it and wave at the tourists?"

Francois said, "Of course. And next time I will let you sit here and you can take the controls some, that is if Chris keeps flying so well."

As we were already heading northwest, it was only necessary to turn slightly to the right to put the Eiffel Tower straight ahead. We passed it at two thousand meters, the altitude given us by flight control, which put us too high to have any tourists see our waving. *Tant pis*, we did it anyway. A minute or so later, air control signaled us to descend to 1500 meters and told us to not go higher, given the descent paths of some incoming airliners. That was all the better for even better views of the rest of Paris, and I turned right more or less over the Arc de Triumph. It was wonderful to see the symmetry of the line from it down to the Place de la Concorde, with the Louvre just beyond, as well as Notre Dame slightly farther and just to the west.

I asked Francois and Valerie where else they wanted to go. Francois said, "Why not continue as you are and fly by the Charles de Gaulle Airport at Roissy. That is, you will have to turn a bit more to the right and go northwest about five kilometers to avoid the closed space right over it, but we can see it well with the visibility we have."

Valerie said, "In that case, maybe I'll see some planes taking off for London. Could that be one over there?"

Francois demurred, saying it was setting up for a turn to the south and Italy or Spain. I asked Francois how flights to Russia were treated on the day of May 9, now a week ago, when he flew there and they celebrated the defeat of the Nazis. He replied that it changed nothing, except for closing certain areas around some airports where there were aerobatics and flight maneuvers to commemorate the occasion.

Valerie asked, "And that one over there climbing to the left, might it be going to London?"

Francois replied, "Yes, I think so. It is too small to be going to America and its flight path if held will take it towards London. Chris, now that we have passed the northern edge of the field, how about turning to the right after another hundred meters or so, And then do another right to aim at the Sacre Coeur church which in a few minutes you will easily see. From there, there are nice views of Montmartre and maybe you will be able to see your house."

That done, in a couple of minutes Valerie said, "Look at that! That must be Montmartre just below and I think that could be the Parc de Monceau over there at about two o'clock. If it is, then our house is just a little way off to the left. Probably on that little street parallel to the bigger street, which probably is the Boulevard Malesherbes. But our street is so tiny, only one block long, and our house is at 15 Rue de Vezelay more or less in the middle of it."

I said, "Yes, I think you are right. Do you see it, Francois?"

"There's such a jumble of streets there, I'm not sure. But, yes, now I see a tiny one block street. So, that makes your day, no?"

With more or less one voice, Valerie and I said '*Exactement*' ! What could be nicer than a bird's eye view of one's home!"

I then lowered the left wing for a turn to the left, saying, "Now I think I will head back for the landing. Do you agree?" They did, and we kept going for another five kilometers or so to the south, and seeing the airfield, I began to descend."

But, at that point, Francois grabbed the stick and pulled back slightly, saying "Keep your altitude of 2000 meters until you fly over the field and make sure they are doing the same runway for landing."

We did, and sure enough, I saw the wind socks now blowing from the south. So, I radioed the tower and they said, "Cleared to land on runway 20." That meant descending to 1000 feet (625 meters). turning left again and flying another kilometer to the east, before doing a turn back to the north on the downwind, another left to the west on base, before making still another left turn onto the final headed south-southwest into the wind. The landing went smoothly, and Francois said, "You did it. I couldn't have done better. Now, let's get back to the hangar and be on our way."

It was close to four and I wondered if we would have rush hour problems with traffic again. But, it was not too bad and

Francois left us off at the Etoile for our metro. Valerie said since it was not even five she would go back to Shakespeare & Co. to see if they had any work for her that late in the day. I asked her if she would like to meet me at seven at the Perigourdine. She suggested eight, and we went our separate ways.

I went home and spent a couple of hours reading and reviewing my notes for the class next day on the march of the U.S. towards Imperialism with the defeat of Spain in 1898. Then, I again took the metro via the change of trains at Etoile, and got off at the Louvre stop. That was on the wrong side of the river, but I always loved taking that walk from the Palais Royale to the front side of the Louvre, and through it to the Cour Carré on its back side. That in turn led to the pedestrian only Pont des Arts, which is by far the most beautiful way to cross the Seine. Then it was an easy ten minutes walk up the river to the Perigourdine bar restaurant. Valerie was already there and greeted me lovingly. We got a table in front which looked towards the other side of the Place St. Michel, and off to the left a little farther on, Notre Dame.

We ordered our wine, and I asked Valerie what she had thought of our flight. She said, "As I have said over and over, I found it very wonderful. I especially liked the take-off and climb out. And then all the sights, from the Eiffel Tower to the airfield at Roissy to seeing Montmartre, and even our tiny street. I couldn't believe it. Francois seemed to like your flying, and I hope we can do it again before too long."

"Right on! But, that will be after our date with Keith, next Wednesday, the 23rd. Do you think we should invite Francois to that dinner?"

"Yes. If he is there, maybe you will be less bothered by Keith's attention to me and the flirty remarks he makes."

"All right. I'll call Francois to see if he can join us for that."

After paying for our drinks, we walked to the Parcheminerie, a restaurant on the tiny street of the same name a two minute walk away from the Seine on the other side of the Boulevard St. Michel. It had been recommended by a friend back in New York, who had lived next door to it a few years ago. He said the food was delicious and modestly priced, and that it was on one of the oldest streets of Paris. We found the description accurate, with everything delicious and there was great service. I especially appreciated our waitress, a charming young lady almost as pretty as Valerie. But, at my urging we left before having a dessert and headed home. I wanted a good night's sleep before my class.

The class went well, with the students seeming more interested as we approached contemporary problems. There were questions about why the U.S. could not have allowed Spain to keep its territories. I pointed out that maybe that could have happened except for their blowing up of the battleship *Maine* in February, 1898, and the American sympathy for the Cuban revolt against Spain, which had started several years before that. As so often in history, the ironies were immense. The Cubans started their revolt which was much like that of the U.S. against Britain a little over a century earlier, but now the European powers were backing Spain. The Spanish, however, failed to protect their colonies, and the United States easily won the "splendid little war." It acquired also the Philippines and got dominance over Puerto Rico with the departure of Spain. America also was now an Imperial Power. The class over, I could look forward to teaching the interesting but terrible march toward the "Great War" of 1914-1918, our next subject. As if that was anything to look forward to, but such are history classes. So often it seemed you go 'from one catastrophe to another.'

After another drink with Claudia at the Hotel St. Paul bar to discuss our classes, I returned home, and Valerie greeted me with a simple meal. I called Francois and asked him if he would like to join us for our dinner with Keith on May 23. He said yes, and that I would have to tell him after we found out where and when it would be. I asked Valerie when she thought Keith would be in Paris, and she said he had left word he would arrive Monday, the 21st. That meant we wouldn't know until two days before our Wednesday dinner. I called Francois back to see if he would be in the Tuesday before and he replied in the affirmative. So, l would be able to tell him in time for the dinner.

The twenty first came rapidly, and that evening Valerie told me Keith had proposed to meet us at the celebrated Lasserre restaurant at the Rond Point of the Champs Elysées on the Avenue FDR, in the Eighth Arrondissement at eight o'clock on Wednesday, the 23rd. I called Francois just after and told him. He said he would see us there, but wondered how expensive it would be. I said no doubt, very, but Keith, being rich and charging his company, would probably pay.

When we met at the restaurant two days later, Keith was wearing what looked like a Saville Row suit and the whole works, boutonniere, tie and spats. He greeted us with the news that the Paris office of the International Wine Shop, Ltd. would be opened with a grand soirée on Thursday,

June 16, starting at six. He said Valerie as the manager should get it ready for that, starting on Monday the week before. He asked her if that would work well with her resigning from Shakespeare & Co.? She said that it should be good, and she would tell the company tomorrow, giving them over three weeks' notice. She said, "How exciting, and thank you, Keith. Now I get to work in a different area, while doing two of my favorite things, Paris and Wine."

Just then, Francois came in, and I went over to lead him to the table we had been given, nicely located in the back, left corner. I did the introductions, and Francois took his seat on the room side. Valerie said, "Keith just told us that his company, The International Wine Shop, will be opening a new office in Paris. He has asked me to manage it with his help, between there and London. To celebrate the opening there will be a soirée Thursday night, June 16, at six. It's on Rue de la Chaise near Sevres-Babylone, and I hope you can come."

Keith followed that up with, "I insist on it and want to be able to say that a distinguished pilot of Air France will be there. At least, that's what Chris and Valerie tell me you are. D'accord?"

"Certainly, I would love to. But, I have to see what my schedule is. I hope there is no conflict."

I asked if he could change his flight if there was a conflict, and Francois said he could try, but that sometimes it was difficult. That over, we looked at the menu and Keith signaled a waiter to order the wine. Asking our assent, which we readily gave, he chose a St. Emilion that he said was supposed to be very good. We all started with seafood salads. After that, Keith and Valerie had their specialty of *Turbot au Romarin*, meaning that fish with rosemary. Francois and I did the lamb specialty, with herbs and mushrooms. The restaurant was one of the best in Paris, with two Michelin stars, and the meal lived up to its reputation.

Valerie asked Keith to tell us more about his company. "Naturally, I am curious about it now that I will be working there, and in addition wine is such a fascinating subject. I am sure all of us would like to hear whatever you can tell us, all the more so as we are now so enjoying this superb St. Emilion."

Feeling quite mellow, Keith finished eating a big bite of his fish and some of the accompanying spinach, and began to talk. "Well, to begin, you recall wine is why Chris and I met, and hence why we are all here. I started working at the International Wine Shop about twenty years ago, after finishing at Cambridge, with a master's in economics. Since I knew some French from summers on the Cote d'Azur with my parents, they put me into the European section. But, the company is quite global, now doing a lot of business with America, Australia, Chile, Asia, South Africa and all over.

Rather quickly, if I do say so myself, I was put in charge of France, the biggest of all our markets. Now, I will have the great talents and charm of Valerie to head the Paris office."

As he said the last phrases, he smiled archly at Valerie, and then quizzically at me. No doubt he was wondering how I would take him being the boss of Valerie. I looked back at him and said, "Keith, as I told Francois, I am very much in love with Valerie, and hope you don't give me trouble by flirting too much with her. And please don't give her too much difficult work either."

Keith said, "You will have to see, or rather believe what Valerie tells you, *'n'est-ce pas?*" I nodded with a skeptical look, and was glad when Francois spoke. He asked, "Do you mostly buy French wines, or Italian or other?" Keith said, "Some of all, but mostly French, and in addition, we sell some British products here, such as special cheeses, leather goods and woolens." Valerie added, "So, we do all kinds of things, but specialize in wines. Is that it?" Keith nodded and asked if we would like dessert. We asked to see the menu again. Looking at that, I said, "Maybe we can share two of the maple walnut crème brulées?" They agreed, and we did, afterwards asking for the check. As hoped, Keith paid, saying he would charge the four hundred euro bill to the Company. We thanked him profusely, and stood up to go our separate ways. Thus ended one of the best meals I had ever had, and I guessed it would be hard or impossible to ever top.

The next weeks were wonderful, with lovely weather, nice walks, and interesting teaching. Ah, the pleasures of Paris in springtime. I spent two classes on World War 1. The first subject was that old standby for teachers, the causes of the Great War. We began by citing the rising anger of the various countries. Those included, France's desire for reversing its 1870 defeat by Germany, Germany's resentment of England's dominance around the world, the rising nationalisms in what would become Yugoslavia, and Russia's resentment of the activities of Austria and Germany in central and eastern Europe. Then, I discussed the growing tensions rising from the Imperialist rivalries in Africa. At Fashoda, on the upper Nile in what is now Sudan, in 1898, France almost went to war with England as it tried to expand eastward into English controlled territories. Then, the Germans challenged the French in Morocco in 1904-5 and 1911. In 1911 also, Italy seized Tripoli from the Turks. Those crises overlapped with the three Balkan crises of 1908 and 1912-1913. They directly involved Germany, Austria, Russia and the Turks, with England and France also supporting their own different interests.

Entangling alliances made compromises almost impossible. Those were the Triple Alliance of Austria-Hungary, Germany and Italy, which opposed the Triple Entente of England, France and Russia. The first began in 1879 when Germany linked with Austria-Hungary, and was joined by Italy three years later. When France made a treaty with Russia in 1894, and England joined France in 1904 and Russia in 1907, the die was cast. The final spark came June 28, 1914, when a Serbian assassinated the Austrian heir apparent, Archduke Francis Ferdinand.

Events moved inexorably toward war from that point. Austria decided to crush Serbia, and gave it an ultimatum, July 23. But, already angry at the 1908 Austrian annexation of Bosnia and confident of Russian support, the Serbs were defiant. Austria declared war on Serbia July 28. Russia mobilized the next day, and Germany, taking that as an act of war, declared war on Russia August 1. Germany had hoped England would not come into the war, but when Germany invaded Belgium and France on August 3, England and France declared war against Germany and its Alliance the following days.

Laying out all those details ended the class, and next I would have to trace the history of that terrible war, which took close to ten million lives. When I did that, I told the students I would have to race through the remaining subjects, with almost no details, so that we could finish the course by Thursday, June 21, the last day of classes. That meant how World War 1 ended as well as the Russian Revolution. Then, came the 1920's, the rise of Hitler, Japan and World War 11, over the next four classes. The last classes would have to skim over the Cold War, the other wars from Korea to Vietnam and Iraq, as well as the political history of the later twentieth century.

Such skimming is hard work, but by now I was somewhat used to it after over ten years of teaching such courses at Baruch in New York. Being in Europe, with different preoccupations and students, I naturally fell farther behind with my teaching than usual. So, I was not surprised at the rush of my last month of teaching. During the last sessions I sought out Claudia to find out what plans she had made for the bike trip. She said she and Guy would like to leave in the first week of July, and asked if Valerie and I and could do that. I said I would check, but doubted Valerie could, since she had just started a new job at the Wine Shop. After the last class, I told Claudia I would call to let her know if I could join them. I also asked her where a good place to get bikes was. She said, "I know of a good one in the Fifth Arrondissement near the Metro Censier Daubenton. It is on the Rue de Fer à Moulin and called simply Velo. By the way, that is the most common French word for bicycles and comes from the nineteenth century word *vélocipede*."

I thanked Claudia and headed home. When I got there, Valerie said she was now sorry that she had just started her job, because she would very much like to do the bike trip. But, she also liked her job and was certainly not going to jeopardize it by going off on a trip so soon after starting. She asked me if I wanted to go on my own, and tell her about it afterwards.

I said, "You are such an angel. I really would like to go, but are you sure you wouldn't mind? You know how much I love you, and there's no way I'm going to mess that up with Claudia. Besides, now she loves Guy Fillon, and he is going along. So, how will it be if I set out with them on Thursday, July 5. That's the day Claudia specified when I last talked with her. We should be back about a month later. What friends will you be seeing while I am gone? On the other hand, don't tell me, so I won't get jealous."

"Well, with Guy going with you and Claudia, who knows? In any case, I will certainly see Keith again, now that I am working in the Paris office of his company. And you never know what new types I might meet. Do you want me to flirt with them to keep your interest?"

"In fact, I am more confident of you now. After our wonderful trips and seeing how well you do everything, including seducing me, I think I won't worry too much. Shall we do a tumble to confirm our love?"

I led her to the bed and it was another one of those times when you think you are in paradise. Valerie seemed to love it as well and we went out for another good dinner at a restaurant recommended to me by Claudia. It was the Perroquet Vert just to the west of the Montmartre Cemetery. It had been a favorite place of Jean Gabin, Yves Montand, Edith Piaf and other celebrities. To get there, we took a fifteen minute walk up the Rue de Monceau, with a zigzag past the Rue de Rome to the Rue des Dames, and on it to just past the Avenue de Clichy to reach the Rue Cavalotti, where the restaurant was. It was a charming bistrot with the usual posters, mahogany beams, pastel walls and French windows. We had a nice, simple dinner and did not see any celebrities that we recognized. We had to imagine the previous celebrities with the Artichokes Piaf and Entrecote Gabin. The dinner over, we made our way again to Montmartre's Place du Tertre where we had several glasses of a delicious port. That was at our favorie bar restaurant there, Chez la Mere Catherine. I was again astonished that though it had been founded in 1793 at the height of the Revolution, it still continues as a flourishing bourgeois establishment.

The next days passed calmly, except for having to rush through my last courses. One day off, I went to the Velo shop on Rue de Fer à Moulin and bought my bicycle. I had asked Valerie if she wanted me to get one for her, but she said she should do it in order to get the right size and features, and might do that before I got back.

CHAPTER NINE

A BIKE TRIP WITH CLAUDIA AND GUY

As arranged, at one o'clock on July 5, I met Claudia and Guy at the Gare de Montparnasse for our 14:13 train to Chartres. We found our *voiture* in the train, hung our bikes on the hooks going into it, and took our seats. We had decided to start our bike trip in Chartres to ride our first 89 kilometers in comfort, and we arrived on time at 15:33. Since, unlike Claudia and Guy, I had not been there, I asked them if we could at least see the Cathedral. I had read that it was the *"reine des Cathedrales de France."* They agreed, saying they hoped I could do it quickly, as they wanted to stay in a *gite,* or shelter they thought was about two hours away by bike.

After our arrival we made the short walk from the station to the Cathedral across the Boulevard de la Resistance. I was immediately impressed by its *portail Royale*, or royal gate. My guide book explained that it, along with parts of the façade, crypt, towers, and stained glass windows, were Romanesque masterpieces from about 1100 which had survived a fire in 1194. After that came the Gothic masterpieces of the rest of the church. Like most visitors, I was stunned by the magnificence of the interior, the choir and transept, and especially the 12th and 13th century *vitraux* or stained glass windows. I told

Claudia and Guy I was ready to leave after about half an hour, and we made our way back to the station and got our bikes.

We set out towards Orleans and found the *gite* two hours later about half way there. It was simple but comfortable enough with about a dozen beds. There were only two other couples there, who, fortunately, did not snore. The next day, we used our coffee maker for a simple breakfast with the bread we had brought, and set off by ten for the several hour trip to Orleans. It was great fun biking with such pleasant companions and seeing the lovely scenery of fields, streams and forests. At meal and rest times, it also greatly helped my French since that was what Claudia and Guy spoke almost all the time. We did a simple lunch, and afterwards looked briefly at the Maison de Jeanne d'Arc. She had stayed in that house in Orleans for several days at the time of her inspiration to break the English siege of the city which climaxed some five hundred years ago, May 8, 1429. We also rapidly cased the early sixteenth century Cathedral Ste. Croix, which also earned stars in the Michelin guide for its grace and charm.

From Orleans, we set out to the southwest towards Blois, the first of the Loire River chateau we wanted to pass by, if not visit. We had discussed over lunch if we also wanted to go another 25 miles east to the famous Romanesque Abby of Saint-Benoit sur Loire, but decided against that as Orleans had already been a detour to the east for us. Since we would be seeing so many wonders, we thought now we should as much as possible stick to our planned itinerary.

Blois was sixty one kilometers away, and we arrived about four hours later in time to find a cheap room for three at the Anne de Bretagne hotel, next to the chateau. The hotel was named for the daughter of King Louis X1 (r.1461-1483), who as the wife of King Louis X11 (r.1498-1515) helped to rule an expanded France after her father's death in 1483. We did an early dinner, and discussed what we would do the next days. Though Claudia and Guy had seen Chartres, they had not seen all the other chateaux of the Loire valley. We decided we would do the most recommended ones. With our guide books, that would mean the cathedrals of Blois, followed by those of Amboise, Chenonceaux, Azay-le-Rideau and Tours. We thought we might skip the last since Tours had fewer attractions than most of our other sites. Bypassing it, we could go on to Angers, and from there to Puy du Fou and Poitiers.

I interrupted at that point to ask if Puy was a word that meant something. Guy explained that it was a corruption of a latin word for mountain sometimes used in France. Claudia said that after Poitiers she wanted to go to the Michelin starred cities of Saintes, Perigueux, Sarlat, Rocamadur, Conques and Carcassone. She said that finally we could go to Montpelier, Nimes, the Pont du Gard, and Avignon. From the last we could take a train back to Paris. Guy said that he thought we were going too fast if we wanted to do even a three week trip. Three weeks would mean getting to Avignon on the twenty sixth for the train back to Paris. We decided therefore to do more days in some of the cities, such as Angers, Poitiers, Carcasonne, Nimes and Avignon. Claudia suggested we write down the schedule of the rest of our trip when we had the time. I proposed we do that the next morning before we did the Chateau de Blois. They agreed and we went back to the hotel for sleep.

The next day, we rose by eight and were at the Chateau de Blois by eleven, among its first visitors that day. The chateau was built of brick and stone in the early 1500s on the orders of Louis X11 and Francois the First, both of whom resided in Blois. Its gracious style, court and terrace overlooking the St. Nicolas church and the Loire earn it the coveted three stars in our Michelin guide. The Italian style had been favored for the Francois *1er* wing and some of its statues make it a *chef d'ouvre* of the gothic architecture of the late French Renaissance. The chateau contains several museums, including one founded by the great nineteenth century magician, Robert Houdin, a native of Blois. He inspired the famous magician Houdini's assumed name. We were properly impressed.

After an hour or so there, we went to get our bikes, stored in a room in the basement of the hotel, and set out for Amboise about 23 miles to the southwest. Although the Chateau d'Amboise also had many interesting things to see, I was even more anxious to see the last residence of the great Leonardo da Vinci, the Manoir du Cloux, also known as the Clos Lucé, just off to its side. Charles V111, the son of Louis X1 and husband of Anne de Bretagne, passed his childhood at the Chateau d'Amboise and renovated it after 1489. Its fine chapel, works of art and beautiful view of the Loire make it another must- see of the Loire Valley. We examined the gardens, ornaments and statues there before walking the short distance to the Clos Lucé. It had been a medieval fortified manor before being converted into a mini chateau. Leonardo stayed there after his arrival in late 1516 or early 1517, and it seemed a surprisingly simple residence for the last habitat of such a great man. But, I thought that was only another evidence of his greatness, with his preference of the essential over the ornate.

Born in 1552, Leonardo Da Vinci grew up in Vinci, a village of fifty house-holds forty five kilometers to the west of Florence, about half way to Pisa. At about eighteen he was sent to Florence to study with the noted artist and sculptor, Verrocchio. He quickly surpassed his master, especially in painting, and went on to great achievements in innumerable fields. They included studies of the human body, of architecture, urban planning and water works. Aside from painting masterpieces such as the Last Supper and Mona Lisa, he came close to inventing the airplane, parachute and submarine, and was certainly one of the most brilliant people of all times. Then, about 1516, it is not known exactly when or how, at the invitation of the French King, Francois the First, he moved to the Loire valley of north central France to spend the last months of his life. Accompanied by disciples Francesco Melzi and Jiacomo Caprotti (Salai), several servants and mules, they somehow made it safely to the Manoir du Cloux. Fortunately, no accident, blizzard or storm harmed them, since, incredibly, they were carrying the Mona Lisa, St. Anne,

St. Jean the Baptist, and other masterpieces. It is known they traveled some three months from Milan and across Alpine passes to Grenoble and Lyon before reaching the valley of the Loire.

There is very little information on the more than two years Leonardo spent in France, before his death at Clos Lucé on May 2, 1519. It is known that he assisted with court spectacles, and designed chateaux and canals, for a recompense of 700 golden crowns a year. No doubt, at 64 he knew he was nearing the end of his life, and his greatest works had been done in his native Italy, mostly Florence and Milan. By 1517 his left arm was partially paralyzed and he ceased to paint since he was left handed. But, the king, under whom things Italian became all the rage in France, knew of the greatness of Leonardo, and urged by his sister, succeeded in getting the great artist to the Manoir du Cloux. Once there, King Francois loved to spend evenings with Leonardo, though one wonders how they communicated. Was it with an interpreter or did they understand enough of the other's latin language to have conversations? Another Italian, forty eight years younger, hired by the same king of France, the sculptor Benvenuto Cellini, testified that Francois indeed spoke some Italian.

After reading with fascination what we could about these wonders, we unlocked our bikes from one another and set out for the famous Chateau Chenonceaux. Since there was frequently nowhere to properly lock our bikes, we came up with the idea of locking them to each other. That way, any thief would have to take all of them, and fortunately no one did. Chenonceaux was less than ten miles to the south-southeast and after a light lunch we arrived and checked into the relatively cheap Relais

Chenonceaux. It was only about four in the afternoon which gave us almost two hours to wander through the beautiful Chateau and examine its lovely gardens overlooking the Cher, a tributary of the Loire. Built by Francois the First after 1515, a little later it was furnished and improved by two of the great queens of France, the near contemporaries, Diane de Poitiers (1499-1566) and Catherine de Medici (1519-1589). The two queens each designed a garden on either side of the Chateau which came to bear their names.

Walking from our hotel, we approached the Chateau Chenonceaux by an impressive alley of plane trees which led to a drawbridge over a moat to the dungeon, controlling access to the Chateau. It was in the form of a bridge over the Cher and one is astonished at the interaction of the water with the beautiful building, as if it were a ship in full sail. As we were examining the handsome chapel, rooms and hallways, Guy held our attention with a narration of how a finance minister of three kings, named Bohier, had managed to buy the property in pieces over twenty years and then destroyed the previous edifice except for its dungeon. His wife, Catherine Briconnet, oversaw most of the building of the magnificent new Chateau over the Cher. She, the two queens and three other owners over the next centuries became known as the 'six femmes' who were most responsible for the beauty of Chateau Chenonceau.

After a peaceful night in our hotel, including conversation about all the beauty we had been seeing over a good dinner and nightcaps, we set out the next day for another top rated chateau built over a river, Azay le Rideau. It was on the Indres, another tributary of the Loire, twenty seven kilometers to the southwest of Tours. Our guidebook spoke of its "unforgettable impression of harmony and elegance," even if it was less grand than Chenonceau. We agreed as well with its characterization as one of the greatest successes of the Renaissance. It had been built by another financier, Gilles Berthelot, from 1518 to 1527, helped by his wife, Philippe Lesbahy. But in 1528 King Francois confiscated the Chateau. Moreover he forced his enemy Berthelot into exile, where he died.

After an hour admiring the spendours of Azay le Rideau and its gardens and views, we did the fifteen miles west-northwest in the direction of Angers to the next Chateau, Langeais. Built in the 1460s over the Roman and Medieval forts that were there, it houses impressive furnishings and tapestries. It became even more famous after 1491 as the site of the marriage that year of King Charles VIII and Anne de Bretagne. Guy entertained us with more stories from the history of the times as well as of the period of the earlier Hundred Years War, with its many battles in the region. He explained that he knew a lot of such stories because of his teaching. Even though his specialty was philosophy, he did quite a lot of French history to do with explaining the progress of culture and thought before the Enlightenment.

After a quick tour of a half hour at Langeais, we got on our bikes and set out to the southwest for a few miles to Ussé, the fifteenth century Chateau on the Indre close to the Loire that was used by Perrault for his story of the Sleeping Beauty. You could easily see why looking at the beautiful white towers which must have served Disney for many of his creations as well. Next, it was northwest to Saumur, the "Pearl of Anjou," about twenty miles to the west. Its charming old town and fourteenth century Chateau overlooking the Loire seemed less interesting and we soon left for Angers, another forty miles to the west. Since it was still late afternoon, that meant getting there in time for a good sleep. With the help of our guides we found a reasonably cheap, well located hotel, the

St. Julien, not far from the Cathedral of Angers. By the time we had unpacked and rested a bit, it was too late to see the Cathedral and we ate and turned in early.

The next morning, it was only a few steps to the Angers Cathedral, which St. Louis had built from 1228 to 1236, making it one of the oldest of the Loire chateaux. The seventeen towers of the Angers Cathedral, up to one hundred fifty feet tall, made an imposing structure. It housed a magnificent painting of the apocalypse over three hundred feet long, which stretched along several walls of a special hall built for it. After some minutes observing these latest wonders, we went back for our bikes. As we did so, Guy told us more stories, including one that Henri Plantagenet, the king of England, who married Eleanor of Aquitaine in 1152, had spent much time in Angers, as had her son, Richard the Lion Hearted. In 1199, Richard died nearby at war with Philippe Augustus, who had been his companion with Frederick Barbarossa on the Third Crusade. That took place 1189-1192, seven years before Philippe Augustus and Richard went to war against each other.

Getting our bikes, we headed south for the next stop, Le Puy du Fou, about forty miles off to the southwest. We ate our sandwiches midway and arrived there towards three o'clock. After briefly looking at the Musée du Vendée there, we decided against waiting for its famous *Son et Lumiere*, or sound and light show, featuring various battles against the Vikings, British and others. Changing direction, we headed east-southeast towards our next stop, Poitiers, a city of close to 100,000 people. We got there in time to see an ancient church, the Eglise St. Hilaire le Grand, which was on our route into the city. It had been started already in the second century and took its name from the fourth century bishop, the teacher of St. Martin who spread Christianity throughout western Gaul during his bishopric at Tours before his death in 397.

We found the Hotel Europe not far away and ate at the St. Hilaire restaurant back towards the church. The restaurant was in a part of the church constructed on earlier ruins from the twelfth century. It had a classic cuisine according to our guide book. That book also mentioned Charles Martel's victory over the Saracens after they had attacked Poitiers and burned the church of St. Hilaire in 732. Guy, who obviously enjoyed his role as the person most cognizant with French history, gave us more details about that over our dinner at the hotel. He started by saying, that that had been one of the great 'might have beens' of history, preventing the Islamization of Europe. Claudia summed up our thoughts about that, saying, "Wow! Imagine how things would have been if we all had had to bow eastward towards Mecca for our evening prayers just now."

The next day, we looked at some more Romanesque churches in Poitiers, including Notre Dame la Grande in the center of the charming city. It had a three star façade with lovely bas-reliefs of biblical stories. Then, we walked the short distance to the twelfth century Cathedral

St. Pierre, and almost next to it, the oldest Christian building in France, the fourth century Baptistére St. Jean. Centuries later it was transformed into a small church. We went through the rooms of the two structures, admiring the sculptures, paintings and other objects. By two in the afternoon, we made our way to a restaurant recommended by the Hotel.

It was almost next to the Hotel de l'Europe and called the Three Pillars. It had round tables surrounded by interesting carved woodwork, and we all ate their specialty of ravioli with langoustine au basilic. Understandably, after that we looked forward to sleeping back in the hotel. More walking through the streets and an early evening and bed followed. We needed some rest after our strenuous days of biking and sight seeing.

Partly because of that and partly because Poitiers was such a charming and interesting city, we decided to stay on for another day before continuing our trip. We did more walking around its lovely streets, and spent an hour in the Musée Ste-Croix, next to the Baptistére St. Jean.

The following day which happened to be the national holiday was Saturday, July 14, and we left comfortably towards ten, going now to the southwest towards the small town of

Saintes. It was an important Roman city on the Charente River which housed many interesting remains as well as medieval churches and other sites. The Latin poet Ausone died there and in the middle ages, the Plantagenets controlled Saintes. In the twelfth century, they built there the Cathedral St. Pierre, which was an important stop of pilgrims on the way to Santiago de Compostella. After several hours of looking at those sites, we set off to the southeast.

First came Cognac, a town of 20,000 about twenty miles east on the Charente River, which housed the great liquor houses of that name. Even though it was only mid afternoon, we decided we had to have a cognac in the city it came from. After that we were not too drunk to get back on our bikes and head for Perigueux another sixty or so miles further southeast. That meant getting there some time in the evening, which was not difficult given the time of sunset in July. Even though that day was the biggest national holiday of France, we found a hotel which had space. The hotel was more or less on our way, and was aptly named the Perigord for the area it was in. We were given a room which had been a stable, but was comfortably furnished and quiet since it was on the back of the hotel. Its front looked out on on the busy Rue Victor Hugo. We did a meal and some extra wine nearby, in the midst of *Bastille Day* revelers. But after an hour of that we turned in early.

Back in the room we read our guide books and found that Perigueux is the capital of the Region of Perigord. Its principal church had been begun in the sixth century and became the Cathedrale St. Front, finished towards 1173. The next morning we went to it and saw its Byzantine style domes and cupolas above a large structure in the form of a Greek cross. I said I thought it looked reminiscent of St. Marc in Venice, as well as no doubt of some ancient churches in Constantinople. After seeing its beautiful interior, we walked through the oldest part of the city off to the north of the Cathedral. There were remains of ancient Gallo Roman structures and handsome Renaissance houses. We especially admired an impressive Roman tower of the first century as well as the Musée de Perigord filled with prehistoric, Roman and medieval remains.

At a café, where we stopped for a bite and some wine, I told my companions that I had read a charming detective story, set in Perigueux. It is called *Tout le Monde l'Aimait*, by the writer using the pseudonym Exbrayat. It narrated how a beautiful and popular woman, Hélène Arcizac, had been murdered and then how the detective, Gremilly, unraveled the alibis of the leading suspects among her ex-husband and lovers. He did that as he wandered the charming streets of the town. He found that all the suspects had reasons to kill her, because behind her charming and seemingly kind appearance, Mme. Arcizac was a schemer and sorceress. Finally, on the last page of the novel, he discovered it was one of the lovers, a notary, named Dimechaux, who had strangled her in her sleep. Claudia said she thought that sounded like a good read, and wondered if she could find a copy. Guy said he had read some Exbrayat and also found them mostly very good. I wondered if Claudia liked my account of it, as I imagined that, in fact, she resembled Hélène Arcizac to some extent. Despite that, I doubted she would meet a similar end.

I looked forward greatly to our next destinations which would take us deeper into the Dordogne region. Biking farther southeast, we would come first to Les Eyzies de Tayac. After that would come Sarlat and then Rocamadur, all exciting ancient and medieval towns. Les Eyzies, like the far better known Lascaux about twenty or so kilometers to its northeast is also on the Vézere River, a tributary of the Dordogne. It is a principal site for the prehistory of France. Although without the etchings and rock carvings of animals found in Lascaux, the caves of Les Enzies contained many evidences, including arms, pottery, and tools, of habitation there tens of thousands of years ago. Its site overlooking the Dordogne river and cliffs, crowned by oak and juniper trees, was very beautiful. But Claudia said she didn't really care that much about Neanderthals and other pre-humans, and so we skipped going into the Musée Nationale de Préhistoire. We gave a brief look at the troglodyte village, however, as it was on our way heading east to Sarlat, several miles to the north of the Dordogne. We arrived there an hour later, in time for dinner, and left our bikes outside the cemetery almost adjoining the fourteenth century cathedral. We found a restaurant nearby, and afterwards, walked the streets of Sarlat. It was a site that had often been used in historic films because of the many Medieval and Renaissance houses there. We found a room in the Hotel Madeleine at the northern end of the old city, and had a good night's sleep.

It was a good thing, because our next stop, Rocamadur, was a longer trip, some fifty kilometers to the east-southeast, and on the other side of the Dordogne, to the south. Moreover, it was one hundred fifty meters higher than Sarlat and at the end of a canyon, dominated by a stunning cliff ascending another hundred fifty meters above the Cité Religieuse of its name. It became one of the leading stops of pilgrims, both for itself, and because it is on the way to Santiago di Compostella. After the discovery of twelfth century tombs near a chapel dedicated to the Holy Mother, there had been much debate about who the first settlers were. Opinions range from Neanderthals to hermits, and later officials. In any case, numerous miracles were reported at Rocamadur, and by famous people. The latter included the English king, Henri Plantagenet, French kings, Louis IX (St. Louis), and his mother, Blanche de Castille, Philip the Fair, Philip VI and Louis XI, as well as Saints Bernard and Dominique. The site, now home to only 627 people, became so popular that on occasion in the thirteenth century up to 30,000 pilgrims were said to be there at one time, sleeping where they could. Many climbed on their knees up the steep incline and the 233 steps of the *Via Sancta* to prostrate themselves before the altar of the *Vierge Noir*. It had been blackened by the smoke of innumerable wax candles lit to honor the site.

Those were details we read in our guide books after we found a room in the Hotel Le Belvedere, a mile away from Rocamadur. From the hotel there was an astonishing view of the site with its chapels, old houses, and mountains all around. We had a bit to eat and walked towards the village up above, which was accessible only to pedestrians. We climbed to the Chapel of the Black Virgin, and did some prayers and meditation. Then, we descended into the lower village, where we found a nice tea house. There, we bought some souvenirs and planned our trip for the next day to Conques, another three star site, almost sixty miles farther east.

After walking back to the hotel and a good night's sleep, we arrived in Conques shortly after one. It was another village perched in the jagged hills of the region of Quercy, which was an important stop for pilgrims on the way to Rocamadur and Santiago di Compostella. Its most famous building was the eleventh and twelfth century Abbatiale Ste.-Foy. It housed an eardrum (*tympan) in a* space between the stone and an arch above), said to be a masterpiece of Romanesque sculpture. We spent a few minutes there observing it and other treasures, and then went through the arcades to a tenth century cloister. It contained impressive gold work said to be the most complete *orfeverie* of French religious art. Some of it was indeed stunning. Claudia said she especially loved one of the rosaries because of its varied colors. But, we spent only a few more minutes there, before heading back to our bikes, which we had left at the entrance to the village.

Discussing as best we could from our bikes the wonders we had already seen, we headed to Carcassone, almost a hundred miles to the south. As it was mid afternoon, we decided to spend the night in Albi, the town about midway to our destination. Its name was given to the Cathar heretics, the Albigensians. They had been mercilessly massacred and suppressed in the thirteenth century on orders of the Inquisition. It was a crusade ordered by Pope Innocent III in 1209, and was one of the worst episodes of Medieval Christianity. The Cathars were 'true believers,' but of a creed influenced by Manicheism. Their final destruction came in 1244 at Montsegur about fifty miles to the southwest of Carcassonne. Guy informed us of these details, as well as of many more about the massacres, and how northern French lords used that internal crusade to expand their holdings in Languedoc and the other southern regions involved.

The next day, as we approached Carcassonne, we were amazed at the magnificence of the walls and towers enclosing that city of some 40,000 people. The fortifications had been begun in the third and fourth, Gallo-Roman centuries. In the fifth century, the Visigoths arrived and then in the eighth , the Franks. The counts of Toulouse controlled Carcassonne for four centuries after that, and further enlarged the walls, as did Saint Louis and his descendants in the thirteenth and later centuries. We decided to stay in the Bristol Hotel which was on our route into the city, just on the other side of the Canal du Midi to the north of the walled city. The Canal linked with the River Aude to its east, giving the city good access to neighboring areas. After undoing our things, and showering, we found our way to a recommended restaurant in the center of the city, the Auberge de Dame Carcas. To get there from our hotel took a twenty minute walk, passing through the principal entrance into the walled city, the Porte Narbonnaise. After eating we returned to the hotel, and decided to spend another day in the magical city of Carcassonne. The afternoon passed well with more walking and tourism, and dinner at another good restaurant.

The next morning, we went back to the old city but entered through the Porte d'Aude on the west side of the Cité. The views from there were even more striking than they had been from the east. The Porte d'Aude was almost next to the place we wanted to see next, the Chateau Comtal. Originally a palace, it was transformed into a fort by St. Louis, taking its place with four other royal forts in the city. It was graced by numerous towers, and we climbed to the top of the tallest tower as we had been told it had the best view of the city. The view was stunning, with the inner wall and its towers surrounding the houses of the inhabitants of the city. Guy told us how after 1835, Viollet-le-Duc had restored Carcassonne, as best he and his workers could. According to some their work was not entirely in accord with the history and traditions of the city. After a few minutes, we descended and explored the narrow streets, admiring many of the buildings. We made our way to the Basilique St. Nazaire, built from the eleventh to fourteenth centuries over the Roman ruins. Partly in ruin, beautiful statues and stained glass windows survive. After the usual prayers and sightseeing there, we walked back through the city, via the Chateau Comtal and then through the Porte Narbonnaise back to our hotel. We did a small lunch, nap and more walks before an early dinner and wine. That put us in good shape for the last of our wonderful trip.

In the morning, we checked out of the hotel, and getting our bikes set out for Montpellier. That was another 90 miles to the east, and we expected to arrive well before nightfall. As the sun still set well after eight in the evening, that could be done without too much effort. We found a room in the Parc Hotel in the northwest of that city of over 200,000 people. Unpacking, we went to a nearby bistrot, as the hotel had no restaurant. We got back to the hotel by eleven and enjoyed another good night's sleep.

The next morning we set out for the Promenade du Peyrou with its beautiful view of the medieval part of Montpellier and the Mediterranean. We finished the cups of coffee we had brought with us after pouring some into paper cups to take with us. I managed to spill half of mine on my trousers, but as they were dark grey, the spot almost blended in. Claudia said she could get rid of it entirely when we got back to the hotel. We rested a bit from our climb to the promenade, while enjoying the view of Montpellier and the Mediteranean. Then, we descended to the bottom of the hill to observe the Arc de Triomphe across the street. From there we walked towards the *Place de la Comedie*, through twisting, narrow medieval streets. Impressive seventeenth and eighteenth century buildings, called *hotels particuliers*, or private hotels, lined those passageways. After walking through the Place de la Comedie, we did an early lunch at the *Cercle des Anges* restaurant a few blocks toward our next site, the Cathedrale St. Pierre. That cathedral had been built in the fourteenth century on the remains of a tenth century church built by founders of the city, who were named Guilhem. From there it was a short walk to our hotel.

In the early afternoon, we set out for the town of Nimes. "How far away is it?" Claudia asked.

I said, "It's about thirty three miles to the northeast."

"Why are we heading there?"

"Well, it was an important Roman town, with a colosseum and an amphitheatre, built in the first century."

"Oh, I'd like to see that place," she said.

Arriving there the evening of July 22, we stopped at a café to check our guide books for a hotel. We decided on the Amphitheatre right next to the *Arenes*, the Colosseum built by the Romans at the end of the first century. They had a room and we unpacked, bathed and rested a bit before going to the *Lisita* restaurant almost next door. Our guide book said it was one of the best in the city, and with its location the choice of '*tout Nimes.*' We ate well and had a nightcap nearby, observing the guests and scene, which included views of some good looking people as well as of the walls and towers all around.

The next morning, we walked the few steps to the *Arenes*, and admired its massive oval structure. It is considered one of the best preserved of all Roman colosseums, although it had to be restored in the nineteenth century. From there we did the ten minute walk to the other three star attraction of the city. It is called *Maison Carrée*, but resembles more the Parthenon. Built in the late first century under Augustus, its Corinthian columns and graceful lines are much admired. After being a stable and the Hotel de Ville of Nimes, under Louis XIV it came under the protection of Augustinian monks who maintain a monastery nearby. We then walked to the beautiful Jardin de la Fontaine. It has myriad lovely flowers and plants and surrounds a square pond fed by the famous spring called Nemausus. The first inhabitants who lived there took the name Nimes from that of the spring. Almost next to the Jardin de la Fontaine, we had a nice lunch in the terrace restaurant, overlooking another attractive garden, in the Hotel Imperator Concorde. We took a leisurely walk back to the hotel. The next day we would bike to the Pont du Garde, some fifteen miles to the northeast.

Arriving there by eleven or so on the 23rd, we were again stunned by the view. This time, it was of the three tiered aqueduct that bore water from fifty miles to the north, all the way south to Nimes. Constructed in the first century, of blocks of stone weighing up to eight tons each, it is considered one of the wonders of antiquity. The huge stones had to be hoisted hundreds of feet up over and over again. With a slope of 34 centimeters per kilometer the aqueduct carried 20,000 cubic meters of water a day to Nimes. Cut numerous times during the many sieges of the city, the aqueduct was more or less abandoned by the ninth century, but it was restored in the middle of the nineteenth. Its gracefully erected superimposed stones now seem almost perfectly in place and amaze visitors. We walked along pathways, observing the three levels of the aqueduct. The highest level was 22 meters high, the middle one 20, and the lowest only three. The top level had numerous small arches, and the middle and lower ones six larger arches, stretching across the valley of the Gard River from our viewing points.

After an hour of looking, resting and walking, we set out for our penultimate stop before taking the train to Paris. That was the astonishing series of cliffs and escarpments called *Les Baux de Provence*, about fifteen miles to the east. From its mines came the metal known as bauxite, from which aluminum is extracted. We left our bikes chained together in the valley and walked up the steep trail to the village of that name on a plateau 592 feet above sea level. Finding a bench there, we read in our guide books some amazing information. By the eleventh century, the local lord controlled seventy nine towns and villages, and boasted to have never been made a vassal by any other lord. By the thirteenth century the leader, Raymond de Turenne, became known as the '*fleau de la Provence*' (the scourge of Provence) for his practice of throwing prisoners from his chateau into the void beyond.

The town of Les Baux de Provence was also known for its *Cours d'Amour*, frequented by amorous troubadours and adventurers from all around. In 1632, Louis XIII and his minister, Richelieu, destroyed the chateau and took control of the turbulent fief. The chateau, churches and houses were restored in the 19th and 20th centuries. We walked first to the ruins of the chateau, and then took the *grand rue* past the *ancien hotel de ville*, some interesting houses, and the principal church, the medieval Eglise St. Vincent. It had a handsome Renaissance tower which made it easy to find. It was at the other end of the village, and finally we walked to a look out on the edge of the cliff. From it could be seen to the south, Arles, and also Aigues Mortes, the port on the Mediterranean established for his crusades by St. Louis after 1240. We had to go back to the trail we came up in order to get back down to our bikes. That trail went 900 meters to the other side of Les Baux de Provence, and taking it we continued to luxuriate in the views of this incredible town and its surroundings.

With luck, we found a room in the hotel, Les Baux de Provence. The hotel had one of the highest ratings in our red

Michelin Guide, for being very agreeable and quiet. Moreover it had with a superb restaurant, the Oustau de Baumaniere,. We took full advantage, with naps, showers and a best meal yet. That included their specialties; ravioli with leeks and truffles, lamb chops au basilic, and red snapper. Each of us took one of those incredibly good dishes, and exchanged bites.

For our last stop before getting on the train to Paris, we biked to Avignon, twenty nine kilometers to the north. In some ways, we had saved our best place for last. To get to it, we had to cross the Durance River, a tributary of the Rhone, which runs through the center of Avignon. We arrived there towards dusk and the view was wonderful. That is, once we got as far as the splendid Palais des Papes, and before that it was like any attractive French town. Late as it was, we had a glass of wine in a bar and got out our guide books to find a hotel. We decided on the Garlande, which was relatively inexpensive and only about ten blocks south of the Palais des Papes and its square, between two fourteenth century churches, the St. Pierre and St. Didier. The hotel, in two parts renovated from older structures, was charming and comfortable enough. Undoing our stuff, we found a nearby restaurant and turned in early.

The next morning, we studied our guide books over coffee, and decided to start our tour by walking about a half hour north to the overlook of the city from the top of the Rocher des Doms. It was reached through a handsome garden, which we enjoyed in the clear morning air. We had an interesting view of the Rhone as well as of the Pont St. Benezet, leading to Villeneuve les Avignon. This was the bridge of the famous song, '*Sur le Pont D'Avignon*,' though we did not see anyone doing the '*danse tout en rond,* as a line in that song had it. The once 900

meter bridge now had only its first three quarters still intact, and it was odd to see it with its broken off end. Next we walked back through the garden toward the twelfth century cathedral, Notre Dame des Doms. Going through it, we were in front of the magnificent Palais des Papes.

We had seen in our guide books that it was really two palaces. In 1134, Pope Benoit XII ordered the building of what became the *Palais Vieux*. We entered that one first, and it was in the form of an austere fortress protecting a cloister. Guy informed us that its austerity had to do with Pope Benoit having been a Cistercian monk opposed to luxury and show. We passed through the Chapelle St. Jean, admiring its frescoes, and the Consistoire, and climbed to the second floor to walk into the *Palais Neuf*. That newer palace had been built in more elaborate style by Pope Clement VI over twenty years after 1342. In all there were seven popes in the 'Babylonian Captivity,' as critics called the Avignon papacy from 1305 to 1377. Guy explained later that it got even worse after that, with the Great Schism of the church from 1378 to 1417, including a brief period when there were even three popes. Finally, there were the compromises needed to end the dispute and ensure the dominance of Pope Martin V over all of western Christianity. He returned the Papacy to Rome with his election in 1417 and died there in 1431.

Claudia said she especially wanted to see the Pope's bedroom, and we threaded our way through the maze of halls and chapels to find it. It had beautiful blue walls with rich decorations and mosaics of birds, branches and trees. As we continued walking we were most struck with the mid fourteenth century frescoes relating the life of St. Martial in the chapel of his name. There were other marvelous frescoes, courtyards and halls as we completed our tour of the Palais Neuf.

We did lunch and decided we would stay one more night in Avignon, to be able to wander its streets and admire the buildings especially the Palais des Papes. Moreover it would give us one more evening together to enjoy and reminisce about our trip. In the afternoon we went to the Musée du

Petit Palais, to see its medieval sculptures and paintings. It was a short walk back to the hotel and we prepared for a gala last night of our trip, before taking the midday train on the morrow, July 26.

We went to a recommended restaurant, called Christian Etienne, just off to the side of the Palais des Papes. As well as more modern ones it had ancient rooms, supposedly from the thirteenth and fourteenth centuries. We chose their specialties of codfish ravioli and red snapper, and found them as good as you might guess. Paying our bill, we decided to walk over to the Pont St. Benezet and see if we could go on it, to dance or not. We could not, and so walked along the bank of the Rhone for about ten minutes to the south, and then set off into the center of the medieval town. We found a sympathetic bar next to the Hotel Danieli, which was quite close to our hotel. We discussed the many wonders of our trip over several glasses of Bordeaux, and turned in close to midnight, thinking we would need some rest for the problems of getting our bikes stored on the train for the trip home.

We biked to the station two hours before the two o'clock high speed train to Gare du Lyon, Paris. As expected, we had to pay a little extra, some ten euro each, for the bikes but were surprised at the reasonableness of our tickets, which were close to another hundred euro each. Remarkably, the train arrived in Paris only three hours after departure, slightly after five in the afternoon of July 26. Later, I figured out that meant a speed of 230.4 kilometers per hour or 144 mph to travel the 685 kilomers or 428 miles from Avignon to Paris. Wow! I wondered why we as the richest and most scientifically advanced country had trains that were so much slower, and often nonexistent.

I debated whether to call Valerie to inform her of my arrival in Paris, but decided to just go and surprise her. Claudia told me to call her when I figured out what I would do the next school year, and Guy told me how much he had enjoyed our trip. He said, "Aside from Lance Armstrong, I didn't know Americans could bike so well." I thanked him for the compliment, kissed Claudia on both cheeks, and jumped on my bike, with an imitation aviator wave good-bye.

It took me close to a half hour to get home, and I was so glad to lock my bike and store it in the back of our small garden. I was even happier seeing the radiant smile of Valerie as she came to embrace me. She said, she'd had a hunch I would be arriving today, though I'd said it might be a day or two later. "Don't you think that's a good sign? That I had a premonition as to when you might arrive? She said, "For me, that means, maybe, I really do love you."

CHAPTER TEN

MY NEW LIFE WITH VALERIE

"Cherie, I am so glad to see you and feel your good vibes. Maybe, I will never leave you again."

"That might be a bad idea. For then, I could be less eager to embrace you when you get back." She said that as she walked across the room to wrap her arms around me. I decided to strike while the iron was hot, and led her straight to our bed. Clothes off, the love making was even better than I remembered it. No doubt, that was in part because I had been away for three weeks. We lay in bed for another half hour, and then decided to get up to prepare dinner.

As we did so, I asked her, "What's new?" I wanted to do that before she could ask me for a blow-by-blow account of my bike trip. New for her, she said, were that she had bought a bike and had had some more encounters with Keith. But, she said, she had kept them platonic and moreover had broken up with Mark Goden. "That is good," I said. "I never liked him and couldn't understand why you ever saw him. And I'm so glad you bought a bike. We'll have to do that a lot in coming days. Now, do you want to hear about my trip?"

"Of course I do. But let me finish doing this lamb dish first. I bought it just for you."

"How wonderful! And take your time. I just like to look at you, and tell me what I can do to help."

"Well, you might as well set the table, all right?"

I did so, and opened a nice bottle of Cote du Rhone before taking my seat and pouring our glasses. Valerie served the plates with haricots verts and lamb, and we dived in, hungry as we were. At least, I was, and Valerie seemed to be also. We finished more quickly than usual, as normally we both eat slowly. Leaning back in my chair, I decided to first make a confession and ask the advice of Valerie before telling about my trip. "You know, beloved, the trip I did with Claudia and Guy has convinced me that I really do love you, and only you. Last autumn and spring, I flirted some with Claudia, though we never consumated anything. But, on the trip, I came to think she was not as great as I had thought. Now, I think maybe I want to marry you. What do you think?"

"Why get married? You already have been and didn't like it, and I don't think I will either. We can just live together, and have the best of both worlds. Love and freedom, don't you think?"

"I can see why I love you so much. You are always so frank, and so often say unexpected things that please me. I've decided I don't even mind your political conservatism any more, since I've become so apolitical. Now, why don't we go to bed and sleep over it."

We did and the night couldn't have lasted long enough. There was not only love making, but cuddling and quiet talk. We woke about eight and went back to sleep until nine, our favorite time to get up.

The next days, I felt good after all my biking exercise the previous weeks, but also worried. Every time I thought about the future, I became nervous trying to decide what alternatives I had. Since I had become so fond of France, and was in love with a lady who felt the same way, by far the best solution would be to find a job here. But, how? There is high unemployment anyway, and new openings almost always went to French citizens. It was now July 27, and unless I could come up with something, I would have to be back in New York for my Baruch job by the beginning of September. I thought my best plan would be first to go back to the Institut d'Anglais and see if there were any possibilities. If not, then I would try the Herald Tribune to see if they had any openings for a novice journalist. If that failed, my last resort would be to decide between getting odd jobs here, such as bar tending or teaching English, or I would have to return to New York. I wondered what my luck would be with getting Valerie to do that, especially now that she had a job she seemed to like in Paris.

As August was fast approaching, and as everyone knew Paris almost shuts down for vacation then, I went early that afternoon back to the Institut d'Anglais. Predictably, they told me all that all their positions for the *Rentrée*, as they call the beginning of the school year, were filled. They suggested I apply for another year sometime in the future. I went by Claudia's office, and she was there. She sympathized with my lack of success, and said she would recommend me for any opening that came up in the coming years. She went on to say she was leaving the next day with Guy for a few weeks vacation in Haute Savoie. We wished each other all the best, and I told her to say *bonjour* for me to Guy.

The next day, a Saturday, I proposed to Valerie that we go back to the Latin Quarter for drinks and dinner. She agreed, and since it was raining we did the Metro. We took our favorite route there, with the metro to the Palais Royale and then walking through the Louvre and across the Pont des Arts. We wandered up the Seine and stopped at the Perigourdine for some wine. We got seats in front and savored the view of Notre Dame, which as has been said, is to the forward left one block to the other side of the Place St. Michel directly in front of the restaurant. After a second glass of our Sauvignon

Blanc, I proposed a restaurant, called La Tourelle, just across the square at 5 Rue de Hautefeuille. Valerie agreed and we walked to it. Given a table in the back left corner, we could survey their incredible collection of *affiches*, as they call the posters, on the walls. They had a different sort of escargot, with not only garlic but basil and other herbs. We ordered and then them. They were delicious as were our main courses of filet de sole and turbot. We agreed one could not go wrong with such a combination of dishes. When Valerie asked if she could have some of my Turbot, I told her, of course. Then I took some of her sole, since it is our custom to share bites as we had already done with the escargots.

After a few bites, I got into what was most on my mind. I told of my fruitless search for a new job at the Institut d'Anglais and about my letter to the Herald Tribune. I asked her for other ideas.

She said: "Why don't you become a bartender or waiter. At least you could try. Then maybe we could start getting free meals."

"You're so right. That's a great idea. I might also ask at some nearby *lycée* if they need an English teacher. Have you noticed any on your walks? I have noticed the one on Rue St. Antoine, the Ecole de Francs Bourgeois, and the even better known Lycée Henri Quatre in back of the Pantheon. I could start with those, but no doubt would have better luck with some lesser known ones."

Valerie pointed to her jaw indicating to wait till she had finished eating her bite. After chewing for what seemed to me a long time for eating fish, she said, "Yes, there is one I passed on the way to the Eglise du Dome at the back end of the Invalides. It's called something like the Lycée Duny or Dunuy. That church, by the way, is very beautiful."

"I don't know it, and should go. I once walked by it, but it was closed and I couldn't go in. Meanwhile, what should we do when we finish here?"

"I'd love to meander some more over by the St. Severin Church. After that maybe we could have a night cap at one of the Greek bars on the Rue de la Huchette."

"Good. If we don't find one we like there, we can go to the Trois Mailletz a little further over. When I was last there, they had a fantastic pianist. His fingers flew without stop every which way, and he got incredible applause."

We paid our bill, and started to walk across the Place St. Michel. On the other side of it we took the Rue St. Severin for a block, then turned right for a few paces to admire the church and its courtyard. After that we had to go back the other way for a few hundred yards and turn left to be on the Rue de la Huchette. On that street, we saw one or two possibilities, along with dozens of restaurants, each vaunting its dishes and prices. I was glad we had already eaten and since we did not much like the bars we passed, I proposed we go on to the Trois Mailletz. That meant reversing course to the end of the street, and crossing the Rue St. Jacques. Then it was straight ahead for a block or so, before the few steps to the bar.

All the seats up front by the piano were taken, but, we found a table in the back. We asked the *serveuse*, or waitress, for a Pastis each. The drinks came and really packed a wallop. I wondered if the waitress had done doubles, and was drinking them herself, since she could barely walk a straight line. We decided to switch to Cote du Rhone wines after our first Pastis. The pianist was there and kept us happy with impressive keymanship and some lovely melodies. When he stopped for a break, I went over to the Maitre D' and asked if there was any chance of them hiring me as a bartender. He took my name and said he would put it in his file, and call me if anything came up. I asked him why the bar was called the Trois Mailletz. He said it went back to the middle ages and had been a word that meant hammer. So, his guess was that it was named for three workmen who brought their hammers there for drinks. I thanked him warmly, and went back to our table.

After we finished our drinks, I proposed we head home by the La Tourelle restaurant which also had a bar. Getting there, I asked about a job, and was surprised to hear the lady in charge say they were looking for a replacement for a guy, who had said he was leaving. I asked her what I should do to get the job. She told me to come on Monday at eleven and to work with the guy who would be leaving at the end of the week. "He can teach you what you need to know in a few days, which you can supplement with what you know. If that works, you're hired."

I was glad Valerie was there as my witness as I could hardly believe my luck. I asked the lady for her name, which was Claire, and thanked her as effusively as I could. As soon as we left, I hugged Valerie, and said,

"Can you believe that. Maybe, I am getting your luck."

"Maybe it's because our love is going so well now, and maybe now we can stay in Paris. But, what about the long term? How long do you think you want to be a bartender?"

"Don't be so practical. We can enjoy it as long as it lasts, and if I like working there, I will write the history chairman at Baruch, asking for another leave of absence. If that is refused, I will have to decide if I go back immediately or quit. Anyway, let's enjoy the rest of the evening and the coming days."

We did another wine at the Perigourdine just across the *Place St. Michel* to celebrate. Getting home early, we got a good night's sleep. Sunday passed normally and we spent it preparing for the first week where we would both be doing regular jobs.

On Monday, July 30, Valerie had to be at work at ten, and so left before I did shortly before eleven. I took the metro at Monceau in the direction of *Bobigny-Pablo Picasso* for a change at *Barbes-Rochechouart* for the *Place St. Michel*. I saw that the connection to *Port d'Orleans,* the direction I needed to go, was at the opposite end of the train from where I was. That seemed almost always to be the case, given the usual bad luck for such things. Still, it was a short walk, and arriving at *Place St. Michel*, I went up the stairs of the metro station out onto the sidewalk for the few paces to the restaurant.

My new place of work, the restaurant, *La Tourelle*, was on the corner of a narrow street just off of the Place St. Michel, leading towards the *Boulevard St. Germain*. It was in a handsome and ancient looking building, with a small tower above the roof to the left of its entrance. When I arrived, I found the barman I was to replace was named André. He seemed a very sympathetic guy, though every now and then we had language problems. Since I already knew how to do the simple drinks. I asked him if there was a book for cocktails and mixed drinks, or if you just had to learn by trial and error. He told me to get the *Dictionnaire des Boissons*, but guessed that I would learn even more from trial and error. I asked him what happened when you made a bad drink. He said "You have to pour it out and start over again." He told me there was usually an hour or so off after lunch, before we had to start preparations for dinner. But sometimes he said, "People keep coming in, and there is no time off at all." That made me think I would probably have to move closer to the restaurant if I kept the job. André went on to say that I should expect to work until about midnight most nights. French eat quite late, though not as late as the Spanish and Italians, he said. Dinner is most often about nine, but on special occasions can go on to 2 a.m or so. I asked how often that was, and André said it was quite rare, but had happened a couple of times in the two years he had been there.

Thanking André for his information, I turned to the *patronne*, Claire,

and asked her what she wanted me to do first. She told me to go behind the bar and study where the drinks were kept. She said, "The wines are normally put higher up on the shelves and the stronger liquors down below." I thanked her and went behind the bar.

I had barely gotten there, when a customer came in and asked for a Ricard with ice. Fortunately, that popular apertif was right behind me and I poured the drink, giving with it also a glass of water as I knew was the custom from when I had ordered that drink as I often did. The client looked to be in his thirties, and proceeded to down his Ricard in rapid fashion with swallows of the water as he drank. He got up and went out, saying that he had needed a *requinquant* or 'pick me up.' I continued to look at the other bottles, ranging from Chartreuse, Compari and Drambuie to Maker's Mark bourbon, Black & White scotch, Pernod, Tanqueray gin and others. When Claire came over to ask me a few questions, I stopped and turned around. She said she had never been to the U.S., but wanted to go when the Euro went up relative to the Dollar. At the time, the dollar was still worth more than one euro. I told her I well understood the problem, as when I first came to France the dollar was worth over ten francs, or close to a euro and a half, but then had sunk to close to six by the time of the switch to the Euro.

At that point, a tour of young people started coming through the doors. The guide said they came from Australia and wanted a table for twenty. Not only that, but just after them four older men, probably in their sixties, came in and said they had only an hour to eat before they needed to get back to their office. André guided the French guys to a corner table and asked me to start putting tables together for the twenty Aussies. As I started to do so, I noticed a particularly attractive woman in their group. She was one of those statuesque blondes, looking as if she had stepped out of an ad for a swim suit. I told myself to not get caught staring at her, and with André's help completed putting the four tables in a row along the back wall. Then, I went over to the group, with another glance at the beauty and showed them the table. The guide, a middle aged and balding man, told them to take their seats as they liked. I noticed the pretty woman sitting between two of the more attractive men. I couldn't resist asking the guide how long they planned to be in Paris.

He answered, "So far, three days. We do two more, and then go to Avignon, before Nice and Italy."

"That sounds like a nice trip, and enjoy it and your meal," I said smiling at him, before again taking a look at the woman and her suitors.

Switching back to French, I asked André who should serve them?

He replied, "It will take all of us with so many, but you start with the Australians. I hope the *serveuse*, Alice, gets here before long. She is already an hour late, and I will do the four Francais." He had barely finished speaking when Alice came in and rushed by us with '*bonjours.*' She disappeared into the back to put on her *tablier*, or apron. We guys had to make do only with our shirts. Since I was the only English speaker, I went over to ask for the orders of the Australians. The guide asked them all to speak up, and they ordered. Most chose the chicken special, with a few taking the pasta of the day, the Tagliatelli con Pesto. I said. "*Tres bien, et comme ca*, you will preview your Italian dishes." The guide answered, "We have already been doing that," as he also ordered the tagliatelli.

But, when the food came I started hearing complaints, one after the other. Some said the pasta was not *al dente*, and the beauty said, "This chicken tastes like goat, or something." One of her suitors, said "I agree, and let's just leave it on the plate and hope they get the idea."

Hearing that, I went over and asked if they wanted to make new orders? The guide said, "No way, we have to be on our way in half an hour for a tour of Vaux le Vicomte, and I don't want to skimp on that sixteenth century Chateau. Addressing his group, he told them to "eat up, as we have to be out of here very quickly."

I said, "As you wish," and went over to talk to Claire about the problems the Aussies seemed to be having. She said to ignore them and hope they didn't bad mouth us. In fact, even before this episode, I had begun to wonder how much longer I could stand being a bartender and waiter. It was tiring being on your feet all the time, and so far I had not much liked the clientele. Except for the beauty, and now I could see she was someone who seemed to complain all the time. On the other hand, I liked André a lot, and Alice and Claire, who were brunettes, well enough.

Other clients kept coming in and before long the Aussies left. We finished the luncheon guests about four, and I went to a nearby library for a little rest and more reflection about the job problem. It was opposite the Eglise St. Severin, which was why I knew of it, that being a favorite church. It is called the Bibliotheque L'Heure Joyeuse, a name to appeal to young people, who were there in great numbers on their way home from school. I decided I would have to give my bartending job at least a few more days, but talk to Valerie about the possibility of her accompanying me back to New York in a week or two. In the library, I got a History of Paris off a shelf and perused it for an hour or so, Feeling somewhat rested, I made my way back to La Tourelle.

It was close to six, and André told me the only couple there were two Americans, who had just arrived. He suggested I could deal with them for their orders and early dinner. He asked why Americans ate so early? I told him, I didn't know, but that since my time in Europe I had adoped their custom of dining about nine, since I agreed that seemed superior to earlier eating times.

In fact, the American couple seemed sympa. They were from Chicago, and both teachers. They said they had just discovered Paris and loved it. They remarked that that was another reason to love teaching, since, although they had less time off than University profs, they could do summer trips all the time,. I said I agreed with them, and was myself a professor of History at Baruch College in New York, now doing a sabbatical year in Europe. I asked, "What can I get you?"

The woman said she would start with an omelette and then do a filet of sole. The man said that was just what he was thinking, but that maybe instead of the sole, he would try the lamb chops. Saying very good, I made my way to the kitchen and gave the orders. I guessed the American couple were in their forties, but our cook was a fiftyish man. I took him to be French and asked him where he was from. When he said, Lyon, I gave a nod of approval, knowing that Lyon was reputed to have the best cuisine in France I left him to his work.

As I went back into the dining room, I noticed Alice talking to a table of four in rapid French. Some of them looked very familiar, and I wondered if they could be movie stars. I asked Claire if she knew them. She said, "No, but the older one is a famous star, Jean Rochefort. I think the two girls were in a very good movie with him that I just saw, Le Placard. That is a story about a man getting fired from a condom factory, of all places. But, he prevents that by saying he is gay. Can you imagine?"

André, who overheard us passing by, stopped and said, "It's one of the funniest movies I ever saw, and I liked it so much I looked up the names of the actors. I think the two girls are Michele Laroque and Alexandra Vandernoot." Turning to me, he said, "It's a recent movie, and you should definitely try to see it. Indeed, the guy came out of the closet as the title indicates."

As I was saying I appreciated the information, I noticed another couple coming in and taking seats at the bar. Since André was dealing with the table of the four French actors, I went over to take the orders of the two new comers. They ordered White Russians, and I found the Kahlua and Vodka for that drink.

After I had made that marvelous but very sweet drink topped with cream and was carrying it to them, I saw the man reach for his arm, lose his balance and fall off the stool. The woman jumped to his side and I ran over, yelling for assistance. The man said he had just had a dizzy spell and lost his balance, but now felt all right. He said he had a history of angina, and that that had given him the sharp pain in the arm and the dizzy spell. But, now he indicated he would like help to get back up on the stool where he had been. André and I lifted him back there, and the couple began to drink their White Russians. Before long, the man moaned and again fell off his chair. The woman yelled to leave him where he was on the floor and call for an ambulance. Claire did so, and André and I kept vigilance over the prostrate man. His lady, who looked in her 60s, sat beside him and stroked his hair. Having understood from his accent that the victim was anglophone, I asked him if he wanted to keep lying down, or be propped up, while waiting for the ambulance. He replied, "Please, help me to sit up." As André and I did that, placing him with his back to the wall, the lady said, "We are English and just over for a brief fling, and now this happens. How awful! I just hope they get here soon."

In about a minute, a policeman came in, saying that the *Service Medicale d'Urgence*, or SAMU, would arrive shortly. André asked me if I knew you had to call the number 15 for that in France, in case you ever have to. I thanked him, saying I only knew that you called 911 in America for any emergency. Four medical people from SAMU arrived about two minutes later, and one of the two nurses examined the patient. She nodded to the men, who then placed him in a chair which they carried out to the ambulance parked by the door. His lady got in also, and the ambulance drove off. Everyone in the restaurant looked very relieved. Some of them almost looked as if they were going to applaud. Instead they resumed talking and went back to eating.

A new couple came in and took seats just to the left of where the victim and his lady had sat. I hoped the same scenario would not be repeated, and was glad when they ordered two glasses of white wine. I was so glad it was wine which is so much easier to serve than having to make cocktails. They said they would eat at the bar and ordered a bottle of Bordeaux to accompany a meal of celeri remoulade, escargots, lamb and red snapper.

It was now about 9:30, and I still had another couple of hours

to pass, either at the bar or serving customers at tables, before I could head home. But, there were no new crises and it was not an especially busy night. I was able to leave just after eleven and was glad to find Valerie still up when I got home. She said, "I knew you would be coming home late, and so had dinner with some friends near where I work."

"Not with Keith, I hope."

"Certainly not! With a lady colleague, named Florence. She is our secretary and a very nice person."

"That's good. And how much will it bother you, to have me coming in most nights about this time or even later. Maybe we have to look for an apartment closer to where we both work."

"We'll have to see. As for the lateness of your return, how do you know I don't like being alone at night?"

"If that is the case, I may have to quit my job and go back to New York."

"Come on," she said as she walked over to give me a kiss and lead me to the bed. "Let's enjoy the rest of what's left of this evening and worry about the rest when we wake up."

"All right, but I've decided I can't continue being a barman and waiter. Unless, I can get a job at the Herald Tribune, I think I will go back to New York and my job at Baruch. Is there anyway you can accompany me?"

Valerie smiled and said, "In fact, I am also getting tired of my job. Too many books, and too much talk about wine. As much as I love Paris, I would love to get to know your city."

The next day, I resolved to give Claire notice that I would have to leave her bar-restaurant in another several weeks, probably after work on August 18.

When I did that, Claire's response was, "*Merde*! That means I have to find someone else right away, since as you know André is leaving Saturday."

"I'm sorry. But, I have decided I have to go back to my job in New York."

"Well, I can see you lied to me when said you wanted to try your hand at bartending and waiting. *Je suis tres faché*, and wonder if all Americans are so unreliable."

"*C'est comme ca,*" I said as I turned away and went back behind the bar. Fortunately for me, a man came in at that very moment and took a seat at the bar. He asked for a whisky on the rocks. As soon as he had it, he started drinking and pulled out Le Monde, which he folded over his lap. I was glad I had recalled that the French called Scotch 'whisky.' The rest of the day went normally, except that Claire kept giving me dirty looks.

The remaining days were calm, although the very next one, August 1, was the day of the *grands departs*, as they call the beginning of the summer vacations. I decided I could get to work late that day, and therefore went by the *Herald Tribune* to see if by chance they might want a forty year old novice reporter. In that unlikely case, I would be ready for it after I stopped my restaurant job. The *Trib* guy asked me to send in my C.V. and come back in two weeks for some interviews. I thought that sounded encouraging, and decided to redo my curriculum vitae and send it to them the next day. A few days later, I made an appointment for Wednesday, August 15, to see if there was any chance of getting such a job. That day arrived, and before work I went over to see if there was any possiblity of a job with the *Herald Tribune*.

They said there was nothing available at the moment, but would let me know if anything turned up. I thanked them, and after work went home for more reflection and discussions with Valerie, I realized

that now I had only three more days at the bar/restaurant before quitting on August 18.

After lunch the next day, I went to another favorite library in the area to refresh my memory of historical subjects before going back to teaching. That was the *Documentation Francaise* on the Quai Voltaire. It was a fairly long walk, up the Rue St. André des Arts to a right on the Rue de Seine, and a left at the river onto the Quai Voltaire. It was at the end of that street beyond the Rue de Bac, and the walk took close to a half hour.

In the journal, Histoire, I found a recent article on China by another acquaintance, Lucien Bianco. He was a Savoyard and long time resident of Paris, as a Professor at the *Ecole des Hautes Etudes* on the Boulevard Raspail. The article was an interesting account of the peasants and the Chinese Revolution, on which subject he was a specialist. I made a note of the issue of the magazine and thought I would have to come back to the library if I could not buy it, since I had to leave by five to get back to the restaurant.

That evening went well, and the next day I decided to try out a new routine for my last days. I would try to stay behind the bar most of the time, and go out to serve as little as possible, in part to avoid the dirty looks of Claire. That of course depended on the customers, but most of the time it was possible. I needn't have worried, in any case, as Claire had already found a new bartender who she said would come in the day before I left. She told me to work with him, saying, "He is an Italian trying to learn French and should be a good replacement for you. You are both étrangers and more or less *sympa*."

"Do you know where in Italy he comes from?"

"Milan, wouldn't you guess."

"And you? Are you Parisienne?"

"Not at all. I'm from Poitiers, but have been here a long time now."

"You're kidding. I was in Poitiers a few days in July on a bike trip I took with two French friends"

"How did you find it?

"I thought it the most interesting of all the towns we passed through, and there were a lot of those. But, Poitiers seemed something else. To see its great churches and learn its history, including the stopping of the Saracens in 732 make it extraordinary.

"I'm glad you think so, and here comes our first client of the day, an old habitué. Greetings, Claude. How have you been?"

Claude took his seat and launched into a long conversation with Claire about his shoe store nearby on the Boulevard St. Michel and then about many mutual friends. Or at least that was what Claire told me later he had talked about. I learned that his store, again with the name André, was the very one where I had bought several nice pairs of walking shoes. Claire brought him a *Spaghetti Carbonara* for his lunch, while Alice and I served the other tables.

The rest of that day went calmly and the next day was my last day of work at La Tourelle. When I got there in the mid morning, the Italian was already there and looking as if he already knew what to do. I asked him, if he needed any information, and he said, "No, but I'm glad to meet the person I am to replace. What is your name?"

"Chris, and yours?"

"Mario."

I said, "Please let me do the bar now, and you can help Alice and Claire. Here come our first clients of the day."

They were an attractive young couple who took seats catercornered, saying they preferred that for talking. I guessed their talk would be intimate from the way they were looking at each other. They were English, and as I approached to give them menus, I overheard the girl asking, "Don't you love Paris? Anyway, I want to go to that museum of the Middle Ages after lunch and go dancing tonight."

I interrupted to say "Excuse me, would you like to see the menu?"

They took them, and the guy said to his lady friend, "Those are great ideas, and I see you proposed a restaurant quite close to that museum. At least, the guide book says you get to it off of the Boulevard St. Michel."

I did not hear her response as I walked over to the bar from the table they had taken in the middle of the room. I took a seat on the chair I had placed behind the bar, to sit down when I could. I didn't understand how people could stand as long as so many jobs required. For me with a periodically weak back, I could only stand a half hour or so without sitting, or I would get a back ache.

When I saw the English couple put their menus down, I got up and went to get their order. She ordered the Salade aux Fruits de Mer to start, followed by a Turbot, and he the Escargots and Sword Fish. When the dishes came, I could see that they continued to court each other, and I was reminded of Valerie and myself. Love is so wonderful I thought.

That banal but true idea was interupted by a new arrival at the bar, demanding, "*S'il vous plai!*" I rushed over and he barked, "Un Ricard!" I poured, saying, "*Un peu de patience s'il vous plait.*" He replied that he only had an hour and didn't see why there was no one else at the bar. I wondered what had happened to Mario, who just then ran in from the back, no doubt after a visit to the toilet. Mario said in English with his Italian accent, "*I'ma so glad you gotta your drink.* Enjoy it."

With that bit of comic relief I thought I was very glad it was my last day and I wouldn't have to worry about such problems any more. But, I was also glad to have seen the film actors previously, and wondered if Valerie and I could go to see the 'closet' film, Le Placard, possibly the next day. The lunch over I took a break with another pleasing walk over to the Jardins du Luxembourg, followed by a stroll over to the apiculture center, recalling my meeting Valerie there almost exactly a year before. When I got back to La Tourelle, the first dinner guests were already arriving and the evening passed normally. I happily said my goodbyes and walked to the metro at Chatelet.

When I got home about midnight, Valerie greeted me with the statement that she had told Keith she would have to leave by the end of work, August 25. Do you think we can get tickets to New York for the 28th,» or some such day? If I understood you correctly you are supposed to start teaching September 11th at the latest."

"Yes, you remember correctly, *cherie*. I will go to Air France Monday, and hopefully there will be no problem."

We had another good *fin de soirée*, with a wine or two, love making and sleep. Before the latter, I wondered how much I would miss all the wonderful things we had been enjoying in Paris, from the walks to the museums, food, wine and general sightseeing. But, I comforted myself by thinking that Valerie would accompany me back to New York.

The next day, a Sunday, we discussed how we should pass the last days, which were only a little more than a week off. Valerie said she wasn't worried, since she would only have a day or two after stopping work. She said that Keith had protested her giving only one week notice, but not too much as he seemed to already have another lady in mind to replace her. I said, "That's super. Do you think we have to do a farewell dinner with Keith? If so, maybe the Saturday night after you stop working, would be good."

"All right, I can propose that. Maybe, you can invite Francois to join us as well."

"An excellent idea. I haven't heard his news since before my bike trip. And this afternoon, how about going to see the movie recommended by the staff at La Tourelle. It's a comedy, called Le Placard, for the 'closet.' It's about a guy being fired who came out of the closet to save his job, by saying he was gay."

"Sounds amusing. Where is it playing?"

Looking in Pariscope, I found that it was playing on the Champs Elysés. "It's at the Gaumont Ambassade, at six, 8:15 or 22:20."

"Perfect. How about at six, and dinner after, maybe at Ladurie, or somewhere nearby."

We passed the rest of the day quietly. After lunch, I sat at my desk, and took out my calendar, to write down that I should go to Air France on Monday to get our tickets back to New York. After that, I thought I could go back to the library, La Documentation Francaise, and read some more of Bianco's article, for my china course at Baruch College to start in only three weeks or so. Then I will have four days from the 21st to the 25th to go to other libraries and museums, or just walk around my favorite big city.

Returning from that Valerie and I left at five, walking to the Champs Elysées via the Rue de Miromesnil. That led to the Rue de Ponthievre, which turned into the Rue du Colisée. And that last street hits Champs Elysées close to our cinema. We got there before 5:30 and bought our tickets before going to a café, looking towards the Arc de Triomphe where we had a glass of Sancere. We went into the theatre in time to get good seats, on the mid left side. I always insisted on an aisle seat to have room to stretch at least one of my long legs.

The film was only a little over an hour and a half long, and as advertized was terrifically good and funny. The actor Jean Rochefort, who I had seen at La Tourelle the last day of July, played the president of the condom factory, where much of the movie takes place. Another well known actor, Daniel Auteuil, plays the part of the guy being fired from that factory. After work the day he learned he was being fired, he told a neighbor in his vast apartment building that news, and how depressed he was. The neighbor told him not to be discouraged and to fight back. He proposed that he say he was gay, and make that known to the management, which could not fire such a person, since much of their business was selling condoms to gays. That neighbor manipulated a photo to show Auteuil caressing another guy and mailed it to Rochefort. The secretary who opened the envelope showed it to her companion, and they both broke up with laughter. But they had to disguise what they were laughing about when a third well known actor, Gérard Depardieu, who played another guy working at the factory came in. The two actresses playing the secretaries were the two ladies who had been with Jean Rochefort at the July 31 dinner at La Tourelle. The movie continued with cavorting, maneuvering, and hilarious scenes, one after the other. Those included various scenes where Depardieu tried to befriend Auteuil in order to prove he was not the anti-gay his previous remarks had indicated, lest he lose his own job. Another scene was filming the Auteuil character making love to one of the secretaries, and being observed by Jean Rochefort and the Japanese clients he was leading through the factory. It became possible for Auteuil to keep his job when his secretary proved that the photo showing him making love to a gay had been faked. The movie ended with the employees all keeping their jobs, and Auteuil finding out that his neighbor who told him to come out of the closet was himself gay.

Valerie and I were still laughing as we made our way across the Champs Elysées to the Restaurant Ladurie. We agreed we had never seen a funnier movie. Valerie added that she had never seen better acting or directing to do with getting every last joke out of every scene. Over the dinner, we continued to recall various things from the movie, and then got into more discussion of how much we would miss Paris. But, I also assured Valerie there was plenty to enjoy in New York as well, and that I would in some ways be glad to get back to teaching, as well as to the city I had lived in more than any other. Our dishes of sole and turbot, following a risotto, and ravioli aux morilles seemed a fitting sendoff for our last week in Paris. After a nightcap at the Deauville, we returned home close to midnight.

On Monday, August 20, I walked over to Air France on the Champs Elysèes. When my number came up, I went over to the lady to do my ticket. She said the first choice of a flight to New York for two on Tuesday, August 28, would not be possible, but that later days might be. I chose a flight leaving at 13:15 hours Thursday, August 30. When I got home that night, Valerie was happy with my choice for the flight to New York, saying she had always liked to travel on Thursdays. Now we had only the last three days of that week in Paris, and would have to pack the following week.

The next days, I mixed libraries with museums, gardens and long walks through favorite parts of the city. Since I had finished the Bianco article about the peasantry in China at the Documentation Francaise on Monday afternoon, on Tuesday, the 21st, I went to the library of the Centre Chine on Boulevard Raspail near the Rue de Cherche Midi for more reading to do with my China course. In fact it was there that I had met Lucien Bianco some ten years earlier. I went back to Centre Chine Wednesday as well, and on Thursday, I decided to go back to some other favorite places. I went to an exhibition about bicycles at the *Conservatoire National des Arts et Metiers*, To get there, I walked from home to the Villiers metro stop, and took the number 3 train to Reamur Sebastopol, which was only a block or so from the museum. The Conservatoire gives a panoramic overview of the history and techniques of machines, from the steam ship and locomotive to airplanes, as well as cameras, phonographs and computers. It contains a melange of exhibits and also of remains of old church structures dedicated to St. Martin, bishop of Tours in the fourth century. That is explained by its location on Rue St. Martin in the Third Arrondissement. The exhibit on bicycles gave a fascinating history of the development of bikes and velos over the past two centuries.

Then, after lunch in the cafeteria of the Conservatoire, I decided to take the number three metro further East to the famous cemetery, Père Lachaise. After wandering around its graves of distinguished artists from Balzac to Colette, Sarah Bernhardt, Edith Piaf and Chopin, and so many others for about an hour, I took the metro line number two to the Jean Jaures stop. I went there to be able to walk down the Canal St. Martin to take my metro home from the Bastille. That canal's water starts from well above the Jean Jaures stop, flowing from the Canal St. Denis and other sources all the way to the Seine at the Arsenal, just beyond the Bastille. It took me over a half hour to get there, and reaching the Arsenal, I called Valerie to see if she wanted to meet me for dinner at Boffinger, the restaurant back towards the Bastille. But, she had not come in yet, and remembering she was to eat out, I dined at the Petit Boffinger across the street from the more expensive parent restaurant. After a good and relatively inexpensive meal there, I took the metro to the Etoile and the number two metro back to Monceau. Valerie greeted me when I got home about nine.

She confirmed she had already eaten, and asked me what I was going to do the morrow, Friday, the 24th. I told her I would like to go back to places, like the Cernuschi Museum almost next door. She said she envied me, and wished she could go also. "But, I have to work through Saturday, and then we will do the dinner with Keith and Francois. For that, how about doing the Recamier, another one star restaurant, and quite close to my office, as it is on the Rue Recamier, which is parallel to the Rue de la Chaise where I work.?"

"Marvelous. I would love to try another good Parisian resto, and will call Francois to tell him. Shall we do it at 20 hours?"

"Yes. Eight o'clock will be perfect for me, working until just before then, and I will tell Keith."

It all worked out perfectly, and the next day I got to the Recamier Restaurant about five minutes to eight. I was able to wait for Valerie and our guests on the terrace of the restaurant on the short street off of the Rue de Sevres. The Rue Recamier ended in a cul de sac just beyond the terrace, and I could almost see the back of Valerie's office building as I had determined where it was on a map before coming. I had also found in my Larousse Encyclopedia that the restaurant was named after a Madame Recamier who was famous for the brilliant salon she maintained nearby, prior to her death in 1849.

Keith was the first to arrive, followed shortly by Valerie. We went into the interior of the restaurant and took our seats at the indicated corner table. When I saw Francois coming in about quarter after eight, I went over to lead him to our table. He apologized, saying his flight back from Moscow had been almost an hour late. Keith said, "In that case, I'm surprised you got here at all."

"I wouldn't miss it for anything. I have known this restaurant for a long time, and you are favorite new friends of mine."

"Thank you so much, Francois. I am glad to see you remember Keith after our meeting two months ago, and certainly, Valerie and I will always remember you. The flights we did were terrific and I've always loved talking to you. But, this might have to be our last meeting for awhile since as I think I told you, we are going to New York next week. I have to resume my teaching job, and Valerie says she is looking forward to living in New York."

She added, "Indeed! We Londoners think of New York as our younger sister, but I have yet to see it. And you, Keith?"

"Many times, but I have to say, I much prefer the European cities. So, I am lucky that that's no problem given my job. The same must be true for you, Francois, n'est-ce pas?"

"Yes. I love flying to the European cities, but I have also enjoyed my trips to New York. You know, for us airline pilots, it's no big deal to fly to a city like New York. Or Beijing or Tokyo for that matter."

Valerie asked, "Why aren't you an airline pilot, Chris, so we could go all over the world whenever we wanted?"

"Obviously, I never got that far with my flying. But, I was happy a professional like Francois could see that I am able to pilot a plane for a little anyway. Now, maybe we should order and enjoy our dinner."

Keith immediately raised his hand, saying in a loud voice, "*S'il vous plait. On peut commander.*"

A waiter rushed over, and we sarted by ordering the wine. Keith did that, choosing a Chateauneuf de Pape. He said that it was one of his favorites, and that he would insist on treating us to this dinner, hoping we would come back often to Paris.

"You needn't worry about that, since it's our favorite city. Moreover as a teacher, I have summers off, so it won't be long before we're back.

But, you really shouldn't be so generous with your treats, Keith. You've already taken Valerie and me to a bunch of places."

"It's my pleasure, and a part of my business as well. Just keep ordering wines, and hopefully some of them will be from my company."

Our food arrived and the specialties were as good as cracked up to be. Valerie again did the Oeufs en Meurette she had so much loved when we did our trip to Burgundy the previous September, and we guys had that other great Burgundy dish, Escargots. For the main courses, Valerie did the Brochet, or pike specialty, with sauce Nantua, and I, the Boeuf Bourguignon. Keith had his favorite dish, Ris de Veau, and Francois, an Entrecote Steak. The vegetables were also out of this world, with carots, haricots verts, peas, and turnips.

Valerie said, "How are we going to survive in New York, if we can't get food like this? I never had a fish as good as this."

"Don't worry, my love. There are numerous great restaurants in New York, many of them with French chefs. And didn't you see the stories about some California wines besting Bordeaux ones, when done with blind tasting."

Keith came in hearing that to say, "I'm not sure I believe those stories, and in any case everything to do with food and wine is so much more expensive in the U.S."

"I will have to give you a report next summer about this competition over the superiority of wining and dining in New York, as against Paris," Valerie said with a radiant smile.

I blew her a kiss, removing my fingers to say, "Valerie has such a great gift of defusing disputes like this one. And, since it is already ten, I propose we pay up here and have a nightcap nearby. I know of a good Italian bar restaurant just a block away, on the Rue de Cherche Midi just off Boulevard Raspail. I discovered it just a few days ago when I was reading for my course, at the Centre Chine not far away."

We went to it, and had some more conversation over Porto and Sambucca. I tried to insist on paying for the bill for the drinks, but both Francois and Keith reached over for it. Keith said, "Since you teachers are all so poor, let's do it 'Dutch.'"

"All right, Valerie and I accept with pleasure. Since I won't see you two for several months, let me say how much I have loved our times together. And till the next time."

Valerie said, "The same goes for me. If you come to New York, be sure to give us a call."

That reminded me to give them the telephone number of the apartment in New York I had sublet. They already had my e-mail address.

The bill paid, we stood up, embraced and went our separate ways. Valerie and I arrived home not long after midnight. The next day was Sunday, August 26th, and we were to leave already on Thursday morning, the 30th., for our one fifteen flight to New York that day. Waking up about nine, I greeted

Valerie with a *bonjour*, and said I would start our breakfast. We discussed our options over the bread and coffee.

"How long do you think it will take us to pack?" I asked.

"Not that long for me. I have only a mid sized and big bag, and those winter coats to worry about. And you?"

"Well, I have to get my trunk sent. I will call and hopefully schedule the pick up for Wednesday at the latest. That's for all the books I brought over and the ones I bought here for the teaching. I suppose I will leave some behind, and we can put our coats in that small trunk, and I can easily fill the rest. Then I also have two bags. Maybe after breakfast I should start on doing the trunk, and after lunch why don't we go to Cernuschi Museum and walk in the Monceau garden?"

"A good idea! I might as well start arranging my things, while you start on the trunk."

So, we set about our respective jobs in the apartment. It was small, but there were four rooms and our stuff was mostly in different ones. We both kept looking out the bigger window at the street below, and Valerie launched into a paean about it.

"Now, we can remember Vezelay all the better. It was so wonderful seeing that incredible Basilica Ste. Madeleine and the other marvelous sites there, and here we are ending our ten months in Paris on the Rue de Vezelay. What could be better? I hope I won't be too disappointed in New York."

"Don't worry. You will be enthusiastic about quite a few things in New York. That's one of the many things I like about you, Valerie. Your enthusiasm for the things you like." I said that as I walked over to give her another hug.

We spent about three hours knocking about the apartment, with me putting stuff in my trunk, and Valerie just wandering around, opening a drawer here and there and sitting down to read from time to time. After lunch, in order to get to the Musée Cernuschi, we walked out to the left on Rue de Vezelay, jogged a quick right and two quick lefts into the Parc de Monceau. The Museum was right there, just to the left of the entrance. I especially wanted to see again the splendid statues the museum had from the middle ages in China. There were marvelous Sung Dynasty camels, horses and people in varying poses from different walks of life. On the way in, Valerie exclaimed, "There's that incredible Japanese Buddha welcoming us inside the museum. Usually, they only have those guardian statues on the outside." We passed a wonderful hour in the museum, recalling many times what we had seen there on our first visit the previous autumn.

Going out into what they called the Parc Monceau, but which seemed really more a huge garden, we circled left and clockwise around it. We remembered to first look at the plaque in honor of the first parachute jump, which had been made October 22, 1797, by André–Jaqcques Garnerin. That was just a few paces outside the museum. Then, we continued on the paths that circled the Parc admiring many beds of flowers, as well as occasional columns and statues. We finished going by a Rotunda, followed by a horse shoe shaped pond with a Colonnade at the end, not far from where we exited the Parc. We debated if we would eat out or in, and decided to eat at home.

"That way we can do restaurants our last three nights in Paris," Valerie said.

"Won't that be terrific. I already have some proposals. Do you want to know what they are?"

"Very much so. And maybe you want to hear mine. Then we will decide, or flip coins."

I embraced Valerie and we finished walking back to 15 Rue Vezelay.

Since it was Sunday evening, I proposed we do what had become my habit. That was to eat cereal, often raisin bran, with fruit and brown sugar.

Valerie said she agreed that was a good idea, but asked me if I had bought any cereal, sugar and bananas or whatever.

I said I had and she asked me to explain how Sunday night cereal had become a habit.

"Oh yes, the cereal and sugar is there, and I'm surprised you haven't noticed it. I guess because I put the box in the back of an inside shelf and the bananas in the front. I ate cereal quite a few times when you were not around, and that habit started back in Asheville. My mother did that Sunday nights to minimize the dishes to clean, Sunday nights being when the servants were off. Being in North Carolina, we usually had at least two black servants around when I was growning up there. Now, the parents tell me they can only get help for special occasions, and are cooking their meals all the time. In any case, I got in the habit of doing the Sunday night cereal, and think it has the additional virtue of changing what you eat at least once a week. Moreover, bran is a rich source of the fiber they say you are supposed to have. It did not take us long to finish and we discussed the things we still wanted to do before leaving Paris.

"You know, it came to me a few days ago that we have not yet done two of the *must sees* in Paris," I said. "That is the Orsay and Picasso museums. I can't believe we have put them off to the end. We should have thought of doing the Orsay after doing the Jeu de Paume, which is practically next door. All the more so, as it was from that small museum between the Place de la Concorde and the Tuileries that all the Impressionists paintings were moved to the Orsay. But, fortunately, we still have three days to see them. Let me look in Pariscope to see when the museums are closed, so we can plan for that."

I looked in Pariscope and found to my delight that the Picasso Museum was open on Monday and closed Tuesday, and the Orsay the opposite. I told Valerie and she said, "Well, our luck continues. So, let's do the Picasso demain and Orsay on Tuesday. Then we will have Wednesday to finish with packing and final stuff."

"Wonderful. I'm glad we did the Cernuschi for the second time today and have tomorrow and Tuesday for the other museums. For our last restaurant dinners here, I propose we return and eat at Chez la Mere Catherine in Montmarte tomorrow evening. Or, on second thought, we should probably save that for our last evening, to facilitate getting to bed early the day before our flight. So, maybe tomorrow should be the Bistrot Mazarin or Perigordine. What do you think?"

"Let's do the Bistrot Mazarin, or maybe try to find something new. Someone at work told me to do the Laperousse Restaurant."

"A great idea, but let's get to bed now to be ready for all that." It was still relatively early, and I was happy to think we could get a good night's sleep and be in shape to finish our final tourism and packing over the next three days.

Monday morning, we resumed packing, and a little later, I called DeBaux Transit to ask if they could get my trunk Wednesday morning. They said they could and would arrive by midday. Relieved to hear that, I went over to the icebox and got out our luncheon cheese. Calling Valerie, I said, "Let's eat. I've got the cheese and will get the avocado and wine." After doing our usual halves of the avocado, some cheese and wine, we lay down for a brief nap and caress. Then, we got up to make our way to the Musée Picasso.

We arrived there before four, via the metro to the St. Paul stop in the Marais, followed by a walk to the Picasso museum which is just off of Rue Vieille du Temple. In addition to the obligatory viewing of the self portrait of the great artist and masterpieces such as *Les Demoiselles d'Avignon,* we were most struck with his paintings and sculptures of actors, nudes, and acrobats. One of the latter included his son and is titled, *Paul, the Harlequin.* The nudes were a mixture of beauty, strange positions and shapes. We were also impressed by the private collection of the artist, including some splendid Braque, Cezanne and others. It was interesting to read the highlights of Picasso's biography. He left Barcelona at 23 to travel to Paris where he spent most of his life. His last years were spent near Mougins at the foot of Montagne Sainte-Victoire in the south where he died at the age of ninety two.

After an hour or so in the museum, we walked back to the other side of the St. Paul metro stop as far as the bar on the Rue de l'Hotel St. Paul. I hoped Claudia would not be there, and she wasn't, no doubt because she was still on the vacation she mentioned taking with Guy in Haute Savoie. Some thoughts about them ran through my head, but I was very glad I was with Valerie and had not ruined that possibility by my flirting with Claudia.

After several drinks and some conversation about what we had just seen, as well as what we had to look forward to on the morrow at the Orsay Museum, we headed to the Bastille metro stop and the return home. As intended, after washing up and a bit of rest, we made it easily to the Bistrot Mazarin and had another great meal. The return home by metro from Odeon to La Motte-Picquet with a correspondence to Bir Hakeim, the Etoile, and Monceau, was now almost routine. It enabled us to get to bed before midnight which we wanted to do in order to be ready for our last two days in Paris.

The next day, it was easy to get to the Musée d'Orsay since we only had to do one transfer, at Pigalle for the line to the Solferino stop, which is close to the museum. We followed our guide books to concentrate on the great nineteenth century painters more or less chronologically. That meant starting with Delacroix and Ingres before getting to Degas, Manet, Monet, Renoir, Van Gogh and all the others. As great as they were in this museum, I regretted that they had been moved from the Jeu de Paume, where I had seen them on my first trips to Paris. They seemed even more impressive in the intimate setting of the Jeu de Paume museum. Once the former Orsay railroad station closed and was converted into the Orsay Museum by late 1986, it was the only place to see most of the Impressionist artists. But, greats such as Delacroix, Monet and Rodin, also had their own museums. When I told Valerie about seeing the Impressionists at the Jeu de Paume, she said, "I am so sorry I didn't see the old Jeu de Paume on one of my earlier trips. I remember my parents saying they wanted to do it, but then as I recall my father got a call to return to London before we had wanted to go, for some business emergency. He worked in a small haberdashery off of Bond Street, and there had been a fire or something."

"I hope not too much was burned or destroyed."

"No. I think just a few dresses and suits. I remember I was very angry at having to stop seeing Paris, which I loved even then. But now, I have spent this incredible year here with you."

We embraced and holding hands, went on with our tour of the museum. On the ground floor, we spent quite a few minutes looking at the rural scenes of Jean-Francois Millet and landscapes by Camille Corot and Gustave Courbet. In addition to the Ingres and Delacroix, there were many pictures by the great artists Cezanne, Degas, Gauguin, Manet, Monet, Pissarro, Renoir, Sisley, Toulouse-Lautrec, Van Gogh and others. We especially liked Renoir's *Bal du Moulin de la Galette*, with its dancers and pictures of lively conversations you could almost see and hear. Then, there were the famous *Dejeuner sur l'Herbe* by Manet, the *Cathedrales de Rouen* by Monet and so many others. After several hours, we began to feel a bit exhausted looking at so many masterpieces. I proposed we exit and walk along the Seine to the Quai Voltaire.

Valerie agreed, and said, "You know, it's our next to last night. So let's try the Lapérousse restaurant tonight. It's been highly recommended and is close by, I think. Then, we can do the Montmartre restaurant tomorrow for our last dinner in Paris, this year anyway."

"Perfect, and I think we will pass a bar or café before getting to Laperousse, where we can do an apertif and discuss what we have just seen."

Going down to the river, we turned right just above it on the path off to the side of the Quai d'Orsay. The stretch of the left bank highway to our right passed by the Assemblé Nationale before giving way to the Quai Anatole France. That turns into the Quai Voltaire near where the restaurant is. As we walked we had a Macon Blanc each at the first bar on Rue de Bac and then Sauvignon Blancs at the next one a few blocks further along, just past Rue Bonapart on the Quai de Conti. The latter turned into the Quai Grands Augustins where we found our restaurant at no. 5l, just before the Pont Neuf. Fortunately, Laperousse had space and we were given a nice corrner table. The dining room has elegant mahogany tables with small oval and oblong windows. I was glad we had a corner table as the tables in the middle were mostly full and rather noisy.

As soon as we were seated, Valerie asked to know the specialties of the day. We both shared a salad and had the Gratin de Langoustines for the main course, with delicious Crepes Mona, for dessert.

"We will have a hard time matching this, but I may know of one place in New York that does something similar. However, as Keith said Saturday, everything to do with wining and dining in New York is more expensive. And that restaurant surely is. It's Le Bernardin and I only know it from when a rich friend took me there. He is an architect I grew up with back in Asheville, who has succeeded in New York and made a pile of money. We dined there about three years ago, and I think they had Langoustines since they are a seafood restaurant."

"Well, I'm sure we'll eat well enough. And we can always come back here, if our money holds out that is. Speaking of that, how do you think my chances for getting a job will be in New York?

"I'm sure you can get one as soon as you ask. Do you think you want to continue working with wine, or go back to selling books, or what?"

"Maybe I'll surprise you and do something quite different, work in a clothing store for instance. I might want to imagine better what my father did. But, then that might be so much more boring than the book or wine trade."

"Whatever you want. Now, let's enjoy this wonderful food now that it's here."

We did, and passed over an hour savoring the dishes as we continued to talk about this and that, from time to time looking around at the other people in the restaurant. Most were middle aged and well dressed, and quite a few seemed handsome and interesting. Fortunately, we knew no one and could finish our meal without interruption. When it came to the bill, it was expensive, but less than it might have been and certainly less than it would have been at Le Bernardin in New York. The bill paid, we walked out and up the Seine to the Pont des Arts, reversing our usual route from the Right Bank. We again admired the beautiful views both ways from the bridge; to the Eiffel Tower and Grand Palais to the West on our left, and to the Palais de Justice and Notre Dame to the East on the right. Walking through the Louvre, we reached the metro at Palais Royal and took it to the FDR stop. Since it was our last night to see the Champs Elysées, we got off and headed to our favorite bar there, the Deauville. Doing only one Marie Brizzard anisette drink each, we arrived home by foot before midnight.

So here we are down to our last day in our favorite city, I thought on waking up in the morning. I looked at Valerie who was just waking up, and again thanked my lucky stars that we were in love and that I would still be able to be with her and look at her mornings in New York.

"*Bonjour!* How long will it take you to finish your packing, and what do you want to do before we go to Montmartre for our last evening?"

"*Sais pas.* I will tell you over breakfast. Now, let's get dressed."

While Valerie was doing that, I went to make the breakfast as was my habit still in my pjs and robe. We discussed what we would do our last day over the croissants and jam. I said, "The people said they would pick up my trunk by noon and I can finish packing the rest while waiting for that. If you can finish your packing this morning, why don't we do another last outing this afternoon. I vote for going back to the Jardins du Luxembourg and celebrating the first anniversary of our meeting at the apiculture center. Or would you rather stay close and do the Parc Monceau?"

"By all means, let's redo our anniversary. We must revisit the site of our getting into trouble with each other. Can you swear to not cause any more troubles?"

I decided not to respond to such a provocative remark but got up and give her a kiss, taking my plates to the sink on the way. Valerie did the few dishes and we rearranged our suitcases for the final packing.

"Don't forget to leave out what you want to wear tomorrow for the return to New York."

"Don't worry, I'm not that scatterbrained, and won't be if you don't upset me again."

"Oh, come on. Since my bike trip cleared my head, I have been such a good boy, and I don't think there have been any problems. I hope you agree. "

"Well, make sure that continues."

"D'accord, and see you for lunch in a couple of hours."

I made good progress and had almost finished packing, when I heard the door bell sound about 11:45. I went down and sure enough it was the people coming for my trunk.

"*Bonjour*. You are right on time, since you told me you would be here by noon."

"*C'est normal*," said the senior of the two guys. He was in his thirties and the other looked only about twenty. They were both sympa and rapidly brought up the two-wheeled cart to put the trunk on. That done, I gave them the additional papers confirming the address of where to send the trunk in New York, and they went on their way.

After our last lunch in the apartment, Valerie and I headed out. We walked to the Etoile and took the metro to Nation with a change to the line to *Austerlitz at La Motte-Picquet*. That way, we could look out of the metro as it went above ground to cross the Seine, and then walk to the Luxembourg gardens from the Mabillon stop.

The walk from there up the Rue de Seine and Rue de Tournon brought us to the Palais du Luxembourg, now used by the French Senate. We turned left and then right to enter the Jardin and walk by the Fontaine de Medici. As so often before we found chairs there to look at the great statue of Cyclops at the end and the frolicking carp in the pond. After a few minutes happily observing that, we wandered west by the circular pond in the center of the garden. Many children and their mothers or nannys were playing with their sailboats or balloons, and we liked seeing some old men who clearly enjoyed watching the children. We climbed the steps off to the west and looked at the different spectacles from the top of the stairs. They ranged from other children riding ponies, to people playing tennis, to still others playing checkers and chess. We turned left to pass a merry go round and bowls game before we arrived at the apiculture center.

"Can you believe that it was only a year ago that we met here? I feel as if I have known you all my life."

Valerie replied, "I was thinking that about you until you started flirting with what's her name. Look at those bees circling each other. That's the way you were are with women."

"Please try to forget my stupidities with Claudia and others, Valerie. Even if Claudia had not found her boy friend, Guy, you wouldn't have had to worry. As I told you, on our bike trip I got over that flirtation. Now, let's just wish them well. As said, Claudia told me that they are doing a vacation in Haute Savoy. I will write Claudia and ask where. Then maybe we can do that trip next summer."

"We'll see. And I am happy you suggested we come back here. It's not everyone who has such an interesting place to celebrate their anniversary. Imagine we are the bees. But, I guess that would mean we would always be with people, which I wouldn't like."

I saw some other people coming, and stepped over to embrace Valerie before their arrival. I whispered to her, "You know, I really do love you. Now, let's go home and get ready for doing Montmartre."

That meant taking the Rue Vavin exit from the Jardins du Luxembourg and making our way to Boulevard Montparnasse for the Vavin metro stop. Before entering the metro and seeing the Rotunde bar/restaurant we decided, as we had a year earlier, to stop there for a glass each of Sauvignon, with more toasts to our good luck. Then we took the metro in the opposite direction to get to the Raspail stop, where we could get the number six line to the Etoile. That way, on the line from Nation to Etoile you can enjoy its above ground trajectory most of the way, with the incredible view of the Eiffel Tower as you cross the Seine.

We arrived home in time for a nap and baths before setting out for Montmartre about 7:30. We did our usual metro on the number two line to Pigalle, and then the 12 line to Abesses for the walk to Place du Tertre. It was a nice evening and as usual in Paris even in the summer with a nice temperature. I said, "It's less cool in Paris than London or Stockholm but a lot cooler than New York in July and August. Do you know why?"

"It's because of the west to east winds, *n'est-ce pas*? That's why I understand California is also cool in the summer. Do you think we might do some summers in California?" "Yes. I'm sure we will, and I'm glad to see you also know your metereology. Now, let's enjoy our last evening in Paris. I propose a vin blanc, maybe right here."

Seeing Valerie's agreement, I led us over to a table at the bar on Rue Gabrielle. We were passing that just before reaching the Place du Tertre where the restaurant was. We ordered and Valerie proceeded to tell me more things about her job at the International Wine Shop.

"I really loved its location on Rue de la Chaise. There were not only great restaurants all around for some really classy meals, but it was so easy to slip over to Bon Marché for whatever shopping you wanted to do. I remember one day when we treated some Germans to lunch at the nearby famous restaurant, Arpege. They were so impressed with the lobster and pigeon dishes, that they told Keith who was with us, that they would order all of their wines from us for their restaurants."

After more conversation, we made our way to the Place du Tertre and settled in to eat at Chez la Mere Catherine. We got our favorite table at the side of the dining area opposite the restaurant. It was just in time since as soon as we were seated, we noticed several groups of people coming in and taking seats all around us. Again, I was struck by the inscription, Fondé en 1793 at the height of the revolution, and the contrast of that with the flourishing present of the restaurant.

We both did salads, and Valerie ordered moules while I did the duck specialty. The Cote du Rhone wine that I ordered arrived and we ate as well as we ever had. I asked Valerie if she wanted to hear more about my apartment in New York, and some of the restaurants near it. She said yes.

So I went on, "The apartment, which I have sublet until August 15, is on West 55th street. That is not far from a favorite

French restaurant, La Bonne soupe, and there are also Italian and Indian restaurants just a few steps away. So, we can eat well there as well."

"I am starting to look forward to living in New York more every day. At least I speak English and won't have a problem with that. Even though my mom is French, here in Paris there are many times when I get lost. Maybe they speak a more modern version of what mother spoke when I was growing up. Anyway, these mussels are so good. How is your duck?"

"*Pas mal*, though you can tell it is farm raised and not wild. I have had the wild ones a few times here as I did often back in North Carolina, and they are quite superior. I guess I just like that wild taste. And, by the way, you might find the English spoken in New York quite different from that of London. But look at that!"

Two guys were coming by just off to our left, doing their fire eating and blowing routines. I had been told they were able to do that by ingesting a gulp or two of kerosene or flammable oil into their mouth, and then aspirating it as they lit it with a torch. The pillars of flame went out and up ten or more feet. However they accomplished it, it was a colorful end to our meal. We each gave them a coin and thank yous.

We got up and walked back around the Sacre Coeur Church to Rue Lamarck. We then followed that street in a circle to the Lamark-Caulaincourt metro stop at a place called Caulaincourt. We were home before midnight, which was just as well since we wanted to leave by ten to get to the Charles de Gaule Airport in plenty of time for our one o'clock flight. A nice round of lovemaking helped us to sleep soundly, and we were up by eight in the morning.

After breakfast, dressing and final packing, we decided to take the RER Train to the airport. We pulled our suitcases over to the metro at the Monceau stop, and took it to Barbes-Rochechouart for the number four line to the Gare du Nord. There, we discovered a problem. On the panel beside the tracks, was a message saying the Train to the plane was 'e*n retard.'* We rushed over to ask at the ticket window how long the delay would be. The agent said he did not know, and that we had to wait. That meant finding two seats and watching our bags as we wondered what to do. Fortunately, I had brought a pack of playing cards, and I took them out of my side pocket. I asked Valerie, "How about a game of gin rummy while we wait?"

She liked the idea and I shuffled and dealt the cards. Valerie won the first three of five hands, and it was already almost eleven. I proposed we do another round or two and hoped the train would come in time for us. Valerie asked if we should do a cab, but I suggested we wait to 11:30 or so, and then decide. I won the next three of five games, and as we were playing the second new hand for the playoff, we saw that the train was coming. I shouted 'Eureka!' We should be at the airport in a half hour or so which will be an hour before departure time."

The train arrived, and as we staggered on board, Valerie said, "I almost hope we miss the plane."

"Oh, come on! Now, I am adjusting to the idea of being back in New York. I really look forward to seeing some friends and colleagues. There will be no problem thinking what to say, since we have so many stories from this incredible year."

"That's fine for you, but I have no friends there. Maybe, you will pay my way back to London before long?"

"As soon as you get a job, tell them you will start a month later and it's a deal. That way, I will be sure that later you will be getting the money needed to pay for the trip."

"You mean, from now on I have to pay for everything I do?"

I leaned over to kiss Valerie and immediately pulled back to say, "Of course not. As much as I love you, you needn't worry. That is, unless, I lose my job."

The train gathered speed and soon came out of its tunnel. That was at the east end of Paris. Nothing of interest appeared until about a minute later when I could make out the back of the Sacre Coeur Church on the hill of Montmartre. I said, "Look. There's Sacre Coeur, and it was only last night that we walked around it for the umpteenth time."

Valerie leaned over and put her head against my shoulder, saying, "I guess Montmartre is the part of Paris that I will remember best from this fabulous year. For me that means the Place du Tertre, Chez Mere Catherine, and Sacre Coeur most of all. But, there were so many other things as well, the museums, restaurants and all the walking we did."

"Very much so, my love, and to my knowledge, Paris is the best of the big cities for walking. New York has some good walks too, but the sky scrapers are far less appealing to look at while walking than beautiful buildings and churches, of which there are more in Paris. Or, maybe it's because Paris is so much smaller than New York, that you can see its wonders that much more easily. And there are far more flowers in the Paris gardens and parks than in those of New York."

"So, are you trying to make me regret going to New York?"

"Certainly not! And look, there's the Stade de France. Too bad we can't see inside it to know if there is some game going on."

"Maybe this year we should have gone to see some football games. I even played a bit as a girl in London, but I didn't think it was that interesting a game."

"Well, as I'm sure you've heard, we call it soccer, even though what we call football is really more hand ball. That's another example of how we Americans change words, or did so earlier when we were so isolated. Your football is the most widely played game on earth, but I must say I prefer watching our football. There is so much more action, and I especially like the pass plays."

"Nevermind, Before long you can watch American football all you want. Do you play tennis?"

"Occasionally. I like the game a lot, but was never very good at it. And you?"

"The same. I play not very often and badly." Valerie said this smiling, while sitting up suggesting we get ready for the arrival.

"But, this is the first stop at the airport, *Terminal Un.* We have to go to *Terminal Deux.*"

Another two minutes and we heard the announcer say, "*Terminus,*" meaning last stop. We got out and rolled our bags to the up escalator, of which we had to do two to get to the main floor where all the check-in counters are. It was quarter after twelve, and the female agent said, "You almost missed your flight. If you had not arrived by 12:20, we would have had to put you on a later flight."

I said, "Our train was late, and fortunately arrived just in time."

The agent smiled and checked our bags. We walked to the designated gate, *Porte* 36, and waited in line to do the security. Late as we were, there were not many people ahead of us waiting to put their bags through the scanner. When we got to the waiting area, they were just announcing the boarding of the flight. "Air France *vol 06 en partenance pour* New York."

Grabbing the hand of Valerie, I spun her around and embraced her, saying, "Now, we are going to start new chapters in our lives, and I am so happy I can do that with you."

"Me too."

It was the shortest reply I had ever heard Valerie give, and I embraced her harder before letting go. We headed hand in hand to the boarding of our plane.